Stormclouds Book III
Prequel series to the Harbingers fantasy novels

Stormbird

Jane M. Wiseman

Shrike Publications

Albuquerque and Minneapolis

Shrike Publications
Albuquerque, New Mexico
Minneapolis, Minnesota
www.janemwiseman.com

Publisher's Note: This is a work of fiction. Names, characters, places, and incidents are a product of the author's imagination. Locales and public names are sometimes used for atmospheric purposes. Any resemblance to actual people, living or dead, or to businesses, companies, events, institutions, or locales is completely coincidental.

Book Layout © 2017 BookDesignTemplates.com

Stormbird/ Jane M. Wiseman . -- 1st ed.
ISBN 978-1-7332998-5-5

As sun grows warm,
The cuckoo brings the storm.
The cuckoo in April,
She opens her bill.
The cuckoo in May,
She sings the whole day.
The cuckoo in June,
She changeth her tune.
The cuckoo in July,
Away she must fly.
If you should hear her in September,
That would be something to remember.
If you should hear her in October,
Tush, shut your mouth, lad. You're a liar.

—based on a traditional rhyme from weather folklore of the British Isles

Contents

A Map of the Known World

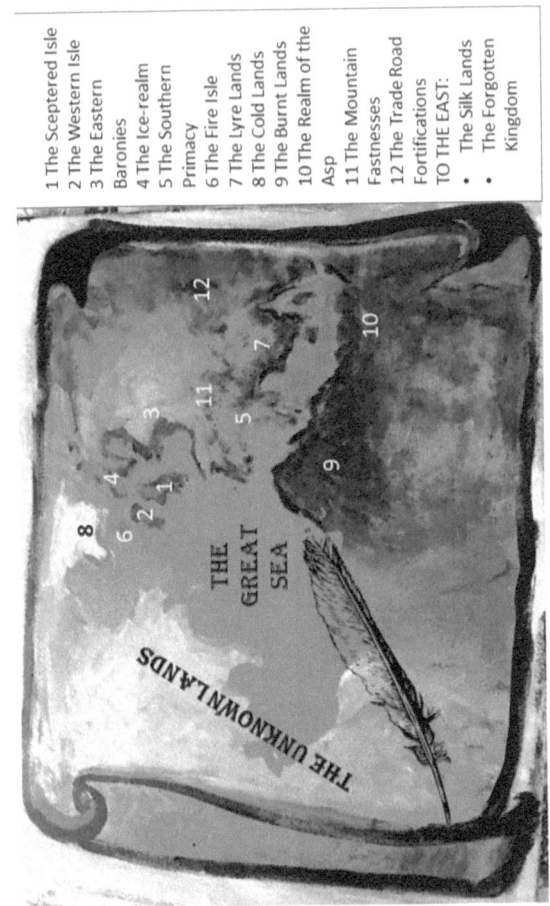

1 The Sceptered Isle
2 The Western Isle
3 The Eastern Baronies
4 The Ice-realm
5 The Southern Primacy
6 The Fire Isle
7 The Lyre Lands
8 The Cold Lands
9 The Burnt Lands
10 The Realm of the Asp
11 The Mountain Fastnesses
12 The Trade Road Fortifications
TO THE EAST:
• The Silk Lands
• The Forgotten Kingdom

THE UNKNOWN LANDS

THE GREAT SEA

The Stormclouds/Harbingers Fantasy Novels

Stormclouds: The Prequel Series

Book I, A Gyrfalcon for a King
Book II, The Call of the Shrike
Book III, Stormbird

The Harbingers Series

Book I, Blackbird Rising
Book II, Halcyon
Book III, Firebird
Book IV, Ghost Bird

Betwixt and Between: The Companion Series

Book I, The Martlet is a Wanderer
Book II, The Nightingale Holds Up the Sky

Stand-alone novel in the Stormclouds/Harbingers fantasy world:

Dark Ones Take It, being the origin story of Caedon and his brother Maeldoi, the Dark Rider

All available at amazon.com for paperback and Kindle.

Underneath the Spheres,

Springtide to Harvestide:

Seven Turnings of the Moon

CHAPTER ONE

Storm's Coming

Wat

Wat stood high on the cliffs above the coast, Eris beside him. "What do you think?" he said.

"We should get to shelter," she replied. "Looks like it's going to be a big one."

"The first storm of spring," he said. "Gowk storm."

She looked over at him, her brows arched. "You believe such things."

"The cuckoo returns at the first of spring, and with her come the spring storms. Everyone knows that," said Wat.

"Well, whyever they come, Dark Ones take it, the timing is bad. If we don't grab those dispatches—" She held up a sudden hand. Pushing a jet-black lock of her hair impatiently off the smooth honey of her forehead, she leapt behind the boulder where they were standing and crouched there. "Get down, for Dark's sake," she hissed.

Wat had heard it too, the creaking and jingling of harness, the faint sliding and scrambling of hooves on steep, stony ground. The noise this horseman was making grew louder and closer.

"Wait, Eris, are we sure—" Wat was saying, shifting uncomfortably as the rider came around the bend into sight just below them.

Eris had already risen from her crouch. As the man went by, she had already drawn her arm back and, turning hand, arm, the line of her shoulder into a fluid, death-dealing blur, had already let fly one of her knives. It connected with the rider in a solid thunk. As he twisted with a shriek to look up and over his shoulder at them, making futile scrabblings at his back, Wat and Eris both released more of their knives. Their target fell from his horse with a wet smack like a bag of oats falling from a high shelf onto the storeroom planks. The startled horse shied, reared, nearly went over the steep embankment on the other side of the road, recovered its footing, and sped off riderless down the path.

Wat and Eris picked their way around the boulders and down the hillside to stand over the man, who lay in the roadway twitching, his mouth open in a soundless scream. He looked desperately up into their faces. Staring into his eyes, Eris leaned over and slit his throat. The arterial spray splattered them. Their target's feet briefly drummed against the loose stones of the roadway, and then the man went still, gazing sightless at the sky.

Crouching down to some clumps of grass, Eris cleaned the knife she had used to finish him. She and Wat kicked the man over and tugged their throwing knives out of the meat of him and sheathed them in the belts at their waists.

Wat stopped suddenly. He turned aside to retch into the gully beside the body. He wiped his mouth with the back of his hand, shaking, and began rubbing at the blood on the front of his tunic.

"You've gone soft, Wat," said Eris.

"Suppose it hadn't been our man," said Wat, when he could speak.

"But it was." Eris was kneeling now, searching the dead man. She yanked a leather case from underneath him, where it was jammed half-protruding from a deep pocket of his cloak. "Here it is. The dispatches are in here. I can tell by the bear." Eris didn't know her letters, but she knew this seal. They both stared down at the crest of a bear, rampant, burned into the leather. "Audie's royal crest," she said, her lip curling in scorn.

Actually, thought Wat, *that's Artur's crest*. But Audemar had taken it over, along with the rest of the realm, after he had had his brother Artur assassinated.

"We need to take the dispatches to Conal and Avery before the storm rolls in," said Wat, peering up into the sky, where black thunderclouds had come boiling up.

"Let's get out of here, then," said his sister, and they began rapidly hiking up into the hills, leaving the western slope that descended steeply at their backs to the coast. They clambered over the eastern slope, the landward side, where Avery's army lay camped in a meadow near a mountain stream. This stream tumbled down the eastern slope from the boulder-strewn heights of a small high lake across a grassy bald, eventually reversing course westward around the shoulder of the mountain toward the cliffs above the sea, and over them with a roar.

The crash of the waters as they foamed down into the sea came at Avery's forces faintly where they'd set up their tents in one of the broad meadows a little way down from the summit. From there, they could see in three directions for miles, and the sea was at their back. They were safe as houses there.

But the growl of the thunder, and the lightning flashes, were getting closer.

By the time Wat and Eris reached the tents, rain was sheeting down on them. Wat was glad of it. It washed some of the blood off him. He stopped and lifted his face to the sky, opening his mouth. The rain rinsed the taste of vomit from him. He spat.

"Come on, ninnyhammer. I'm getting drenched." Eris tugged him in the direction of Avery's tent, and they sloshed toward it, bent over against the gusts of wind and rain.

Avery must have seen them coming. He stood at the tent flap, holding it open, and as they rushed within, he gathered them both up into his big cloak and hugged them to him.

"Brother. Sister," he said. He put out a finger to smooth the sopping hair off Eris's face.

She shrugged out from under his arm and strode to the fire in a brazier at the center of the big tent.

"We got the dispatches," Wat said from the other side of Avery. "Nine Spheres, Avery, we've soaked you through."

"Do I care? I have my family with me, and you are both safe," said Avery the prince, looking over at Wat with fond eyes and releasing him from the shelter of the cloak. "You're the one who is soaking wet, Wat," he said. He fingered the spatters of blood on

Wat's tunic. "Looks like you had some trouble. Go over to the fire with your sister. She has the right idea."

Wat picked his way around some small groups of other soldiers toward the fire and crouched down there by Eris. He was shivering, but he knew it was not the cold that was making his hands shake and his insides churn. He held his hands out to the warmth of the brazier, as if the fire could warm that other cold feeling, the one in his gut.

"Why do you always shove Avery away, Eris?" he said to her after a moment, in an undertone.

She shrugged irritably. "This brother-sister thing he's always pressing on me. He's not my brother."

"He is, though," said Wat.

"Not in any way that matters. You're my brother, Wat."

Wat wondered whether Eris would ever get over what their father had done to her, when she came of age. Branded her, as if she were cattle. But he failed to see what any of that had to do with Avery. Avery was the true-born son of the king, Wat and Eris only the king's bastards by two different mothers, but as far as Wat was concerned, Avery was his older brother, and he loved him. He tried to feel more sympathetic about Eris. He knew he felt guilt over what had happened to her. No one would have ever branded him, the son of the king's concubine. Eris was only the child of a bondservant.

He looked up to see Conal watching them somberly.

"Conal!" he exclaimed, leaping to his feet. He rushed to him and embraced him. Conal was a solid presence in a world gone unsteady.

Wat had noticed this about himself. He wanted to be where Conal was. Conal knew important things, and he was willing to teach them to Wat, just as he had taught Wat's older brother, his full brother John. And the other members of The Rising, of course. Prince Avery, Wat's and John's half-brother. The Earl Drustan, who wasn't really their brother but might as well have been. Their friend Rafe. Conal had trained all of them in the arts of war. He loved them all like brothers, except for Avery. Conal loved Avery in a different way, the way a man might treasure another man, deeply and passionately.

"Wat, it's good to see you. Avery and I were worried." Conal looked past Wat to Eris. He acknowledged her with a nod. "And Eris. I'm glad the two of you are back."

"We got the dispatches," said Wat. "Where's John?" He looked around for his brother.

"Not here yet."

Eris stood up then and came over to Conal, pulling the leather case from beneath her cloak. She handed it to Conal and went back to her seat at the log pulled up to the makeshift hearth. In this wet weather, the smoldering turves of the fire threatened to fill the tent with choking smoke. After a moment, she stepped to to the tent flap and fastened it open. She stood looking out into the rain.

"Good work," Conal was saying to Wat, his eyes still on Eris. "Looks like there was trouble."

"Yes," said Wat.

Conal turned his attention to Wat and waited.

"We had to kill a man, to get the dispatches."

"Ah," said Conal.

"We tried to intercept them, but that didn't work, so then we had to waylay the courier, and—"

Conal nodded.

"Eris says I've gone soft," said Wat.

"Why's that, Wat?"

"Just—I don't know. I hesitate when I should act."

"And you hesitated, back there?" Conal indicated the mountain with a jerk of his head.

Wat nodded.

"Why did you?"

"Suppose we didn't have the right man," said Wat. He avoided Conal's eyes.

"That would have been a very bad thing," said Conal softly. "But Eris didn't hesitate?"

"No."

"She was sure of her man, then."

"I suppose," said Wat. "And she was right. Turned out he was the one with the dispatches. He was the courier."

"Lucky, eh?" said Conal. He looked past Wat again to Eris, his eyes narrowing.

"Yes, because if we had done what I wanted, making sure of him, he would have escaped us," Wat said. "Possibly." He stopped, feeling miserable. "Probably."

"Yes," said Conal. "Probably. A balancing there. Act one way, and you've got your man. Or maybe instead you've killed an innocent person. Act the other way, and you've let your target escape. Or maybe instead you've avoided doing a terrible injustice, as bad as the injustices you've set out to correct."

"Suppose he'd gotten away from us."

A burst of laughter interrupted them. Men shouldering into the tent, slapping each other on the back. Everyone was still in a state of exuberance over their battle against Caedon's army. They'd forced Caedon to flee south in defeat. In disgrace.

Caedon's had been a force much bigger than theirs, but they routed his men through a lethal combination of Conal's and Avery's tactical and strategic skill aided by John's uncanny powers. Wat shied away from thinking of those. He'd caught others glancing at John with something like fear, but John was Wat's older brother, almost like a father, not old enough to be his father, but the only one he'd really known. Wat loved him dearly and looked up to him. If he had strange powers, well, then. Wat turned back to what Conal was saying.

"In war, many matters turn on just this kind of chance," Conal said. Wat listened to the older man while he thought about the dilemma he and Eris had faced on the mountainside. He needed to listen, and listen hard. Conal knew all about weaponry and fighting, but he knew a lot more than that. War was about a lot more than that, and of them all, Conal understood the most about those other matters. "The results of guessing wrong can mean disaster, especially in the kind of war we're fighting," said Conal. "But Wat. Sometimes you just can't tell."

"So I suppose Eris was right to kill the courier, and I was wrong, to want to wait and make sure. Chance it, just in case. Eris was right," Wat said, trying to convince himself it was so.

"Was she? Is that what you should have done? There's a lot to be said for speed and shock, for acting quickly in the midst of chaos. Sometimes, in war, you don't have the luxury of careful decision-making and checking to be sure you're right. But sometimes you do."

"How do you know which?"

Conal shook his head. "Do you ever know? But maybe, if you live long enough and fight hard enough, you develop a second sense about these matters. It's just—" He paused and considered Wat carefully. "It's never perfect, and you have to live with that," he said at last.

"Or die with it," Wat heard him mutter as he turned away to take the dispatches to someone else who'd look them over. Conal didn't know his letters, as the rest of the Six did.

But what Conal knew. Wat drew in his breath. He'd stake his life on what Conal knew. Conal might not be a gentle, but he had as much honor as any of them. More.

And what am I? Wat thought. *Not a gentle either. Betwixt and between.*

CHAPTER TWO

The Recent Unpleasantness

Caedon

G iving himself permission to relax with a cup of wine, Caedon sank back with a sigh of pleasure into the leather and furs of the carved chair in his favorite room, the walls filled to the ornately carved rafters with books on long shelves. Books and parchments on every available surface, stacked into every available nook and corner.

In the end, none of the unpleasantness of the botched battle mattered. The resounding defeat of the troops Caedon led. How they trickled back, beaten and diminished, to the royal seat in Tambourne.

The upbraiding Caedon had to endure from his monarch. The threats. Threats! from Audemar, that silly pig of a man. The clumsy attempt at a trial for treason. *Pfft*, thought Caedon with irritation. He held the wine cup up appreciatively to the light. It was made of that rare glass the Ice-realm's ships brought back from the Great City of the Lyre Lands. This one was studded all around with prunts in an interesting design. Caedon ran his finger over the design and took another swallow of the wine. A fine claret from the Baronies. He had it shipped across the Narrows from the vineyards of his guardian, the Baron Gilles de Rais.

Caedon put the cup carefully aside. He had been in no real danger during Audemar's fit of pique. The judge and jurors were easily bought off. The worst of it had been the malicious interference of the queen. *Ailys*, Caedon thought with contempt. He wondered whether he should have pandered a bit more to her sense of self-importance, but he brushed the thought impatiently away. Ailys had gotten what she wanted, hadn't she? But nothing was ever enough for the woman, murrain take her.

But when he thought of the long boring slog he'd had to make back into Audemar's good graces, he sighed. At least the king hadn't confiscated Caedon's manor, as he threatened. Because what he would have found there— Well. If it had come to that, Caedon would have just had to appeal to Gilles. That would have been messy and much more than unpleasant. Much, much more. But his breach with Audemar hadn't come to that. Caedon had handled things.

This Rising led by Avery and his friends. It was a gnat-bite only. They'd fought their battle, that little ragtag group. They would have lost if not for John, their mage, even with those interesting bows Caedon had devised.

Caedon's eyes strayed to an odd engine of war in brackets on the wall of his study. It was a type of bow never seen before. Caedon had thought the bows would make a big difference in the battle's outcome. Gilles had told him about them. Crossbows, they were called. Something Gilles had seen on one of his trips to that different plane, the one with the saintly maid. Gilles had explained them to Caedon, when he had returned to Caedon's own plane, and had drawn him a little diagram. Then Caedon had engaged weaponsmiths to forge and craft the bows, and the bolts they shot. He'd even taught himself to use one so that he could help train the bowmen.

"Those cumberground bows of yours. Pah," Audemar, scowling and red-faced, had said after the battle and the failure of the crossbows to matter. "How much gold of mine did you spend on them? And you're the whoreson knave who's supposed to have the brains."

But they are fine bows. A fine idea, Caedon had thought, while bowing silently to his monarch. A few kinks to be worked out there. Maybe a re-design or a different strategy for their use.

John and his powers, though. That was another matter. No point in explaining John to Audemar. Audemar had heard the grisly stories about what John's powers had done to Caedon's army but of course hadn't believed them. Had scoffed at them as a bunch of superstitious claptrap and excuse-making. "I remember another time John was supposed to have shrieked during a battle and caused a rout. What fopdoodle would believe such nonsense?" Audemar had said. "I thought it then, and I think it now. What kind of army have you mustered for me? An army afraid of some jack-minstrel, just some bastard," he had muttered.

Caedon had seen for himself, though, and up close, the time Gilles had taken John to his great hall and had forced the bastard to use his powers. What John had done then, and what he'd done during the battle, were deeply disturbing to Caedon. Not all the blood and gore. He was used to that. But what it meant, that John had these powers and that Caedon hadn't been able to stop him from using them. That's what he found so disturbing. He'd been worried until he talked it over with Gilles.

"John is finished," Gilles told Caedon, when Caedon made his springtide trek over to the Baronies, to pay his respects to Gilles. And to pay his tribute. "I doubt John will be able to use his powers again. He isn't trained. He doesn't know his own strength. Just the same, with John you do have a loose end to tie up, my dearest boy, and I want you to let me know when you've done it."

Will I be punished? thought Caedon nervously.

"Only a little," Gilles said as he read Caedon's thoughts. Then he had reached out to Caedon, and had drawn him close, and had—

Caedon shuddered at the memory. But Gilles was right. His punishment was not very severe. It only added a few extra days to Caedon's usual fortnight of recovery after a session with Gilles.

Best of all, Caedon's wards, the ones he'd thrown up around his secret, had held. Gilles didn't know. He still didn't know. Even after the act of punishment, which had weakened Caedon beyond the usual, Gilles didn't know. Caedon had made sure to throw the wards up well before he came into Gilles's presence. Else he was a dead man for certain.

In spite of Gilles's displeasure, more at Caedon's failure to deliver John to him or to get rid of John than about the actual defeat, which he cared little about, he had given Caedon rich rewards.

"One day, my dearest boy," he had said, caressing Caedon, "you will be the one in power. You'll be my viceroy in those lands. That silly king thinks he controls them. He does not. You do, in actual fact, and soon you'll control them in name as well."

"In your name, Most High One, although of course no one will realize it. And then you'll rule from the Baronies to the Sceptered Isle and beyond," Caedon had replied. "You'll rule the Ice-realm too."

"Lands past even that," said Gilles.

Caedon tried to think what he could mean by these lands. The little Fire Isle, to be sure. And that explorer's outpost in the Cold Lands. That's what Gilles must mean, although these small holdings were hardly worth Gilles's while. Westward past that, there were only travelers' yarns and fables.

"But they aren't just yarns and fables," Gilles whispered. "They are true. The vastness of the Unknown Lands to the west. Those lands lie within my grasp. In coming years, explorers in the Cold Lands will bring back word of them."

Caedon's eyes had opened wide in surprise.

"The world is a bigger place than you can imagine, Caedon, and I will take it all, with you as my instrument. And so," said Gilles, "although you yourself are not a mage, you'll need more of my powers to sustain you, my boy. Let me teach you."

Now that Caedon was back across the Narrows in his own manor in the hills above the Dourdin River, he thought what he would do first with the new powers.

Rafe, of course. New tools for controlling Rafe and harvesting more of his essences. Caedon thought about how long he would drag the process out. Not much longer, he decided. Once he was finished with Rafe, he'd send the shell of the lad over to Gilles for whatever last purpose Gilles might make of it.

He loved the lad, but Rafe had turned traitor.

I loved him, Caedon whispered furiously to himself.

He decided he needed a better grip on his spy in Avery's camp, too. She'd served him well so far, fueled only by her own resentments. But what would happen if she came up against something she couldn't handle?

What would happen if in the course of her duties for Caedon she'd have to damage that young man directly, the youngest of The Rising's leadership, Walter. They called him Wat, and if Caedon's spy had one weakness, Wat was that weakness. She protected him fiercely.

Wat was the middle brother of the set of brothers Caedon so longed to crush. Caedon had eliminated the youngest, along with his mother, but he'd failed with the other two, including John, the oldest.

That would change. He'd go after them both, and his spy would help him do it.

He had sent one of his other servants off to summon this spy to him. She was here now, they told him.

A discreet knock came at his door.

"Has she come?" Caedon looked up from the parchment he was studying.

"Yes, my lord Caedon," said the servant at the door.

"Send her in."

The man ushered a young woman into his private audience chamber.

"Eris," he said.

"My lord Caedon," she replied, bowing. But not very low.

"You understand," Caedon told Eris, after the preliminaries—her bowing, his gracious acceptance of her courtesies, such as they were, her handing over of a packet of information she had searched out at his command. "I must make sure of you, if we're to work together further."

"What do you need from me, my lord. I've given you everything you've asked. I'm done here."

Caedon ignored her words. "This last task troubled you deeply. I'm right, aren't I?" When she said nothing, he stood and said again, more insistent. "Aren't I?"

"Don't think you can intimidate me, Lord Caedon," she said.

"Just answer me."

"Yes. I brought you the information you wanted. Then you nearly killed my friend. My brother."

"It was unavoidable. You're a soldier, Eris. Surely you know that unpleasant things, unavoidable things, happen in time of war."

"You lied to me. You said you wanted John's whereabouts. You'd wait until he had stolen back to his house, you'd stake it out, and you'd take him there. You didn't say anything about killing his mother, and Wat, and that little boy."

"Sentimental about children, are you?"

"No," she said. "I don't care what you did to that child. But Wat's mother was kind to me. And Wat is my friend. My brother," she insisted again, glowering at him. "You lied to me, and John escaped you anyway, and Wat nearly died."

"So you want out, now," said Caedon.

"I won't help you any more," she said. "You've rewarded me. I thank you. Now we're done."

"Oh, I don't think we are, mistress," said Caedon softly. "You don't just walk away from this." He had the satisfaction of seeing a flicker of uncertainty in her eye. Not much. Just enough for someone trained to it, like himself, to notice.

He stepped to the door and motioned to two men outside. They came back into the room with him. He nodded to Eris, seated before the fire, as she looked over her shoulder at them in confusion and the beginnings of fear.

"Bind her," he said.

Although she fought and bit, the two tied her with stout ropes to the carved chair where she had been sitting. Then they left.

"You'll kill me now," she said to Caedon, her voice filled with loathing.

"By no means, mistress. I've seen how useful you can be. They all trust you. Prince Avery's sister."

"He's not my brother."

"Yes, he is, as you know very well. Half-brother. What does it matter. He trusts you."

"He's too trusting. They all are," she spat.

"Indeed. You have the right of it, Mistress Eris. But if you're to continue to work for me—"

"I'm not."

"—you need instruction." He stood up from his own chair and moved to stand over her. "Since I doubt you'll take this—" he paused. "this. . .instruction. . . willingly, I have had to have you bound."

"You swine," she said.

"You mistake me, mistress. I want nothing to do with you in the way you imagine. Hmm," he said. "I'm thinking you may bite, though." He moved to stand behind her and gathered up her hair in one hand, while she twisted and fought to get at him with her teeth.

"Hold still, mistress," he told her, and bent over her right ear as he gripped her head hard between his hands.

He insinuated himself through her ear into the crevices and folds of her brain.

For a moment, she thrashed and fought. Then she went completely rigid.

He proceeded with his work, and when he was finished, he withdrew from her ear a long, thin thread of her. He coiled it into a leather pouch, letting her see as he did it.

"There, now, mistress. I own a little piece of you."

She stared at him with wide frightened eyes.

"You see?" he said. He stepped back hastily as she leaned to vomit over the side of the chair.

When she had finished, he said, "I'll have you taken to a healer. I haven't done much. Not so very much, this time. You should be recovered in few days. If I have to repeat the procedure, you won't come out of it so well. You'll obey me now."

"Yes," she said, but he was fairly sure she didn't understand what she was saying. She was in a kind of semi-trance.

"When you've come back to yourself, I'll give you my next task. You and I understand each other, I think. We both have unfinished business with John. He escaped us once. He must not again." He snapped his fingers under her blank gaze. "Do you hear me?"

She nodded.

"I won't have to repeat this little act of reaping, if you obey me."

He stepped to the door again, and the same men came in to haul her off. "And send someone in here to clean up this mess," he called after them. He shut the door and stepped over the puddle of vomit, wrinkling his nose in disgust.

CHAPTER THREE

The Ends of the Earth

Dru

Dru stared into the fire, brooding. Beside him at the hearth stones, Elsebet stroked his hand. The girls were safely asleep.

"I know you still think about what happened to John's family."

"You can read my mind." He pulled her shining head over onto his shoulder and kissed the corner of her mouth.

"I know you blame yourself for putting John so near danger. You couldn't have known," she said to him.

"Still," said Dru grudgingly, because he did still blame himself, "it was a good thing he was near by. Otherwise his young brother would be dead. But the rest of them were slaughtered. You know his mother—" Dru swallowed hard. He moved away from Elsebet and rolled his shoulders, trying to unkink the tension. She reached over to pull him back close to her. "John's mother was as much like my own mother as—well, not as much as she was his and Wat's mother, I suppose, , but near enough," he said. He said it to Elsebet, but really, he was talking to himself, an accusing self inside him. "She mothered me, and she mothered Avery, too. I keep wondering whether my message to John somehow tipped off our enemies." Then, grudgingly, because he didn't want to let himself off the hook, "Someone in our midst is spying for Caedon, looks like."

He closed his eyes, as if that would make the swarming thoughts go away. Caedon and his ruffians.

What they'd done to Cicely, the kindest woman he'd ever known, taking on the task, unasked, of helping him grow from boyhood to manhood after his own mother had crossed that river to the Land of the Dead.

What Caedon's thugs had done to that little boy, John's youngest brother.

What they'd almost done to Wat and John.

"Makes me want to go over there and do something about it," he said in a savage whisper. "I'm beholden to Avery, though. I can't go off on revenge trips of my own. One day, Avery will unleash me on Caedon. But at least we beat his army and sent his soldiers whimpering back to their master. Too bad that pig Audemar didn't have Caedon executed for his sorry role. Something dark protects that man."

Elsebet began massaging the tension out of Dru's shoulders. "I don't want you going after Caedon on your own, either. I'm with Avery on that," she murmured. "It's too dangerous." Then she added, "When Rafe met us on market day the last turning of the moon, he told us Caedon isn't even in Tam Fort any more. He's back at his manor."

"Rafe does more than ten of us put together," said Dru. "But I worry about him more than any of us."

"And John," said Elsebet. "You worry about John all the time."

"It was so good to have him here with us. All winter. I didn't want him to leave. When we were boys, we were almost never apart. John, me, Avery. Having John here, I almost felt as if the world could be a happy place again. Now that he's gone, I fear for him." After a moment, Dru looked up and abruptly stopped talking about it all. With an effort he swallowed, steadying his voice. "Sweetheart," he said, and put out his hand.

Mirin was standing on the other side of the fire.

He wondered how much of their troubled talk she had overheard.

"I can't sleep, Father," she said.

"Come here and sit by us," he said to her. He and Elsebet made room for her, and soon she was nestled between them. "Is your sister awake too?"

Mirin shook her head no.

Dru gazed down at her affectionately. He loved her as much as if she were his natural daughter. Whenever he looked at her, the first heady days of his love for Elsebet came rushing into his memory. He glanced over her head at Elsebet and the two of them smiled at each other. The child was growing up. Soon she'd cross the boundary from girlhood to young womanhood. Already she was doing an adult's work to help keep the household together.

Right now, though, sitting wedged between them, she re-minded him of the little girl she used to be, not so long ago.

And now there was Jillian, who followed Mirin everywhere and tried to do everything her older sister did.

When he thought of Wat's and John's little brother, around the same age as Jillian, and how Caedon's men had brutally slaughtered the boy, it almost undid Dru.

He forced himself to talk of ordinary things.

At last all three of them went to bed, but Dru didn't sleep well. He was plagued with bad dreams. He lay thinking of John and his family. He thought of his own carefree boyhood with his friends, and reflected how differently his life had turned out from the way he'd expected it to. Sometime during the night Elsebet half-roused and cradled him to her, and then he could sleep.

In the morning, he felt in a better frame of mind. He'd go out and look over their strip of cropland and see what he might need to do as the growing season began. What tasks he'd need to com-plete so everything would be ready and tidy before the heavy springtide work of plowing and planting.

I'll get some of the harness for the village ox and figure out how to repair it. And then I'll take some pieces of wood to make Elsebet a new joint stool to replace the one that broke down a fortnight ago. I haven't seen to that yet. He began to whistle to himself.

Elsebet, stirring the kettle at the fire to make their porridge so they could break their fast, looked over at him, a smile playing about her lips.

Jillian was jumping around excitedly, exclaiming about the poppet her mother had made her, and the little house she planned to create for it underneath the quickthorn hedge that formed part of the village enclosure. The hedge was just beginning to leaf out.

Mirin was putting on her boy's things. "I'm going to snare us a rabbit. We haven't had meat in a sen'night," she said. Then she paused and looked up at Dru. "Father, are you going to make a rebec for me, the way John asked you to?"

"I am indeed," said Dru with a grin. "I always keep my promises to my brother."

"John is your brother?"

"We didn't share the same parents, so no, not in the way most people think about it. He may not be my real brother, but he's my true brother. Think about it, Mirin. Real and true. Real is what the world thinks. True is what is. Deep down, what is. My brother wants you to have a rebec. And so you shall."

"I want me to have one, too, Father."

"And. . ." Dru teased. "My daughter wants you to have a rebec, and so you shall." He ruffled up her hair and pulled her close to him for a hug. "In fact, just yesterday," he told her, "I saw the tree I'm going to carve it from. The pear tree down at the edge of the meadow, the one that got blasted with lightning during the gowk storm."

His heart filled with love as he saw how thrilled Mirin was at his words. He'd carve the rebec, as he promised Johnny he would, and then Mirin would be able to continue the music Johnny had taught her. Dru saw how important it was to Mirin. And it had been very important to John. Strangely important to him.

"Gowk storm," Elsebet was saying with a laugh. "I haven't heard that since I was a child."

"What's a gowk storm, Mother?" said Mirin.

"'As sun grows warm, the cuckoo brings the storm,'" Elsebet quoted. "The first cuckoo of spring brings the first spring storm. The old folks always said gowk for cuckoo. So the storm is a gowk storm."

"I saw a cuckoo in the woods the last time I went out," said Mirin.

"We had that fierce storm, just after," said Elsebet, nodding solemnly at her daughter, who was looking skeptical. There was a twinkle in Elsebet's eye.

But Dru wasn't paying much attention. He was remembering the day last harvest-tide, late in the season, when he'd heard a faint hallooing outside their cabin.

They had all stopped what they were doing. Dru and Elsebet were ever on the alert for a moment like this. Though they'd never discussed the need for vigilance with the girls, both children had picked up on their parents' unease. Even Jillie, young as she was.

Dru moved quietly to his weapons, his knives, and sheathed them in the scabbards at his waist. He'd had them out the day before, oiling them and sharpening them on the whetstone.

Elsebet gave him a warning shake of the head, looking from one daughter to the other, but Dru saw they were too occupied with listening to notice what he was doing and become alarmed. He stepped outside the cabin. Someone was coming down the path from the village toward them.

The figure waved.

"John!" Dru cried, the tension dropping away. In an instant, he was down the path to meet his friend, the man raised like a brother with him and with Avery, John's half-brother. Dru and John stood in the middle of the path, embracing, and then Dru was leading John to the cabin, and John was exclaiming over Mirin, who had stepped out to see what was going on. Elsebet and Jillian came outside too. Soon they had all gathered around the hearth stones, and Elsebet was getting out the spare wooden spoon and bowl and passing pease porridge around for everyone.

"How is Wat?" Dru asked John in an undertone.

"He's doing well. The arm's strong, as I think you saw at the battle. The wound ended up healing well, no festering. He'll have a bad scar, though."

"Not the only one with a bad scar," said Dru, scrutinizing the side of John's face.

John laughed. "Good thing I don't hope to attract the ladies," he said. "It's strange, though. I thought I was going to have to start using a disguise during my performances, especially after the incident. But this scar is my disguise. Nobody looks at me. They all look at that. I may as well be invisible. It's a great thing for the work, Dru."

Dru looked over at John, worried. His scar didn't seem to bother him in the least. *If he could love again*, thought Dru, for maybe the thousandth time.

The girls were chattering away with their mother. Dru turned to John. "Brother, aren't you ever going to get past Lyn? I don't mean entirely, but—"

"No," said John, and smiled at Dru.

"So stubborn," Dru muttered.

"Some of us are lucky in love," said John, looking over at Elsebet.

"And some of us won't even try."

"Elsebet," said John, talking past him. "Remember when we sang that duet? Back at that lovely house of Dru's?"

"I do," she said.

"Shall we try it again?"

"Why not?" she said.

He already had his rebec out and was tuning it.

"The porridge not even cold," said Dru, rolling his eyes.

"What's that?" said Mirin, stepping up to John to see.

"This is my rebec," said John. He looked up at her, where she stood bent over his instrument. He went quiet. Then he put the instrument down beside him. "Elsebet," he said. "Let's sing the duet later."

"Fine with me, John," she said. She busied herself with cleaning-up tasks.

"I was just about to take a walk over to our strip of crop land. I hope you're planning to stay for a while," said Dru.

"Just a day or two. I'll come out there with you. There's something I've come to talk over with you."

"Something important, or Avery wouldn't have told you where to find us," said Dru quietly. They'd all agreed. No one but Avery would know where Dru and his family lived. It was safer that way. Not unless there was an overriding emergency.

John gave a small affirmative nod. His expression was grave.

Elsebet went out to the well, and little Jillian skipped alongside.

"Let me get a few tools I've put up here in the rafters," said Dru. "I'll need to see whether I'll have to oil them for the winter, or—"

Below him, John sat looking at Mirin. "This is my rebec," Dru heard him tell her. "Would you like to hold it?"

"Yes, please," she said. Dru stepped down from the rafters with his hoe. He looked over at Mirin with tenderness. He saw how her eyes were shining as she reached for John's instrument.

Dru watched as John put it in her hands and showed her a few things about the strings.

"Dark Ones take it, looks like we'll have another musician in the family," Dru teased, and Mirin looked up at him, delighted. "Mirin has Elsebet's voice," he said to John. "And now I can see how fascinated she is by this fiddle thing of yours. I can see it in your eyes, Mirin. You can't fool me."

Mirin grinned at him.

"Dru," said John. His voice was hesitant. "Would I crowd all of you if I stayed longer?"

"Stay as long as you like, brother," said Dru. "Stay all winter." But he glanced again at John, then stared at him hard. John's gaze was riveted on Mirin, as if he saw something uncanny there. And then a change came over him.

Dru watched, puzzled. There was something in John's expression he couldn't quite fathom. It seemed to him as if John were looking at something no one else could see. Something far away and profoundly sad. Dru felt a chill creep up his arms.

He knew that look of John's. It always meant something spooky was about to happen. Something connected to John's uncanny powers. Those insights of John's didn't come out often, but when they did, Dru knew he had better take notice. Whether John's look portended a good thing or a bad thing, that he didn't know and, he suspected, neither did John.

He thought again of the battle they had fought, and how John's powers had defeated Caedon. He thought of the battle long ago, when Dru and Avery and John had gone over to the Western Isle to fight in King Ranulf's war. If not for John and his powers, they'd all be dead. Conal too.

He thought of the terrible thing that had happened to Avery, in boyhood, and how John had gone straight to Conal, to summon help. For a long time, Dru hadn't understood how John had known to do it. Later, he realized.

He thought of the time he himself had forged the brooches of the Six Proud Walkers, the leadership of The Rising. How he'd planned to forge only five, with five gold bars in the backing, because there were only five of them then. "Forge six," John had said, and didn't even realize what he was asking. Later, they'd all understood. The sixth of them was Wat. John had known, deep down, but he hadn't even realized what he knew. That was the way of it, with John.

What was John? A mage, maybe. Dru shied away from thoughts like that, because that's not how he saw the world, but it must be true. And John didn't even know what he was, or didn't at first.

John had never wanted it. Wherever his powers came from, they tormented him, even when others—Dru, all of them—owed their lives to John and his magicks.

Dru promised himself he'd help John with whatever John needed. He glanced over at John, where he sat still staring at

Mirin. Whatever that look of John's meant, Dru vowed he'd help John with the consequences.

He realized he'd go to the ends of the earth for John, and that John would go to the ends of the earth for him. It had been so all their lives, and it was that way still.

CHAPTER FOUR

Overdue

Wat

Wat, Eris, and some of the other young recruits were waiting for their training with Conal to resume. The day had grown warm. They were sitting together during a break Conal had called in the training.

"You wouldn't need this training if you'd been allowed to go to the king's arms master as a boy," Eris was saying. He knew she blamed Avery for it. Unfairly. Avery had had nothing to do with the king's decision not to allow him to train with Conal, as John had been allowed to do.

"And you, Mistress Eris, you wouldn't need this training if you weren't just a girl," Wat needled her back. *Keep it light,* he thought to himself. *Don't get angry. She has some need to think and say these things, Child knows why.*

She thumped him on the arm, hard, and he swatted at her lazily with the flat of his practice sword.

"Ow," Eris said in a high, silly, affected voice. "That's going to leave a bruise."

They both laughed. Underneath, Wat wasn't laughing. He missed the special training he had gotten from Dru, and he missed the closeness with Dru himself, now that Dru was back with his family and away from the camp, but the training with Conal was the core. Conal's knowledge of combat was unsurpassed, and he was an excellent teacher. Dru had taught Wat the skills of knife, garotte, stealth. Conal's training focused on more usual combat skills. The short sword. The broadsword. The shield. Combat from horseback.

These were all the skills Wat had lacked as a boy when he wasn't allowed to train with the sons of the nobility. But John had been allowed. And now Wat was behind. He was determined to catch up.

The bow, though. That was a far different matter. John had gotten him his first bow when he was eight. Even sons of yeomen were expected to know how to wield a bow. Wat and John, bastards, weren't nobles, and they weren't yeomen either. *Betwixt and between*, Wat thought. But Wat had practiced for several candle measures with the bow just about every day since, and now, with Conal's training, he'd gotten really good at it. When he went into battle with his bow, he had cut his long, fair hair off short, like Conal's. He didn't want it tangling in the bowstring.

"You're right," Wat said now to Eris, picking a piece of grass and sucking at it, trying and failing to make it whistle. "I wouldn't be so behind in my skills, if I'd been allowed to train like John." *May as well let her talk about it,* he thought. *Let her get it out.*

"That's because Mistress Cicely was the king's favorite, when John was born. By the time you were born, the king had tired of your mother. He paid attention to John. None to you," said Eris. Then she added, "That's why you can't trust them. Any of them. All friendly and brotherly when they can use you. When these people can't, or when they don't need you, they kick you to the midden."

"I know all about my mother and the king," said Wat. Now he wanted Eris to stop talking about it. Now he wished he had just let it drop after Eris had brought up his lack of training. His mother had been King Ranulf's concubine. And Eris was right. By the time Wat was born, Ranulf had lost interest in his mother.

None of this was Avery's fault, as Eris was always implying. Now that Wat's father the king was dead, one of his sons, Audemar, sat on the throne. But Audemar was a usurper who had assassinated his older brother Artur, Ranulf's heir. The Rising was the youngest brother Avery's attempt to make things right and avenge Artur's assassination. *Who is more trustworthy than Avery?* Wat thought. *Who nobler?* Eris was wrong about Avery.

"If you mean Avery, when you say you can't trust them, you're just wrong, Eris." Wat said it out loud. Eris needed to understand. He felt a deep loyalty to Avery, and nothing she could say would undermine it.

Eris had her own resentments, and she seemed determined to fan the flames of his. To try, anyway. "Sometimes I wish you and I could step away from all this," said Eris, sweeping her arm wide, indicating the whole camp.

"Not to be part of The Rising?" Wat looked over at her, worried about what she might be thinking. This was new. It went beyond resentment.

"Just be on our own. You and I, on the road together, doing whatever we'd a mind to. We have the skills to keep ourselves. We wouldn't be a part of any of these big conflicts, not Avery's, not Caedon's, not Audemar's. To the Dark Ones with them, all of them."

Wat gave her a half-smile. Her dream of a carefree life did have its enticements. But it was the dream of a child. They weren't children any longer. He and Eris both had their responsibilities. And Nine Spheres, he thought, Eris was good at hers.

The night before, Eris had come back from one of her scouting expeditions. She excelled at this work. She'd be gone for days at a time, and then she'd return with information for Avery and Conal.

She didn't bring back the same kind of information Wat helped John collect, on John's expeditions. His and John's information-gathering was all about the way people in the villages were ground down by Audemar the king's oppressive laws, the whispers around castles and manors that gave Avery some inkling of Audemar's vulnerabilities.

Eris's spying was different. The information she collected was about troop movements, locations of caches of weapons and supplies, the whereabouts of someone Avery might want Dru to go after with his stealth and his knives.

When she came back this time, she seemed changed, some-how. Wat wondered if she had fallen ill. Her face looked thin and drawn, and her eyes had a strange glitter. So now he was troubled by what she was saying, and especially by her disenchantment with The Rising.

"I want to be part of it," he told her.

"Well," she said. "Of course you do, now that they've drawn you into their cozy inner circle."

"Eris. Caedon's men killed my mother. They killed Aedan. They tried to kill me and Johnny. You think I'd walk away from The Rising?" He was beginning to get angry. "I watched them, Eris. I watched the killers when they butchered my mother and brother. I watched them when they—." He had to stop talking for a moment. The emotions that caught him were too overwhelming. But he went on. "The people who care about me are here. Rafe helped Johnny save my life. Avery and Dru and Conal welcomed me here."

She put out a hand to him. "I know," she said, unexpectedly hesitant. "I know that's how it feels to you. I wish you could see that's not how it is for me. I wish you could see how easily these people could change their minds about you. How easily they're using these obligations to manipulate you. I just wish you and I weren't in it, that's all. It's dangerous for you, Wat."

"Of course it's dangerous. Dangerous for you, too. We're in danger every day. Do you want out? I think if you did, you could tell Avery that, and he'd understand."

"You think he'd just let me walk away, knowing what I know? Good way to get my throat slit," she said, smiling grimly. "And what I mean by dangerous and what you mean are two different things. You're thinking of the dangers of battle. Of the sword. I'm thinking of other dangers."

Wat didn't know what she meant by that, but he was truly shocked. "You think Avery would kill you? Avery? He's your brother," he said.

"Yes. I suppose he is my brother," Eris said, and looked away. "But if I left, you'd come with me?"

"I'll never leave," said Wat. "Avery is here. John is here, and Conal. Dru and Rafe come and go all the time. They're my family, Eris. Nine Spheres, they're your family."

"I don't feel the same way you do about them, Wat," she said quietly. "It's different, for me. Don't you see?"

Wat thought about Eris's experiences, in girlhood. He had known all these men, from infancy practically, because John was his older brother. His mother raised Avery and Dru, one of them a prince, one of them an earl, but both of them motherless, right alongside John and Wat, her two bastard sons by the king. The three older boys had been inseparable, and still were. In childhood, Wat had looked up to all three of them, and all three of them had played with him, teased him, taught him.

Eris was right about herself, he saw. That hadn't been her experience, not at all. But then, he thought in confusion, why join The Rising, if she felt that way.

"You're my family, Wat. You're all of it. Not these men," she said, her voice low and bitter.

"Johnny is one of these men, as you put it, Eris. I love Johnny more than life." Then Wat wished he hadn't said it. A black look came across Eris's features and just as suddenly left. What was that, Wat wondered. Jealousy, maybe.

"You should listen to me, Wat. None of them can keep you safe. Not even John. I can."

Before he could think about the strange thing Eris was suggesting, that he was in some kind of mysterious danger only she could save him from, Conal was moving among the trainees, clapping his hands sharply.

"Look alive, varlets," he called to them all. "Enough lollygagging." But Wat saw the twinkle in his eye as he strode past.

It was time to begin their session again. Wat turned away and didn't answer Eris. When he looked over at her, later in the session, he saw she had passionately entered into the exercises Conal set them. *Nine Spheres*, he thought. *Eris is one of Conal's best students.* Quick. Dangerous. Strong. *Much better than I am*, he thought.

Afterward, as he walked to his tent mopping the sweat from his neck and chest with his wadded up tunic, Eris caught up to him.

"You'll keep my words to yourself? What we talked about earlier?"

"Of course," he said. He gave her a quick embrace. "We're family. You're right about that. You can tell me anything, Eris. We may not always agree, but you're my sister, and we've been friends from birth, practically. I love you."

At the camp's central hearth, Avery stood talking to a few other men. Wat saw Conal was with them. He and Avery both looked over in Wat's and Eris's direction, and Avery motioned Wat over.

"Run," said Eris under her breath. "Run to your masters, boy."

"Eris—" said Wat.

"Go on. His Highness needs you."

With a troubled heart, Wat approached the fire. Avery and Conal were looking grave. Had they overheard something of Eris's disenchantment? Would they question him about her, he wondered. He'd never betray her confidences.

The reason for their grave looks rested on a completely different matter, and it terrified Wat when he learned of it.

"Wat," said Avery. "John was supposed to come into camp two days ago. He's overdue."

Wat had been waiting for John to come back to the camp. He'd been hoping, now the battle was over and the mopping-up done, that he'd be released to travel with John again. He found these long roaming journeys with his older brother were as reassuring to him as anything could be, now that his mother and Aedan were gone, his home taken away, his wounds healed. The outer wounds, anyhow.

The brothers traveled the countryside together. Wat juggled and performed acrobatics, just the way Silly Shep, the king's old jester, had taught him. That attracted the attention and the crowds. Then John played and sang. And the haunting, beautiful strains of John's music got them entry just about everywhere.

The two of them collected information and brought it back to Avery. They also ferried messages between Avery and far-flung members of The Rising who couldn't easily get to Avery. They got information to Rafe, and he gave them information to bring back.

Of all of the Six, Wat realized, Rafe must play the most dangerous role. He was their double agent in Caedon's very household, and he also spent a lot of his time at the castle where one of Caedon's minions kept the Princess Diera, daughter of the assassinated crown prince. Diera, Wat's childhood friend, and—odd to think of it this way, since she was a bit older than he was—Wat's niece. But only the Six knew this about Rafe. The others thought he simply roved the land, spying for Avery.

Wat and John, together. When he was a boy, he dreamed of going with John on the adventures he was sure John was always having. In the midst of a bad time, that dream had come true, and he felt more than his wound healing when he and John sat close together at their campfire and quietly talked over the day's accomplishments. Or when he lay with his head pillowed on his arms, looking up through the trees at the stars hanging from the Spheres on their golden chains, and listened to the music John played just for the two of them.

"John's overdue," Avery said again. "It's probably nothing. But if he's still not here in another day or two, I'm going to send you off to Rafe so you and he can track John down."

Wat nodded. He could see by looking in their eyes. They were worried. Otherwise they'd never have brought this up to him.

"Don't fret, lad," said Conal. "You and Rafe will find him. We know where he has been working."

Rafe had helped John get out of a terrible situation over in the Baronies not so long ago. Wat knew this. Wat knew how important it was to get to Rafe.

Three days later, just after breaking his fast, Wat made ready to go south. Then he'd turn up the Dourdin River to the castle where Rafe was assigned by Caedon to watch over Diera.

Eris stopped him as he was heading out of camp. "Be careful, Wat," she said, and he saw a strange uncharacteristic panic in her eyes. "Wait. You're going off to do something dangerous. I can tell. I'll get Avery's leave to go with you."

He lingered on the path out of the camp. Eris came back soon.

"I'm not to go," she said, her face dark as one of the thunderclouds always massing about these mountains. "Conal has some other thing he wants me to do."

"I'll be careful, Eris. You know I will."

"You're too soft, Wat," said Eris. "You need me with you."

"I'm not. I don't." He was annoyed now. He shrugged away from her and headed down the path without looking back.

That night, bedded down in his furs underneath the stars on a little forested hill, he thought about what she had said to him. *Too soft*, he thought. *Am I?* Everyone treated him gingerly, after what had happened to his family. After what he had seen and suffered. But during the battle, hadn't he proven his courage and ability? Hadn't Avery himself invited Wat to become part of The Rising's leadership?

In the morning he woke to birdsong and mild springtide weather. He was going south, and it was getting warmer. All around him, the calls of the spring cuckoos rang out, insistent. *The male bird*, thought Wat. *And there's the female.* A bubbling rill of sound underlying the repeated two-note calls of the males. Every springtide, as he, Eris, and their friend Keelie had roamed the forest outside Tam Fort, they'd heard these birds, and their hearts had lifted, because it meant spring had come. They could toss their heavy cloaks aside, run bare-legged through the meadows ablaze with primrose, dog's mercury, celandine. Splash through the little river below the fort. He thought of Keelie, long dead. How amazed she'd be at the turn his and Eris's lives had taken.

Keelie's death. That had been the beginning of it all, thought Wat. Everything was fine. Their lives were good. Then that horrifying act. The violent death of a young girl. Nothing was the same again, not for him personally, and not, he realized, for the realm either. *It's as if her death started something that hasn't stopped yet*, thought Wat. *Would it ever?* He unrolled himself from his furs and began folding them tightly into his pack. Time to get going. He hoisted the pack onto his back, and began walking.

He knew where he was going. He and Johnny had come this way together many times, because they always stopped to collect information from Rafe on their way back to Avery.

Rafe couldn't get away from Caedon's scrutiny, not too easily. Less and less so. Sometimes he made it over to the nearby market town to talk to Dru.

Wat knew Caedon had some kind of sinister hold on Rafe. He remembered what John had told him, after the battle. *Get to Rafe*, John had urged him. *Tell him my farwydd says his Child stands with him.*

Whatever that might mean to Rafe, Wat knew by John's tone that it was a serious matter.

At the time, Wat had been frightened. Why couldn't John himself tell Rafe, the next time they both saw him. That's what Wat had wondered. And now. Wat felt a chill take him. Now John might be missing, and Wat was going to Rafe alone.

John knew things he shouldn't have been able to know. John had strange powers.

Wat swallowed hard. Was this one of the things John had known, that Wat would have to get to Rafe when maybe John wouldn't be able to?

Then he thought of John's other powers. The blood and horror of the battlefield when John strode out with his rebec and opened his mouth to shriek. How the enemy went down before him like barley scythed in the field.

Bards and their powers. Everyone loved the songs they sang, the music they brought into the dull lives that ordinary people led. But everyone feared them a little, too. Most minstrels and bards were exactly what they seemed. Jolly folk. Entertainers. Every now and again, though—

And John, it turned out, was one of the dangerous kind.

Thinking of his brother as dangerous. It was a strange notion to Wat. But Wat had been on the battlefield that day. Wat had seen.

The fineness of the day stopped these thoughts at last. Wat walked along the roads and paths, looking around him, eased by the green of the surroundings.

He figured it might take him a fortnight to walk to the Dourdin, and then up it to the castle where Rafe did his work. In the meantime, maybe John would come into camp. Avery promised to send John on to Rafe, if that should happen, and then Wat and John could resume their circuit from there. It was a good plan.

After almost a sen'night of walking, using his bow to take down small game on the way, finding streams of clear water where he could fling himself full-length onto the mossy banks to drink, Wat had convinced himself that he'd surely find John with Rafe. His heart lightened. He stayed away from towns.

Gradually his thoughts turned darker. He was striding along the verge of a broad road leading south when, behind him, he heard the creaking and clanking of a wagon. He stepped to the roadside to shade his eyes. A lone carter. Looked to be some yeoman farmer.

Wat stepped into the road to wave the man down.

The man pulled his ox up and peered over the side of the cart suspiciously at Wat.

"My good man, I'm headed south on this road. I'll pay you well to let me ride along," Wat said to him, holding up a coin for the man to see.

The man took it, turned it over, bit it. "Good coin, young master." His expression cleared.

"I'll pay you another like it when we reach your destination," said Wat.

"I'm heading to the next town only, but hop up onto the cart, if you will."

Wat did so. He braced himself against the back-board of the cart among the man's boxes and bundles, and they jolted off.

After a number of candle measures, when Wat had not robbed the driver, or committed any manner of violence, and when Wat felt he'd be shaken to pieces before the journey was done, the driver looked over his shoulder at Wat. "Come up here on the seat with me, if you will," he called back. "The ride will be easier."

Wat gratefully crawled over the back of the wagon and up onto the wagon seat with the driver. "My thanks," he said.

The driver was a taciturn, grizzled peasant who had no need to converse. Wat was glad of it. He didn't want to have to make up some story about where he was going and why.

The next town turned out to be quite a distance away, the coin well-spent. "Thanks, my good man," said Wat as he jumped down from the wagon at the gates of the prosperous-looking town. Wat squinted at the palisades surrounding it. He thought he recognized it.

As promised, he handed up a second coin to the driver. The man pulled his forelock, apparently deciding Wat was some sort of gentle, the Lady knew why. Wat didn't wear his hair like a noble any longer. He cut it short like a peasant. "You two knotheads," Avery said to him and Conal, to tease them. But Wat didn't want his hair tangling his bowstring, and Conal refused to grow his hair long. "I'm no gentle," Conal would mutter, with an irritated little grimace at Avery's grin.

Now the driver nodded to the town gates. "Withiel," he said.

Wat nodded. Withiel. Yes. He did recognize it. He and John had come through here and played at one of their street fairs. He thanked the driver again and watched as he angled his wagon to head through the gates.

Then Wat kept down the road past the town, as it followed a river.

He didn't stop in the town. He'd have to show a parchment to get into the place, and he had none. When he and John toured these towns, sometimes the guards would let them in without parchments, especially if there were something going on, like a street fair. The guards could see they were minstrels and players, and rules were frequently relaxed for such traveling folks. Johnny the Traveler. That was John's stage name. And he, John's partner, was Kenning the Juggler.

But sometimes he and John would have to set up their wagon and perform outside the gates. It all depended on the mood of the guards and whether something dangerous was going on in the region. However much Wat might long for a real bed and a real meal in one of Withiel's taverns, he wasn't in his player's costume, a frippery thing of green with a frippery cap. Wat had copied it from Silly Shep's costume. King Ranulf's jester had taught Wat all he knew of acrobatics and juggling. Even the Six-Ball Shower, his most famous trick.

Without his player's costume and the performance wagon he and John drove from town to town, Wat knew he'd never be admitted to Withiel when he couldn't show proper identification. Not in these times. Then again, he could spare not even a candle measure. He needed to get to Rafe, and fast. As fast as possible. He was feeling more and more uneasy about his brother. He only hoped he was heading in the right direction along the river.

As Wat walked up the road paralleling the river, he came around a bend to the spot where a second river poured into it. *Thank the Lady*, he thought. He knew where he was now. Just a bit upriver from the smaller town where Cwenegund the healer had treated his wound after Caedon's attack on his family. Cwenegund, Keelie's grandmother. He'd known her since childhood.

When John and Rafe had gotten him to her, half-dead after the attack on his family, she'd hugged him to her, exclaiming and fussing and crying over him. Then she'd patched him up good as new, made him lie still for a fortnight and more, and forced broth and ale down him when he didn't want to eat.

He'd just wanted everyone to leave him alone, back then. He just wanted to turn his face to the wall and stare at it, or doze, or fight off the frightening dreams that swarmed into his head the moment his eyes closed. Cwen wouldn't let him be. No matter how sullen he acted, no matter how hard he tried to drive her, and everyone, off from him, she refused to let him get away with it. So at last he healed.

John wouldn't let him alone, either. He sat by Wat as time burned by in candle-measure after candle-measure, unless he had to go away for a few days on a mission. As soon as it was over, he was right back by Wat's bedside.

Occupied by thoughts of John and how John cared for him, Wat turned up-country. He thought of Cwen and her granddaughter Keelie, his and Eris's fast friend—Diera's friend, too—as he walked. He thought of Keelie, murdered at only fourteen, before she'd had a chance to live. When he was small, the world had seemed right and good. Then it had turned dangerous and vile. Keelie murdered. Now, too, his mother and younger brother. The world had transformed into an ugly place, and Wat was not sure how to live in it.

He tried to drive these thoughts away. They were too difficult.

Finally, after a hard day's traveling, he reached his goal and was no longer out on the road alone with his thoughts. He had ordinary tasks to do now, and he rushed to do them. They displaced the terrible images that haunted him.

He came to a small village. He recognized it as the village just outside the castle where Rafe watched over Diera. He paid for a bed in one of the villagers' houses, and in the morning, he'd headed up the path, pushed the rusted creaking village gate aside, and made his way to the castle. He'd see Rafe. Rafe would know where John was. Everything would be fine.

"Hold," said one of the guards. "Your business here, fellow?" This man wasn't confusing Wat with a gentle.

"I'm Master Leofric's brother," said Wat. He and Rafe had settled on this story the year before. Leofric was the name Rafe used at the castle. Wat had put up his hood so his and Rafe's very different coloring wouldn't seem so obvious. Rafe was dark-haired, his skin a pale, delicate olive, his cheeks so pale that the dark beard always showed through a bit, as if Rafe always needed to shave. Wat was fair-haired and ruddy-cheeked. He'd tried to grow a beard once, like Avery's, but had shaved the wispy thing off in disgust. He overtopped Rafe by a head. They looked nothing alike.

The other guard stationed at the gate glanced over at him and acknowledged him. "You were here a season or so ago, maybe," he said.

Wat nodded.

"I'll send for Master Leofric. Wait here," he said.

Not much longer afterward, Rafe was at the gates. "Brother!" he exclaimed. To the guards, he said, "Tell them in the household, if you will, that my brother and I have gone over to the tavern in the village."

Then he stepped into the roadway. Wat had to keep himself from staring. Rafe looked gaunt and unwell, the cheekbones standing out sharp against the pallor of his face.

Rafe took Wat's arm, and they went down the roadway together until they were out of sight of the guards. Then Rafe steered Wat down an overgrown pathway to a quiet clearing where they could talk.

"Rafe, have you been ill?" said Wat anxiously.

"In a manner of speaking," said Rafe. Before Wat could wonder what he might mean, he was staring at Wat intently. "Where's John?"

Now Wat's heart sank into his shoes. He had convinced himself Rafe would say to him, *Oh, Johnny went off to this village or that one or*— But now Wat saw it wasn't so.

"I was hoping John was here. I was hoping you had seen him. We were hoping," said Wat. He watched the tiny flame of panic kindle in Rafe's eyes.

"No," Rafe said. "I haven't seen him since he brought word of plans for the battle. I expected to see him afterward. I expected to see you both, and hear your account of all your mighty deeds. Caedon has certainly fallen from his high horse because of them." Wat could see Rafe was trying to smile.

"Nobody knows where John is," said Wat, a deep alarm settling on him now. "Unless our paths crossed, and he's back at camp by now. When I left, he was five days overdue."

"Let's hope he's following you," said Rafe quietly.

"Suppose he's not."

"I have a few things I can do to find something out," said Rafe. "Stay around here, in case he arrives soon, and in the meantime, you can take messages for me up-river. You know Lorel and Torrin? Their village is near by. They're doing fine work for us, operating out of that village. And Dru should be along in about a fortnight, I'm thinking."

"Good," said Wat. "Just tell me what you need, and I'll do it." Then he added, "Dru may know something. Avery sent Johnny off to Dru, and as soon as he returned, he and I were supposed to resume our circuit of the street fairs and the taverns and the manor houses."

"John went to Dru?" Rafe moved over to a tumbledown stone wall at the edge of the clearing and slouched against it, as if casually. But Wat realized the real reason. If Rafe didn't have something to lean on, he might fall down.

"Yes, to warn him. Someone is getting information about us to Caedon. We think whoever it is may have discovered Dru's whereabouts." Wat scrutinized Rafe with concern. Wat realized Rafe was even weaker than he had first thought.

"No one is supposed to know Dru's whereabouts," said Rafe. "I don't even know. It's somewhere pretty close to here, though. I meet him sometimes at the market town down the road."

"Yes, that's all I know about where he is, too," said Wat. "But Avery knows. I think he's the only one who does know." Wat stopped. "Except now John does. And, I suppose, Caedon's traitor. When Avery realized Caedon might know where Dru is hiding, he sent John to warn Dru."

"Someone is betraying us to Caedon," said Rafe, looking stunned.

"Yes," said Wat. Then he had a bad thought. "Do you think you may be in danger yourself, Rafe?"

Rafe smiled and shook his head. "Not I. I'm as safe as a mouse in the cornerboard. Caedon knows who I am already. He knows where I am at all times. Nearly all times," he added with a laugh as he saw Wat's expression. "Don't worry. You and I are fine here. No one's lurking about. But Caedon knows he can get to me whenever he likes and deal with me however he likes. He knows

I favor The Rising and would betray him in an instant if I could. There's the rub, Wat."

"What do you mean? Why are you still alive?"

"He thinks he controls me totally, and because Diera trusts me, he thinks he can control her through me. He used to think he could use me to get false information to The Rising or to get to The Rising through me, but now he sees he can't."

"I still don't understand. Just because Diera trusts you? That's the only reason you're alive? And he thinks he can control you. But how?"

"It's hard to explain that, Wat. You know Caedon and I were sent over here to the Sceptered Isle by our guardian, that powerful noble, Gilles de Rais, the one with lands in the Baronies. You might not know the most important thing about Gilles, though. He has powers. In fact—" Wat saw Rafe was carefully gauging his expression. "Gilles is a mage," he finished quietly.

"Like Johnny," said Wat, shuddering.

"In a way, I suppose." Then Rafe shook his head. "Not like Johnny. Johnny's powers are nothing to his. And Johnny uses his powers for good."

"Caedon? What about him?"

"Not a mage. But Gilles lends him his powers. That's why Caedon thinks he controls me. He thinks the things he can do to me will keep me in line. But they won't. And that's what he doesn't know."

"And is that why you—what are they doing to you?" Wat burst out.

"No need to know that, Wat," Rafe said softly. "Just that it won't go on much longer."

"John will stop it."

"If only he could."

Wat suddenly remembered. "Johnny gave me a message for you, a message from his farwydd."

Rafe, who had been leaning against the wall with shoulders hunched, looking down at the grass under their feet, turned his pale face slowly in Wat's direction.

"His farwydd said to tell you that your Child stands with you."

Wat stopped, astounded at the transformation in Rafe. Rafe's eyes widened. Then he turned aside, sank down into the grass at the foot of the wall, and wept.

Wat stood uncertainly clasping and unclasping his hands.

Finally Rafe wiped his eyes on his sleeve. He turned back to Wat with a smile, leaning his arms on his knees and looking down again. "I'm so weak. My feelings are all out in the open for anyone to see. Sorry, lad. Caedon has weakened me mortally, I think. But your message gives me hope. Unexpected hope," he ended with a whisper. Then he looked back up at Wat in alarm. "John told you to tell me this."

"Yes," said Wat, moving to sit down beside Rafe in the grass.

"Why not bring me the message himself."

"He told me," said Wat, remembering, "We soldiers give these messages to others all the time. Just in case. That's what he said to me."

"He told you this before the battle," said Rafe, relief flooding his features.

"No, after."

Rafe went silent. He held out a hand to Wat, and Wat steadied him while he got to his feet. Wat saw with fresh alarm how very ill Rafe was. He saw Rafe could barely stand.

"Wat," he said, low and fast. "Something has happened to your brother. I'm going back to the castle, and I'm finding out what it is. Then you and I will search for him. Agreed?"

"Yes," said Wat, his heart beginning to pound. "Something has happened?"

"I'm pretty sure of it. We need to act fast."

"What could have happened? What do you know, Rafe?"

"Listen, Wat. Did you know I got your brother out of a bad spot, over there in the Baronies?"

"Yes, he told me something about it. Caedon's men caught him and tortured him, and you got him out. That's how his leg got injured."

"That's what he told you."

"Yes, and then he visited his farwydd, because our father the king had made him promise to go to her."

"That's right. But there was a lot more to it, Wat. Caedon did those things to John, but he did them on Gilles's orders. Gilles wants to possess John, to own him. To study him. But if he can't have him, he wants him dead."

Wat felt a chill when he realized what Rafe was saying. How it might explain why John had disappeared. "Caedon may have grabbed Johnny." He put out a hand to steady Rafe.

"I'm guessing he has," said Rafe, "and I know how to find out if I'm right. The easiest way to find out will put me in the hands of a healer for a fortnight, and we don't have that kind of time. Besides, Caedon might kill me the next time he. . . does what he does, and then I really will be useless to John. So I'll go about it the hard way." Rafe straightened up, shaking off all weakness. "Go back to that little village, Wat. Wait for me there. This should take me maybe a day, maybe less. I'm hoping less. I'll find you there. Then you and I will get John."

A Quiet Glade

Wat

Wat and Rafe sagged against each other, saying nothing. Wat couldn't talk, not if all the Dark Ones in their dark realm swooped out of it after him. He could see Rafe felt the same. They just stood leaning together, underneath the trees in the little glade where they'd finished burying John.

The last few days had passed in a haze of horror and grief. Wat could scarcely fathom it. Yet all around them, the birds were singing. Cuckoos. Skylarks. Wat looked down at the spade in his hands and tossed it on the ground.

How is it, thought Wat, *that the world underneath the Spheres is so glad when I feel as though someone has scooped out whatever lies inside me, and trampled on it, and left me to walk the lands as if I'm some alien thing made of wood or stone. At least,* he thought, *John lies in this peaceful place, and I know where he is. Not like Mother, or Aedan. It* was as if those two had been wiped from the face of the earth. As if they had never existed at all.

"Somebody needs to get word back to Avery. And get word to Dru." Rafe spoke at last.

"I'll head back, then," said Wat. "Only Avery knows where Dru is."

"And that betrayer."

"Yes."

"Suppose," said Rafe, but then he stopped.

Wat knew what he was about to say, and he knew Rafe couldn't say it, because it was too terrible to say. Suppose the killers had found Dru and his family, the way they'd found John. Wat didn't say it, either. Instead, he said, "Do you figure you and I managed to kill Caedon?"

They both thought about the chaotic moments the day before when they had gotten to John too late. Caedon was lurking over John's body, and they struck him and stomped on him and damaged him as much as they could. But they couldn't stay to make sure of the job, because there lay John, and the guards were just down the corridor, and they had to get John's body up the hidden narrow passageway out of the castle before anyone stopped them.

"John," Wat said. "John," he said again, just a raw sound bursting out of him. Rafe put a hand on his shoulder. They'd gotten John out, and then they realized he wasn't dead. The memory of that moment of sudden hope jolted Wat as if someone had shot him with one of Caedon's cursed crossbows. John had died in Wat's arms at the edge of the forest.

"He was well out of it by then, Wat," Rafe whispered. "He wasn't feeling anything at all by then. No pain."

"We were too late," said Wat.

"He knew, Wat. He knew it would end that way. The farwydd told him."

"It was a cruel thing she did, then," said Wat bitterly.

"He told me it freed him. He told me he wasn't afraid of anything any longer, after she told him that."

"The old slag. She should keep her vile thoughts to herself."

Rafe held Wat while he raged. At last Wat made himself still.

"Anyway, Wat," said Rafe with a sigh. "No, I doubt we killed Caedon."

"At least we could have done that much," said Wat. "We failed John, and then we failed him again."

"We tried. But listen to me. Gilles protects that man. Trust me on this. We may have damaged Caedon terribly, and I hope we did, but he'll keep on living, if you call the slimy trail he makes across the earth living."

Wat remembered how, after the battle, they'd all shot their arrows at Caedon while he floundered in the river. How they'd all missed, even when he swam straight under the bridge where they stood with a clear shot at him. He nodded reluctantly. Then he looked over at Rafe in alarm. "Do you think he recognized you? We had hoods and I doubt he knows what I look like, but he—"

"If he didn't recognize me, he'll soon think it through. He'll realize."

"You need to come back with me to Avery. He'll kill you."

"I'll never leave Diera," said Rafe. "Tell Avery this, though. We've got to get her out, and soon. I have suspicions about Caedon's plans for her."

"Rafe. You have to leave," Wat said more urgently. "Caedon will kill you."

"Count on it," said Rafe.

Wat looked at him bleakly. "Don't tell me. Your own slag bitch of a farwydd warned you of it."

"No," said Rafe with a choked kind of laugh. "I know in other ways. But maybe I can buy my life dearly from Caedon, through means he won't be expecting. I'm going to make him pay, Wat."

"Rafe," Wat whispered miserably. "Losing John. Then losing you? You think I'll just walk away?"

"I'm telling you to, Wat. I'm ordering you to. Dru's safety depends on your getting to Avery as soon as you can."

"It will take me a fortnight."

"No, it won't. You'll go a'horse. Wait right here while I steal you one." With the shadow of his roguish grin, Rafe thumped Wat on the back and leaned down to pick up the spade. He shouldered it and slipped away through the trees.

Alone in the glade, Wat moved to the mound of raw earth they'd heaped over John's body after they had heaved it into the pit they'd dug. Wat dropped to his knees. He fell on the mound, and now that he was alone, he released his grief. He lay racked with sobs. He'd been too late. He hadn't been able to save John. His mind reeled back to that day in his family's dooryard, when John had arrived in time to save him. Caedon's soldiers had driven Wat back to the wall of their house, and Wat had only an upended wooden bench between himself and them for protection. Then, as if he were one of the eala in the stories, John had appeared out of nowhere. John couldn't save their mother or Aedan, but he'd saved Wat.

Wat tried desperately to think of John as he'd been, always almost luminous, especially when he played his rebec and sang. Lanky. Shy. But completely in command of himself. Not the bashed in, torn apart, battered object he and Rafe had seized away from Caedon and had dragged through a sewer.

Another memory came at him, pierced him to his core. He was very young. He and John had been tussling. *You're a growing boy, and you'll overtop me soon. Then I'll have to come crawling to you for protection from my enemies*, John had teased him. *I will, Johnny. I'll protect you*, Wat remembered saying. He was just a little boy. John had grinned at him, tousled his hair. *I'm counting on it*, John had teased. *Promise*.

"I promise." That's what Wat remembered he had replied. He whispered it aloud. "I promise." He had made his brother a promise, and he hadn't kept it. The glade quieted around him, and the light of late afternoon began to slant through the trees. Wat got up and dusted himself off. He made himself busy gathering brush and leaves to pile on the mound. Suppose Caedon found it. Suppose he desecrated this holy place. Such a thought was agony to Wat.

Wat didn't think of the gods very often, and he didn't think of them now. Their mother, his and John's, had believed in the Lady Goddess. Everyone else, his father the king, Avery, Dru, even John—and Rafe, he supposed—had all reverted to the old gods, the Children. Most of them worshipped the Child of Earth, although Rafe's was the Child of Sea. Wat supposed he must be a child of the Child of Earth, as John was. Who She was, exactly, and why She might care about him, and why he should pay any attention at all to any pronouncement out of Her farwydd's sunken old mouth, those matters Wat found difficult to consider seriously.

But this glade where the broken shell of his brother lay was a holy place. He did know that much. *If I know anything at all, I know that,* he said to himself.

There was one other thing he needed to do. Wat moved to the edge of the glade and retrieved his pack. He'd emptied it of his furs and extra tunic so he could fill it with the shards of John's rebec. Somehow, in all the craziness, as he and Rafe had scouted around for the best way out of Caedon's dungeon, Wat had spotted it tossed on the castle's midden just outside John's cell. And Wat had grabbed all of the pieces.

I'm going to rebuild this instrument, he told himself. Dru had taught him many things about dealing death with knife and garotte. But Dru was no natural killer. Dru was a maker, and Dru had taught Wat that skill, too. *I can't put the broken pieces of my brother back together, but I will fix this,* Wat promised himself.

The light was almost gone when a crashing through the underbrush told Wat someone was coming. It was Rafe, taking a big brown rouncey at a walk through the trees and into the glade.

Rafe swung off the horse and handed the reins to Wat. "Child go with you, Wat," he said, helping Wat to mount. "Get to Avery as quick as you can. And listen to me. Listen to me hard, Wat. If you're too late to save Dru—" Rafe paused to catch his breath. Rafe was so pale. So weak. Wat saw the strength he had been able to summon up, when they went in to try to get to John, had faded out of him. Wat didn't want to leave him. He knew he had to. "If that happens, Wat," Rafe gasped out. "If you're too late. Remember this. It won't be your fault. None of this is your fault. Do you understand that?"

"I was too late for John," said Wat. *I promised*, he thought, *and I failed*. "I'll never be right with that." *I'll never be right with leaving you here, Rafe*. Wat turned the horse and rode off into the gathering dark.

CHAPTER SIX

Ripping the Heart Out

Caedon

Now at last, Caedon exulted, The Rising wouldn't be able to rely on John. Caedon had his sources, his one treacherous source in particular. Eris. She had helped him locate John. *Doing as she is bid*, Caedon thought with satisfaction. It had taken her two more lessons to reach the point where Caedon knew he could rely on her. Then at last John had lain secure in the prison of Treddian's castle.

Caedon thought about the rest of it. He forced himself to think past the horror of what the intruders had done to him, when they'd gotten to John, and the long recovery.

He thought backward past all that. Thought of the wonderful moment when he knew he had John in a cell, locked up awaiting Caedon's handiwork.

The possibilities had seemed endless. Boundless.

Rafe awaited his attention, too. He needed to go one way or the other with Rafe. No more waffling. The lad was delicious meat to him, but he had turned on Caedon and Gilles. Caedon was going to have to think about that one, how to do it for utmost pleasure and utmost revenge.

Rafe owed everything to Gilles, and this is how he repaid him.

Caedon thought with a twinge of the day he himself arrived in Gilles's household. He thought of how Gilles had stared at him, examined him. He thought of the deep hunger he had seen in Gilles' eyes that day, and how Gilles had shunted aside the boy Rafe, his favorite, to install Caedon in that place of honor. Suppose the root of Rafe's betrayal was some long-held resentment.

But no. Caedon thought about it. Resentment, no. Rafe had turned on Gilles, and on Caedon, because he was a traitor who yearned for the other side.

As for Drustan, and Avery and Conal. Mere gnat-bites.

Again Caedon forced his mind back to that day, the day he had John within his grasp. So close. He had been right there on the point of possessing John.

Caedon remembered humming to himself the snatch of an old song he'd heard somewhere. *Now he'll begin, oh he'll begin,* he hummed. *To your heart he enters in.*

When he had realized what he was doing, he remembered standing frozen with fear. No music. None of that. He recalled how he had shivered. How, with an effort, he had pushed the music out of his mind. He shut himself from it. He distracted himself thinking of the next interesting task.

Time to see to John, he had said to himself.

Caedon recalled that by then, there was not much of John left to see to. Caedon had destroyed John's body, pretty much. Caedon remembered strolling through the keep of Treddian's castle. After what he went through afterward, he was glad his memory of the time before those two men attacked him was still this clear. Patches of detail stood out. He remembered nodding pleasantly to a guard he knew. To a servant whom he had found useful. To a boy he had his eye on.

Then he'd come to the dungeon level of the castle, and there was the door to the cell, a long, high-ceilinged room more like a stone-walled storeroom than a cell. But there was space in this room, space for the things Caedon wished to do to John, so Caedon had had John taken here, not to one of the fetid cramped places where prisoners were usually held.

Caedon remembered opening the door. John's broken body lay on the stone-flagged floor, clinging to life. Fragments of John's musical instrument, his rebec, were scattered there. Caedon had crushed the rebec with his boot while John could still see him do it. Caedon had shuddered to spot the splintered wood.

get rid of it get rid of it get rid of it

Foolish, he knew. Its voice, and John's voice, were silenced. Just the same, he recalled opening the door of the cell again and calling out into the corridor. An old jailer came tottering down it toward him. "Good man," Caedon had said. "Take those broken shards of wood off to the midden and toss them in."

"Aye, lord, I'll do 'ee." The jailer had puttered into the cell and swept up the fragments, stepping around John, and had headed out into the corridor with them. Caedon remembered averting his eyes so he wouldn't have to see.

After the last sounds of the jailer's footsteps had faded down the corridor, Caedon was able to draw a ragged relieved breath. He had prowled around John's inert form. A stubborn core of John refused to give in to him. *This is taking too long. Just end it,* he'd told himself. But it infuriated him that he still encountered this last resistance. He prodded John with the toe of his boot. John didn't even moan. He kicked John. Nothing.

In any way that meant anything, the man was dead.

But Caedon knew. If he could only thread his way to that core, the payoff would be the crowning sweetness of his life. In a supreme act of confidence in him, Gilles had given John to Caedon. Caedon wanted to extract the most he could.

He crouched down beside John and reached out his hand. He touched John. *Still warm,* he thought. *Still breathing.* John had been a beautiful man, that disfiguring scar notwithstanding. Beautifully made. A beautiful face. A beautiful voice.

Caedon shied away from thinking of John's voice. Shied away from some things he had witnessed, and heard, at Gilles de Rais's manor when he and Gilles had John chained up there.

John was not beautiful now, not the battered exterior of him.

Inside John, there was a beautiful core.

Caedon tried to brush the stiff, blood-encrusted hair away from John's smashed-in face.

If he could only thread his way to John's core. Then it would belong to Caedon. It would be part of Caedon, what had been John's.

He would kill them all. All those brothers. The little one was already dead, and he hadn't made the most of it. He'd done what he could, sending the body off to Gilles. What benefit there was had gone to Gilles. Caedon tamped his resentment down.

Gilles had graciously given John to Caedon, and now John was almost dead. One brother was left. Someday, he'd possess himself of that one, too. Everything that had belonged to John Caedon would take into himself.

But here lay John, and what would Caedon do about it? He stood and examined John from head to toe. The best entry point. Where would it be, and why was he thwarted of it?

Caedon shook his head in annoyance. A scrabbling sound broke his concentration.

What was that.

The sewers of the castle gave out directly here. High above him, on the upper levels of the castle, a slit allowed the residents to pour the contents of their chamber pots directly down from the castle's upper story, its big sleeping chambers and halls, to the sewers beneath his feet. In this room, the masonry had deteriorated, so you could step over to the long wall of the cell, part of the outer wall of the castle, and look up into that shit- and garbage-smeared conduit. It meant this particular part of the dungeon reeked of the worst odors of the castle.

There it was, the scrabbling sound again. Rats, probably. Caedon didn't like rats. He didn't like music, and he didn't like rats. They both gave him the horrors.

But the noise was too loud for rats.

What was it?

Caedon stepped over John's body to look. And was bowled over by two men hurtling out from the jagged stones of the crevice and into the room. One of them dealt Caedon a tremendous blow to the head, and he went down.

Lying with his face ground against the stones, Caedon struggled to scream out. He struggled to get up. A kick from someone's boot silenced him. Another vicious blow. Then he did scream.

He blinked to try to clear his head. Everything was blurred. There were forms of men, black-clad, hooded men, two of them, yanking and tugging at the body. They dragged it to the crevice and disappeared into it with John.

The dungeon's guards came running in then and rushed to Caedon. He pointed incoherently at the crevice, but they didn't understand. They hauled him away to a healer, and he must have fainted, because when he came to again, it was night.

Over the next several days, he learned that mysterious men had indeed made away with John. One of them even retrieved the fragments of John's fiddle thing out of the midden.

Caedon lay silently fuming in his bed while healers hovered around him, spooning broth into him, administering potions.

But gradually he came to some kind of peace with what had happened. Surely John was dead. Surely his musical instrument was shattered beyond repair.

Eris managed to slip away from Avery's camp to visit him. She told him John was gone. It was over. "John's death broke them," Eris assured him. "Avery is the leader of The Rising, but everyone says John was the heart of it."

Caedon knew now. That heart was stilled.

As Caedon got better and gradually pieced together the disjointed shreds of memory coming back to him from the chaotic events in John's cell, one of the blurry figures captured his attention. Against the screen of his mind's eye, Caedon scrutinized it.

In a dark fury, he realized he knew it.

Rafe.

Caedon was resolved now. No mercy for the fellow. Rafe was done for. Caedon did hope to gain the maximum benefit from his essences, though. He wouldn't tell Rafe, until the very last, that he knew what Rafe had done. Meanwhile, he'd give Rafe no respite.

He'd feed. And feed. And feed.

The seasons had clicked along to springtide when Caedon had crushed John and was then attacked by the two mysterious men. When he realized about Rafe, it had taken Caedon several more turnings of the moon to recover enough to carry out his resolve. Not until the turning of the next moon was he able to function as he used to, at least a little.

It should have taken him many turnings longer, a season, more than a season, but Gilles sent Vigilia, the dead witchwoman Labinia's sister, to see to him. Labinia had helped him many times before. Vigilia was as skilled as Labinia had been. Caedon silently thanked Gilles for training her, for enabling her to produce her clever potions and spells.

As Caedon got better and was able to summon Rafe to him, he rapidly gained strength, too, from the rich juices. As his own vigor increased, he felt a grim satisfaction watching Rafe dwindle.

He pressed it and pressed it, allowing no time between for Rafe to regenerate his energy. Rafe was becoming a hollow-eyed shell of himself. Caedon saw Rafe realized what Caedon was doing to him.

But Rafe had become too weak to fight back.

CHAPTER SEVEN

Hounds and Hunters

Wat

Wat followed Avery to a quiet spot in the camp. They sat down together. Avery motioned someone else over to join them.

A young woman walked toward them, older than Wat. Maybe a bit older than Eris, he decided.

"Please talk with us, mistress," said Avery, indicating a spot on the log where he and Wat sat. "Wat," said Avery. "I want you to meet someone. She came into camp just this morning, while you and Eris were off on your mission." He turned to the woman. She was tall and thin. Her upright bearing, as if she weren't used to bowing to others but instead used to others bowing to her, made Wat wonder whether she might not be one of the gentles.

It was rare to see a lady of the nobility, even the lesser nobility, in these rough surroundings.

Hesitantly, she sat down beside Avery.

Wat wondered what she could possibly be doing in the camp.

"Rhiane, this is my brother Wat," Avery was saying to her.

"Well met," she said, giving Wat a little smile.

"Wat, Rhiane is a singer," said Avery. "She wants to join us, and I thought you and she could team up. Then you could continue your information gathering."

Wat felt himself tensing. *No,* he thought wildly. *It's too soon. I can't do it.*

Avery put out a hand, steadying him. "Wat," he said quietly. "It's your decision. Whatever you want to do will be fine. Just think about it, if you will."

Wat nodded and gave the young woman a numb smile. He turned back to the fire. The spring rains had come hard again, but now the weather was clearing. He shouldered out into the early evening, where the clouds were just beginning to part, revealing here and there a star hanging from its golden chain.

He'd been out scouting again with Eris, a very quick mission that took them only to the next village and back, nothing very taxing, no violence.

Avery had made that clear to them, as they headed out. "No violence," he said firmly. "No killing."

Eris's lip had curled. "Sometimes there has to be. Brother."

"Sometimes." Avery had nodded. "Don't let it happen this time."

Wat knew what Eris thought. *Wat is soft, and they are babying him.* He could read it in her face.

Later, Conal had shaken his head, when Wat told him that. "If that was her thinking, she was just wrong," he said. "We need to be careful around these villagers up here. They know one false move will bring Audemar's men savagely down on them. If they think that of us, too, they'll just see us as one of the dogs in a dog fight. One dog is going to overtop the other, and the dogs don't much care who else gets bitten in the process. But that's not why we're here."

Now that Wat was back from the scouting expedition, he was wet through. His clothing had dried out a bit, at the fire, but he still felt sodden and chilled. He found his own tent, and his dry clothes. The other lads who shared the tent with him were elsewhere, probably eating their dinner, and he was glad. He didn't want to eat. He couldn't eat. He wanted to be alone. He wrapped himself in his furs and tried to sleep.

It was impossible. He couldn't sleep. He hadn't been able to sleep since that terrible day. Actually, when he felt himself finally slipping into sleep, he feared to sleep, maybe worse than after he'd been wounded. At least then, his nightmares about his mother and Aedan had coiled themselves into his fever dreams, and nothing seemed very real.

But his nightmares about John were all too real. Again and again, in his dreams, he had just reached John, and was reaching out a hand to him, when something thwarted him, and John was pulled back away from him by some dark force. Then he'd wake to discover his nightmare was the truth.

Worse, Wat felt uneasy now around Eris. They'd always been close. But now somehow things had changed. She was harder. Angrier, even with him. She'd muttered a few words of sympathy about John, but after that, she didn't talk about what Wat had been through.

Today, Eris was sent off again, alone.

Wat had been glad, in a way, because he didn't want to talk about what had happened to John, and the attempt he and Rafe had made to get to him, and how they'd failed. Eris didn't really understand, and he couldn't tell her everything, anyhow. He couldn't reveal Rafe's role in it all. But he was worried the others thought he was too damaged and hurting to go off on any but the simplest missions.

Now he was starting to feel better about it. Avery had kept him back, not because he thought Wat couldn't handle the difficult work of The Rising, but to introduce him to this woman, Rhiane, so he could resume the tasks he and John had undertaken. Then, after introducing her, Avery would let Wat decide. Wat saw Avery wanted him to think about how much he could take on, and how soon, and make that decision for himself.

He could accept Rhiane as his partner, and then the two of them would go off on the circuit he and John used to follow. Only this time, he himself would be in the lead. Was he ready for it? That's what Avery wanted him to think about. If he wasn't, he realized Avery would probably just keep sending him out on the scouting forays with Eris.

Unlike Eris, Avery and Conal understood what he was going through, because they were going through it themselves. A deep, devastating sorrow. And Rafe had understood, back at the grave.

The day Wat returned to camp on Rafe's stolen horse to tell Avery and Conal, they had reacted in grief and horror. Wat flinched away from the memory of their faces as he had gotten his news out of his mouth.

Somehow he had been able to tell them. It all seemed like a bad dream that he could recall only in stuttered fragments. His words. Their faces. The way his voice had broken. The way they'd tried to comfort each other. The despair that had settled over them, almost a physical thing.

Avery was John's brother and lifelong friend. As for Conal, Wat hadn't realized the depths of his feelings for John until he saw how hard Conal took the news. Then Wat understood. Conal had acted somewhat like an older brother to John. A beloved mentor. He was devastated, just as much as Avery and Wat were.

Of course Avery and Conal had each other for solace, and Wat could see how much they helped each other. But they hadn't neglected Wat. They'd both gently probed Wat's raw feelings and had offered him silent support. When they sat quietly together, the three of them felt some kind of mutual comfort. Wat supposed Eris might feel shut out of this circle of grief and was relieved whenever she went off on one of her expeditions so she wasn't around to feel jealousy. She hadn't really known John.

Wat had gotten in the habit, after the evening meal, of coming to the fire and just sitting there staring into the flames. Pretty soon, all three of them would be there together, even though no one mentioned it. If they talked at all, they talked about their fears for Rafe and Dru.

All three of them worried about Rafe, grieving on his own. But Wat realized something. "Not all alone. He has Diera," he told Avery and Conal. He remembered then Rafe's directive to tell Avery his premonitions about Diera. "Rafe says we need to get

Diera out of Caedon's hands as soon as we can," said Wat to them.

They all worried about Dru most of all. "Dru doesn't even know, unless Rafe has been able to get to him somehow," said Conal as they sat together earlier in the evening.

By now, Avery had sent someone out to find Dru. Wat had wanted to go himself, but the other two had overruled him.

"You're in no position to do that, Wat. You've just been on a forced march around the entire countryside for a full turning of the moon. You're exhausted," said Conal. "You've seen terrible things, and you've gone through a terrible ordeal."

Wat thought with a deep knife-thrust of anguish about John's final moments before making that journey across the river to the Land of the Dead. Wat had felt his brother's last slight movements, had seen him take his last few breaths, one or two noisy, rattling breaths that for an instant made Wat wonder if he were trying to speak or maybe coming back to himself.

Then a long pause.

A slight, shallow breath.

After a while, another.

Then nothing at all.

By then, Wat had seen a lot of death. He knew his brother was gone. Underneath his own hands, he felt John go.

They're right, he thought. *I've known terrible things. And inside me, I'm in terrible trouble. Conal and Avery both see that. So now because I can't get myself in hand, I'm failing Dru too.*

Dru would find out through some courier. *Some stranger, probably*, Wat thought.

"But Elsebet will help him through it," Avery whispered.

"My bigger worry is whether the betrayers have found where Dru is hiding," said Conal.

"You'll have to reveal Dru's whereabouts to someone," Wat had told Avery, that first day back. "But suppose he isn't trustworthy. Send me."

"I'll find someone trustworthy," Avery had said. "And Wat. Think about it. You've already told us. The reason Dru is in such danger is that Caedon undoubtedly already knows. There's nothing to betray."

So someone else was on his way to tell Dru about John.

Wat felt a kind of despair. By now, Caedon might have realized that Rafe had taken part in the rescue of John's body and the infliction of his own injuries.

Wat recalled, in the moment, the direct brutality of his feelings as they overtook him. He recalled the savage satisfaction that had thrilled through him as he had stomped and kicked Caedon. *If I've gone soft, as Eris tells me I have, my body must not have gotten the message. Not during that,* he thought bleakly.

Now, a sen'night later, they had gathered again to talk. "I just hope our message has reached Dru," Avery said, with a grim look at Conal. "We should have gone ourselves."

"We're at a delicate moment in the negotiations with this village overlord up here," Conal said after a moment. Standing to one side, Wat saw that Conal was filled with guilt. "I think the man is on the point of turning to our side, though."

"Will Dru understand?" said Avery, his voice dropping low.

Conal nodded. "He will. He knows what we're up against." Conal looked over at Wat now. "Don't torment yourselves, either of you," he said. "There's torment enough to go around."

"As soon as we've finished, we'll head south to Dru," Avery decided. "Just a small party of us. Me, you, Wat. A few others. I'll want Eris with us, as soon as she has returned."

"She's due back today," said Conal.

"Good, then. And we'll need maybe a few more. You pick them, Conal. We'll set up near that village where Cwen lives. I know a little house up in the hills above the village that we can use as a temporary base without attracting attention."

"Torrin and her friend Lorel would be solid support for us," said Conal. "I'll choose them."

"Good idea," said Avery. "We'll swing by their village for them on the way. We'll do as Rafe suggests, get Diera out of Caedon's hands. And there's another thing we can do, while we're in the Riverlands and up into the high country above the rivers. We'll hunt for Domgall and Ryce." He turned to Wat. "Con and I keep hearing rumors that Audemar has them stashed some place."

Domgall and Ryce, Wat breathed. The princes, Artur's children. Domgall was his heir, the true heir to the entire realm.

"Why in the Nine aren't they dead?" said Conal. "I was expecting that would be Audemar's first act, killing them."

"Thank the Nine he didn't," said Avery. "That boy is our legitimate monarch."

"Some say—" Conal began carefully.

"I know what they say, Con. I'm not blind and deaf. Everyone, my enemies and even some of my friends, say I want those boys dead, too. They say The Rising is just my own attempt to usurp the throne. Brother against brother, me against Audemar, and the throne goes to the winner. Remember those rumors Caedon spread? That I was Artur's assassin?"

"That kind of thinking is what we must combat, with these village strongmen. That's why we need to be out there, changing minds," Conal said, nodding.

Wat was floored. "People really think that?"

Avery put his hand on Wat's shoulder and squeezed it. "People do. Power is all they know. That's the only motive they recognize, so they see it in me."

"The knaves," said Wat.

"Don't say that, Wat. It's all they've ever known. All their leaders operate out of power and fear. Let's show them something different. Something better." Avery looked down at his shoes as they sat by the hearth fire. He looked up again. "So we assume the princes are alive, and we go after them."

"Actually," said Conal slowly. "They could very well be dead, no matter what we've heard."

Wat realized something. "Conal, remember what you said about dogs and dog fights?"

"Yes."

"I know why the princes could still be alive. They're the bone two dogs are fighting over. Two hounds, snarling over the same prey."

Avery and Conal looked over at Wat, their eyes puzzled.

"I'm guessing Caedon has them," said Wat. "I'm guessing Caedon is using them to bargain with Audemar. Don't you see? Caedon has them. Audie wants them. They're spoiling for a fight over it. A big one."

Conal began to laugh, although it was a bitter sound. "The boys may be alive indeed. You know a lot, Wat. Don't give me that *everyone thinks I've gone soft* cack. You're smart and you're capable. We all know it. John knew it."

So it was decided among them. Avery and Conal had some work to do first. They needed to organize their next campaign, the one that would take their forces driving south, carving out more territory from which to challenge Audemar. Once that was accomplished, they'd head out to the hills above the Riverlands to conduct their search for the princes and to plan Diera's rescue.

After that conversation, Wat felt his spirits rising. They weren't going to sit here in the north and dither and do nothing. They'd take action, and he'd take action with them.

In the meantime, he needed to sort out his feelings about working with this new singer, the young woman named Rhiane.

He decided he had mulled the situation over long enough. Too long. In the morning, he'd give Avery his answer.

That night, bad dreams woke him several times. Faceless men with swords. A lot of blood. He tried not to cry out. He'd disturb the others sharing the tent. In the morning, he felt a little better. But he wondered about himself and his restless sleep. The other young men in the tent were looking red-eyed and weary as they climbed out of their furs and headed to the fire for something to eat. He guessed they were finding it pretty hard, being his tent-mates.

Wat was hungry, too. He too crawled out of the tent to break his fast.

Across the camp, he spotted her. Rhiane, the singer.

He remembered his resolve of the day before, to come to a decision about her. He supposed it was time he considered Avery's words. He supposed he should put his private grief aside. The

Rising needed his abilities, and Avery thought this woman could help him carry out his work. Wat supposed he should do as Avery said. He saw Avery wasn't going to order him to do it, although he could. He still might.

Wat had seen Avery order other men to do things they didn't want to do. People close to him. Wat remembered a time Avery had ordered John to do something he really didn't want to do, and John had done it, even though it had cost him dear. It was because of his oath, thought Wat.

Wat hadn't taken an oath with the other members of the Six, but he was one of them now. He supposed that meant he needed to do what Avery was urging on him. He fingered the gold brooch at the shoulder of his cloak, the brooch of the Six Proud Walkers. *This is my oath*, he thought.

He had a responsibility. John would want him to step up and take it on. *That's what he would do, if he were still here. I'll talk to Avery, then to her*, he decided, glancing again at the young woman, who had come to the main hearth fire of the camp with bread and cheese. He caught her eye and raised a hand in greeting.

I'll talk to her, thought Wat. *But breakfast first.*

When he went to Avery, Avery put a hand on his arm. "This is hard, Wat. No matter what you decide to do, or end up doing, it's going to be hard."

Wat nodded. "I'll do it, Avery. John would want the work to go on, and he trusted me. He made me his partner. John wouldn't want me backing away." He stopped and swallowed hard. "I miss him every day. Every moment."

"So do I," said Avery. They stood together quietly. After a while, Avery said, "Tell me how I can help. Do you know where you'll go first?"

"I'm not sure. Johnny was the leader. He knew where we should go. What we should do."

"Now you're the leader, Wat. That girl won't know what to do. You'll have to teach her."

"She's older than I am. She probably thinks I'm just a boy," said Wat. "Will she do anything I say?"

"She'll have to. You'll have to make her understand. You're one of the Six, Wat. We're relying on you."

"Suppose I can't do it," Wat burst out. "Suppose I let all of you down. Suppose I can't fill John's shoes. I'll never be able to."

"Wat," said Avery. He took Wat's hand in his and looked into his eyes. "Brother," he said. "Who made you one of the Six."

"You did. You and Dru."

"No. Think, Wat. Who did?"

After a moment Wat said, low, "John did."

"Yes. And he didn't even know he was doing it. There was something inside John, something powerful and strange."

They sat silent, remembering the blood, the death. All the horrifying effects of John's power on the battlefield.

"Of course we saw it. We all did. How terrifying it was," Avery continued. "But that was just the big showy part of our brother's power. Most of it was hidden. Quiet. He knew things, Wat. He knew about you, and the role you are going to play. He knew how hard it was going to be for you, and he asked all of us to help you. We need to trust that thing John knew, all of us. You especially."

"Yes." Wat felt a new determination harden inside him. "I will."

Avery took Wat by the hand and looked him in the eye. "I'll help you however I can. Conal will. Dru will."

Wat had sworn an oath to Avery, just as good as. Now it felt as though Avery were swearing an oath to him. "And Rafe," Wat added. "Rafe will help me."

"And Rafe. Maybe especially Rafe."

"I think—" Wat hesitated. "I think Rafe knows who our true enemy is."

"Not Audemar. Audemar too, of course. But we've all long known it. Caedon stands behind Audemar. How that happened is a mystery to us, but Caedon. It's really Caedon."

"Avery." Wat stopped, troubled. "What I mean about Rafe. Rafe knows. Yes, Caedon. But Caedon's powers come from somewhere else. It's no mystery to Rafe. He does know."

"Gilles."

"Yes."

"We're fighting something maybe we're not equipped to fight. That's what you're telling me."

"That's what I think Rafe knows," said Wat.

"We had John, in that fight. Now we don't."

"I didn't get to him in time," Wat said bitterly. "When Caedon and Audemar sent men to kill me, John got me out. When it was my turn to get John out, I failed."

"Oh, brother. You must—" Avery paused, and Wat could tell it was because he was trying to collect himself. "You must stop hounding yourself over this."

Hounding myself, thought Wat. One part of himself was constantly hunting down another part, cornering it, snarling at it, biting at it, and that part of him could never escape the hunter. The hunter gave him no rest. The hunter promised him, *I'll destroy you.* Avery was right. Wat did want to go on. He wanted to honor John. *But to do it, I must stop this. This hounding.*

"You must stop blaming yourself," said Avery, taking him by the shoulders.

"I can't," Wat whispered. Then he stood up straighter and looked Avery in the eye. "But as for the work, going about the countryside performing, and gathering information under the cover of it, working to the utmost of my abilities and strength for The Rising, that I can do. I can and I will."

CHAPTER EIGHT

Feeding

Caedon

Caedon began positioning himself to be indispensable to Audemar. Very delicately, he began to hint that if Audemar wanted the young princes Domgall and Ryce to do with as he liked, he'd better consider giving their sister the Princess Diera to Caedon.

Audemar was starting to knuckle under. Because now Audemar was beginning to see it. Caedon had the princes safe in the cells underneath his manor. What might Caedon do with them? How might Caedon use them to undermine Audemar's reign?

It was gradually occurring to Audemar. Gradually, because Audemar was so thick.

It was dawning on him that if he tried to take the boys from Caedon by force, they could very well end up instead in the hands of people who would reveal to the kingdom—to all of the little people of the kingdom who liked him just fine—and to the powerful of the kingdom who looked the other way and benefitted as Audemar systematically bled the realm dry, just what kind of scum Audemar really was.

The kind who would assassinate his own brother to get to the throne. The kind who imprisoned little children. *And damaged them*, Caedon thought. The dreadful shape those boys were in could be made to lie at Audemar's door, not his own. What would Audemar's subjects do then, all of those who went to their beds every night convincing themselves they were decent folk? How would they be able to face themselves? In a situation like that, how easy it was to blame one's own failings on someone else. On Audemar, if Caedon managed the situation well.

Of course, that change in the opinions of the people wouldn't happen by itself. People were able, Caedon found, to overlook the most heinous behavior, even crimes, if their own interests demanded it. But Caedon could work to change those opinions. He was especially good at that. It was one of the reasons Gilles had honored Caedon by granting him this mission in the Sceptered Isle.

The next step required Caedon to seize Diera for himself. Caedon had placed her in the castle of one of Audemar's minions, the Earl Treddian, close by Caedon's own manor. Supposedly, the earl was holding her there until Audemar could decide on a strategic marriage for her. But Caedon was the one who really controlled her. By now, Caedon had made the Earl

Treddian his own ally. Caedon had Diera. That was reality. But Caedon knew he needed the appearance of it, too, if his plans were to succeed.

Give me Diera, Caedon was telling Audemar in everything but words, *and I will give you the princes. Then you can make a looming problem disappear.*

Gilles stood behind him in this. "Do whatever it takes to marry this princess. Then you can easily try again with her," he told Caedon. He was referring to Caedon's report, seven years earlier, that Diera's child by him, the child he had forced on her, had died of plague. *You still owe me a boy-child*, Gilles reminded Caedon. *And I'd like one coming from her.* He didn't want to bother with the princes. They were too ravaged by now, and older than Gilles liked them. Much too old. By now the little one was twelve years old, and the older one was close to manhood—or would be, if he weren't so utterly defiled.

Meanwhile, The Rising was a troublesome thing for Audemar, but Caedon could tell that the resisters would not be able to worry him for long. After the great victory the rebels of The Rising had won, they started becoming less of a problem.

"How can this be?" Audemar said when Caedon reassured him. "They won." He scowled at Caedon. "Because of your incompetence."

Caedon chose to ignore the insult. He swallowed hard and took a conciliatory tone with the king. "They did win. Your Highness is right about that. But they won at great cost. Now they're running low on funds, my king. When you're feeling the same pinch, all you need do is tighten down on your subjects and squeeze a little more out of them." Caedon didn't mention how he himself would never run low. He had Gilles.

The Rising, though, was becoming every day more impoverished. Not just in coin. They'd lost John. They didn't know it yet, but soon they'd lose Drustan and Rafe. Little by little, Caedon was making crippling inroads on them.

Caedon thought it over. Avery, the leader. Avery had appealed to that uncle of his, the one in the Baronies, and the man had given him gold. Avery wouldn't be able to keep going back to this man. Avery's money problems were pressing him, and soon they'd be pressing him hard. Conal, his right hand, was still there to give him support. Caedon didn't underestimate how much support.

Conal wasn't just Avery's lover. He was as skilled a man around weapons and weapons training as anyone could find. Ranulf the Fourth had seen it. Avery's and Audemar's father had appointed Conal to the post of Royal Arms Master at an unusually young age.

As for Caedon, he knew himself to be one of the most skilled with a sword in two realms, and he knew this without self-congratulation. It was simply true.

Conal was his equal, though. Easily his equal.

Part of Caedon yearned for a neutral world where he and Conal could match themselves against each other. His blood rose at the thought. Too bad they lived in the real world instead, where that match-up would never happen, unless by chance in battle.

Probably not, though. The days of The Rising being able to field an army were over. Caedon wondered if Conal knew that. He wondered what Avery and Conal would do about it.

Interesting, he thought, *how success in war depends, not so much on skill with weapons, bravery, all that claptrap, as on more mundane matters.* The possession of wealth. The use of public influence: the ear of the people, the eye of the people always on one. The movement of materials. The ability to build structures like bridges.

The general of the Old Ones knew these things. Caedon had read his book, full of important information and, beyond that, the general's canny shaping of his own image so that people would come to gaze at him and admire him, let him have his way with them. That man knew how power worked, and with that knowledge, he had made the Southern Primacy, at least for a while, the center of the world.

Gilles has studied the general's book, thought Caedon. *And so have I. When I was a boy, it was the first book Gilles showed me, to teach me.* The general had brought his analytical mind, from the first, to the problem of how to control the territory that was now the Baronies. *All those lands,* the general had written, *can be divided into three parts.* Then his book showed how he had conquered that divided land.

And then the Sceptered Isle. He'd conquered it, too. On the pretext that its people were helping his enemies, the warlords across the Narrows, he had landed his ships in the marshlands near where Lunds-fort now stood, and had taken the lands there for his own.

With Caedon's help, Gilles would soon possess those lands himself. With Caedon's help, Gilles would undermine Audemar and then defeat him. Avery was a mere distraction, far too weak to fight Caedon and Audemar, and by the time Gilles had come to take over the Sceptered Isle, Avery would be long since finished.

As Caedon thought this through in his roomful of books, he stepped to a small table. There he had laid out the game board he'd bought from a trader traveling from the Great City of the Lyre Lands. The squares of the board were black and green. An army of green game pieces faced off against an army of black pieces. But the green pieces were fallen over. They were few. The black army had encroached on them, and soon the black army would sweep the board.

Caedon stood toying with one of the black game pieces. He reached out his hand and swept the rest of the green pieces off with a clatter onto the floor.

A servant stuck his head into the room. "Shall I clear that up for you, my lord?" he said.

Caedon waved him off, and the man went away. It's not that Avery lacked ability, Caedon thought. That he had in abundance. No. What he lacked were resources. As the general of the Old Ones had known, that was paramount.

Caedon took stock of Avery's assets. If Avery were wise, he'd be doing the same. Avery had Conal, his right hand. Between them, Avery and Conal had demonstrated strategic and tactical skill of a high order. Avery still had Drustan, his left hand, his stealth weapon. *But,* thought Caedon with satisfaction, *now that I know his whereabouts, Avery won't have Drustan for long.* Best of all, John, the heart of The Rising, was gone.

Rafe, Caedon puzzled. Bending down to pick up one of the green pieces, turning it over and over in his hands, he thought about Rafe's role in The Rising. Was Rafe the brains of it? Caedon thought of the pale husk of himself Rafe had become. That couldn't be it. *Rafe,* he thought with scorn. Rafe was The Rising's vulnerable underbelly. With his talons, Caedon was soon to rip that underbelly open and spill the guts out onto the cold ground.

Well, he thought. *Not exactly rip him open. Drain him dry. Devour him from the inside out.*

Caedon recalled seeing once, at the celebrated university in the Primacy, as he stopped there during a journey he had undertaken to the city of the Old Ones, a great glass jar. In it, a famed doctor of the philosophic arts had coiled a mammoth parasitic worm, slits for eyes, a hungry sucking mouth. He imagined the worm out of its jar, its dead white skin pinked with the juices of its victim. *I'll devour Rafe like that worm,* Caedon thought.

Caedon tossed the green game piece aside.

The very next day, he went to Treddian's castle and called Rafe to him. Rafe was hovering near Diera, as always. *The poor fool,* thought Caedon. *There's his biggest vulnerability, that silly girl.*

"Master Leofric," he said loudly, using Rafe's name around the castle. "I need your services. Can the good earl spare you?"

Treddian looked over from his hearth, where he sat at ease with his wife and daughters. He waved a hand genially in Caedon's direction. "Take him, Lord Caedon. We can do without him for a while."

With satisfaction, Caedon noted the despairing look that passed between Diera and Rafe.

Rafe came over to Caedon and knelt.

"You and I need another of our sessions," Caedon said to Rafe privately.

Rafe didn't even raise an objection. Caedon thought he probably would, and looked forward to the play of emotions he'd see on Rafe's face. Fear. Anger. Desperation. They both knew it was too soon. Rafe hadn't properly recovered from Caedon's last feeding. Rafe disappointed Caedon. He looked up into Caedon's eyes and nodded in mute obedience, his face a pale mask.

"Good," Caedon murmured. "Let's get to my manor. I'm hungry."

Once there, he went straight to his private rooms. He heard Rafe's quiet tread just behind him. As soon as they were alone, Caedon stepped over to the door and barred it.

"Take off that tunic and stand there," he said to Rafe, pointing.

Rafe pulled his tunic over his head and dropped it at his feet. He went to the post in the middle of the room, where Caedon usually wanted him.

"Hands behind you."

Rafe put his back against the post and his hands around the other side of it.

Caedon stepped around it to tie Rafe's hands together there. He knew he wouldn't have to bind Rafe further. Rafe had become too weak to put up much resistance.

"Look how well I'm walking now, Master Rafe," said Caedon, coming back around the post to face him.

Thanks to the potions I got from Vigilia. He thought with regret of Labinia, Gilles's witch woman, found dead a few seasons ago. He was pretty sure John had had something to do with killing her. But Vigilia was in possession of her sister's big wooden chest of potions, and she had made good use of them after the attack those two, John and Rafe, had made on Caedon. Otherwise, he'd still be lying abed. Labinia had been very useful to him, although she maybe knew too much. It was fine to have Vigilia there to tend him instead.

"I'm nearly healed of my injuries," said Caedon.

"I'm glad to see it, lord," murmured Rafe.

Caedon laughed scornfully. "You think in here we need to continue our little mummery? I know who caused these injuries, Rafe."

Rafe said nothing. He didn't suppress a smile of triumph, as Caedon thought he might, or a gasp of panic when he realized Caedon knew. He just looked down miserably at the floor.

A good thing, too, thought Caedon. *Or I'd be tempted to finish you right here.* But, he thought with an irritated sigh, he needed Rafe through the marriage negotiations with Audemar.

"You know what I'm doing, don't you," said Caedon, coming near Rafe. "How I'm depleting you."

"Yes," Rafe whispered.

"You robbed me," Caedon said. Rafe did not look up. Caedon knew what he would see in Rafe's eyes. Rafe had set out to rob Caedon. Rafe had meant to do it, and he had succeeded, and he was glad he had. He had robbed Caedon of John. It was always possible Caedon might have reached that inner core of John. At the very least, he would have sent John's body to Gilles, a rich gift that Gilles would have appreciated very much.

But Rafe had snatched John away.

That thought filled Caedon with such fury that he realized if he put hands on Rafe right now, at this particular moment, Rafe would be a dead man.

Caedon took another turn about the room. He must not give way to his rage. He needed Rafe.

He came back to stand in front of him. "This isn't the end for you, not today, much as I'd like it to be. A murrain take you, Rafe. John was three of what you are. Five," he burst out.

"I know it, lord," Rafe murmured.

Caedon wanted to throttle the lad. He didn't even want to feed, he was so disgusted. He just wanted to stomp Rafe's guts out, the way Rafe and that other one had stomped on him. He wouldn't, though. Somewhere inside him, Rafe wanted him to do exactly that. He wouldn't give Rafe the satisfaction of a clean death, the kind Rafe had seized for his friend.

"I'm not ending you today," Caedon got out between gritted teeth. "You know why?"

Rafe shook his head no.

"I need you to help me with Diera one last time. Will you do it?"

"You know I will, Caedon," said Rafe, raising his eyes and looking directly into Caedon's. Caedon saw the depths of the hatred and contempt there.

He dealt Rafe a stunning blow to the side of the head.

Rafe took a while coming out of his stunned state.

Oh gods, Caedon thought. *He's trying to goad me into killing him. I must not let him thwart me, not again.*

When Rafe lifted his head at last, shaking it from side to side in bewilderment, Caedon moved to him again. "You dare speak to me in that manner? You dare raise your eyes to mine."

Rafe said nothing, just looked down. His eyelashes were long and lush, the ivory of his skin almost translucent except for the faint flush over the cheekbones. When Caedon had looked into Rafe's eyes, he'd seen how gray and wide they were. *Sea-Child eyes*, Caedon thought.

A shame Gilles had never let him take pleasure in Rafe, when Rafe was a boy. Caedon would have enjoyed that.

Now it was too late for that kind of pleasure. Caedon liked them young.

"Diera," said Caedon close to Rafe's ear. "I want her for my wife. Audemar, of course, has other ideas. You'll help me keep Diera calm and tractable. If you can't or won't, you and I will end it here."

"I'm yours, Lord Caedon," Rafe murmured tonelessly, but Caedon saw how unnerved Rafe was that Caedon's mouth was hovering so close to his ear.

Caedon reached over and tucked a strand of Rafe's long dark hair back into the band that held it off his face. He let his fingers linger on Rafe's cheek. He saw how Rafe had to stop himself cringing away.

"Comment tu te sens, Raoul," Caedon said softly to him.

"Pas terrible," whispered Rafe.

Caedon stepped away to get a better grip on himself. There was something about Rafe that moved him, in spite of himself. In spite of everything.

He came back to Rafe, where he sagged against the post. "I know about you and Diera," said Caedon. "Don't think it has escaped my notice. And I don't care. I don't care what the two of you do together. Just as long as the two of you understand you belong to me. You know it. She may not. She must be made to know it."

"Yes, lord," Rafe whispered. He looked over at Caedon, then quickly down again.

Caedon read alarm in his eyes. That was a good thing. Rafe, alarmed. Frightened and cowed. That he could use.

"Lord, you won't. . .you don't want to. . ."

"Feed on her? No, that's not my preferred food. C'est toi, Raoul." Again he ran a finger down Rafe's cheek. Rafe did flinch away from him this time.

Caedon turned aside. "No, I want to breed with her," he said briskly.

"That child. Her son. He died."

"That's right, and now I need others."

"You'll give them to Gilles."

"That's not your concern."

"What must I do, lord?"

"Tell her to prepare herself. I have means at my disposal to convince Audemar to give her to me. It would be so much easier if she were cooperative. Make sure she is."

"Yes, lord."

"And there's another thing." Caedon looked Rafe up and down, coming around to face Rafe and tap a speculative finger against his bare chest. He toyed with the amulet Rafe always wore on a thong about his neck. He patted it back in place. "I can't have people going around commenting about you and Diera. You must take a woman. I have the very one."

He stopped to think about it. "A girl from the west that I procured for Audemar last year. He's tired of her now. I'll bring her here."

Caedon prowled the room, planning and making mental notes of how to go about it. "I'll make her Diera's maid. Then it will look like a natural thing to people, when they see you always standing near Diera, in that cloying way you do." He came back to Rafe and poked his chest again hard, with his index finger. "Pay court to this maid."

"Pay court to her?"

Caedon looked at him, exasperated. "You know what I mean."

"Suppose she doesn't want to—"

"Nine Spheres, Rafe. They all want to. That's your particular genius, as the Old Ones would put it."

"But suppose I—"

"Make yourself do it. I order you to. Or, fine, if you won't, we'll end it here, you and I, and I'll find someone else to mind Diera." *There*, thought Caedon. *That flummoxes the lad every time. Now he'll do what I want.* "When I get children on Diera, I don't want anyone speculating they're your spawn instead of mine. In fact," he said, realizing this would be just the thing, "I want you to get her maid with child."

"Sometimes that doesn't happen."

Caedon stepped to Rafe and stared at him coldly. "Try," he said.

But then he thought, with fresh vexation, that he'd have to hold off after this session with Rafe, at least for a little while. If his new idea was going to work, Rafe would have to have his strength. "Try," he said, even more emphatically.

"Yes, lord," said Rafe dully, not seeming to understand the advantage to himself. "What's her name."

"No point in telling you now. You'll forget totally, after I've done with you today. I'll remind you when you come back to yourself. And now, make yourself ready."

Rafe closed his eyes and tensed.

"Not like that," said Caedon, annoyed. "You need to relax."

"I can't," said Rafe. "I try, and I can't."

Cadeon sighed. "Very well. We'll do this the hard way, but you know it makes your recovery more difficult."

Oh, well, he thought. It would take a while to get the girl over here and settled in. By then, Rafe would be healed and up to the task. Still, it was too irritating. Every time. Every single time.

"Don't you understand?" he demanded of the lad.

"Yes," Rafe whispered.

"Nine Spheres. Relax!"

"I can't."

"The ear again," said Caedon, disgruntled. The nasal canal would be so much quicker and easier, and he'd have so much more control. But Rafe had an unpleasant habit of seizing up, and then that passageway became close to impenetrable.

When I finally do end it, thought Caedon, *I'll just open a vein.* Too fast to allow Caedon much control, if he expected the lad to be alive at the end of it. That was the difficulty.

Of course, he thought, stepping back for a moment, scrutinizing Rafe. A vein was indeed the quick way to end things, but was it the most pleasurable? He'd have to ask Gilles for some tips.

There was that full-body thing Gilles liked to do, through the pores.

He noticed Rafe staring at him in a state of increasing panic. Gods above and below. The lad was going to work himself into such a state that Caedon would have to spend a candle measure and more on the insinuation phase.

He gave Rafe an exasperated shake, and then he moved in to feed.

CHAPTER NINE

A Pretty Bird

Wat

I'll explain what we do, shall I?" said Wat to Rhiane, his new partner. They were sitting together at the camp's big hearth fire in the mild spring evening, light still streaking the sky, soldiers still moving from tent to tent with the day's last tasks to accomplish.

When she nodded, he continued. "My brother John and I would—" He stopped to collect himself.

Then he began again, schooling himself to sound perfectly ordinary and matter-of-fact. "John and I traveled the realm. He was the main act, and I was the one who warmed up and drew in the crowds. I'm an acrobat and juggler." He thought for a moment. "Johnny hardly needed a warm-up act. Johnny the Traveler. He was famous."

"I heard him once," said Rhiane. "His voice was beautiful."

Wat nodded. "He played well, too. He had a rebec." Wat thought miserably of the broken shards still in his pack. He'd start working on them, he promised himself. That very day, he told himself.

He knew why he hadn't. Every time he thought of doing it and opened his pack to look at the broken thing, it reminded him of John's broken body, and then came a grief so overwhelming it unmanned him, and he had to turn away. But he'd do it. He'd repair John's rebec. He would.

"Your brother played beautifully, too. I don't play an instrument," said Rhiane. "I just sing." She shrugged.

"Try something now."

"How about *She moved through the fair*?"

"Try something else." Wat's mouth had gone dry. That was John's signature song.

"How about this?" She stood up, opened her mouth, and sang.

The cuckoo is a pretty bird, he sings as he flies,
He brings us good tidings, he tells us no lies.
He sucks the sweet flowers to make his voice clear,
And the more he cries cuckoo, the summer comes near.

A-walking, a-talking, a-walking was I,
To meet my true lover, he'll come by and by,
To meet in the meadows is all our delight,
A-walking and talking from morning till night.

O, meeting is pleasure and parting is grief,
An inconstant lover is worse than a thief,
A thief, he will rob you and take all you have,
An inconstant lover brings you to your grave.

Come all pretty maidens wherever you be,
Don't trust in young varlets to any degree,
They kiss you and court you, poor girls to deceive,
There's not one in twenty a girl can believe.

Come all you fair maidens, take warning of me,
Don't place all your love on a green growing tree,
The top it will wither, the roots they will die,
I'll wander forsaken, the cuckoo. . .

She drew the note out.

The cuckoo knows why.

"That's nice," said Wat, when she finished. She had a pleasing voice. It wasn't like Johnny's, but it would do.

He realized he himself would have to take a more active role in the performances. *And by now, I've had a lot of practice,* he reassured himself. He decided that before heading out again, he'd go to Silly Shep, show him all his tricks, and get some pointers.

"But I don't play an instrument," Rhiane said.

"Listen. With Johnny, we could get ourselves into important places and in front of important people. But he and I realized pretty early on that singing at street fairs and in taverns brought us just as much information, and maybe in a safer way. You and I will do well. We don't need to be the most sought-after performers in the realm. It will be fine if we're just ordinary."

Wat wasn't sure how much he believed that. It would have to do. They didn't have Johnny.

Just himself and this girl.

Then he said, hastily, "I don't mean to insult you, mistress. You sing very well."

"I'm here to help The Rising," she said with a show of determination. "I'll do what I can. I'm not Johnny the Traveler. We both know that. I'm not insulted."

He looked at her carefully now. He thought she must be a good-hearted girl. She hardly looked like the type who would join an armed insurrection, though.

She laughed at him, although the laughter didn't reach her eyes. "You're wondering why in the Nine I'm here," she said.

"Yes." *May as well be honest with her.*

"We come from the western coast. Up the coast north. Not too far from here. My sister—" She stopped and looked down at her hands. "The king's men took Bertrys. She was just a young girl. They took her to the king's tent, where he was on campaign, and they—"

Wat put out a hand to her. "I'm sorry," he said softly.

"I don't know where she is now. Our parents died of plague a year or more ago. I'm all she has, and now that king of ours has taken her."

"He's no king of mine," said Wat.

Rhiane nodded. "I realize it now. No king of mine. My parents believed if they worked hard on our lands, and didn't harm anyone, and paid their share to the overlord, and collected their share from those beneath them, then the world would stay basking peacefully underneath the whirling Spheres as it always does, the right ones on top always in command of it."

She drew a deep breath. "My parents thought it was nothing to do with the likes of us who those on top happened to be. Let kings and lords sort that out amongst themselves. My parents thought the ones on the bottom should stay there, where they're meant to be, obeying their betters. Us in the middle, just as the Lady ordained it, should mind our own business. But—"

She paused for a long time. Wat wondered if she would say anything further, after such a lengthy outburst.

She resumed. "But that turns out to be wrong. My parents were wrong. Things have turned upside down, seems like. And now I'm a woman, a girl no longer, and I'll go my own way."

"What about your lands?"

"Taken by the king's tax collector when our parents died and we couldn't pay. And then, as if that weren't enough payment," she said, her voice turning bitter, "they took Bertrys too. Our brothers are both dead. Our little sister is staying with some people in the countryside, to keep her from harm."

"Well, then," said Wat at last. "We'll leave within the sen'night."

As Rhiane walked away from him, Wat remembered with a chill something John had said to him, soon after the battle. "You'll meet a young girl, Wat. A girl who makes beautiful music. I want you to look out for her." He remembered promising Johnny he would.

At the time, he thought John meant someone they'd meet on their travels together. But now he saw that couldn't be what Johnny meant.

John was gone.

Maybe he meant this. This partnership with Rhiane.

Was Rhiane a young girl? The way Johnny had spoken of her, Wat had thought he meant someone younger. And while Rhiane had a nice voice, he didn't know if John's words of praise for the young girl he'd meet really did describe Rhiane.

Wat looked over doubtfully at his new partner. But maybe John did mean this woman. This Rhiane, trying to make her way in the world after her family was torn apart.

Wat knew how that felt. Not exactly in the same way, but he did know some part of the pain Rhiane was feeling.

Whether John's words meant Rhiane or not, Wat was resolved. She'd be his new partner, and they'd try to resume the work he and John had done together for The Rising.

On the day they decided they were ready to leave, Avery was there in the spring dawn to see them off. "Stay safe, Wat," he said, embracing Wat.

The prince turned to Rhiane. He smiled and held out his hand to her.

She curtseyed and kissed it. "Your Highness," she said.

Wat had brought the wagon around, and he helped Rhiane up onto the seat. He looked the ox Millicent over carefully, making sure her harness wasn't galling her.

As he made to swing up onto the wagon seat himself, Avery stopped him.

"Wat," said Avery, speaking low. "Our messenger to Dru has come back. Dru and his family are fine. I thought you'd want to know."

"Thank the Children," said Wat.

Avery stepped back, and Wat guided Millicent out of camp down the road south.

As they came to the first turn, a figure moved into their path from beneath the trees.

Wat pulled on Millicent's lines, and she plodded to a stop.

"Eris!"

Eris came to the wagon and stood looking up at Wat. "Heading out on your circuit?"

"Yes." He indicated Rhiane and introduced her.

Eris nodded briefly in her direction, barely civil.

"What about you? Back from your latest mission?" he asked her.

"Just last night. Too late to come to you and tell you. I'm glad I caught you before you left," she told Wat. "I didn't want you to leave before I had a chance to speak to you. Be careful, Wat."

He looked down at her tense expression and laughed. "Avery just told me the same thing. Everyone worrying about me."

"After what you've been through—"

Wat talked past her. "I'll be fine. This is nothing Johnny and I haven't done many times over. Don't worry about me, Eris."

He and Rhiane went on.

Eris dwindled behind them to a small dark figure, and then they rounded another bend and she was gone from his sight.

He was glad he didn't have to talk over his new arrangements with Eris. Endless talk, endless admonishments from her.

Be careful. Don't trust anyone.

On and on. Nine Spheres, she was only a bit older than he was, but she acted like a woman grown and treated him like some green boy.

He and Rhiane made camp before the first town where they would perform, a smallish town with a little village fair. "This will be a good place to try out our act," said Wat.

She nodded and began helping him set up. She was singing a cheerful song that made him think about sun and summer. *Summer is a'coming in, loud sing cuckoo.*

Wat was starting to feel good about what they were doing now. It wasn't summer yet, but it soon would be. Rhiane's song told it right. The sounds of the cuckoos were bursting out of the woodlands as they passed.

They'd been practicing every day on the road, three or four days now, and they had worked the kinks out of a few parts of their performance. Wat had checked the wagon over and made sure the box bed where they slept was sturdy enough to bear their weight.

He and Johnny would pull it up at the fair and use the top of the box bed built into the wagon as their stage. But the bad times had come, and Wat hadn't used it for several seasons.

He made sure all of the boards were sound and undamaged. His acrobatics were pretty vigorous. He didn't want to go crashing through a rotten board and destroy his ankle or knee.

Nights were the hardest for him to manage.

It was strange sleeping rolled up in his furs on one side of the box bed while some woman he barely knew lay rolled up on the other, hardly a hand's span between them.

He cursed himself for a fool. He was disturbed by her presence. He'd never been with a woman.

She was pretty, but he wasn't especially attracted to her.

So he told himself.

At night, in the dark, his body was telling him something different. After the third night, when he blinked in the light of dawn filtering through the slats of the box bed, he turned over to haul himself out of his furs and caught her staring at him.

"Should we just get it over with?" she said to him.

He looked at her in confusion.

She laughed. She rolled over on her back and stretched. "I was in love once. Thought I was. He left for a soldier and I never saw him again."

Then she turned back to him and her eyes widened. "Holy Lady. You've never done it, have you."

Wat felt himself coloring up.

"Want to give it a try?"

"No," said Wat. He tumbled from the furs to climb out of the box, and she laughed again.

"Looks like you do," she said softly. "Let me show you how."

Afterward, Wat wasn't sure whether he was relieved or the reverse. He was pretty sure he had made a fumbling mess of things.

"Don't worry," she said. "Practice makes perfect."

That day, while juggling, Wat dropped two balls. He never did that.

He cursed himself viciously.

"It's just a little village fair," Rhiane consoled him, after.

"It's not just a little village fair," Wat said unreasonably, between gritted teeth.

But eventually, he got the hang of things.

CHAPTER TEN

Suspicious Minds

Wat

Wat and Rhiane were heading back early. Something had happened. Something alarming.

"Avery needs to know this," he told her. "We aren't so very far away. We can loop back, deliver our news, and then we can start out again."

"We shouldn't keep going?" Rhiane raised her eyebrows.

"I think we need to get back," said Wat.

"I don't think we should," she said, strangely insistent.

"We're going to, though," said Wat, overruling her. He told her about the suspicious message he'd received.

She just shrugged. She probably didn't realize what this information might be implying. "You're the leader."

It was clear to him she was angry.

By now, their love-making had dwindled away. *Probably I'm not any good at it*, Wat thought, ashamed. It's not as though he were in love with her. So he wasn't sure why he should care.

But they worked pretty well together onstage. Before the performance, she would put on one or the other of two pretty kirtles she owned. One was blue and plainer, but the blue brought out the blue of her eyes. The other was yellow with beautiful bands of red and green embroidered flowers. "The last of my belongings from home," she told him.

He would put on his green Kenning the Juggler costume. He'd prance and leap and somersault before the people gathered in front of their cart. He juggled. There was a complicated routine he did, passing the balls under first one upraised leg, then the other. He used to do this to the music John would play on his rebec, but without that, he simplified the act a little. Then he ended with the astonishing Six-Ball Shower.

After that, Rhiane would step past him to the front of the stage and sing. People seemed to like the act. The two of them collected a tidy little pile of coin with each performance. Usually just coppers. Sometimes a silver penny or two.

They made their way to one of the larger towns, their first major performance. At this town, all the performers took turns on a wooden platform the town had erected, so he and Rhiane weren't even restricted to the small performing space on the top of their wagon box bed.

On impulse, Wat got his bow afterward and competed in the archery competition. He came away with one of the prizes, and he smiled as he trickled his winnings into the leather bag of coin they'd take back to Avery. Rhiane's eyes, as she watched him compete, were bright. His skill with the bow seemed to have shown her a different side of him.

Afterward, as they strolled back through the booths and wagons toward the place they'd tethered Millicent, Rhiane spotted a shiny trinket.

"Look!" she exclaimed.

She was standing before a peddler's tray of fairings. She held up a glittering bangle. Wat eyed it. It was gold, or maybe just some kind of gimcrack gilt. On it was a bird. Its round eye was picked out in blue enamel.

"The cuckoo," she said, dimpling. *The cuckoo, he's a pretty bird*, she sang, looking him up and down.

The peddler grinned, showing a blackened tooth. "Buy something pretty for the pretty maid?" he wheedled.

She had their bag of coin, and she held it up and waggled it at him and gave him a winsome look. Her eyes were really very big and blue.

"No," Wat said shortly, and strode away. At the edge of the fair, he looked behind him and saw she was still dawdling along by the peddlers' carts. "Rhiane," he called.

She looked up. Even from that distance, he could see how angry and disappointed she was.

He waited until she had caught up to him. She took her time about it.

He grabbed her by an elbow and steered her over to their wagon. He shoved her against it, and she stood there refusing to look at him, sullenly regarding her shoes.

"Rhiane," he said. "This coin doesn't belong to us. It belongs to The Rising."

"Peddler wasn't asking much," she muttered. "It wasn't much. Just something pretty. Take your hands off me."

He stepped back hastily. "I know the price wasn't high, but no, we can't spend this coin on tawdry fairings. We need to take it all back to Avery."

"We barely have enough to eat." She handed the bag of coin to him, and he took it. "There. Take it all back to your masters."

"Look," he said. "We'll get down river to a house I know. A woman sympathetic to The Rising lives there. She'll feed us. She'll practically force food down us. We'll gorge ourselves before we head out again. In the meantime, we need to save every copper."

Looking back on it, he realized that was the moment the stranger had come up to him and tugged at his tunic.

Wat turned around, startled and a bit alarmed.

"I knew your brother John," said this man. "Why isn't he with you?" He glanced past Wat to Rhiane. "I enjoyed your songs, mistress," he told her.

"Thanks," Rhiane muttered.

"John and I don't perform together now," said Wat carefully.

"I was asked to give him this," said the man, thrusting a parchment into Wat's hands. "Will you see he gets it?"

"What is it?" said Wat. He glanced around covertly. The man could be setting him up.

"Dunno, lad. I don't know my letters. Just a fellow gave me good coin to get it to your brother. Seems to me I've discharged my duty. Seems to me I've earned the coin, now you have the parchment." The man walked away.

Wat took the parchment and unfolded it. *Caedon knows.* That was all it said. It chilled Wat. It might be a warning for John, come too late. Or it might mean something else. He'd have to take it to Avery and see what he thought about it.

So then, over Rhiane's objections, Wat had made them turn around.

He might have made a different decision if they had reached the Riverlands already. But they were still close enough to get back to camp with only a day or two of hard traveling.

He and Rhiane turned Millicent and went plodding in the opposite direction they'd come. Throughout the day, whenever they stopped, Rhiane kept wandering off along the roadside and was slow to get back to the wagon. She claimed to have lost something and had to look for it. She claimed she was feeling a little sick and needed to get some air. She lagged and delayed. Wat was beginning to get angry about it.

He was about to work himself up to talking to her, giving her a direct order, insisting on cooperation, when they heard a rider behind them, coming up fast. Wat's heart always began to beat harder, when something like that happened. *It's nothing,* he told himself. *There's no reason anyone would be after us.* The message had made him jumpy, though.

The horseman swerved his rouncey around them and dismounted.

"Dru!" shouted Wat. Before Millicent had even stopped moving, he was off the wagon seat and had flung himself into Dru's arms. He was sobbing against Dru. "They killed him, Dru," he sobbed. "John. They destroyed him. We didn't get to him in time. They— they—"

Wat paid no mind to the girl on the wagon seat.

Dru waved an arm in her direction and walked Wat a little way into the woods. He sat him down. "I know," he said over and over to Wat. "I know."

Wat leaned against Dru until he was still. He'd never done this to Avery and Conal, and he loved and trusted them just as much. But somehow, seeing Dru had unleashed the grief he'd been keeping tight inside.

"There, lad," said Dru softly. "There, now."

"Sorry," Wat muttered.

"Don't say that to me, Wat. I feel the same. John was my brother as sure as he was yours and Avery's. Maybe not the way the world counts these things, but it's the way I count them. I loved him, Wat. Loved him more than life."

"What will the world be like without Johnny in it?"

"A bad place," Dru whispered. "A bad place for my girls to grow up. A bad place for you to be a man. So we must work to make it a better place, Wat."

"How can that be?" said Wat. "I look around me, and I only see the bad."

Dru didn't answer. After a while, he said, "I hoped I'd find you on the road. You must turn around, Wat. We must get to the Riverlands, and then head up into the high country beyond." At Wat's questioning look, he explained. "Avery, Conal, and a few others have gone there, to a house Avery knows about. There are some things we need to do, and we need a base closer to Caedon."

"Look what a man gave me. This is why we had started heading back to Avery. To show him." Wat fished the parchment out of his belt pouch and handed it to Dru.

"Yes," said Dru. "Yes, good impulse. I'll lead you to where Avery and the others have gotten us a small cottage to use. You can show him this, and then he'll tell you his plan. I'll accompany you. We should get there in a sen'night or so." ·

"Millicent doesn't move very fast," said Wat.

"Maybe leave her here at this town? I'll pay for her keep. You can get her later."

"But three of us on one horse. We can't do it."

"I'll engage other horses. Let's go, Wat."

When they went back to the road and told Rhiane, she looked even angrier than she had before. "Just leave me in the town," she told them shortly, throwing Wat a scornful glance that filled him with a burning shame. "You can get me on the way back. That way, you'll just have to hire one horse."

"No, mistress," said Dru, his voice going hard. "You're coming, too."

She had shrugged and hadn't raised any more objections.

She minds Dru. Not me. I'm just a boy. A boy who falls apart at the least little thing. That's what she thinks of me, said Wat resentfully to himself. He carefully avoided her eyes, and he saw she was avoiding his.

Wat tried not to wonder where Dru had gotten the coin for it all—boarding Millicent and the wagon, hiring two horses. Dru did have it, though, and in a little less than a sen'night, the three of them were into the high country up the Dourdin River.

They followed a winding trail to a small stone cottage. Over the hills to the west of them, the last of the light had just gone, and the lone beacon of a rush torch shone out ahead of them to welcome them.

Avery was out in the dooryard. "I heard the horses," he said, helping Rhiane off hers and embracing Wat and Dru. They all went inside and sat at the hearth, eating from the big kettle there. It was crowded. Avery was there, and Conal. Torin and Lorel, two women who had joined The Rising together, were there. Eris was there, too. And now the three of them.

The cottage was one fairly small room, although a log with steps cut out of it led up to a platform loft that extended halfway over the lower space.

One slit of a window let in light and air. Right now a soft wash of moonlight was spilling through it into the cottage.

"In the morning, I'll explain how matters stand," Avery said to Wat. "For now, everyone," he called out, including them all, "get some sleep."

Avery and Conal mounted the log steps to the platform above. The rest of them rolled themselves in furs on the rough boards beneath.

Wat chose a corner and headed to it. He spread out the fur robe Dru had handed him. As he turned to straighten it, he saw Rhiane standing uncertainly in the middle of the house near the hearthstones. She looked over at Wat, as if she might head to his corner, but as she moved toward him past the place where Eris sat sprawled against some packs, she tripped over Eris's outstretched leg and went down hard. Rhiane pulled herself up to her knees, looking a little stunned, and everyone stared over at her, startled.

"Sorry," said Eris. Her voice was lazy.

Eris tripped her. She did it on purpose, thought Wat.

Rhiane got to her feet, nursing her shin, and turned to Eris. Wat saw her eyes blazing in the firelight. Eris was looking back at her, a small smile on her face, her eyes appraising.

"Over here, Mistress Rhiane," said Torrin. She strode to the girl, took her by the hand, and brought her to the corner she and Lorel had staked out as their own sleeping place. "Sleep here beside us," she told Rhiane. Her voice was perfectly even, but Wat could see the warning look she threw over her shoulder at Eris.

Wat rolled into his furs and faced the wall. Whatever was happening, whatever petty grudge Eris was holding now, he didn't want to know about it. After Rhiane's difficult behavior of the day before, after his own emotional outburst in front of her, Wat was feeling uneasy around her. Just the same, it troubled him, watching Eris harass her. Eris hadn't needed to cause trouble. She was always doing things like that. Stirring things up. He loved her, but she was difficult to like sometimes. Always had been. He burrowed his head into the furs and tried to escape into sleep.

The next morning, after they'd all had some of the porridge Dru prepared at the hearth, Avery explained his plans to work on finding the princes and getting Diera out of the hands of Caedon. "Wat," he said. "Some of the others of us have already talked this out, but this is the first time you've heard of it. We have these two important tasks to accomplish, both of them about Artur's children and their legacy. If we can restore that legacy, we'll accomplish a lot."

Wat saw these words were inspiring to Torrin and Lorel. He found them inspiring himself. The Rising was working to restore justice in the realm. As for Eris—but, he said to himself, who ever knew what she thought about anything? She kept her feelings to herself.

He thought Avery and Conal both looked weary. It gradually occurred to him, as the talk went on amongst them, that much of the assembled force in the north had dwindled away.

Dru confirmed it the next morning, when Wat went to him with some of his misgivings. "The Rising is not in a good place, Wat. We won a great victory, but we don't have the funds to keep going the way we have. A lot of the men have families and farms. It was plowing time when they began to leave, and planting came right after. If we could pay them—but we can't. Many of them have gone home."

The cottage was quiet as they talked. Torrin and Lorel were putting their things to rights. Eris was nowhere in sight. Wat found himself wishing this peaceful interlude could go on forever.

He and Dru sat together on the log outside the cottage that served them all for seating. "I can still head out and take care of some things, at Avery's orders," Dru said after a moment. "I'll do that. Avery and Conal have this task to do, with Diera. They're trying to locate the whereabouts of the princes. And then they're also trying to build the force in the north back to fighting strength. If they can do it, we'll bring the men south and try to mount an attack late in the summer, or maybe early harvest-tide.

But those two—" He cast his eyes over to the place where Avery and Conal stood talking. "They have too much to get done."

"What about me?"

"For now, stay close," said Dru. "It may be Avery will need you to go out again."

"With Rhiane."

Dru looked off into the trees. "She may not be the best partner for you, lad. Avery and Conal and I have talked about that."

"She and I were doing fine."

Dru considered him. "You're not getting close to her, are you?"

Wat knew what he meant. He blushed. "Not really," he said. "Not much."

"Good. She may not be what she says she is."

Wat looked up at him, startled.

"Eris brought back some information about her. It alarmed us."

"She seems fine," said Wat.

"She seems pretty reluctant," said Dru.

"Yesterday, she was," Wat admitted. In fact, he thought, she'd acted a right pain in the arse.

Dru went off to do some quick thing Conal needed from him. Wat didn't want to ask him what this thing might be. He knew Dru's skills. What they were used for. Dru had taught them to him.

Wat practiced with his bow, and then he sat by himself on the old log outside the low door into the cottage. He began thinking about rummaging around the cottage for bread and cheese.

Eris emerged blinking into the sunlight.

"Eris," said Wat. He was still angry at what he'd observed the night before. "What did you tell Avery about Rhiane?"

"Keep your voice down," she snapped. "It's not for me to say. I report to Avery." She deliberately turned her back on him and stalked away down the path to the stream behind the cottage.

She'd hardly gotten out of sight when Rhiane came out, too, smoothing her blue kirtle down around her. She really stood out. The other women were all in trousers or tunic and leggings. Wat wondered if she had overheard what he'd said to Eris, and Eris's reply.

She stood looking around into the trees. "Wat," she said, moving to sit down beside him. "This isn't a good place for me to be. I don't feel welcome here. I thought I'd be helping, but I see I'm not. I need to leave."

"Don't mind Eris," said Wat quickly. "She's always like that. She's pretty prickly. I didn't like the way she treated you last night, and you probably didn't either, but don't mind her."

"That's not it." Rhiane gave him an uneasy look. "It was unpleasant, what she did. But I've been thinking about this for days now."

Wat looked at her for a long moment. "Have you told Avery?"

"No, I was hoping you'd help me do that. I was trying to tell his lordship, but he wasn't listening."

His lordship, Wat thought, puzzled. Then he realized Rhiane meant Dru. The Earl Drustan. He realized he never thought of Dru that way, not any longer. If he ever really had. "I think you should have just told him, rather than make trouble all day long," he said at last.

"I know," she said with a sigh. "I'm to blame. I didn't know how to do it. I should have asked your advice. Now he doesn't like me."

"That doesn't matter. He's a fair man. But he thinks our partnership isn't working out."

"It's not," she said softly. She looked over at him. "Nothing to do with you, Wat."

What does it have to do with, then, he thought bitterly.

"Look. It's that soldier I told you about," she said, as if she had heard his unasked question.

"The one you were in love with."

"Yes. I lied to all of you." She colored up and looked away. "I believe what I told you, about my sister, and the way my ideas have changed. I didn't lie about that. But I lied about wanting to join The Rising. I'm so stupid. I wanted someone to help me travel around, so I could find the man I loved. I could tell, once we'd started on your circuit of the village fairs, that my plan would never work. It was a silly-headed notion, like something out of the stories. The fair maiden heads out into the forest to seek the lover who abandoned her. What was I expecting? Fairy magic?" Wat saw she was talking more to herself than to him. "I might as well go to look for a needle in a meadow."

I'm a fool, thought Wat.

Under her breath, she sang a few bars of a song she liked. *"They kiss you and court you, poor girls to deceive,"* she sang, low. *"There's not one in twenty a girl can believe."* She sat silent. Wat didn't know what to say, so he sat without speaking beside her. "I didn't mean to hurt you," she said to him, without looking at him.

"You didn't," he said shortly.

"So," she said after a moment. "How do I tell Avery I want to leave?"

"Just tell him." Wat got up and started walking away.

"And how do I get out of here?" She sounded desperate.

He shrugged and kept walking.

He had nothing particular he needed to do, so he rambled through the woods, trying not to think about all the problems pressing down on him, or the humiliation he felt now. Although why he should feel humiliated was a puzzle to him. This girl didn't love him. He didn't love her. They'd never had such feelings about each other. So why were his cheeks burning, he asked himself.

He decided partnering with a woman on his missions was too complicated. Once she was gone, he'd tell Avery that he wanted to work by himself.

He thought about John's admonition to him. *You'll meet a young girl, a girl who makes beautiful music.* He thought about how he had figured Rhiane was that girl. *I suppose she's not*, he thought.

But then he thought maybe, if another like girl who matched John's description did show up, he might ignore what John had asked of him. Would that be acceptable, he wondered, to ignore and push aside something John had asked of him?

Throughout the morning, he walked without purpose, trying to drink in the springtide air. All around him called the cuckoos.

It was that time of sweet showers, ending the dry winter, piercing to the root every green thing, so that tender shoots had begun poking up through the sod, carpeting the forest floor. The young sun poured into the world from its place fastened to the

Spheres, bathing everything in light, the rich liquid from which the flowers sprang, as if watered by light.

Small birds filled the surrounding forest with melody, even at night. Through the tiny slit of the window in the stone cottage, Wat had heard the blackbird singing all night long. Once, a nightingale.

This night music reminded him of his childhood, when the world seemed fine and glorious. When it seemed as though nothing would ever go awry.

His mother loved him.

And I never thought about it, Wat said to himself. *I just knew it. Something that was always there and always would be. So I thought.*

His brothers. How much he loved both of them.

His friends, Eris and Keelie. Later, Diera.

Then someone killed Keelie, and the world changed.

Now, it was as though the world had up-ended. *Rhiane is right*, thought Wat, remembering what she had said about the world seeming to turn upside down after her parents died and her sister was taken.

He was suddenly afraid for Rhiane. He couldn't say why.

He turned and headed back to the cottage. He'd tell Avery to help Rhiane leave. She just wanted to find this man she'd lost. She hadn't lied to Wat about it. Not really. She'd told him she loved the man.

He thought with a blush about his fumbling attempts at lovemaking. *She enticed me*, he thought bitterly.

Then he thought, *I didn't have to accept the enticement. It's not as if my heart is broken.*

But, he thought, she had lied to Avery, and about a very serious matter. She'd lied about wanting to join The Rising, and now she knew a lot of things about Avery and the rest of them that she shouldn't know.

Still, he thought *It's not as though she bears us ill-will.*

He remembered what she had said about her life and how Audemar's men had destroyed it. Destroyed her sister. Surely she posed no threat to The Rising. She was a sympathizer.

Besides, she has learned she isn't cut out for this life.

Who was?

If she had another way to live, and she wanted to live that other life, let her, Wat thought. It was clear she was gently brought up. Why should she want to jolt around the worst roads in the realm closed up in a wagon box with a callow young man she didn't know and didn't even particularly like.

My pride is wounded, he told himself. *That's all there is to it.*

Now he saw why Rhiane had wanted to be left in the last town they'd passed, instead of coming with him and Dru. She saw she'd be better off on her own. She wanted a quick way to end their arrangement.

At the fair, she had been happy, at least for a little while.

He was sorry he hadn't let her buy the bangle she wanted. She was right. It would have been cheap. She had little enough happiness in her life, and the bangle might have given her a small moment of joy.

As, consumed with these thoughts, he trudged up the path, he spotted Avery, Conal, and Dru standing outside the cottage. Their expressions were somber.

He came up to them. "Avery, I've been thinking—" he burst out.

"Wat," said Avery, holding out a hand to forestall him. "Sit here with us. We have something to tell you."

They all sat down on the log together. Wat felt a sense of dread pressing down on him.

"Wat," said Dru. "Remember what I told you about Rhiane?"

"Yes, but Dru—"

"No, just listen," said Dru. "She's betraying us to Caedon. Eris has found it out."

"No," said Wat. "I don't believe that."

"Part of her plan was to befriend you," said Avery. "If Dru hadn't stopped the two of you and made you turn around, she would have led you into a trap."

"No." Wat shook his head stubbornly. "She doesn't want to be here with us, but it's not the way you think."

He saw Avery and Dru exchange glances. "Listen, Wat," said Dru. "The information Eris brought us was conclusive. She's a traitor. She may be the traitor who led Caedon to John."

"I doubt that," said Conal.

The other two looked at him. Wat could see they were surprised.

"What did you think of Eris's information, Con?" said Dru. "If you have doubts, tell us."

Conal looked uncomfortable. Finally he nodded. "The information was persuasive. They're right," he told Wat.

"The parchment that fellow brought you," said Dru. "Did Rhiane's behavior change, after she saw he had given it to you?"

Wat reluctantly nodded. "I suppose so," he said. He thought about it. "It was right around that time."

"We need to act," said Avery.

"Act how?" said Wat. His blood was beginning to pound in his ears.

"You know how," Avery said to him.

"I'm her partner. I should be the one to deal with it," said Wat.

"No, lad," said Avery. "Let Dru do it."

"You're all calling me one of you, but you don't believe it. You think I'm a child," Wat burst out.

Dru took Wat by the shoulders and turned him to look into his eyes. "Wat. I'll do it."

"That's an order, Wat," said Avery, and he rose with Dru. They walked off together under the trees.

Wat sat morosely looking at his feet. "They're going to kill her, aren't they."

Conal said nothing.

"It's not right."

Conal put his hand on Wat's knee and squeezed it. "She's a traitor, Wat."

Wat looked up at Conal. "You don't even believe that."

Conal looked back at Wat, and Wat could see he was troubled. "I'd say she couldn't be. My gut tells me she isn't. Sometimes the gut tells you wrong, lad. The evidence is clear. I can't argue with it. She was about to take you straight to Caedon. If Dru hadn't gotten to you, you'd be dead. You know what Caedon is capable of. You and Rafe know better than any of us." He and Wat sat silently together. "No telling what other damage the girl has done," Conal said at last with a sigh. "No telling what she might still do, if Avery lets her walk away from here."

"Couldn't we just lock her up?"

"Not practical. Not in the situation we find ourselves. She knows who we are. She knows about this place. Avery and Dru will deal with her. It's their decision, and their job to do, not yours."

Then Wat thought about the bangle. That's when her behavior had changed.

Before the note, not after.

He tried telling Conal this, but Conal just shook his head.

The weather had turned harsh again. Wat sat shivering close to the hearth fire. There was nothing for him except waiting for Avery's further orders. Dru had sent Lorel to retrieve Wat's ox and player's wagon from the little town where Dru had found Wat and Rhiane, and now Lorel had come back.

All Wat really needed to do was see to Millicent, make sure she was fed and groomed. Today, in the wet weather, he went out to check the box bed for leaks.

He stooped into its dim interior. Over in the corner of it lay Rhiane's yellow kirtle with the colorful embroidered bands, crumpled up. Wat smoothed it out but snatched back his hand as if the cloth had burned him. He should throw the kirtle away. He found he couldn't touch it. He couldn't even look at it. He climbed out of the box and onto the wagon seat, promising himself he'd deal with it some other day.

Then he jumped down and went over to Millicent, where she stood patiently eating oats from a trough under a crude little shed roof. He leaned against her solid flank. She felt good to him. He breathed in the innocent animal scent of her.

He didn't know where Avery and Dru had taken Rhiane. He had a pretty good idea what they'd done.

Avery had come back, alone.

A little while later, Dru had walked back up the path. He had gone straight to the bucket at the door and had drunk a lot of water out of it. He'd rolled himself into his furs and had slept the rest of the day, all that night, and into the next day. Nobody dared disturb him.

When he woke that next day, he had been dry-eyed and brisk. But Wat thought he saw signs that Dru was deeply disturbed. *Maybe I'm imagining it*, thought Wat. *But I don't think I am.*

Wat had never seen Rhiane again.

Something in Dru's eyes told him, *Don't ask.*

He thought about the skills Dru had taught him, and shuddered.

At the time, using knife and garotte had seemed like a game. They didn't seem so now.

Wat looked at his own hands. Would he have been able to do what Dru had no doubt done to Rhiane? He'd brashly told them all she was his partner and he should be the one to deal with her. Could he have done it? He doubted he could.

But then he thought about what he had done to Caedon. *Under the right circumstances, I could do it*, he said to himself. *If only I'd succeeded, with Caedon.*

He thought of John and his powers, the unearthly shriek ripped from his brother by some unknowable arcane force, and the men it had killed. Hundreds of them. Just common soldiers enlisted into the army of the king. Enemies or not, none of them deserved to die, especially not like that.

He thought of the haunted expression in John's eyes, the last time he'd seen his brother, at least the last time he'd seen him conscious, moving around walking and talking in the world underneath the Spheres, and he realized where that expression had come from.

The wet day went slowly by, rain starting, pouring down in torrents, lessening, stopping. Beginning again with a low growl from the sky.

Torrin and Lorel left, Lorel to look into acquiring some new horses, Torrin on some other errand.

Avery, Conal, and Dru were off somewhere.

Eris came into the cottage, her clothes dripping. She stepped to her corner, stripped out of the wet things, and pulled on dry clothing. Then she came to sit beside Wat at the hearth.

Wat moved away from her.

"Wat," she said softly. "You're still brooding about that. About that girl."

"I hope you were sure," said Wat. He knew his tone was vicious. "If you're wrong, that girl is dead because of you."

"Wat!" she exclaimed. "She would have led you to your death."

"You know this."

"I do know it." She threw her arms around him and pulled him close. "How could I let you walk into a trap? And the Lady knows what else that woman was telling Audemar's people about us."

"Telling Caedon," said Wat. He spat the name out. "That's the one she would tell, if she were a traitor."

Eris turned away from him and stared into the fire as the turves smoked and crumbled.

"Yes," she said quietly after a long moment. "Telling Caedon." Then she said, "Did you love her?"

"Who?" said Wat, startled. "That girl?" He couldn't bring himself to say her name. "No," he said.

"Oh. Looked to me that maybe—"

"No," said Wat. "You might be right about all the rest. You're wrong about that, if that's what you think."

"Oh," she said. After a silence, she said, "A good thing. She wasn't worthy of you, Wat."

Wat looked over at her and saw she was taken aback. "Rhiane didn't fancy me, either, you know," he said. "She loved some soldier she wanted to find." He saw he had surprised her. "I guess you don't know everything about her, after all. What a shock. You being so smart and canny and all."

He got to his feet and heaved out of the door into the rain.

He walked down the path, fast, and he didn't stop when he heard her calling after him.

CHAPTER ELEVEN

Trade-offs

Diera

Diera studiously ignored Caedon. The man was trying to get her attention, as she sat with the four daughters of Earl Treddian in the castle where they kept her. Caedon had a young woman by the hand.

It was too provoking. He refused to be discouraged. He must see how much she loathed him. Everyone must see it.

"Your Highness," said Caedon, and bowed low, right at her elbow. He had the strange young woman in tow.

The hypocrite, thought Diera. "Lord Caedon," she said coldly.

"I've brought a new servant for you."

"I don't need any more servants."

"Oh, but Lady Treddian and I agree that you do."

"Diera, my lovely girl. You need a lady's maid. You can't keep sharing Mildburg's. The earl and I are about to agree on a husband for her, and she'll need her own," the earl's lady called over to Diera. "Lord Cadeon, how delighted I am to see you in health."

"Thank you, my lady. My recovery was swift, thanks to the excellent healers you and the good earl provided me." He turned to the girl now, tugging her forward by the arm. "Bertrys, this is Her Highness the Princess Diera, your new mistress," Caedon said to the blooming girl beside him.

She bowed low to Diera.

"Rise," said Diera indifferently.

"Leofric." Caedon turned to Rafe, who was standing beside Diera. Diera tensed. What game was the fellow playing? Now all her senses were on alert. She knew Caedon and his churlish ways too well, by now.

"Yes, lord?" said Rafe.

"Take Mistress Bertrys to Diera's rooms and show her around. Show her where she's to sleep."

"Yes, lord," said Rafe. He motioned to the girl and led her off.

"This, I suppose, is another way you've arranged to keep your eye on me," Diera said in an undertone to Caedon.

He laughed. "So suspicious, Your Highness. Can't I do you a friendly office without my motives questioned at every turn?"

"No," she said.

He put his hand on her knee as if for an affectionate pat, and she tried to keep herself from cringing away from him.

"Don't try to thwart me, Diera," he said in an undertone. "You won't succeed."

Thank the Children he left her side then, and soon he called for his horse to be made ready. He made his bows to the earl and his lady, to them all, and left for the castle's outer bailey, where the stables were.

Diera was quick to excuse herself to go to her rooms. No telling what that girl was doing in there. Going through her things, no doubt. But as she moved down the gallery pierced with tall windows that overlooked the bailey, she saw Caedon, below, talking to Rafe. She quickened her steps.

In her rooms, the girl was sitting passively with her hands in her lap.

"Mistress Bertrys, is it?" said Diera.

"Yes, lady," said the girl.

"Just so we're clear. I know Lord Caedon has set you to spy on me. The less we have to do with each other, the better. You do what you need to do to satisfy Lord Caedon, and I will do what I need to do to keep him away from me."

The girl colored up and looked over at her resentfully.

Rafe came in then. He bowed to them both.

"Leave us," said Diera to Bertrys.

"Lord Caedon says I'm not to."

"But I say you are."

"Your Highness. If I may," said Rafe. "I'll talk to Mistress Bertrys privately."

Diera couldn't fathom his expression, but she nodded.

"Mistress, will you follow me?" said Rafe.

Diera was amazed to see that the girl did without further objections. However Rafe managed it, Diera was grateful. The girl was giving her a headache, and she'd been in Diera's rooms less than a candle measure.

Not much longer afterward, Rafe returned without the girl.

"How did you get that silly girl out of here, Rafe?" Diera cried. "I'm grateful to you for ridding me of her."

"Bertrys has been given to believe she and I are allies in the keeping of you, Diera," said Rafe. He looked weary.

"That's pretty clear. What else do you know about her and what Caedon wants her to do? Tell me, if you can. Quickly, while we're alone. I doubt we have much time."

"No, we'll have the time. I sent little Bertrys off on a complicated errand."

"What errand?" His expression frightened her a little.

"There were sweetmeats I enjoyed, as a child. The making of them is time-consuming. She has gone off to make some for me."

"Rafe, what's going on?" said Diera. Something very odd, she was beginning to realize.

Rafe looked away. It was clear he didn't want to answer. Finally he said, in a choked kind of voice, "She was brought here for you, yes. But she was also brought here for me."

"To spy on you?"

Rafe didn't say anything.

"Why, Rafe."

"She thinks she's—" Diera could see he was having a hard time getting the words out. "She's been brought here to be a wife for me. I'm supposed to be courting her."

"Rafe."

"This makes me believe my time being able to protect you is coming to an end, lady."

"Rafe, don't talk to me like this."

"Let me tell you what I know."

She summoned all her resolve to stay calm. "Do that, Rafe."

"Caedon is planning to force Audemar to give you to him. He plans to marry you."

Diera saw she wasn't even surprised. "Go on," she murmured.

"He wants you to bear his children."

"After his first little experiment in that line went awry." She felt the rage building in her now.

"This time, it will be a known thing, not the secret villainy he practiced on you earlier. With Audemar's endorsement and a publicly acknowledged marriage, he can have that."

"He wants power," said Diera. "He thinks I'm the way to get it."

"That is certainly one of his motives," Rafe said. She saw how carefully he was picking his words.

"And what else? What else is he trying to do? How does this girl figure into things?" she said sharply.

"People have begun to notice my devotion to you, lady."

"Stop calling me that. Yes, I see it. This girl will divert them into a different way of thinking. You'll be seen as besotted with her."

"No one will then be likely to misconstrue. . ." Diera saw again how carefully he was trying to put things. ". . . misconstrue the parentage of any issue you and Caedon may have." Then he burst out, "You see how I've failed you yet again. I love you, and everyone sees it, and now it has led to this."

"Do you regret what we did, that afternoon?" she said, moving close to him and putting her hand on his arm.

He raised his eyes to hers. "Never. Never think it, Diera." They were in each other's arms then. "But this. This is too dangerous a place for us to be. . ." He moved away from her.

She pulled him back closer. "I don't care."

They tumbled into her bed.

Later he raised himself on one elbow and began twining strands of her dark curls around his finger.

"I must leave, Diera. I must end this."

She had been stretching languorously under him, smiling, loving the feel of her bare skin on his, loving the scent of him, the scent of their love-making, but now, with his words, a pang of fear thrust itself deep into her gut. "I know we need to part before that girl finds us here." She stopped. She saw that's not what he meant by *ending this*. "What are you talking about, Rafe? Some of the things you've told me make me think that ending your service to me would be terribly dangerous for you. Is that it? Is that what you're suggesting, going away from me?"

"Yes." He stirred and sat up. "But Avery needs me here. He's working on a plan to get you out." He laughed, a bitter sound. "And Caedon needs me here to convince you that you have no choice but to go along with his plans for you."

"Then stay and help me. Here's the person who needs you, right here in this bed. I need you, Rafe." She reached out and stroked him, laying her cheek against his chest. "What's this?" she said sleepily.

"What?"

"This." Diera reached out her hand to touch the little amulet he always wore on a thong about his neck.

"Something from home. Something from my childhood."

"And you always wear it."

"I do."

"A reminder of what's most important?"

"Something like that. I suppose it's a reminder that in childhood I once led an ordinary life, like other boys. Before my parents sent me to Gilles."

Diera was silent for a moment. She was still not sure what it meant, that Rafe had been sent to Gilles de Rais, in boyhood. "What can I give you to remind you how important you are to me, Rafe?" she said at last. "To make sure you stay by me always."

"You know what that will mean, if I stay by you? You know what it means, that this woman is here? She's part of Caedon's plan. I'll have to—" He swallowed hard.

She leaped from the bed and pulled a robe around her, understanding what he was trying to say, trying to calm the sudden fury rising in her. "I'll kill that woman with my own hands. Who is she, anyway?"

"Her story is sad," said Rafe. "She was seized by Audemar's men for Audemar's pleasure. Now she has been discarded. Now Caedon is using her." He swung his legs off the side of the bed and began feeling for his clothing. He pulled on his tunic and tucked the little amulet down the neck of it. "She mustn't find us like this. However sad her origins are, she's Caedon's creature, and Audemar's. She'll go straight to Caedon if she sees us like this. Not that he doesn't know how I feel about you. In fact, that knowledge makes his plan to use Bertrys even more intriguing to him. He loves cornering people who are in his power and putting them in impossible boxes."

"This girl's story is indeed a sad one," said Diera. "She's very young."

He stepped to her and pulled a robe around her, tugging her close to him again "Whatever I'm made to do, I love only you, Diera."

"You'll fall in with these plans?" Diera knew her voice must sound incredulous. "With this girl?"

"Or I can end it. If I do, I fail Avery. If I don't, and stay here, I may be able to help Avery, but I'll certainly find myself serving Caedon. Either way, I fail you. Caedon has cleverly seen to that. I need to end it."

Diera searched his face with her eyes. His phrase *to end it* sent a chill up her body.

He didn't just mean going away. He meant something more sinister.

"Rafe, when you say that, I feel such fear I don't know what to do with it. What do you mean, when you say that."

"Caedon has certain ways to—" He stopped. Clearly he didn't know how to go on.

"I've noticed how pale you look, how you seem to be wasting away before my very eyes. This last time you were away, I was terrified, and when I saw you after, even more. I know Caedon is damaging you. Is he poisoning you, somehow, the way he poisoned Grandfather? But look at you now. You were so pale. Like death. You look so much better, Rafe."

Rafe pulled away from her. "I must go." Over his shoulder, he said to her, "Yes, I'm better. Caedon thinks he needs me better. To— you know. Court that woman."

"Court her." Diera felt the rage rising in her again.

"Yes." He stopped, his head drooping. "So what must I do? I'll go to Avery, tell him I won't be able to go on."

"You'll leave me. Leave me in Caedon's hands."

He was back beside her in two strides. "Diera. I can't stay here and be a party to Caedon's plans. I can't make love to some girl I despise. Or to anyone, no matter how friendly or unfriendly I might feel about her. Unless that one is you." He hesitated and reached out to smooth her hair away from her forehead, looking as if he wanted to drown in her eyes. "If I don't do what Caedon wants, he'll end me. I want him to. Enough. Avery is going to get you out."

"I mean nothing to you."

"You mean everything to me. That and my oath to Avery. But when Caedon killed John—"

"My uncle?" Diera cried.

"Child help you. You haven't heard."

Diera felt the blood drain from her cheeks. Rafe pulled her down to sit on the bed again.

He sat beside her, tucking her head against his shoulder. "Wat and I tried to prevent it. We tried so hard. We were too late."

Diera heard Rafe's voice break. She gripped his hand. "Wat," said Diera, trying to smile. "He's my true friend. When I was a lonely girl, he befriended me. You, too, Rafe, as much as you could. When you go to all of them next, tell Wat I grieve with him. Tell Avery."

She felt she might faint, but she steadied herself. "Caedon," she whispered. "There's no evil that man won't do."

"Some dastardly villains nearly killed him," said Rafe, low. "You may have heard."

"Yes, although I didn't know why he was attacked. As he lay injured, I was hoping the Dark Ones would have pity on us all and take him on off with Them to Their dark place. But the Dark Ones are pitiless. Alas, here he is, back with the living, and he looks to be just fine."

"Wat and I were those murderous villains. We were here in this very castle's prison to get John out, and when we saw we were too late, we turned on Caedon in our grief and fury, and we beat him. We held him down and stomped on him the way you would if you encountered a poisonous serpent. We had hoped we'd succeeded in killing him. But he survived. Caedon has protections, Diera. I of all people should have known that. We damaged him. We weren't able to kill him."

"Protections?"

"It's hard to explain. Our guardian Gilles protects him. And the two of them are destroying me, little by little. Now, even more. Even faster. Caedon knows I'm one of the two men who tried to kill him."

"Why not arrest you? Why not have you tried and executed?"

"Eventually, he'll kill me. Not in some public way. He'll do it by stealth. He doesn't want anyone to know our connection with each other, and with Gilles. A public denouncing and trial would bring that out. At present, though, he still hopes to use me. Against you, Diera. Otherwise, I'd certainly be dead."

"Can't we ride away from here? They don't watch me so carefully any longer."

"They do. You just don't see them doing it. And now, with Caedon's plans—"

"I'm trapped here. I'll never marry him, whatever he does to me." She looked over at Rafe, suddenly resolved. "But maybe, if I traded myself for your life—"

"That wouldn't be the way of it, even if I agreed to let you. I'll never agree to that, my dearest one." He folded her in his arms again. He buried his face in her hair.

Then he gently led her to the bench before her hearth fire and sat her down there. He brought a cloak and enfolded her in it. "Avery is getting you out. I'm helping him, and so is Wat. So is Dru. We're all working out a plan. And now I must go."

"Go off and eat those sweetmeats little Bertrys has prepared for you," said Diera. Then she wished she hadn't. Her tone had been mordant, and she saw how it cut Rafe.

She rose from the bench, throwing the cloak aside, and kissed him again. "I can't let you out of my arms," she murmured against his shoulder. "Better go." She gave him a little push with her fingers against his chest.

He backed out of the rooms, not taking his eyes from hers. "Don't give in to despair, no matter what Caedon does. I love you, Diera." He shut himself out into the corridor.

I won't marry Caedon, Diera said bitterly to herself. *No matter what he does, I won't do it.*

She sat back down beside the fire and realized she was wrong. *That's what I told Rafe. But I was lying to him, and to myself. Yes, I'm going to do it,* Diera thought. Rafe said he would never agree to such a thing, but Diera knew the decision was her own.

Me for Rafe, she thought. *I'll tell Caedon tomorrow.*

CHAPTER TWELVE

Proposal

Diera

Diera waited until Rafe was elsewhere. She saw with pain how he exchanged looks with Bertrys. How fluttered the girl was to be around him. Silly wench. Diera would enjoy having her killed. Except.

She thought about it.

Her Child would not want her to habor vengeful thoughts about such a pathetic foolish child. The flat glassy blue of her eyes. Her buxom curves, like a delicious piece of fruit ready to be picked up and devoured—a ripe, juicy pear, thought Diera—as the girl posed herself enticingly sway-backed. The carefully crisped curls, like golden wires. The high plucked forehead, the whole effect worked on for many candle measures so she'd look like the damsels of the stories.

The girl was as much a victim as she herself was, Diera scolded herself. More, because Bertrys didn't even realize how she was being used. Diera felt ashamed. But she couldn't stop herself looking at the girl with dislike, and treating her coldly.

As was his custom, Caedon had come from his manor nearby, late in the day, to dine with the earl and his family. Now the board was cleared, the trestles removed. Diera, the earl, his lady, his daughters, and Caedon all sat before the big hearthstones.

"Bertrys," she said. The girl came to her and curtseyed. "I'm feeling a chill. Please get my wrap from my rooms."

"Yes, my lady," said Bertrys, curtseying again. She left the room swiftly.

Probably glad to get away so she can hunt Rafe down, thought Diera. She prayed to her Child she could stop tormenting herself with such unworthy thoughts.

Now, she said to herself. She looked over at Caedon. "My lord Caedon," she said.

"Your Highness." He turned his malevolent amber eyes in her direction. Diera was infuriated to see a hint of amusement there.

"Her ladyship congratulated you, yesterday, on your speedy recovery from your injuries. Let me add my own."

He inclined his head.

"I hear you were set upon by terrible men who damaged you in villainous ways," she said, summoning up a look of concern. Now, she saw, she had angered him deeply. He understood at once she knew who had done it. He saw at once she was taunting him.

"They didn't succeed, as you see, Your Highness," he said.

"The Lady be praised," she said with a simper. *Good*, she thought. *That has enraged him further.*

"Indeed," called the earl's wife to Caedon. "The Lady took you under Her protection, Lord Caedon. Have the villains been caught?"

"Not yet, your ladyship. They will be soon. I know who they are," said Caedon, his eyes never leaving Diera's. "When they are found, I'll make sure they are put to brave tortures and torments before they are killed."

Diera's mouth turned dry. She remembered what Rafe had told her about John. What Caedon had done to him. She saw Caedon was watching her, noticing her reaction. His eyes blazed with suppressed fury, and something else. What was it.

A strange kind of pleasure.

"You have a fearsome reputation against enemies of the king," said the earl's lady.

"As is my duty, your ladyship," Caedon replied.

"Shocking they should attack you so brazenly, and in this very castle."

"Shocking indeed, your ladyship," Caedon murmured. He rose and stepped to Diera. "A word, Your Highness, if I may." He led her over to a window embrasure away from the hearth.

"Just what game are you playing with me, mistress?" he snarled at her, as soon as they were out of earshot.

"You forget yourself, Lord Caedon," said Diera, but inwardly she was cringing, thinking maybe she'd gone too far.

"So? What do you have to say for yourself? Your Highness," he corrected himself, his tone scathing.

"I don't answer to you, Caedon," she said.

"You do. Soon it will be clear to everyone that you do. Tell me why you're taunting me. You know who did it, don't you."

"Of course I do. You must still think of me as a simpleton of a child, as I once was. I see exactly what you're doing, and why."

"Your lover told you this, did he?"

"Yes," she replied. She saw she had astonished him, at least a little.

"You're very brazen, lady. Beware the consequences of that."

"What consequences are those?"

"I could have you killed."

"Do it," she said.

"Instead, I'm going to marry you."

"What will my uncle have to say about that?"

"Audemar will come around. He already has, pretty much. Prepare yourself. And yes, I could have you killed, and might do it, especially if I realize I've wed a shrew. I could even more easily have him killed."

"Who, Audemar?" she said with an arch smile. "I believe you've just spoken treason, Caedon."

"You know exactly what man I mean."

Diera stepped closer to him now. Time for the second part of her plan, now that she'd angered and roused him, made him realize how difficult she could be, what a nuisance she might prove.

She looked up into his eyes. His very strange eyes. "Suppose I tell you I'll go quietly along with whatever plans you have for me,

Caedon? Suppose I say I'll agree to anything. Bearing your children, and without all the fuss and bother you went to last time, too. Suppose I say I won't resist, even if you decide to kill me. I'll stand there and let you do it."

"Suppose you do," he said, looking at her warily. Then he understood, and a smile began to play about his lips. "Oh, I see it. No, Diera. You won't be able to bargain with me for Rafe, besotted fool that you are. No," he said, and took her hand and brought it to his lips and kissed it mockingly. "I own you, mistress, and need no bargain with you to make it so. If you cause trouble, that will be a gnat-bite only."

As she snatched her hand from his, he laughed. "And I own Rafe. There's no trade here, Diera. I own both of you. You have nothing to trade for him."

"You'll kill him."

"Indeed yes. Not while he's still useful to me, though."

"You think he's useful because he keeps me in line."

"I do, yes."

"But you just said I was a gnat-bite only. Any trouble I gave you would be only a gnat-bite."

"That's true." Diera watched with a sense of despair as Caedon pretended to think it over. "So, really, by your logic, and even by my own, I don't need Rafe after all. Thank you for schooling me, Diera. How have I been able to think through my problems without you? You'll make an admirable wife."

Diera sagged back. This plan of hers was not working.

"Time to bring Rafe to account for his villainy toward me now, I think." Caedon was continuing to talk, pretending to ponder, as if he were thinking something through. "The sooner the better."

Actually, thought Diera, *he is mocking me*.

"Rafe's will not be a pretty end. Did he tell you what I did to John?"

Tears sprang to her eyes. She lunged at him to hit him. Part of her knew very well such a gesture was utterly futile. Another part of her acted before she could think.

Caedon grabbed her by the wrist and painfully twisted it until she cried out.

The others at the hearth looked around, startled.

Caedon smiled over at them and pretended to smile at Diera. He loosened his grip and released her. "Better not goad me too far, mistress," he whispered in her ear. "I'll keep Rafe for my own purposes, as long as I feel like it. When I don't, he's a dead man. And you may begin thinking of your own case the same way. You have your owner's permission to start thinking about that now."

"What must I do? What can I give you, to keep Rafe safe from you?"

Caedon just laughed.

"Suppose I refuse to give you children."

"I doubt you'll be able to stop me from getting them on you, mistress."

"There are ways, you know, to rid a woman of an unwanted babe."

"Ways you'll be carefully guarded against using."

Diera glanced behind her. Suddenly she realized the window embrasure was wide, deep, and far off the ground.

"Don't even think it, Diera," said Caedon quietly. "If you go, he goes. And in more pain than you can begin to imagine."

"He can get away from you," she whispered.

"He'll never get away from me. I have a hold on him. When I say I own him, I mean it in the deepest possible sense. Not in the ordinary way I own you, as effective as that is. With Rafe, it's not ownership in any way you can know." Caedon laughed again. "He and that John had made some sort of pact. John was going to help him end it, when he got too weak to do it himself. Now John is gone, and I'm the one who made sure of that. Nothing can help Rafe, and he knows it. You can't help him. He can't help himself."

"Who are you? Who is this Gilles you serve?"

"Wouldn't you like to know." Caedon turned away from her now. "The Rising," he said. "Those fools believe they're fighting Audemar's injustices. And here all along the thing that menaces them is huger and more powerful than they can possibly understand." He looked back at her and gave her a little bow. "Only John and Rafe came to know it."

"And now I do," she said.

He made a dismissive gesture. "You're only a woman. John is dead, and Rafe soon will be. Good evening, Your Highness," he said. "Sleep well." And he walked away from her down the dark corridor.

CHAPTER THIRTEEN

Tell Me No Lies

Wat

With no partner, Wat's days of touring the street fairs and taverns seemed to have come to an end. He went with Dru now on his missions. The work was often tedious, surveillance of some minor official, collecting evidence of injustices and petty wrongdoings to make sure The Rising didn't assassinate someone for mere high-handedness, merely infuriating his neighbors.

But sometimes the work was fast, brutal, and sickening. Wat began to get good at it.

As the year made the turn into summer, he wondered whether he might have been trusted, after all, to execute the hapless Rhiane, if her betrayal had happened later in the year.

If it was a betrayal at all. A cold voice in the back of his mind kept niggling at him.

Whether he could have, whether he could have done it well. These were matters of little curiosity to him, although he was glad he hadn't had to test his resolve by doing away with her. When he and Dru agreed they had to execute rough justice on some evil-doer, a rapist, a murderer cloaking his murders in the law, he never hesitated. He was fast. After, he always felt cold and sick.

"It's good that you do, Wat," said Dru to him after one of these episodes of misery. "If you didn't, what would it mean? What we have to do is terrible, but it's necessary. If we began thinking it enjoyable work, or even just ordinary, what kind of men would we be?"

Wat nodded. He didn't want to talk about it. But he thought about Dru, what a tender father he was. How deeply he loved his wife. Strange to have two natures existing in oneself side by side. There was no one Wat loved in that way, no family now. Except, he said to himself, Avery, Conal, and Dru himself. And Rafe. *They're my family*, he told himself.

Rafe was the only person he knew who might share his deep misgivings about the killing they were doing. Rafe was taken by the same bloodlust, when they'd confronted Caedon over John's body. And he knew Rafe had experienced the same revulsion, after. Even about Caedon.

His feelings about Eris had turned complicated. He shied away from what they might mean.

A turning of the moon after Rhiane's disappearance from their lives, he sat staring into the flames of the hearth fire. Avery and Conal were tracing diagrams in the packed dirt of the cottage floor, going over strategies for another battle. Torrin and Lorel were talking quietly together. He looked to Eris's corner of the cottage, where she bent over one of her knives, honing it on a whetstone. Then he looked away again, troubled. He turned back to the task he had set himself that evening, trying to lose himself in it.

His life now seemed to be one episode after the other of heart-pounding, sweat-drenching, nausea-inducing violence separated by long boring periods where he had nothing to do but brood.

At least during these quiet times he had a task that meant something to him. Tonight he was engaged in meticulously piecing together John's smashed rebec. Dru helped him with that, too, when he was around. Right now, Dru had gone home to his family. Wat sat before the hearth with the pieces of the rebec spread out on a cloth, and a pot of glue, and a delicate little squirrel-hair brush. He swore softly to himself, trying to find a piece that fit into the broken area he was trying to repair.

"I don't know why you bother with that," said Eris, getting up from her own task and walking over to look. "No one will ever be able to play it."

"I don't care," said Wat. He picked up another shard of wood and held it this way and that, seeing where it might fit. If it hadn't been so shattered, he knew he would have been able to make it play again.

But it was too broken. Eris was right. He had lied when he told her he didn't care. He did. *You can fix something up, after something bad has happened to it,* he thought. *Lots of times you can. But if it's too badly damaged, you can never fix it. You might make it look whole, but it will be a sham, just the appearance of the thing it was. It won't be able to do its proper work in the world. Not ever again.*

"Let's get out of here," Eris said, intruding on his thoughts. "I'm feeling cooped up in this place."

Wat nodded. He was feeling the same itching anxiety. He put away the rebec pieces. He had built a box to hold them so they wouldn't get damaged further, or lost. He laid the box carefully in a niche in the stones of the cottage's inner wall. He knew he would doggedly keep working on them until they had at least the semblance of a whole. He wasn't sure why. *Eris is a realist,* he thought. *I'm just a dreamer. Just sentimental about some broken fragments of wood.*

When he stepped out of the cottage into the twilight, Eris was looking up at the sky, where a star here and there was beginning to wink on.

"Looks like the weather will clear tomorrow," she said.

The summer chorus of birds was quieting as night drew on. But the woods were not as full of birdsong as they had been in springtide. These days Wat hardly ever heard the cuckoos calling. He listened.

"There," he said. From far away in the forest came the distinctive gowk sound of the male bird.

"Cuckoos," said Eris dismissively. "They're nasty birds. They lay their eggs in other birds' nests, and when the young hatch, they push the other birds out. The real offspring."

"Bastards. They're like us."

Eris looked over at Wat, amused. "True. Maybe I like them after all."

Avery was stepping out of the house just then. Eris walked out under the trees, and Avery pulled Wat aside. He had heard what Wat said. "You really think that?" he said. "Does it bother you, that you're a bastard and I'm not." The firelight from the hearth, glowing past him through the cottage's open door, played softly over his features.

"No," said Wat, and laughed.

"Good, because if any child sat himself down in the nest of the loving arms of a mother not his own, and took all her care for himself, I'm that cuckoo's child. Your mother was as much my mother as yours, at least in the time she spent on me, trying to make me into a better boy and face my misbehavior, love me in spite of myself."

"She did that with all of us," said Wat quietly.

"Yes," said Avery. He put his arm around Wat's shoulder and drew him close. "I miss her. I didn't know the little one, but you must miss him fiercely. I miss John as much as you do. I can claim that."

Then he released Wat and walked away to the shed where the horses were stabled. Wat saw how moved he was. A deep despair swept over Wat like a wave. He wanted to howl and scream at the heavens for the injustices the gods allowed. The wave receded, leaving him shaken. He didn't follow Eris into the cool depths of the forest. He went back into the cottage, meaning to take the rebec out of its box and work on it more. He found he couldn't. He couldn't do anything except brood.

Only one thing helped him, really. That was the thought of how they all might somehow be able to get Diera safely away from Caedon. When he thought of the happier days of childhood, he thought of Diera and Keelie. Eris occupied a more tumultuous presence in his memory. He tried to think back to the day before their father King Ranulf had had Eris branded. She hadn't been as difficult before then. What their father had done to her had damaged her and changed her.

As the summer deepened, the tight feeling always in his chest, like a steel band, gradually relaxed. During the long summer days between tasks, he and Eris sometimes went splashing into the little stream behind the stone cottage, just as if they were still children. Their Child was the Child of Earth. They did not swim. But they splashed in the shallow water and shouted with laughter, and the others, passing along on the bank, looked over at them, smiling, and rolled their eyes.

On such occasions, as the honied skin of her body flashed in the water, Wat sometimes caught a glimpse of the brand on Eris's wrist. Usually she covered it with the left one of the pair of leather bracers she always wore. He made himself look away, if he happened to see it.

It made him angry, when he thought about the injustice done to Eris. It made him want to go after the people who had condoned such an injustice. But then he would have had to go after his own father. Now his father was dead. And he would have had to go after himself. He had always blamed himself, that he'd stood aside and had done nothing.

But what could he have possibly done? He was twelve or thirteen, when it had happened. Just a boy.

One late afternoon, so hot that he had stripped off his tunic and sat sweating in only a loose pair of trousers, he and Eris found themselves alone. Avery and Conal had gone to the market town in the Riverlands to see Cwen the healer. Dru hadn't returned yet from the village where his family lived, wherever that was. Torrin and Lorel had gone home to their own village to tend to some matter involving their families.

"It's good to have time alone together," Eris said to Wat. She had trapped a rabbit, and she and Wat went into the cottage to roast it at the hearth.

The meat tasted good. As the day darkened into evening, a full moon edged up past the trees, and a mild breeze cooled everything off. "Like old times," Wat agreed. Eris was more relaxed than he'd seen her in many a season. Her habitual tension wiped away, she looked young and pretty.

"Remember that idea I had, a season ago, that you and I would leave The Rising and just head out on our own?" she said, smiling.

"Yes. It's an enticing thought. Like when we were children and roamed the forest below Tam Fort, as carefree as a leash of foxes. You, me, Keelie. Later, Diera."

Her expression clouded over again. Wat was sorry he'd brought Keelie up. That was no doubt the reason for her change of mood, he thought.

She turned away. When she came back to the hearth, she had a stone crock with her. "Look what I found the last time I was out scouting. It was on a shelf in some man's house. After I dealt with him, I looked around for anything we might use, and I found this." She unstoppered the crock and held it under Wat's nose.

"Mead?" he said, looking over at her warily. When he and Dru dealt with someone, as she put it, they never searched his house and made away with anything. It felt too much like banditry. He wasn't going to bring up his private feelings about it to Eris, though.

"Not mead. Something better," she said, cradling the stone crock. "Uisge beatha." She set the crock down by the hearth and turned aside to rummage among the cooking things. When she turned back to him, she had two wooden noggins, one in each hand. She set them both down on one of the flat rocks around the hearth and carefully poured each of them a dram from the crock.

"Here," she said, handing him one of the noggins.

He looked at it dubiously.

"Such a baby. Don't tell me, Wat. You've never been with a woman, and you've never had anything stronger than ale."

He downed the liquor in a single gulp. It burned through his throat all the way to his toes. With an effort, he kept himself from coughing and sputtering and spewing it all up. He turned away from her.

"Oh, now I've insulted your manhood."

"No, you haven't," he said softly, when he could speak.

"What about that woman. Whatshername."

"Rhiane?" asked Wat after a moment. He went over to the open door of the cottage and leaned against it, looking out miserably.

"That's the one. Did you think she was pretty?"

"What does it matter. She's dead," said Wat, going back to the fire.

"Did you kiss her?" said Eris.

"Eris, shut up," said Wat. After a while, he said, "I'm tired." He left the fire to roll himself into his furs in his corner. Eris was still at the hearth. He looked over to see her pouring another dram into her noggin.

The uisge beatha was making his head swim. He felt a bit sick. *If I lie very still, the feeling will go away*, he told himself. Underneath was a worse feeling, remembering Rhiane. After a long time of lying in his furs wanting to vomit, he fell into a thick sleep.

In the night, the moon went down, and the cottage lay in darkness. In his dreams, Wat felt that some large animal was pawing him. He dreamed he was dead, and an animal was rooting at him to uncover his grave and worry at his corpse. He moaned and tossed restlessly. The animal prowled away.

Much later, the animal seemed to be back. But suddenly Wat was awake.

There was no animal. There was Eris.

He kept himself completely still.

She was hovering over him. Fumes of the strong drink were pouring off her. She was muttering. From time to time, she put out a hand to his cheek.

He lay not daring to breathe.

"Wat," she was muttering. "Never fucked a woman. Better not, I'll kill her," she was muttering.

She eased her hand under the furs and began patting at him, feeling down his torso.

He tensed and rolled away from her.

"Wat, you're such a baby," she said, crouching over him. "Did you fuck her? Did you?"

Wat sat up carefully in the dark. "Eris. What are you doing?"

Eris didn't answer him. She stood and wandered to the hearth, where the fire had gone out except for some faint embers. He saw her nearly trip over one of the noggins rolling on the floor. She cursed and kicked at it. She went down. After a moment, he heard her hoarsely snoring. He could dimly see her form splayed out on the floor by the hearth.

Lady help me, what's that about, he thought. He got up, stepped around her cautiously, got one of her furs from her corner, and dragged it over to her. He tucked it around her against the night chill and then went back to his own corner.

But now he couldn't sleep. Every time he drifted off, he woke up with a start, on full alert.

Eris didn't move under her fur.

As dawn turned the slit of the window gray, Wat quietly unrolled himself and went out into the morning with his bow and a sheaf of arrows. He began walking rapidly away from the cottage.

Out in the woods, he put in his usual several candle measures of practice with the bow. It was a big bow, as tall as Wat and a fistmeile taller. As he'd been taught, he laid his body into the bow. The strenuous and fluid movements took his mind off everything but his target, a sapling deep in the forest. He slashed it to pieces with his arrows. He retrieved all the arrows, putting them carefully back into his quiver, all but one that had broken. They were too precious to waste.

It was almost noontide before he returned to the cottage. Eris wasn't there. He took off his sweaty tunic and roamed around putting the place to rights, washing out the noggins in the stream, washing out his tunic, too, and draping it across some buckthorn to dry. He heaved the stone crock, now empty, far away into some underbrush.

Later in the afternoon, the others started trickling back. Torrin and Lorel. Avery and Conal. Dru was with them.

"Where's Eris?" said Torrin.

Wat shook his head "I don't know."

All day he had thought about Eris and what she'd done in the dark. What she'd said.

I'll kill her. Eris's words kept coming back to him. *Did you fuck her?* And the strange feeling of her hands on him, her breath in his face.

When she gets back, he thought, *I'll joke with her about getting herself drunk.*

But when she did come back, it was two days later, and he was just preparing to go out with Dru.

He never did ask her what she remembered of that night. If she even did. They never discussed it at all.

Wat let the whole disturbing matter drop.

A few days later, Wat found himself completely alone at the cottage, the only one not out on some job or mission. He'd waked early as several of the others gathered around the hearth, getting ready to head out. Eris was there, being briefed by Avery and Conal. She left first, then the rest of them.

Wat lay on his furs in his corner, his arms folded behind his head, and watched. After they'd all gone, he curled back into sleep. It was too warm to use the furs as a covering. He nestled into them, letting them cradle his body. As the fingers of summer morning sun probed into the doorway of the cottage, its stout plank door standing open now that it was so warm, he blinked awake and lay sprawled out, luxuriating in feeling himself completely alone.

Finally he rolled off his pallet and got to his feet, going behind the cottage and into the woods a little way to relieve himself, then back to the hearth to scoop up the remains of the porridge out of the kettle and eat it.

Humming a little to himself, he hauled the kettle down to the stream and washed it so it would be ready when everyone came back for the evening meal.

I'll take my bow out and see if I can bring down an animal for meat. Maybe even poach one of the king's deer, he thought. *Audie's deer,* he thought with scorn. No one in this remote area would catch him. He thought about all the times in boyhood he'd watched Audemar and his cronies ride out to the hunt and come back some candle measures later, laughing, with a deer stretched out across someone's saddle.

He settled instead, feeling indolent, for the easier task of getting his fishing line and lying stretched full length on the grassy bank of the stream, lazing in the summer morning.

Pretty soon he had a string of fish keeping cool threaded through the gills and attached to a stake in the stream by the bank. The rest of the people at the cottage would have a good dinner waiting for them, when they returned.

Then he did take out his bow and practiced with it.

Later, he spent some time with the puzzle pieces of John's shattered rebec.

He even spent some time practicing his letters with a stick in the dirt. He couldn't let himself forget them. He'd promised Dru he wouldn't.

As the sun's beams began to slant toward afternoon, he went back to the stream to check on his string of fish.

That's when he spotted it. A gleam in the water.

He waded in and reached down. Something glittered there. He picked it up.

His heart stopped.

It was a bangle. A pretty thing, with a little bird on it. The eye of the bird, a perfect circle of blue enamel, seemed to wink out of the bangle at him.

He knew where he had seen it before.

The bangle Rhiane had wanted to buy at the fair. He had said no. He remembered how she had lagged and delayed. Now he realized why. She was using their coin to buy this bangle in secret, after he'd told her she couldn't, and then she had hidden it from him.

Holding it up to the light, he saw writing around the rim of it. *The cuckoo, he's a pretty bird, he tells me no lies*, the words read.

Now he saw why she wanted it. It wasn't just a dainty trinket. It spoke to her. Probably about that soldier she loved and tried to follow. The one who had played her false.

How did the song go, thought Wat as he sat on the bank and ran his finger around and around the rim of the bangle. *A thief, he will rob you and take all you have, an inconstant lover brings you to your grave.*

He brought the bangle with him into the cottage and set it in the niche on top of the box that contained John's rebec.

The others would see it there. They must not. Wat wasn't quite sure why, but he felt strongly that no one should see this bit of foolishness that a poor dead girl had maybe paid too dearly to possess.

He went out of the cottage and searched around in the brush behind it. There. There was the stone crock that had held the uisge beatha Eris had been drinking, that strange night.

He dragged it out of the brush, took it down to the stream, unstoppered it, and washed it well. Then he brought it back to the cottage. The bangle fit inside it perfectly. He dropped the bangle in. It clinked at the bottom of the crock. Then he stoppered it up and thrust it deep to the back of the niche where nobody would spot it.

He was breathing hard when he finished, and he wasn't even sure why.

When the others returned in the early evening, he had prepared fish for all of them. They ate the fish. They ate bread and drank ale. There was a lot of merry talk around the hearth.

Wat cleaned up the remains of the meal and went to his pallet. Ignoring the uncertain glances the others stole in his direction, he turned his face to the wall, pretending to sleep.

He wasn't sleeping. He was thinking, and his thoughts were a torment to him.

The cuckoo, he's a pretty bird, he tells me no lies ...

Did you love her? Did you kiss her? Did you fuck her?

Come all you fair maidens, take warning of me ...

Don't tell me, Wat. Such a baby. Never been with a woman, never had anything stronger than ale.

Wat, never fucked a woman. Better not, I'll kill her.
Did you think she was pretty? Did you kiss her? Did you fuck her?

What does it matter. She's dead.

CHAPTER FOURTEEN

Last Chances

Wat

Avery and Conal looked up when Wat came in. The others were off doing various tasks the two had assigned them. Wat got the distinct impression they'd all been sent away so Avery and Conal could talk to him completely privately.

"Sit here by us," said Avery, patting one of the stones by the hearth.

"We're sending you off to do some important work for us," Conal said.

Wat looked from one to the other. "What is it? Tell me and I'll do it," he said.

"We want you to go to Lunds-fort," said Avery.

Wat looked at them blankly.

"We're bringing the army south," said Avery. "But we can't do it without funds."

"We'll fight Caedon and Audie again," said Wat. "We'll smash them!"

"We will, Wat. With the help of the Children, we'll extend our reach into the Riverlands, rally these people around here to our side," said Avery, grinning at Wat's excitement.

"Why am I going to Lunds-fort?"

"We've had a message from my uncle, Mabire, the one whose lands are in the Baronies across the Narrows. He wants to meet with us on this side of the Narrows, in Lunds-fort, as he visits his brother's children." Avery thought for a moment. "Probably his real reason for coming over is to conspire with his fellow nobles. They're always squabbling with each other over who controls the place. To him, we're a gnat-bite only, but I got him a message some turnings of the moon ago, and I believe he'll answer my plea for more funds. I believe one of his reasons for summoning me is to bring me these funds. Conal and I need to be with the troops, though. You're to go, and then, if Mabire gives us the gold, get it to us as quickly as you can."

"I'll make ready," said Wat.

"What are you doing?" Eris asked him as he rushed around gathering up his things. She had just come back to the cottage.

"I'm not to say."

She nodded knowingly. "They're sending you to Lunds-fort to talk to Avery's uncle."

Wat looked at her, dumbfounded.

"Think he'll listen to the likes of you?" she said, with one of her cynical smiles.

"He'd better. We need the coin."

"When is this battle?" she said.

"Ask Avery. I'm not supposed to say. Besides, I really don't know anything."

"I expect he'll tell us all soon," she said. She sat down at the hearth and watched his preparations. "Be careful, Wat," she said, as she always did. Then she whisked out of the door, and he saw her striding away down the path.

Wat turned to see Conal there beside him, watching too.

"If you and Avery were trying to keep my trip to Lunds-fort a secret," he said, "I don't think you needed to bother. Eris knows all about it."

"I expect she does," said Conal. "Mistress Eris knows a great deal." At Wat's expression, Conal clapped him on the shoulder. "That's what she's good at, lad. That's why she's valuable to Avery." He was silent for a moment. "And she's his sister."

"Eris gets uneasy with all the brother-sister talk," said Wat.

"She's a hard one, is Mistress Eris," said Conal. "But very skilled."

"She's your best student. Better than I am."

Conal nodded thoughtfully. "And Aves— I think when he looks at her, he thinks how wrongly she was treated, when she was a girl. That bothers Avery. Family is really important to him." Conal laughed a little. "As for me. Avery's my family."

"What about me? What about Dru and Rafe?" said Wat, shocked.

"Yes, and you lot," said Conal, giving Wat an affectionate mock-cuff to the jaw. "And Johnny," he said softly. He turned away quickly, but not before Wat saw sudden tears start into his eyes. "Get going, lad," he called back gruffly over his shoulder at Wat.

Being on the road, all on his own, his bow slung over his shoulder, his quiver at his back. Wat was finding the journey a balm to him. He didn't have to think about a thing except where to stop along the way and how to bring down enough to eat. His packs were full of oats for the horse.

It was high summer, and the weather was fine.

Once he got to the border between the Sceptered Isle's land and the narrow fingernail of land along the Narrows that abutted their own realm but belonged to the Baronies, he found it easy to slip across the border. The two realms were not at war, not even in the state of tension that frequently occupied them. The border was laxly guarded.

I don't have to worry about the guards on their side, Wat thought, fingering Mabire's signet ring kept snug in his belt pouch. *Only the ones on our side.* They were the ones who'd throw him instantly into some hole of a cell, if they searched him and found the contents of his belt pouch. The carved little obsidian blackbird of The Rising, the message he carried from Avery, and Mabire's signet.

The road from the border to Lunds-fort made a short journey. As he shouldered through the crowds into the gates of the town, he needed only to show the guards the signet of Mabire. They waved him right through.

Lunds-fort was astounding. Carts, riders, masses of people. Street vendors crying their wares. Soldiers marching five abreast down the broad streets. Officers riding three abreast. It was the largest place Wat had ever seen, and the smelliest.

The stench nearly overpowered him.

But he got himself to the inn Avery had described to him and paid good coin to have his horse stabled. He procured a bed in a room with only four others. An actual bed! He had to share it with only three of the others. One of the men in the room, a prosperous merchant from the look of him, had a whole bed to himself.

It was drawing on evening, so he made his way to the below-stairs tavern part of the inn and bought himself stew and ale.

In the morning, the hardest part of his mission began. "Take this coin," Avery had said, "and find yourself something proper to wear. Don't stint. You can't go to my uncle looking like a beggar lad."

Wat hardly knew how to accomplish this feat. He thought about Tambourne, the town near the fort where he'd spent his childhood. There were tailors' shops, and a bootmaker's. But his mother had made all his clothing, right down to the shoes. And back at the camp, there was a tent full of spare clothing. Whenever you needed any, you went in there and found something that more or less fit, and you tried not to think what dead soldier it may have come off of.

He squared his shoulders and set out to browse through merchants' goods on display in small shops and vendors' carts. He thanked the Children for his schoolmaster at the High Temple of the Lady Goddess. Ranulf the Fourth hadn't allowed him to train with Conal, as he'd allowed John. But Wat had been allowed to go to the schoolmaster, as his brother had.

For a long time he wondered why the king would allow one but not the other. Finally John told him. "It's Uncle Brenci who pays for it," John had whispered. Brenci was Dru's father, a man who loved learning. If not for him, none of the boys, Wat included, not even Avery the true-born son, would have had any sort of learning. Ranulf didn't believe in it, except for his oldest son Artur, and that was only because, or so they said, he'd had a direct order from the Earth Child's farwydd about it. Brenci, of course, wasn't Wat's actual uncle. But as Dru was (not really but truly) his brother, so Brenci was (not really but truly) his uncle.

Thank the Children, the schoolmaster at the temple had been a priest from the Baronies, and he'd taught them all to speak the language of the Baronies. Otherwise, Wat realized, he didn't know how he would have managed in this big confusing city.

Of course, he thought, *that's why Avery sent me. I'm one of the few members of The Rising he trusts well enough, but I'm also one of the few who can speak the language.* In fact, Wat realized, he knew how to speak it better than Avery. Much better than John. That particular schoolmaster had arrived at the temple when the three older boys' own studies were winding down, but Wat had gotten a full dose of the man, and his blackthorn rod. Dru, of course, knew it better than any of them. But Dru, like his father, was a scholar.

Now, as Wat wandered the city's streets, careful after the first mishap not to step into any dung or get urinated on from the overhanging stories of the houses, he tried to think how best to accomplish his most difficult mission, clothing himself.

I don't have time for any tailoring, he decided. He'd find something nice, used. By that afternoon, he owned a stout pair of boots without much wear on them, and they only pinched a little. He found a good-quality cloak with only one patched place, and that on the inside.

"Blue, young master," said the old fripper as she handed it over. "As matches the blue of your eyes."

He found a pair of long-enough trousers that weren't even patched, and a tunic that was actually splendid with rich embroidery. The tunic strained across his shoulders, but only a bit. He knew he must be a country clod who had paid too much for it when the fripper snatched his coin without any bargaining. But it was a wonderful garment, and he had carefully inspected the seams for nits.

The very next day, finely attired, he made his way to the city's fortress to pay his respects to Baron Mabire.

The fort, on the other side of the big stinking lazy brown river that snaked through the city, was where all visiting dignitaries took rooms.

He had to pay good coin to be ferried across the river to get there, though.

He began to worry that he was spending too much of Avery's coin. *I'll leave as soon as I've seen Mabire,* he thought. *I won't linger. Time is of the essence.* He felt a pang of regret, though. The city was so fascinating.

The baron was courteous, welcoming even, though Wat saw right away, with considerable embarrassment, that his fine new clothes (new to him, anyway) were shabby compared to those of the lowliest member of the baron's retinue. And he also realized that his hair, worn peasant-style, probably wasn't giving Mabire the best impression.

"My boy, you remind me so much of your brothers," said Baron Mabire graciously, ushering Wat into a comfortable room with a big hearth. The summer heat outside was considerable, but Wat had shivered as he walked into the fort, and had pulled his blue cloak closely around him. The fort's thick walls kept the place perpetually chilly.

Wat made Mabire a low bow. Mabire motioned to him to stand and walked around him, inspecting him out of shrewd old eyes. "Like Avery," he mused, "but most like Sir John."

"My brother John was killed by Caedon," said Wat.

"I heard. We grieve with you, lad. John was much beloved by my people when he visited my lands. What a beautiful voice."

Wat inclined his head in thanks. "My lord, I came to you right away. Avery—" he stopped. *I'm no courtier*, he thought, his mouth going dry. "His Highness Prince Avery would have certainly come himself, only he and Master Conal are in the field already, bringing our army south."

"They fought a mighty battle, I hear."

"Indeed," said Wat, "and sent Caedon's army howling back to Audemar the Usurper."

"And were you there, yourself, young Master Walter, at this battle?"

"Yes, Your Lordship."

"Let me guess. Your weapon of choice is the bow."

Wat had to grin then. "Yes, Your Lordship."

"I'm an old campaigner myself, lad. No serious bowman but wears his locks shorn. As for a warrior, you can't find a more valiant knight than your brother the prince. I know it well. He fought in my wars." Mabire's eyes dropped to Avery's parchment, and he read it over. "Gold is needed. More of my gold."

"Yes, Your Lordship, and Prince Avery says I'm to thank you for the help you gave us, before."

"I'll help your prince, Master Walter. But tell him this is the last time I will."

Wat saw that for all his friendly feelings, the baron had a hard practical side. He wouldn't throw good coin after bad. They'd have to prove themselves capable of funding their own campaign, after this.

"What of Artur's sons?" asked Mabire.

"We are searching for the princes."

"They're probably dead," said the baron. "Tell Avery not to squander my gold looking for them. That's my biggest fear, lad. That your high-minded brother will go chasing after them when he himself should be taking firm control. It's he who should be king. My gold is best spent there."

Wat knew he should not argue with the old man. He inclined his head.

"And the sister of these boys, Artur's daughter? I hear Audemar has her."

"We're trying to get her out of his hands."

"Good. She'll prove a valuable counter. Avery may trade her to his advantage some day."

Now Wat wasn't liking the baron so well. "The Princess Diera is my childhood friend," he said quietly.

"Oh, aye? Well, that's just fine, Walter." The baron sailed right past the matter of Diera's strategic usefulness and moved on to other matters. But at the end of their interview, he put his arm around Wat's shoulder and walked him to the window.

"My eyes are not as good as they used to be," he told Wat. "Let me have a good look at you. Hmm. Yes. You're the spit of your brothers. Tall. Fair. Broad in the shoulder. You all look like that rascally father of yours."

Wat had to bite back a startled laugh. Mabire meant the king.

"But Avery. He has the spirit of his mother. She was my sister, lad. My sister Emilde. Artur the crown prince, poor soul, looked like her, but he didn't have what was inside her, and that disgusting Audemar certainly doesn't. No, it's Avery her youngest who inherited the fineness of her. They tell me—" and here Wat was surprised to see the old man's eyes fill with tears. "—they tell me this princess, Artur's daughter, is very like her grandmother."

"Diera has dark hair and eyes," said Wat. "She is slender and small."

"That's Emilde. How I wish I could see her, your young princess."

"Your Lordship, the Princess Diera must indeed look like your sister. I was born after her death, so I didn't know Queen Emilde, and besides, my mother—"

The baron placed an understanding hand on Wat's arm.

"But Your Lordship, everyone says so, that she resembles the queen. Diera—" he gulped and began again. "The princess has a noble spirit. She is learned and brave." Wat thought about it.

"She is fierce, Your Lordship. I'm not sure Avery knows this about her, but I do. She and I were friends during some most difficult times."

"That's Emilde." Wat saw how Mabire glowed with pride and love. "Thank you, young Walter, for telling me this. You make an old man's heart glad."

Wat intended to leave the city the very next morning. He'd go to Mabire early, receive the gift of his gold, and be on his way. He needed to get back to Avery and Conal as fast as his horse could take him. With Mabire's gold, maybe they had a chance. Without it, none.

That evening, as he returned to his inn room, he found a messenger with a little parchment.

Attend me tomorrow night at banqueting and pastimes, it read. It was sealed with Mabire's signet.

I'll have to wait until after the banqueting is over before I can leave, Wat thought with despair. *Banqueting and courtly pastimes*, he thought, with even greater despair. He knew his feelings of dismay must arise from vanity but felt them hard anyway. *I have nothing to wear but this.*

Then the messenger handed him a long package. When he unfolded the cloth wrapping, he saw the package was filled with fine clothing.

CHAPTER FIFTEEN

Pastime With Good Company

Wat

When Wat made his way into the banqueting room in Mabire's quarters at the fort, he stopped in the big doorway, his eyes momentarily dazzled. Not only rushlights, but candles. Candles from the Baronies, each burning a tidy little fortune away as the night progressed.

Mabire's gift of clothing fit Wat as if it had been made for him. The new cloak was blue, but it was a rich blue, not the slightly faded blue of his earlier purchase at the fripper's. The new tunic was a lighter blue, linen banded with embroidered silk.

The trousers were scarlet linen, belted with leather so soft Wat couldn't keep from touching it. And under the trousers, the softest of small clothes caressed his body. A novel feeling. With every step, they silkily caressed him. He didn't know how to think of these sensations.

An embroidered band circled his head, hardly necessary, since Wat didn't have the long locks to keep off his face. He wore it anyhow.

As Wat entered the room, Mabire came toward him, his arms outstretched.

Wat bowed low. "I thank you for your gifts," he said.

Mabire motioned him to his feet, beaming. "A handsome lad," he said. "You must let the others see how handsome, not hide it away underneath patched clothing."

"I'm a poor man, my lord," said Wat, smiling.

Mabire grunted. "But rich in other graces," he said. "Come to my board, lad. Eat and drink. Afterward, there will be music and dancing."

"My brother John was raised at court. I was not. I don't know how to dance, my lord."

"I'll set one of these fine ladies to teach you," said Mabire.

Wat blushed, and Mabire laughed. "You look a rustic princeling out of the stories, lad."

Then Mabire moved away to greet some great lord, leaving Wat to head to a window embrasure and stand there uncertainly, shifting from foot to foot.

At board, he expected to sit far below the salt, but servants led him to a place in the middle. To either side of him, fine ladies cast their eyes on him demurely and smiled.

After the board had been cleared, Mabire's musicians struck up a tune for dancing. Wat listened appraisingly. Not as good as John. No one was. John had been the star pupil of Master Electus, King Ranulf's music master, and then, by Master Electus's own admission, grew to surpass him by far.

A sudden silence descended on the gaiety. Some court official announced, in a loud voice, "Her Majesty the Lady Ailys, the Most High and Noble, Queen of the Sceptered Isle, and her companions."

Everyone stood and bowed low as this queen swept into the room. Audemar's wife.

Wat knew a moment of stark fear.

Then he breathed easier. He remembered Ailys as one of the older girls about Tambourne, when he was a small child. He remembered that she had been the friend of the young woman John loved. Odelyn, tragically slain. Everyone knew she was killed because of her improper love for John, and no one knew how much involvement Ailys had had in her betrayal. But everyone suspected there had been quite a bit.

And now Ailys was queen of the Sceptered Isle. Queen Ailys, Audemar's consort. Before that, before the crown prince Artur's assassination, she had been Artur's wife. Diera's stepmother.

Wat breathed easier. There was no way Ailys would remember him, and if she somehow did, she wouldn't recognize him, now he had reached manhood. He quickly scanned the courtiers she had brought with her, and didn't recognize a one, thank the Child.

Mabire was there, greeting her.

He knew she'd be here, thought Wat. *What is his game?*

He didn't have much to worry about. Ailys was seated at a place of honor, near the big hearthstones, where she could enjoy the music to the fullest. Wat made sure he kept on the other side of the room from her.

Later in the evening, Mabire was at his elbow. Wat turned to him with a start.

"Easy, lad," said Mabire in an undertone. "She was here in the city." He nodded toward the place of honor where Ailys sat. "I could hardly let you go back to your brothers without giving you a chance to encounter your enemy and examine her, here on neutral ground."

"What if she had recognized me?"

"I took the chance she wouldn't," said Mabire with an unexpectedly youthful grin. "You don't look like the type to hang around with the courtiers."

Wat had to smile then.

"Here's an opportunity, lad. I'll be interested to see what you do with it."

Wat recalled then the tales Avery told of his uncle. How, the entire time he was at his uncle's estate, he felt Mabire was testing his mettle.

I suppose it's my turn now, thought Wat.

Mabire leaned close to him. "The queen is here because she is meeting with emissaries of Hakkon Hardaxe privately, away from her realm," he said softly. "They say Hakkon might be interested in a bargain. Opportunities in the Sceptered Isle's north, ports for the Ice-realm ships, possession of some of the islands off the northern coast, in exchange for helping Audemar with some quite troublesome rebels who seem to have become a thorn in his flesh."

Wat felt the hairs on the back of his neck prickle. "Nine Spheres," he whispered.

"Suppose you were to return to your brother with more than my gold?" said Mabire. "With information, too."

"My thanks. I'll need to get to Avery immediately with this."

"Come to me in the morning to receive the gold. In the meantime, young Wat, learn whatever you can, tonight, at my hearth."

Mabire straightened and looked about the room. He called out to a young woman passing by. "My lady, attend me here, if you will." As she came over to him and curtsied, he plucked at the sleeve of another passing young woman. "Ladies!" he said, turning from them with a flourish and bringing Wat into their orbit. "Here's my clod-footed nephew, young Walter, and he doesn't know how to dance. Will the two of you teach him as a mercy to our good Goddess?"

One, an ample young woman in yellow, giggled. She leaned over to the other, a strapping blonde, and translated. Then the other one giggled, too. Mabire stepped back, and the two young women closed in on Wat as he backed nervously away from them.

"You'll dance with us, Master Walter," said the one in yellow, grinning. "I'm Douceline. Sigrid will help."

Wat looked over at the other advancing maiden. Sigrid. One of Hakkon's retinue, no doubt about it.

They seized him and hustled him into the circle of dancers, one taking his right hand, the other his left. To the music of rebec, pipes, tabor, and organistrum, a merry group of dancers held hands in a circle, men and women alternating.

"Follow us!" said Douceline, holding his hand high and stepping down prettily on her left foot. On the other side of her, Sigrid did the same. Wat copied them. Then they made a step with the right foot, sliding it to the left. The whole circle made a stepping, dipping wheel that whirled faster and faster to the music. Wat found he could easily keep up.

The dancing was heady and arousing. When the music stopped, everyone dropped hands and stood laughing. "The baron's nephew," breathed Douceline to Sigrid, cutting her eyes at Wat.

He turned to her and grinned. "Only on the wrong side of the blanket."

She leaned over to translate this for Sigrid, and the two were off in gales of laughter. They pulled Wat into another group of dancers. These were making little stamping movements with their feet, swirling their bodies in complex figures around each other to the tempo of a new song the musicians began to play.

It was harder to keep up, this time, but Wat managed, watching his two laughing partners closely. He realized his acrobatics were helping him keep up. As the whole group of dancers wheeled about the room, little groupings broke off and danced their way to the center, usually a man with a woman on either hand. Their feet cut rapid figures across the floor, the two women wheeling out from the man and then twirling back toward him.

Wat watched intently as one man thrust one of the women behind him, bowed to the other, then put his hands on her waist and lifted her high as she raised her arms and cried out. He set her down and pivoted to the other, lifting her as well and setting her down. Everyone stopped to watch, beating time with the music and calling encouragement. Then the little group danced back to the circle.

"Our turn!" cried Douceline. She and Sigrid each grabbed Wat by the hand and danced him protesting into the center of the circle. He felt himself blushing, and not just with exertion.

"Lift her, pretty lad," someone called out as he swiveled to Douceline and put his hands around her waist uncertainly.

"Lift me, Master Walter!" she exclaimed, and he did. He lifted her high, set her down, and turned to the willing Sigrid to do it again. The three of them danced back into the circle and rejoined the joyous heaving mass of dancers.

At last, flushed and laughing, they worked their way out of the circle and Wat took flagons of mead from a servant, presenting them to each of his partners. He took one for himself.

"Thirsty work!" said Douceline, drinking deep from her flagon.

Wat started to do the same. He stopped himself, remembering how his head had swirled after the usige beatha Eris had given him, that troubling day at The Rising's little hidden cottage. He thought of what he really needed to do. He took only a small swallow of mead.

The three sat companionably before the hearth as if they had known each other all their lives. Wat turned to Sigrid. "You come from the North?" he asked.

She nodded. She had understood. "From the Ice-realm," she said haltingly.

"She's here with King Hakkon's courtiers," Douceline burst in. "They'll meet with the queen of the Sceptered Isle."

"Oh, aye?" said Wat.

"There she is. That lady there, in the beautiful clothes," said Douceline, pointing Ailys out to Wat. "If only those clothes were mine." She pretended to swoon, and she and Sigrid went off into a fresh round of giggles.

"Why come here to meet with King Hakkon's emissaries?" said Wat.

"It's a secret, shhhh," said Douceline, and Sigrid put up her own finger to her smiling lips.

"A secret?"

"We'll help that queen in her war," said Sigrid, forming the words slowly.

"Ahh," said Wat. "I didn't know there was a war."

"Those people over there in the Sceptered Isle need to rid themselves of a pack of troublesome rebels," Douceline said importantly.

"Dance," insisted Sigrid, as the musicians began a new song. She stood and tugged at Wat's hand, and soon she and Douceline had dragged him back into the circle of dancers.

Wat was gaining confidence with each new dance he tried. He watched the man beside him swooping toward his lady partner as if he were some majestic falcon, and the lady swirling and dipping about him as if she were a swallow. The man seemed as if he smoothly glided, but the woman seemed to float.

I can do that, he told himself. And he did, first with Douceline, then with Sigrid.

As the music grew ever more insistent, the spots of red on the dancers' cheeks more hectic, everyone's breath coming faster and faster still, he felt as if he had whirled into a bright world of color and pleasure he never knew existed. It was as intoxicating as the mead.

I must stop, though, he told himself. *I need rest. I need to leave tomorrow and get my troubling news to Avery, along with the gold.*

He was thinking regretfully of leaving his two smiling partners when a strong feeling of being watched made him turn his head. Then he quickly turned back away.

Ailys the queen had come to stand at the edge of the circle of dancers. She had looked directly at him, an intense look that frightened him to his core. She didn't know him. He knew she couldn't possibly. But that look told him otherwise.

Murmuring an apology to his partners, he danced the three of them over to the opposite side of the circle, sat them both down on a bench, kissed them each quickly, and backed away into the crowd of pleasure seekers, shouldering his way from the baron's rooms and out into the fetid Lunds-fort night. He got himself to his inn, careful to use every skill Dru had taught him to make sure he wasn't followed.

At the inn, he shed his new rich clothing, tumbled into bed in the smallclothes caressing him like a lover's touch, and fell into a profound sleep. In the morning, he dressed himself quickly in his old patched clothing, folding his new clothes into his pack. He strode through the streets, already bustling with vendors and criers, to Mabire's quarters. Again making sure not to be observed, he presented himself to Mabire's chief serving man.

"You did well last night, Master Walter," said Mabire, coming out to embrace him. He handed him a plump leather bag that Wat could tell was bulging with coin, and gave him the Lady Goddess's blessing. "Go safely, and tell your brother to spend my gold well."

Soon after, Wat was on his horse and headed up-river. He wouldn't cross the border at Lunds-fort. It was too dangerous. But eventually he engaged a farmer to pole him and his horse across the river, and he made his way by back roads and cattle trails across the border into his own realm.

CHAPTER SIXTEEN

Taking the Long Way Home

Wat

Now that he was carrying so much gold, Wat started to worry about bandits, not just Audemar's soldiers. In his old patched clothing again, he didn't look so prosperous. But while he didn't stand out in his stained traveling clothes, the horse was a fine animal, and that alone would attract bandits. He planned to cut across northwest of Tambourne in a more direct way to the place where Avery's army was massing.

Not a candle-measure into the realm, he came to a small village. He needed food. In the center of the village was a tavern, just someone's house with a kettle in the front room and a barrel of ale the goodwife had brewed herself. He wouldn't give himself the time to sit down and have a meal, though. He needed to get to Avery.

He paused in the door to the small room and nodded to the other few patrons.

"May I purchase bread and cheese?" he said to the tavern wench, enjoying the syllables of his own language in his mouth.

As he waited for her to bring him the food, he scrutinized the others in the tavern carefully. He knew he must be on his guard. A small party of travelers, one of them a very big man.

Once he had the food, he rode with it down the path and found a rock where he could sit and eat, and drink from his leathern bottle of water.

A jingle of harness told him others were coming down the path. He put the food away quickly and stood, his hand to his sword's hilt. He wanted these travelers ahead of him, not behind him. He'd wait until they passed.

Three or four practical looking fellows on practical horses. One of them, the lead horseman, was the huge man Wat recognized from earlier, in the tavern. As the horsemen trotted toward him, this big man raised a hand in greeting. The party of them didn't look threatening. Wat gave a brief nod, waiting for them to ride by.

Somehow, instead, the green forest, filled with birdsong and the trip-trapping hooves of the horses on the stones of the road, abruptly upended. Abruptly went silent, went black.

When he came to himself, Wat was on his back in a dark stifling place.

Child help me, he thought, as he gradually became lucid enough to realize what had happened to him. Someone had knocked him over the head. Someone else maybe with the approaching riders. Someone who had circled around and, under cover of the others' noise, crept up on him from behind. Now someone had taken him. . . somewhere. *And Child help The Rising.*

He felt about himself. Of course the belt pouch and the bag of gold were gone. *I keep failing*, he said to himself. *And now The Rising may fail because of me.* But he didn't have a chance to dwell on these thoughts. He tried to sit up, and that left him retching painfully and sinking back down, his head swimming.

He felt his head gingerly. His hand came away sticky with blood.

As he lay thinking viciously over his own failings, he started realizing other things. What had happened to him was no ordinary robbery. Otherwise he would have been left for dead on the road.

These men, he realized, must have lain in wait for him. Must have tracked him through the forest, across the border, and down the road. After they had clobbered him from behind with something heavy, they'd taken him somewhere to hide him away.

Here.

A dim sound came to him. Footsteps. Wat felt his way to the wall of the small room where he was being kept and used it as a support to waver to his feet. He felt his way around the wall to a door, and then, as the footsteps got louder, backed carefully away from it.

When they open the door, I'll—

There was the sound of a bar being drawn back.

The door opened with a blaze of rushlight. Wat threw himself at the big man who shouldered through first. He recognized the mammoth leader of the horsemen along the road.

The man's hand, as large as a ham, shot out and shoved Wat in the chest.

Wat went down.

Now there were three of them, standing over him, staring at him. They didn't harm him. One turned and set a bowl on a joint stool by the door. Another set a noggin of water down beside it. They all backed out of the room then, and Wat, from his situation on his back on the floor, heard the bar rammed to again.

"See? Not dead," he heard one of the men say, just outside.

And another, in a diminishing voice as the footsteps faded back down the corridor again, "But you could have, Bunce, you dolt. . ."

Could have killed me, Wat supposed. Bunce was a very big man.

So they don't want me dead, Wat thought, a little while later. There was a hole between one thought and the next. He realized he might have lain there out of his head again for a bit.

Not robbers, he thought.

Caedon, he guessed. *And he wants me alive because—*

Well, because. He thought of John and what Caedon had done to John.

He crept to the noggin of water and gulped it all down. Then he vomited it all back up. He lay shivering in a corner.

No heroes to the rescue for me, he thought. Not that it had done John any good. But no one knew where Wat was. Wat didn't know, either. He tried to think where they might have brought him. Surely not up into the high country to Caedon's estate and Treddian's castle. Surely not that far. But he really didn't know how long he'd been out. Maybe longer than he thought. It didn't feel that way, though. The room was windowless, so he had no way to tell how much time might have passed. But anyway, Caedon's estate or the castle would be the most likely places Rafe or Dru or the others would look for him, and the more he thought about it, the more he doubted he was anywhere near there.

He felt the flat taste of despair. In flashes, the color and excitement of the dancing only the day before, and the feeling of success and confidence, burst into his head, taunting him. All those bright feelings lay in tatters, leaving a sour tang of failure and shame. The only course of action open to him now was somehow to try to prepare himself for what would come.

He thought maybe the agony of waiting around for the pain was part of the torment Caedon carefully planned for his victims.

Rafe said John wasn't feeling any pain at the end, he thought. Maybe the first painful part of it would be quickly over.

He thought for a long time about what Caedon had done to John, and how long it had probably taken to do it.

Another way might be open to him, he realized. If there was a way to do the job for Caedon before Caedon did it himself—

His thoughts were beginning to turn in that grim direction when he heard noises. More footsteps coming down the corridor.

He dragged himself to his feet again and tensed. They'd be ready for him this time, he knew, and last time didn't go well even when he'd had the element of surprise.

Now it was Wat's turn to feel surprise. The voice outside the thick door between himself and the corridor was a woman's.

"In here?" he heard this woman say.

There was an indistinct response. Wat moved to the door and pressed his ear to it.

"You performed your task well. There's gold for you," said the woman's voice again. Then footsteps going away.

What thing under the Nine Spheres is this? wondered Wat.

A flame of hope kindled in him, and just as quickly died. He didn't know what woman might want to kidnap him and take his gold, but if Caedon didn't have him, he'd maybe get away somehow.

He had to. He might no longer have the gold Avery needed. But he had information that could destroy The Rising, and from an unexpected direction. Hakkon Hardaxe and Queen Ailys, conspiring together against them.

If someone knew he was bringing this information to Avery, that someone would have every reason to seize Wat and prevent him.

Perhaps some enemy of Mabire has me, he thought. Perhaps they've taken me back across the border into Baronies territory. But no, he realized. Bunce and the others, and the mysterious woman outside his door, had spoken in his own language.

He began to pace. He went to the bowl of food the man Bunce and his friends had left and licked it clean.

He suddenly sat down on the floor, staring into the dark and cursing himself for a fool. He remembered the sharp look Queen Ailys had aimed at him, the night before. Of course. She was the person who needed to stop him. And somehow, last night she had seen who he was. Somehow, in spite of all the precautions he had taken, she had sent men after him.

She probably wants to kill me as much as Caedon does, he thought. *But if she does, maybe she won't care how I die. Just cut off my head or stick a knife in me or hang me.*

Probably hang me, he thought. *It's clear I'm not a gentle. No headsman for the likes of me.*

He felt the shame of it. Instead of anguishing over the gold and information Avery so desperately needed and wasn't going to get, Wat kept dwelling on how Ailys would kill him.

He thought of the several hangings he'd witnessed, as a boy. Some miserable flea-bitten felon dragged by a rope around his neck behind a guardsman's horse through the streets of Tambourne to Hangman's Hill. These men did not die pretty deaths. And the deaths of the die-hards were not quick.

Compared to what John had to endure, though. On the whole, Wat decided he'd come out well if a hanging was all he got.

After the third or fourth day of pacing and speculating and agonizing and berating himself in the dark, Wat began ardently wishing for a hanging. Judging from the pains in his belly, they fed him once a day, and the food was vermin-infested. The water was fetid. On the fifth day, his bowels were griping him, and he was too weak to stand.

He felt he probably had a fever. He was hot, horribly hot, and strange dreams had caught him up. *This will work as well as a hanging*, he thought during one lucid period. *I don't deserve to live, anyway*, he thought. Not after failing Avery so spectacularly.

When was it? The sixth day? Later? Wat lost count. The door to his cell was thrown open, and a painful burst of light caught him full in the face. Someone screamed. Maybe himself.

But no. It was a lady. He squinted to see. It was Ailys, or maybe he was dreaming her. She was a hazy shape hovering above him.

She was screaming in rage. "What have you done to him!"

Placating voices of the guards. Then Wat was dimly aware that these voices had turned frightened. Then someone was hauling him out by the armpits, and then.

Then, maybe days later, he woke up to find a healer supporting his shoulders so he could drink some broth, and he was unaccountably clean, and in a clean bed.

"There now, lad," this healer said. "Ye need your strength. The lady will see you tomorrow."

"What lady?" Wat croaked out. That's when he realized two women were attending him.

"Hush it, foolish woman," said this other one, sharply.

The woman who had been feeding Wat rose to her feet, handed the bowl to the other one, and withdrew.

"Never you mind who. Just eat this," said the second woman, taking the first's place on the joint stool beside Wat's bed. "If you do well with this broth, there'll be bread and ale for you later," she promised, whisking away after he had hungrily sucked the broth down.

I've been ill, he thought. His mind collected itself. And the lady was the queen. For whatever reasons of her own, reasons beyond his knowing, she had seen him tended to. He gazed around him. And in luxurious surroundings, too.

She had taken Mabire's gold, that was clear. Now she was making sure the knowledge of her meeting with emissaries of Hakkon Hardaxe, the powerful king of the Ice-realm, was kept from Avery. The train of events was getting clearer and clearer to him. He reviewed what he knew. It was clear that Bunce and his fellows, at the queen's orders, had followed him from Lunds-fort, knocked him on the head, taken Mabire's gold, and locked him up.

Now that he was back in his right wits, Wat set his mind on escape. He needed to get to Avery, confess his failure, take whatever punishment Avery meted out, but most of all, get his information to his brother. It was all he could offer Avery now.

From his bed, he could see the women tending him hadn't even bothered to lock him in. The door to his room was standing a little bit ajar.

But he quickly realized why they hadn't been worried.

He threw back the covers and steeled himself to sit up and swing his feet off the bed. Then he discovered one ankle was tethered by a long rawhide thong to the end of the bed.

His head began to swim and he sank back down. He pulled the rich coverlet back to his chin and lay shivering. *Whatever they did to me has me just as well tethered as this thong*, he thought.

Throughout the day, he alternated between sleeping, when sleep overwhelmed him in its dark irresistible wave, and looking around him at the room. He noted the high window. No easy exit there.

The door.

If he could slip off his tether, he could get to the door and through it, but what was on the other side? He craned his neck to look at his ankle. The cuff around it had a small lock embedded into the leather. Only someone with the key to this lock could unhinge the cuff and untether him.

He was dressed in a kind of short bed gown. He'd never worn such a thing. Wat fingered it under the covers. It felt made of some sort of finely woven cloth. If he could tear it into strips. . . But as he lay there, his body, almost by itself, nestled deeper into the coverlet and into this strange garment, and he couldn't help it. Sleep took him again.

The healer woman, the friendly one, bustled in during one of his sessions of speculation. She was carrying a loaf and a tankard of ale. She beamed at him as he devoured the loaf and drank up the ale.

"A healthy sign," she said. "And now drink this." She held a small bottle to his lips and poured some kind of potion down him.

In the morning, she brought more nourishing food and watched while he ate it. Then she stepped to the door and motioned. The unfriendly woman and Bunce came in.

Wat watched Bunce through narrowed eyes. He had a club at his belt. Wat wanted to get at that club.

Bunce looked down at him and laughed. "Feisty fellow," he told the others. "Look how he wants my club."

"You're not going to get it, so don't even think about it," said the unfriendly woman. She threw the covers off Wat.

With a casual hand, Bunce held Wat down, while the woman took a small key from a bunch dangling at her waist and bent over to unlock the cuff around Wat's ankle. Then, among them, his three minders hoisted him to his feet and walked him out of his room and along the corridor to a big hearth room, where a tub of hot water waited.

The women whisked the bed garment off him as he yelped in protest, and Bunce bundled him into the tub. "You must be clean and sweet-smelling," one of the women said, strewing lavender and other herbs into the deliciously hot water.

"Why?" said Wat suspiciously.

The two women between them dunked him under and washed his hair.

Then Bunce lifted him bodily out of the tub. "I could break you in two with one twitch of me fingers, laddie," he said, "so don't try anything."

Wat did anyway. The queen had screamed at Bunce, when she saw Bunce had mistreated him. Dark Ones knew why, but she'd done it. So he knew the big man wouldn't dare try to break him in two. Wat fought. He summoned up everything Dru had taught him. He fought dirty, going for the groin, but Bunce danced away from him. For a big man, he was light on his feet.

The two women screeched in fright, and Bunce grabbed at him, but Wat was slippery. He made for the door. The women tackled him. They brought him down. Then they forcibly dried him off. Bunce picked him up with one arm and sat him down on a joint stool, none too gently, and held him there while the women combed out his hair. It had begun to grow long.

One of them held his head still while the other one shaved his cheeks. "Hardly necessary," she said.

Wat twisted to get at the razor.

"Careful, lad, you'll slit your own throat," said Bunce, helping to hold him. "Not that it would be such a bad thing. In my opinion, someone should slit this knave's throat," he said to the two women. "But they're not asking me."

The three of them popped a tunic over Wat's head. Bunce kept him from kicking at them while the women pulled on leggings, each taking a leg.

Through it all, Wat had kept completely silent. He kept scanning the room for some advantage, some way to get out of their grasp. But he was too weak.

They got him back to his room and shackled him with the tether again. Wat lay back into the coverlet and closed his eyes, exhausted and furious.

"You've had a struggle with young Walter, it seems," said a voice.

Wat forced himself to open his eyes.

The two women and Bunce, soaked and angry, were bowing low as the queen herself stood in the doorway.

"Do you know me?" she said to him.

Wat decided to pretend he didn't know her. He shook his head no.

"Bunce," Ailys said to the big man. "I want to get a good look at him, but I don't want him thrashing about. Do something."

"Yes, Your Highness," said Bunce.

Wat's eyes widened in shock. He was so surprised that he forgot to fight as Bunce grabbed him by both wrists and tied them. He pulled Wat's arms over his head and tied his bound wrists securely to the carved headboard of the bed. Meanwhile, one of the women had lifted up the coverlet and had tied his unbound ankle to the other post at the end of the bed.

"Fine," said the queen. "You may leave me now. The lad can't get at me, if he's minded to, or try to escape."

With more low bows, her servants left her alone with Wat.

"Now let's see what the gods have brought me," said Ailys, stepping to the bedside.

Wat turned his head away. What did it matter what she did to him. She'd hand him over to Audemar, or Caedon. His brief time of thinking his fate wouldn't be like John's was over.

"Stupid varlets. They put clothes on you. What did they think I wanted you for," she said.

Wat shook his head, hard. He stared at her, thinking he might not be understanding her.

He saw he did.

"You're a pretty boy. You always were. Just like your brother."

"Now you've insulted me, Your Majesty."

She laughed. "So you do know me. I was sure you did. I'm not comparing you to Audemar, silly lad. I mean John. If the king heard you talking this way, he'd demand your head. He doesn't think of you as his brother."

"But I am, aren't I? We share a father, anyway," said Wat, wondering why he was bothering to joust with words this way, trying not to let his anger rise and overwhelm him as she used John's name in her filthy mouth. If he kept a clear head, maybe he could find out something useful. Maybe.

"You're right, to be sure. Clearly, you and the king are brothers. Anyone looking at you can see it, if they have eyes in their heads. Ranulf's get. John. And Avery. Even Audemar, although he's so vile that it's harder to see, in him."

"You don't like your husband."

"Who could?"

Maybe she's actually an ally, thought Wat for a brief crazy moment. But then, at the same time, he realized no. No, she wasn't.

"Every one of Ranulf's sons but Artur, the poor man, has this same big blond handsome look about him." She had moved from standing over Wat to sitting beside him on the bed. "You, though. You're a more slender type, I see." She began toying with his hair as he tried to twist away from her. "I enjoyed your dancing at the baron Mabire's hearth. It stirred me."

She moved her hands down his torso and grasped the bottom of his tunic. She pulled it up and continued her exploring, this time on his bare flesh.

She didn't say a word now, just caressed and stroked.

Wat closed his eyes and turned his head away from her, tensing up.

She moved to his leggings, pulling them down around his ankles.

"Well, well," she said softly.

With humiliation, Wat realized he was aroused. With horror, that she was moving to arouse him further. Then she had possessed him.

He lay sweating and hating himself.

"There. That was good," she said, rolling off him and putting herself to rights.

"You can be sure that won't happen again, Your Majesty," he said between tight lips.

"We'll see about that," she said to him and left him there, uncovered, his clothing disarranged, in a state of shame and fury made even worse when the servants came in to tend to him, and he saw the knowing looks they exchanged with each other.

After they had freed his hands and one of his feet "so you can use the chamber pot, my lad," said the friendly woman servant briskly, they left him alone.

Wat couldn't help it. He cried. He knew everyone said men shouldn't, but he did.

I've cried a lot lately, he thought dully. *Over John. Now over this.* He was consumed by his failure to deliver the gold Avery and The Rising so desperately needed, and on fire with the things he knew. And now this dangerous woman had used him like a beast. Like a thing.

After that day, thank the Children, Queen Ailys left him alone for a while, and he began to get stronger.

She was toying with me. Now she has had her amusement, and she won't be back, he told himself, trying to convince himself it was so.

It was not. She paid him several more visits, but he was on his guard now. He always knew when these visits were about to happen, because his minders hustled him off to the lavender-strewn tub. But he was stronger, and wary. The queen left these sessions frustrated and angry, her eyes snapping.

He kept waiting for her to ship him off to Caedon. She would, as soon as she realized he was never giving in to her again. So he knew he had to get out.

He set himself to lull the suspicions of his minders. Now at least he knew where he was. He was in Tam Fort, and he knew if he could get out of the rooms where they were holding him, he could get out of the fort into the town and away. He knew the place, every jot and tittle. Every hiding place. Once he got himself out into the town, they'd never find him.

Only two minders watched him now: the kind woman and Bunce. Bunce clearly thought keeping an eye on the plaything of the queen was beneath him. The kindly woman was chafing at tending a person who no longer needed her healing skills.

When he was in his cups, Bunce liked to taunt Wat and knock him around a bit, especially if the woman wasn't there to see it and stop him doing it. He knew Wat would die sooner than hide behind her skirts, and he knew he outweighed Wat by many stone. Wat was tall, but Bunce overtopped him. And Bunce was far more massive. Wat could see these thoughts as if they were written in script on the big man's forehead.

Tethered and closely guarded, with nothing at hand to use as a weapon, Wat set his mind on escape anyway. He set himself to wear his captors down.

He set out to annoy and irritate Bunce as much as he could. One morning Bunce came in to see about some errand he'd had to do for the serving woman who minded Wat. Wat made a rude gesture at him, just a little out of his line of sight.

Bunce whirled around. "Do you bite your thumb at me, sir?" he snarled.

"I bite my thumb, sir, but not at you, sir," Wat said.

Bunce was advancing on him menacingly when the serving-woman stepped between them and grabbed up Wat's hand.

"You do bite your thumb," she said accusingly. "You bite your nails. That's a nasty habit, lad."

Wat shrugged sheepishly. He did. His mother had tried to stop him and break him of the habit, but she had never succeeded.

"Put those hands out. Both of them," the servingwoman demanded, pointing to the coverlet.

Meekly Wat lay both of his hands on the coverlet.

The servingwoman picked them up, first the left, then the right, and examined them. "They're clean, anyway," she said grudgingly.

"It's all those baths," said Wat.

"As sweet-smelling as a little girl," Bunce mocked.

"Go out to your post, Bunce," ordered the servingwoman. From her apron pocket, she withdrew a small glittering instrument.

Wat eyed it uncomfortably. What was it? What was she about to do to him with it?

She had it propped on thumb and index finger by two rings attached to two sharp little blades. She picked up his right hand and drew the glittering blades near, extending the little engine on her fingers' ends.

Wat tensed and flinched back.

She slapped his hand. "Be still, Master Wat. I don't want to cut you." Then she sat back in exasperation. "Do I have to bring Bunce back in here and hold you still?"

He put his hand back on the coverlet.

"Such a big baby," she scolded. She took up his right thumb. She spread the glittering forfex wide, then joined the two little blades to nip and clip at the ragged cuticle around his thumbnail.

Swiftly and carefully she treated each of his ten fingers thus, while he looked on in astonishment.

"There now," she said, patting his hands and tucking them back under the coverlet. "Don't bite them again."

"Yes, mistress," said Wat.

"Don't let me catch you doing it."

"No, mistress," said Wat.

She frowned. "Those are very calloused hands, young master. I will bring my pumice stone next time and smooth them out."

"No point, mistress," said Wat, politely. "It's the bowstring that does it."

"You're not going to be shooting anything any time soon," said the servingwoman. She whipped out a little comb and combed Wat's hair off his face. "And your hair is growing out nicely now."

"Suppose you bring me a leather band, to bind it off my forehead?" said Wat, struck with a sudden thought.

"Certainly not," she said, and flounced from his room.

But other attempts of Wat's to annoy Bunce were more successful.

He discovered something remarkable about Bunce, the giant of an oaf who served as his chief guard and most enthusiastic tormenter.

The king's musicians practiced in a courtyard just underneath the place where Bunce sat guard in the corridor outside Wat's room. Across from Bunce, a long bank of high, open, arched windows looked out over the courtyard.

The heat of late summer was stifling, and his captors, not completely devoid of human feeling, took to leaving his door open so a cross-breeze could cool him as he lay sweating under the high single window above his bed. Besides, they too had to be in the stifling little room with him, when they tended to him.

The kindly woman servant entered one day to throw the covers off him and strip his sweat-soaked tunic from him.

"Thanks," he said between cracked lips.

She held a skin of water to his lips and he drank.

"Tch," she said, reaching over to run a finger down the long jagged scar on his left arm. "Looks like you were a lucky lad. Someone took you to a good healer after someone else did this to you." She shook her head. "And there you were, out brawling and fighting when you should have been learning your trade of your master, stonemason or miller or smith."

"You think this is some prentice?" Bunce had come into the room to look, too. He snorted.

Wat turned his gaze to the ceiling. He didn't want them standing over him like that, discussing him and examining him as if he were a slab of meat on display at the butcher's counter.

"This lad, or so they say," said Bunce, turning to his serving-woman, "is one of Ranulf's bastards."

"Oh, aye?" said the woman, her tone unimpressed. "All the more reason he should have been setting a good example, not out there getting himself into fights."

"You stupid wench, they say he's one of these rebels, with the rebel prince."

"Tush, he's not old enough for that, and besides, Bunce, you addle-pated tun of guts, if this lad were a rebel, his head would have long been parted from his shoulders, pretty or no."

"You call that pretty?" Bunce sneered. "All women are stupid cunts."

"La, even the queen, who keeps this pretty lad for her own self?"

"Even she," said Bunce. "Especially she."

"Careful, Bunce, or you'll find your lard-head has been separated from your own lard-shoulders."

Wat gritted his teeth, having to endure this pointless, endless chatter. Day after day, the two of them insulted each other, and he had to listen to it.

But then. Then he learned the important thing to know about Bunce.

In the middle of their flyting, Bunce held up his hand. "Hush it, woman. Listen."

Wat stared in amazement as the man's coarse features underwent an utter transformation. His eyes softened. His slack, cruel mouth pursed up in delight.

From below in the courtyard, faintly, the sound of the king's musicians floated upward.

Bunce sighed, full of longing and pent-up, delicate emotion.

That, thought Wat. *I can use that.*

Wat, finding out this one important thing about Bunce, realized Bunce had not discovered the one important thing about Wat.

Wat's brother John had known the pathway to the Spheres. John's beautiful voice had been that pathway, and the music of his rebec.

Wat, though. Wat was as musical as a post.

Wat could not sing. He did not play. If he had tried, multitudes would have gathered in his mother's dooryard to beg him to stop.

Wat took to humming a little tuneless song. He took to doing it for candle measure after candle measure. And as he hummed, and sometimes sang to himself, he watched Bunce's shoulders hunch up higher and ever higher about his ears.

His plan to irritate Bunce into some unfortunate rash move nearly miscarried, though. After a few days of it, Bunce slammed the thick door to Wat's room and left him in there to swelter.

So Wat stopped doing it. At least while he was in his room.

The queen allowed him, once a day, an airing in the little courtyard below his rooms. Once a day, Bunce would come into Wat's room, unfasten his thong, help him stumbling down the stone stairs, and push him and shove him out to the courtyard.

Wat was regaining his strength. From the courtyard, he could just barely glimpse over its high wall the road that led past the fort's stables and mews. Beyond, it curled around to the house where he had grown up with his mother and brothers. Beyond that, the forest.

The little courtyard was not large, but it had been turned into a charming enclosed garden with trellises made of wattle for roses and other plants. Clearly, it was designed for some lady's pleasure. Wat walked around and around this garden. Every day, he went over to one of the trellises, seemingly to admire the flowers there, enduring Bunce's scornful but increasingly bored surveillance.

And every day, he worked one of the springy osiers of the wattles a bit loose from its weaving into the frame of the trellis.

When he saw Bunce was sufficiently bored not to be watching, he broke off a piece of wattle and laid it quietly under the overhanging vines and stems of the trellis. Then, the next day, another. Soon he had made a pile of sticks around the length of his hand. Next he untangled one of the osiers and began winding it around the bundle of sticks so that, over the space of a sen'night or so, his bundle of sticks had become a strong and compact little rod.

Meanwhile, as he walked around and around the courtyard, as determined as a man grinding at the quern-stone, he hummed. He sang.

Each time, as he came back around to where Bunce sat, he saw the big man hunching his shoulders and cringing away. Bunce had taken to sitting at the entrance to the courtyard, facing outward. Facing away from Wat. *After all*, Bunce seemed to be thinking, *This lad can't get past me, and he has nothing to attack me with, from behind.*

Wat saw that Bunce looked around the courtyard each day before they entered it. Once he removed a large stone. *He thinks I might sneak up behind him and hit him on the head with it*, thought Wat. *As he and his men did to me.*

Wat had several plans going. Several times he attempted to loose the thong that tethered his leg to the bed. Several times he was found out. Once Bunce pushed and threatened him, but at the last few attempts, he had just laughed contemptuously and reattached the thong.

The failure of these attempts didn't dismay Wat. He was going to get out, and he had figured out how he'd do it. He began carefully fraying the seam of his bed garment until he knew he'd be able to rip a piece of cloth from the hem of it. The night before the day he'd decided on, Wat waited until Bunce, seated on a chair shoved up against his door, was snoring just outside. Muffling the ripping sound in the bedclothes, he tore off a long piece of cloth. He set himself to tying tight knots in the cloth, spaced out at intervals, until he had fashioned a necklace-like rope of cloth beads. He tore off another strip and did the same. He tore off and knotted a third strip. Then he tied all the strips securely together and coiled the long thin rope of knotted cloth underneath him as he lay in his bed. In the morning, when he pulled on his tunic, he slipped the knotted strip up his sleeve and wound it around his arm.

By now, the woman servant let him dress himself. She let him put on his own tunic. Then, when she untethered him briefly to let him use the chamber pot more easily, she let him draw on his own leggings. *Why not?* she seemed to be thinking. *This lad's not much of a threat. He has become quiet and tractable, and his nails are very clean.*

On the morning he decided to act, Wat waited patiently for his daily outing.

"Time," said Bunce, thrusting his head into the room. He came in and untethered Wat from where Wat sat on the side of the bed. Then, with a beefy hand in the small of Wat's back, he walked him down to the little courtyard.

Wat strolled around the courtyard, as usual, pretending to admire the flowers. He saw how scornfully Bunce glanced in his direction, but then how the big man turned away, as usual, to sit on a bench in the archway of the courtyard. Bunce had taken to gazing out longingly over the field where the Royal arms master trained the king's soldiers to fight on horseback.

Wat saw Bunce was confident that his prisoner couldn't scale the wall of the courtyard, and of course he couldn't get past Bunce at the entrance. Wat saw how restless and bored Bunce was with this duty. And now Wat took up his customary practice of pacing the courtyard and humming and singing.

Today I'm getting out of here, thought Wat. He moved to the trellis and found the little bundle of osiers he had fashioned into a rod. Making sure Bunce was gazing out to the field with the horses and not into the garden, Wat eased his knotted cord out of his sleeve in a double loop and tied one end around the middle of the rod in a secure knot.

His circuit around the garden took him behind Bunce as the big man sat on his bench in the sun. As Wat padded past Bunce, humming his irritating little song, he was uncoiling the knotted strip of cloth in his right hand, the side of his body hidden from Bunce.

Bunce happened to turn around as Wat passed. "Beautiful day," Wat murmured, easing the cord down out of Bunce's sight.

Bunce grunted and turned back to watch the horsemen.

Wat kept his scuffling walk around the garden path until he was behind Bunce again. Directly behind him. He smoothly pivoted with his cord and threw it in a loop of a slip-knot over Bunce's thick neck. He twisted it tight as Bunce's arms flew up, and with the attached osier rod, he twisted it tighter and ever tighter still. At the same time, he used his whole weight to drag Bunce back, but braced his knee against Bunce's back so Bunce didn't fall flat on the ground and have a chance to twist around to face Wat.

As Bunce struggled forward, his own weight helped Wat's cord do its work, tightening Wat's improvised garotte so rapidly that the man had no breath to call out. For a few long moments, he flailed and floundered. Then, his air supply completely cut off, he sagged, nearly dead. Wat pulled tight on the slip noose the cord had made and abruptly removed his knee. Bunce crashed over backward. Wat danced aside, throwing the end of the cord over a protruding knob in the wall to keep the cord tight and taut. He pulled hard on the cord, sawing it against the stone wall so it couldn't slip off the knob. He let Bunce's full weight finish the job as he fell.

There. Just as Dru taught me, Wat thought, standing heaving for breath over the massive body.

He made sure that Bunce was dead. Then he stepped over the big man and walked casually away from the courtyard, zig-zagged down two alleys, stepped out into the road, and moved down it toward the forest.

The gods had a different idea. Wat figured this out later, thinking it over and overhearing stray remarks. By chance, Wat's other minder, the friendly little woman, had come looking for Bunce with a message from his cousin. When she spotted Bunce's fallen bulk, his bulging eyes and protruding tongue, the blue of his face, she let out a shriek.

Wat heard it and began to run. *Dark Ones take it*, he thought. If he had still been within the walls, he could have found a place to hide. But here he was, out on the road. Even when hoofbeats behind him told him it was no use, he sprinted for the forest, because if he could gain the forest, he knew he could hide there and evade anyone in Tam Fort come looking for him.

A fresh horse covers far more distance than even the fastest man can outrun.

The king's horsemen rode him down and thrust him into a dank cell much worse than his original dark room in less time than the whole strangulation of Bunce had taken him.

They weren't gentle about it.

Wat lay bruised and groaning with misery all that day. His groans were not cries of pain. They were curses and mutterings born of utter frustration.

The next day he was hauled before Tambourne's beadle for murder, and the beadle swiftly sentenced him to hang the day after that.

Head down, he stood shackled between two guards as sentence was passed. He didn't care what they did to him. Not any longer. As the guards pivoted him around to march him out of the beadle's hall, they found a splendidly dressed courtier barring their way.

"What's this?" said the courtier sharply, speaking past Wat to the beadle.

"This man murdered the queen's servant yesterday. I just sentenced him to hang tomorrow," said the beadle testily. Then, seeming to think better of his words, he bowed and added, "Your lordship."

"Release him to my custody at once," said this courtier.

"And why will you interfere with the king's justice?" said the beadle, stung out of his civility.

"The queen commands it. This man is her personal prisoner."

The beadle blanched. "Your lordship, I was not told," he stammered. "Take the prisoner."

Wat's guards stepped aside.

"Come with me, fellow," said the courtier. He didn't watch to make sure Wat followed him. He turned on his heel and strode away.

After a startled moment, Wat followed him at a shuffle. Shackled as he was, he didn't see how he'd escape.

The courtier waited at a small door in the outer bailey of the fort, tapping his foot impatiently. Wat entered the door and the man stepped in behind him. With the flat of his sword, he chivvied Wat ahead of him into a room with a single carved chair.

"Leave us," said a voice. The man withdrew.

Wat recognized that voice. Wearily he turned to face the queen.

She swept past him and mounted to her chair, set upon a dais. "Kneel," she said.

Wat got awkwardly down on his knees.

"What did you think you were doing?"

"Escaping?" Wat offered.

"You foolish lad. Don't you understand? I'm keeping you safe here. You're safe," she emphasized, her eyes flashing.

"Safe?" said Wat. "I'm a prisoner here. You'll turn me over to Caedon, and you know what he'll do to me. I was one of the men who found my brother John. I was one of the two who nearly beat Caedon to death."

"You?" said Ailys. She looked him up and down scornfully. "Hardly likely."

"How do you explain your dead man out there, then?"

She sat watching him through narrowed eyes. "I've a good mind to call the beadle and let him take you off to the gallows after all," she said. "You're nothing but trouble."

"Do it, then," he said.

She sighed. "You're bought and paid for, lad. I'd like to, but I suppose I can't. Not without alienating the seller, whom I happen to need just at the moment."

"The seller?"

"The person who brought me all the gold you were carrying, doing me a very valuable service. Giving me the funds I need for my own enterprises, and depriving your doomed little Rising of the funds they need. The only price I had to pay was your safety. I suppose if it costs me a few incompetent servants, you're still cheap at the price." Before Wat could make any angry outburst, she added, "As soon as time allows, I'll pay you a visit, pretty boy. I enjoyed our last."

"I didn't."

"That's because you need to relax," she told him. "In time, you will. I'll teach you how." She rose from her chair, strolled over to him where he knelt, and ruffled his hair. Then she eyed him sharply. She drew up one of his hands, burdened with its shackle, and stood turning it this way and that. "Just look. What lovely nails you have."

Wat snatched his hand back and clambered to his feet.

"You should thank me," said the queen. "I even tried to warn your brother once."

"Your warning came too late," said Wat, remembering the parchment and the man at the street fair.

Ailys shrugged.

She motioned to a minion who took Wat back to his room, redoubled his guard, and fastened him by both ankles to the bed. When the serving woman visited him later in the day, she told him coldly that the queen had denied him his daily airing.

"Misbehaving lads must learn to behave better," she told him.

Wat lay on his bed day after day, ever more disconsolate and bitter, ever more puzzled about why he was there and who in the Nine Spheres was keeping him. The only optimistic thoughts he had were about the queen's failure, day after day, to make good on her promise to visit him.

One of many indeterminate days later, he woke to find that no one was at his door guarding him. No one came to his room to see about him. No one released his thongs so he could relieve himself. No one brought him anything to eat or drink.

They've forgotten I'm here, he thought. Then he thought, *And I don't even care.*

But his minders hadn't forgotten. They were only lying dead up and down the corridor. When Dru stepped into his room, Wat thought maybe he had finally gone crazy and was starting to see visions, but Dru was real. Dru cut him loose, bundled him into a hooded cloak, walked him down the corridor past the dead people. Wat stepped over the contorted body of the kindly woman servant and looked down at her with a small pang of regret.

"Come on, lad," Dru murmured. Wat followed Dru to a passageway cutting underneath the fort's walls.

"Just a little place we found, some years back," said Dru, gesturing around him at the close walls of the dim passageway.

Wat found he couldn't speak. Dru guided him outside and to the forest verge.

"Here are our horses." Dru pointed them out to Wat.

Dru had to help Wat mount. Wat was ashamed to discover that after a fortnight or more of complete inactivity, he felt boneless as a newt and just as empty-headed.

"Dru. Wait," he said rapidly, coming out of his stupor. "I found something out. I lost Mabire's gold, but at least I have this." He told Dru about Hakkon Hardaxe.

"Good work, lad," said Dru. "Lady help us, what have they done to your hands, you look like a simpering lord."

"You need to take this information to Avery," said Wat.

"You'll tell him yourself. Gracious gods, lad, you smell like the springtide flowers in the meadow."

Wat looked down at the ground in despair. "I can't go back," he said suddenly. Loudly.

He slid off his horse and knelt before Dru. "A better idea. Kill me. I failed Avery. I failed The Rising, as good as if I were a traitor. Just do away with me, Dru. I know you know how. I know you've had to, sometimes."

"Keep your voice down. You're coming back with me. And how you think I'd ever be able to do away with you, as you put it— Wat, I'd sooner cut off my right hand."

At the exasperation in Dru's voice, a wave of fresh shame took Wat. He looked up desperately into Dru's eyes, but Dru wasn't looking back.

Dru was gazing past him toward the fort, scanning its walls.

"I can't go back," Wat said to him, more urgently. "You don't understand, Dru. I let The Rising down. I let someone steal Mabire's gold. I let someone drag me here and give me to that queen."

"We know," said Dru, looking down at him now, a kind look that pierced him to the heart.

Dru swung out of the saddle and slung Wat back onto his mount, talking all the time. Talking quietly and steadily, as one might talk to a horse ready to bolt. "Do you know how overjoyed everyone will be to see you? Do you know how terrified we've been that you were dead? How terrified I was that I'd get into the fort only to find you dead? Avery is counting the moments until you get back to camp. He can scarcely contain himself. We need to put him out of his misery. Let's go home, Wat."

They turned their horses' heads and rode out of there.

CHAPTER SEVENTEEN

Shrewd Trading

Ailys

The queen was none too pleased, but then again, the loss of the lad was a gnat-bite only. What she really disliked was the pestering and pestering of the boy's betrayer.

"Oh, send her in," she told her steward grumpily. "I may as well get it over with and see her."

The young woman, dressed more for a hunt than for a petition at court, was ushered in before Ailys.

The woman made a bare sketch of a curtsey.

"Is this how you approach your queen?" said Ailys. She looked around at her steward and the guardsmen. "Leave us," she said.

"Is that wise, Your Majesty?" murmured the steward at her ear.

"You heard me. Leave." Ailys's voice was cold, and she saw with gratification how her retainers backed hastily away from her carved chair.

"But you," she said to the woman, barely more than a girl. "You, come near. Come here to me. What's your name again?"

"Eris, Your Majesty," said the woman. Her tone was insolent. She took a few steps closer.

Not too close, Ailys saw.

"You feel aggrieved, I suppose," said Ailys after a moment.

"I do, Your Majesty. We had a bargain."

"I'm well shut of that lad," said Ailys. "A score of my men are dead because of him, and no few of the bondsmaidens."

Eris shrugged. "Our bargain was, I give you the gold, you take Wat and keep him safe. We made no mention of what you'd do if he proved a trouble to you. You agreed to take him. If you can't keep one skinny lad from killing your armed men—"

"Quiet, you, before I have your tongue cut out."

"You went back on our bargain, Your Majesty."

"Why do you care? If he's your lover, why give him to me?"

"He's my brother."

"Oh? Oh, aye. Ranulf's pack of little bastards."

"I want my gold back."

Ailys laughed "You'll not have it. You're a fool, Mistress Eris, you know that?" Ailys leaned back in her chair and smiled. "I know exactly what you're thinking. It's written all over you, mistress. You're thinking of going straight to Lord Caedon, aren't you?"

"I work for him, after all."

"And what do you think he'll say to you when you tell him you have been doing little tasks for me? Such as giving me all of The Rising's gold instead of giving it to him."

"He doesn't own me, Your Majesty."

"No?" Ailys eyed her shrewdly. "That would surprise me very much, mistress. Well, well, do as you think best. You'll not get the gold back from me. I kept your lad as close as I could, but he has skillful and loyal friends, and he escaped. A pity. I was enjoying him very much, and then those friends of his had him off me."

"Drustan," Eris spat.

"The young earl? I remember him, when he was just a stripling lad. And what a lovely lad he was, too. Yes, indeed. A pity about your friend, or lover, or whoever he is. My duties took me away from him, or I would have been paying closer attention."

"I told you. He's my brother," said Eris, scowling.

"Hmm. And another of your brothers was that John person, the bastard who got my friend Odelyn killed."

"Oh, did he?' said Eris. "I heard a different tale. I heard it was you got Lady Odelyn killed, because John was her lover, and you knew it, and you told. That was Wat's brother. His full brother."

"Wat. John's brother. Yes, indeed. It explains a lot. Both very pretty men. I tried to help John once, too. But he didn't get the message, or maybe just didn't fall for it. Gilles de Rais wanted to take him for his own, you know. You and your brothers, you're all out there making trouble of one kind or another. You look nothing like them yourself, mistress."

"No. They look like our father. I don't. Thank the gods I don't."

"I hear Caedon caught up with this John and dealt with him."

"Yes," said Eris.

"Caedon is a useful man, in his way," said Ailys. "But he has his blind spots. One of them is me. Did you know that?" When Eris didn't reply, she went on. "He underestimates me. When you run complaining to him about me, you might tell him that."

"He'll laugh, if I tell him that."

"I've no doubt of it, girl. Silly man that he is. He's on his high horse now. He won't be up there forever."

Ailys sat immobile while her ladies in waiting put the final touches to hair, face, gown.

"Finished?" she said with a flash of impatience.

They murmured and bowed, backing away from her out of her rooms.

She swept from them and took the arm of her steward.

When they reached the great hall of Tam Fort, he announced her in loud and formal terms.

Every head turned to her.

The steward led her across the room to her seat at King Audemar's left. At his right sat his most important guest, King Hakkon Hardaxe of the Ice-realm.

Ailys allowed herself a very brief glance in Hakkon's direction. Their eyes met. He acknowledged her with the slightest of nods.

"My queen, here is our brother monarch, King Hakkon," said Audemar.

"I am most pleased to make your acquaintance, Your Majesty," said Hakkon. "The bards are not wrong. Your beauty surpasses any lady's I've seen in the entirety of your realm."

"A pretty compliment, Your Highness," said Ailys.

So they played out a little mummery version of a first meeting.

At Hakkon's side sat his two sons, the eldest, the crown prince Thorfinn, pale and delicate-looking, and his nine-year-old brother Ansgar. Their mother, Hakkon's queen, was an invalid, the victim of some wasting disease, and never traveled from her seclusion in a castle of her own away from Hakkon's capital.

Hakkon was speaking the language of the Sceptered Isle. Ailys looked over at the boys, wondering how much they understood. They both looked bored and sleepy.

After the tiresomely many courses of the banquet, after the pastimes that ended the evening, Audemar's menservants helped him off to his bedchamber in his usual state of near-insensibility.

Hakkon and Ailys sat close together at the hearth stones. "It's good to see you again, Your Highness," murmured Ailys.

"You as well," he said.

"We may talk here without anyone overhearing," she said, waving the servants away. Not before she had appointed one to show Hakkon's sons to their room.

"I value our alliance, Your Highness," said Hakkon, once everyone was out of earshot.

"As do I. Our interests are aligned, I believe."

"I hinted this to you in Lunds-fort, my dear lady, but let me emphasize it now. My information tells me your realm is on the brink of civil war. I'm glad we have this occasion to talk of it further."

"The Rising," she said dismissively.

"No, they're much too weak to pose a threat."

"Who, then?" said Ailys, trying to stifle her surprise.

"Your husband's underling Caedon will soon take arms against his king," said Hakkon.

Ailys felt her lips curving into a smile. *You'll be the most powerful woman in the realm*, Caedon had once promised her, the liar, *and I'll be the most powerful man.* "That has long been his plan," she told Hakkon. "I confess I hadn't seen it coming so soon, though."

"You and Caedon are allies?" Hakkon's voice was careful. He watched her with careful eyes.

"No, my king. Once we were. No longer."

"Good," said Hakkon. "You and I are allies."

"Yes," said Ailys. "That is my dearest wish."

To herself, she said, *Yes, Caedon, I will be the most powerful woman in the realm. The most powerful person. No thanks to you.*

"Caedon thought he was using me," she told Hakkon. "But he was wrong. I was using him. And I still am."

"Caedon, though. He has the backing of Gilles de Rais."

"I'm aware of that, Your Majesty. I have my own arrangements with the baron. Arrangements Caedon knows nothing about."

"Excellent," said Hakkon.

Ailys stared at Hakkon appraisingly. *Lure him into my bed?* she thought. *No, she decided. He's not a man to be lured with such tactics.*

But where was he vulnerable?

His sons, she suddenly realized.

"You know, my king—" She hesitated. "If anything should happen to Audemar, he and I are childless, and I fear for my future."

"Could you marry this Caedon and see to him that way?" Hakkon suggested.

She shuddered. She tamped down her rage at the very suggestion. She saw Hakkon was a completely practical man. He did not mean any insult. It was one among many possible solutions to their mutual problem, as far as he was concerned.

"No, my king. He is of common stock, a jumped-up lord. A mushroom gentle. Besides, he is too dangerous to fob off with some marriage."

"I hear he conspires to marry Artur's daughter."

"As to that. Yes, he may. Then he'll use the girl. But he knows full well he won't be able to use me to consolidate his power. And I know too well how foolish it would be for me to put myself in any way into his hands and under his control. No, that can't be the way of it. It would not serve my interests, and it would not serve yours, Your Majesty."

Hakkon was nodding. "Yes, you have the right of it, I see." He looked at her thoughtfully. "A marriage between the two of us would be just the thing. Alas. I have a wife."

Well, now, thought Ailys. *Does the man have scruples? An ailing wife—easy enough to find a solution.*

But anyway, she thought. *I want my own power. Not to share it by acquiring it through a husband. That's no power at all, just the shell of it. As I know very well.*

"So then," Hakkon continued. "Marriage is maybe not the solution. Did you know there are precedents for a woman to rule as monarch on her own?"

"It's not the usual thing, I believe," she said.

"If we were allies and co-equal monarchs, I would value such an alliance," he said.

"An excellent suggestion, Your Majesty," she breathed. Between the support of Gilles de Rais and the support of Hakkon, such a position was not out of the question. Not at all.

And as she looked over at Hakkon, she saw something else. *I've disarmed him,* she thought. *He imagined I was about to hint, ever so delicately, that he might do away with his wife. But I've done no such thing.*

She saw she had gained his trust, at least as much trust as a man like him could give to a woman like her.

And she laughed to herself, because she knew the nature of his soft underbelly. But she said only, "Shall we work toward a solution like that, Your Majesty? Myself as monarch and your ally? No matter how unconventional others may find it?"

"Yes," he said.

"Excellent. And now I'll have the servants show you to your bed. You must be weary, my king. I saw how your boys were half-asleep at board, the poor sweetlings."

"Ah, they are fine sons," said Hakkon.

"They are indeed. Thorfinn will be king after you. I imagine you are already looking out for a wife for him. I could perhaps share a few suggestions with you, if you wish it," she said.

See there? she beamed at him silently. *If you had one lingering doubt, that despite our age difference I might have suggested Thorfinn for myself, I've disarmed that suspicion too.*

"I have a few young women in mind for him, of course," said Hakkon. "Including Artur's daughter, by the way. But I'd welcome any suggestions of yours, my dear lady."

"I doubt the lady Diera would be a good match, my king. She comes with too much baggage, too many suspicions."

"You're probably right, Your Highness. Any other ladies of this realm?"

"I can't think of a one. But in the Baronies, there are several suitable young women." *Here's a good matter to take to Gilles,* she thought.

Hakkon was nodding at her approvingly. "We will make excellent allies, my dear lady," he said to her.

"That is my fondest wish, Your Majesty," she purred.

"Thorfinn is delicate, like his mother," said Hakkon after a moment. He looked brooding into the fire.

"Did you know that I once had in my employ a famous healer of the Baronies? She met with an unfortunate end at the hands of some ruffians several years back, but she communicated many of her healing techniques to me, and I still have many of her potions. I'll send one home with you, for your prince, if I may. A few drops a day will do him a world of good."

Will take him right out of this world, she said to herself.

Ailys's heart was pierced at the look of gratitude the king darted at her. *You poor man,* she thought. *You're like all the others.*

The younger boy, she realized, would be much more promising material for her, once his father and the older boy were out of the way. She had caught this boy's eye at board. He was young, but his eye was bold and knowing. It was clear he understood not a word spoken by his elders, but in some deeper way, he knew what was going on around him.

Ailys recognized talent like that, even in the egg. *I can shape someone like that*, she thought. *And not tomorrow, not next year, but sometime, when the right time comes, he'll be an instrument, a weapon I will wield.*

"I will take my way off to bed," said Hakkon. "A stimulating conversation, Your Highness. But now I am weary."

"I feel we have struck a profitable bargain between us, and with many more benefits to come," said Ailys, rising and motioning to a servant to come to lead King Hakkon Hardaxe to his bedchamber.

"Indeed, I believe we have, most gracious queen," said Hakkon.

Now Ailys, too, was weary. Her women settled her in her bed.

As she drifted to sleep, she thought of that lad of The Rising who had dropped so unaccountably in her lap and had so unaccountably departed her grasp. A pity, she thought. Just when she was coming up with a novel way of making him her own. A potion Labinia had showed her once. When she had him secure, she might have had a reliable inside source to the workings of The Rising.

But Hakkon and his sons had just opened new vistas to her, much more important than the gnat-bite of The Rising, which was really no threat at all.

A pretty lad escaped from her, a new alliance opening its riches before her. All in all, she thought, a worthy trade.

She decided she'd go to Gilles de Rais in the next turning of the moon or so. Gilles had promised her some things. He'd given her a potion to make her beauty flourish. He'd trained her in its use.

By now, her skills surpassed his dead witch Labinia's, and her even more skillful sister Vigilia's. Far surpassed them both.

She'd use this potion to enhance her beauty, and she'd acquire the young prince Ansgar for her own purposes. She'd lead him down a merry path, until one day she'd lead him instead into a dark wood from which there was no returning.

Shrewd trading, she thought.

She looked at herself in the mirror on the wall. *And I'm the shrewdest of them all.*

CHAPTER EIGHTEEN

A Strange and Bewildering Place

Caedon

H ere you go," said Caedon to Rafe. "Your first test. You and Mistress Bertrys have the evening to yourselves. Go in." He urged Rafe through the door of a suite of rooms in his manor.

"This is where you kept Diera," said Rafe, looking around him.

"Indeed. So these rooms will seem like familiar and comfortable surroundings to you."

"And you want me to fuck the poor girl here," said Rafe, his eyes hard.

"If you care to be crude about it, yes," said Caedon. "Take all the time you need. I'll let you out at dawn." He fussed with Rafe's clothing. "There. You look quite presentable."

"What if I can't?"

"Then your usefulness to me will be over, and you and I will end our arrangement."

"A strong sop to desire," said Rafe.

"Why, Rafe, you've become cynical. Dour, too. I remember a time when you bedded every woman who came across your path."

Rafe stood silent.

"Which will it be?" said Caedon after a moment.

"Send her in," he said.

"That's my gallant lad. Think how pleased Diera will be. By the happy outcome. You by her side still. Less pleased by the means, perhaps."

"Suppose I tell this girl, this Bertyrs, how she's being used."

"Suppose you do." Caedon shrugged. "Let me manage her. She'll see things my way. There will be a rich reward, for her, if you get her with child."

"It seems your object is to kill every possible spark of desire I may have for her, and watch me fail. You could do that more quickly and easily by ending it now, Caedon."

"If you wish." Caedon overlooked the insolent bravado. It was more delicious to watch the lad squirm. All his and Diera's pathetic little plans for escape would be smashed if he didn't cooperate. Caedon knew it, and Rafe knew he knew it.

"Very well. I'm ready," said Rafe.

The stony look he threw in Caedon's direction plucked at Caedon's heart. He realized he was really quite fond of the lad. Caedon merely smiled, though, and backed from the room.

He gestured to a servant, who soon returned with the little Bertrys on his arm.

"My lord," said Bertrys, curtseying.

"You may go," said Caedon to the servant. "Now, Bertrys. You know what to do."

"Let him make love to me," she said breathlessly.

"That's right. But understand something about our poor Leofric. He is misguided. He believes his heart is pledged to his mistress."

"The princess?" Her eyes widened.

"Yes, so he is a tormented man. Of course his love for her can never be. This is not widely known, but I don't mind confiding in you, mistress. Master Leofric has been in my service since his boyhood. For a long time, I have felt an almost brotherly affection for the lad. I understand where his best interests lie. In fact, he puts himself in danger, daring to love so high. It would please me greatly if the regard and tenderness of a good woman made him see better sense and gave him a chance for a better life. Any child of his and yours would receive my patronage. Of course, mistress—" Caedon paused delicately. "You yourself will receive my patronage. Tomorrow, I will interview you and ask for your impressions and suggestions. Between us, maybe we'll be able to help the lad and steer him in a better direction. If he gets you with child, the honorable thing for Leofric to do will be to wed you. You may be sure I'll see that arranged."

Betrys curtsied to him again. When she rose, she met his eye. She understood perfectly what she needed to do, and why. *Maybe not entirely why*, he revised. *But she understands very well that I have an interest in seeing this thing done, a very great interest, and she sees she'll be richly rewarded for bringing it about.*

Then she surprised him.

"My lord, I will most willingly take your guidance in this matter. But may I ask—" she hesitated, blushing.

"Please ask your question," said Caedon kindly, thinking *What in the Nine?*

"How is the king? How is it with him?"

"Audemar?" said Caedon blankly.

"Yes. Is this the king's wish as well?"

Caedon couldn't hide his consternation and amazement. She was desperate to please Audemar in any way she could, even if it meant abasing herself in this way.

Audemar, of all people, had inspired such devotion.

Caedon saw instantly how he could use what he had just learned about her. "My dear young lady. I hoped to spare any delicate feelings you might have on that score. But yes. Yes, this is the king's wish. I'm merely his humble agent."

"Then I will do my utmost," she said solemnly. Her eyes shone with love and firm resolve.

He held the door for her, and she went in.

Nine Spheres, thought Caedon. The world lying helpless beneath those whirling nine was indeed a strange and bewildering place, and the strangest object in it had to be the human heart.

In the morning, Caedon unbarred the door to the suite of rooms.

Rafe came stumbling out, disheveled and furious. "Do I have your leave to go back to the castle, my lord?" he said between tight lips. "Or do I need to make a report?"

"No need," said Caedon. He took Rafe by the shoulder and stared into his eyes. Rafe's own hostile eyes met his full on. "Careful, Rafe," Caedon murmured. "Looks like you've done well, but you're only temporarily in my good graces. What have I told you about never looking me in the eye?"

"Stuff it, Caedon," said Rafe with a bitter laugh. "You got what you wanted."

"Did I? We'll have to make sure of that. Be here at the same time tonight. In the meantime, get some sleep." He gave Rafe a none too gentle shove, wondering how far Rafe's impulse to fight back might go. But Rafe turned away from him with a weary gesture. His footsteps echoed hollowly down the corridor.

Caedon stepped into the little outer chamber. He waited with patience.

After a while, Bertrys came out of the inner bedchamber, patting her clothing, smiling and dreamy-eyed.

"My lord," she said, startled. She sank into a curtsey.

"There's a lovely garden just outside," Caedon said to her. "Let's go there. I want to hear how everything went last night. The servants will bring something to break our fast.

Over berries and hot possets, he heard her account of the previous evening.

"I could see Master Leofric was angry and uneasy," she began, sipping at her posset. "But he was perfectly courteous."

"And?"

"I suppose you want to know whether we performed the act of love."

"Yes." He had to keep from snapping at her or slapping her face.

"We did, my lord."

"Good," he said, breathing easier. "Well done, mistress." He was on fire to know how Rafe had managed it, as distasteful as the lad seemed to have found the task. Caedon glanced at Bertrys's easy, golden beauty and wondered whether, in spite of himself, Rafe had actually been roused to pleasure. She was certainly not to his own taste, the quite narrow zone of his taste, but Caedon knew she would be to many. She was exactly the way Audemar liked them. He wondered how Audemar could have given her up.

Suddenly he realized the probable answer. She had gotten jealous.

"Master Leofric is really a most kind-hearted man," Bertrys was saying.

What a sentimental fopdoodle Rafe is. So he bedded her out of pity, Caedon mused.

Not quite. He did. Then again, he didn't. He was helped into that state of mind by Bertrys and her clever ways. She knew which side her loaf was buttered on.

"All it took was a few tears," Bertrys was saying complacently. Her small neat tongue licked at the posset like a cat's.

"You are a treasure, my dear," Caedon breathed. "And speaking of treasure, I have something here with me I'm sure you will like."

From beside himself on the seat, he took a small carved box and presented it to her.

She opened it and screamed with delight.

This is going well, thought Caedon. *I'm going to enjoy this.*

CHAPTER NINETEEN

Right and Good

Dru

"What we're doing is so dangerous, Elsebet. I'm terrified all the time. Terrified for you, and terrified for the girls," Dru murmured against Elsebet's shoulder.

She pulled him over closer to her in the loft where they slept under the rafters of their small cabin. "I love you, Dru," she whispered.

"And I love you. I loved you the moment I saw you, and I've never stopped."

"When I first saw you, I nearly dropped the ewer of mead I was carrying around to Fylkir's guests," she said, keeping her voice low. The girls were sleeping just below.

"The Children meant it to be."

"The Children." She stirred beside him uneasily.

"My darling. You don't have to believe in Them just because I do."

"I know," she said.

"You should make the trip over to the Lady's temple, in the market town. I'll take you myself."

"Dru. I'm not entirely sure I believe in the Lady either."

He rose on one elbow and peered at her. He could just make out the shining of her eyes in the dim light of moon and stars filtering in through the chinks in the wattle and daub. Deep inside one part of him, he made a note to repair those chinks before the next winter season.

"Do you believe in nothing?"

"I believe in you." Then she cried out, "What kind of god would allow John to be torn apart by that fiend?" She lowered her voice. "What that man did to him." She shuddered in his arms. He held her.

After a moment, she said, "I believe in something. I do. I just can't name it," she said.

"That's fine, then. When I cross that river to the Land of the Dead, my Child will make sure you cross to the same place too."

"Don't say that, Dru."

"Elsebet. This could happen. We know that."

"After what happened to Johnny. Yes, we do," she said.

"Are you afraid?" he asked her, his heart stopped with love and fear for her.

"Of course I am. More afraid we'll be separated. More afraid for the girls." After a moment she nestled closer to him. "And afraid now for the other one, son or daughter," she whispered sleepily to him.

"Elsebet! How long have you known?"

"I wasn't sure. But now I'm pretty sure," she said.

"My darling." He covered her face with little kisses. "My dearest, dearest one."

Soon they were kissing in earnest. He pulled her underneath him, and she stirred against him, breathing quicker.

He stopped. "Suppose we hurt the baby."

"Early days, darling. We won't hurt him."

A son, Dru thought. Then he thought of his daughters. A *daughter*. Whichever the Children vouchsafed them, he'd love that child with everything in him.

In the heat of summer, they were sleeping naked. He ran his hands down her flanks. He moved to her breasts and kissed first one, then the other, gently taking her nipples into his mouth. He was already roused; he felt himself stiffen hard against her now. She rose to meet him as he entered her, first tenderly, then urgently.

When he heard her little cry of pleasure, he released himself into her, burying his face into her breasts, not able to suppress a deep groan of ecstasy.

"Shh, the children," she laughed softly into his shoulder.

He lay spent across her, fondling her and kissing her.

"Nine Spheres, I love you," he whispered.

They lay quietly, glistening with sweat in the heat of the summer night.

She rolled half away from him, and he stroked her hair and nestled her against him.

"Dru," she whispered, after a while.

He was half-asleep. He shook the sleep away. "What, darling?"

"Suppose we could take the children somewhere safer."

"You mean move? Give up these palatial surroundings we've worked so hard for?" he said lightly.

"No, just take the children somewhere. Somewhere safer."

Now he was fully awake. "Where?"

"To Cwen, maybe?"

"Huh," he said. He thought about his life without them, how empty it would be. "I'd miss them terribly."

"I would, too. But I fear for them."

"Maybe we could take Jillian," he said dubiously. "But you know—" He thought it over. "You're going to need Mirin, when the baby comes."

She sighed beside him. "Yes, you're right," she said. "I'll need someone here."

They both knew there was no one in the village they'd be able to rely on.

"Poor Mirin," he said. "She hasn't had much of a girlhood."

"I had none at all," said Elsebet.

Dru felt the familiar surge of anger that always took him, whenever he thought of Fylkir and what he had done to Elsebet. Taking her to wife when she was just barely old enough to be a mother. A nasty old man who used her hard. Getting her away from him was a sacred task to Dru. He knew John had always worried about it. Taking another man's wife. It never worried Dru.

"I want something better for our children," said Dru.

He thought uneasily about his lands and his manor on the western coast. If he hadn't joined The Rising, they'd be living there in comfort. More than comfort. He had been one of the richest men in the realm. All he would have had to do was look away from Audemar's vile practices and oppressions. He and Elsebet could have lived out their days in ease. They could have made an easeful home for their children.

Instead, he had found he couldn't look away. So he had lost everything. Everything the world held dear, anyhow. "Are you sorry we—"

"No," she said, stopping his mouth with her hand. "Never. I want something better for our children, too. Not this. But I want something better for everyone's children, not just mine."

"We're foolish dreamers, both of us," he said, taking her into his arms again. "When they come to adulthood and realize, will our girls ever be able to forgive us?"

"We're giving them something better," whispered Elsebet. "We're doing our best for them. They may not have the luxuries an earldom would have given them, but they are growing up loved. And look at Mirin. She knows her letters, thanks to you. Thanks to you, so do I, and with both of us teaching her, she has become quite a reader."

"She's so quick," Dru said with pride. "I wish we had more books for her. But you're right, my dearest wife. Our daughters have two parents who treasure them. How many can say that?" *Love*, he thought. Riches beyond price. But when he thought of the danger they were all in, he wondered if the price were too high.

Before sunrise, they'd made love again. He decided that no, it was not too high, and yes, he'd pay the price.

Around the hearth fire in the morning, they were sleepy but smiling.

After the porridge, Mirin took out the rebec Dru had made for her and began to practice.

"You are making beautiful music, my daughter," said Elsebet, listening.

Dru glanced at her over their daughter's head. Mirin knew her letters, and she had this gift of music the gods and Johnny between them had given her. He saw Elsebet's eyes, too, were shining with wonder and love.

"Johnny knew something important about Mirin," he murmured to Elsebet when he bent to collect her porridge bowl with the others to take them to the little stream behind the cottage to wash.

He picked up their bucket as he went, and drew enough water for Elsebet, so she'd be able to do the day's cooking and cleaning.

"Now I suppose I'll get the hoe and head out to the fields," he said, when he came back to set the bucket down carefully just outside the cottage door.

Mirin wandered out in her boys' things.

"Going hunting?" he said.

She nodded.

He dipped up a ladle of water for her, and she drank it.

From inside, he heard Elsebet singing.

Bring me a boat that can carry two, she sang. *And both shall row, my love and I.*

"You have your mother's voice, Mirin," he said to his daughter. "You have her gift of song."

"Will Johnny be back soon?" she said.

A cold hand seized Dru's heart. "No," he said softly.

"When, then?"

"I—" he began, at a loss what to say. How to tell her. The world was a cruel place underneath the Spheres.

"Maybe this winter," she said happily. "Maybe he'll come back to spend the entire winter with us, just as he did last winter."

Dru couldn't speak.

Then she stopped and her hand flew to her mouth. Her eyes filled with tears.

"What is it, sweetheart?" he said.

"He won't be coming back, will he?"

He pulled her close. "Are you having one of those feelings you get?"

"Yes," she whispered.

"Don't be afraid," he said. "It's the Children's gift."

"It doesn't feel like a gift," she said.

The mood passed.

She drank more from the bucket, gave him a quick kiss, and moved off down the meadow with her traps and her fishing line.

"Stay out of the river, child of the Child of Sea," he called after her. "Your mother will skin you alive if you come home dripping wet."

She looked back over her shoulder at him and grinned and waved. They both knew Elsebet would do no such thing.

Then Jillian was out in the dooryard, launching herself at her father like a zinging little projectile from somebody's sling.

"Oww!" he exclaimed, catching her and tossing her into the air while she screeched with delight. He hoisted her up onto his shoulders and ran around the dooryard with her while they both pretended he was her horsie.

Elsebet came into the dooryard and stood, hands on hips, shaking her head and laughing.

"Get down here, demon-spawn," she said, reaching up for Jillie. "Look at the snarls in your hair. You'll need to sit still while I comb them all out."

Dru handed Jillie off to Elsebet and bent to retrieve his hoe. "I'd better get some work done before the blackbirds make off with our entire crop," he said, pulling her over to him for a kiss.

Then he stopped. Jillie had escaped from her mother and was running in the sunshine, waving her poppet over her little fair head like a flag.

"Elsebet. What we talked of last night." He sat down at their hearth, and she sat beside him. He stared for a long time into the fire. "I know you'll need help, when the baby comes. But you were right last night. We've chosen a risky path, and for the right reasons. But we can't risk the girls, not after John's warning." He realized now. "We'll send them both to Cwen, and when your time comes, you'll go to Cwen yourself."

"To be separated! No, Dru!"

"Yes. And you'll be with our children there, keeping them safe."

"But you won't be safe."

"I'm not safe, Elsebet. We both know it."

"You fought in a battle I didn't even know you were fighting. You could have been killed, and I wouldn't have even known it."

"But you and the girls would have been safe. And John was with us at that battle. He was our weapon." How could he tell her what that meant? What John meant?

"He's not with you now," she said quietly.

"No." He turned to her and took her hands in his. "Do this for me, Elsebet. Do it for our children."

"Very well," she said, and he saw the tears start into her eyes. "But not til the harvest is in. We're all needed to bring in the harvest, and after that, I'll be big with this baby. Then we'll do it."

"Then we'll do it," he agreed.

As he walked away under the summer sun, the fears that had plagued him the night before began fading away.

They'd made a decision. The children would be safe, and Elsebet would be safe. The world underneath the Spheres was right and good.

He wondered to himself what he should have said to Mirin, though. How he should have answered her question about John.

Maybe she didn't have to know it, what happened to John. Maybe he could protect Mirin from the world's cruelty, at least a little while longer.

But then, he thought, thinking of that moment the force he could only think of as her second sense had gripped her. *In some place deep inside her, she already knows*

CHAPTER TWENTY

Bought and Paid For

Caedon

Everything was going well. As he sat before Treddian's fire, exchanging niceties with the earl's lady, talking politics with Treddian, Caedon was aware of Diera, icy in her disapproval, sitting on the other side of the hearth with Treddian's daughters. A little way off from her, Bertrys plied her distaff. Standing stiffly beside the little maid, Rafe.

Caedon stood up and stretched. "High time I was heading back to my own manor," he said.

"Do you want to borrow Leofric?" said Treddian, with a twinkle in his eye.

"Yes, if you will. Oh, and Bertrys," he said. "Mistress, I beg you to come with me, if your lady can spare you. My cook has a recipe she has promised to share with you. My lady Diera, if you'll permit—"

"Yes," said Diera shortly.

Bertrys rose from her place by the hearth, dimpling.

The earl's lady gave Caedon a wink. Treddian grinned.

"I'll bring your maid back to you early tomorrow," Caedon said to Diera.

Diera didn't bother answering him.

"You can share Mildburg's maid, for the night. You won't mind, will you, Mildburg?" said the earl's lady to her oldest daughter.

"Oh, Momma," said that young woman with a petulant toss of the head.

"I'm sorry, Mildburg. It wasn't my choice," said Diera evenly.

"Such a selfish girl," the earl's lady sighed. "Surely you won't mind a single night, daughter."

Mildburg was silent.

Caedon reminded himself to bring the girl a gift.

He summoned Bertrys and Rafe to follow him. They made their way to the stables, and all got into Caedon's closed cart. The groom waiting for Caedon drove off with them.

The three of them were silent, although Bertrys couldn't stop smiling.

At the doors to the manor, Caedon bade both of them good night and left them together.

After a while, he stole back to the suite of rooms and quietly let himself into the outer chamber. He listened at the door of the inner chamber.

He could hear raised voices.

I hope the wench knows what to do, he thought.

Moving stealthily so as to make no noise, he crept to a spot further down the wall, where a tapestry hung. He pushed it aside and squinted into the inner chamber through the peephole concealed behind the tapestry.

Rafe, in only his trousers, was striding about the bedchamber, clearly distraught. "I'll not be forced," Caedon heard him say in a clear, angry voice.

"You are a terrible man! You don't love me." Bertrys's voice throbbed with unshed tears.

"Well, no," he heard Rafe bite out.

"Don't you see? This is a good thing between us, Leofric."

"It's not."

"Say you care about me."

"I don't."

Caedon pressed his forehead in despair against the wall. He began grasping at alternate strategies. Maybe she wouldn't have to get herself with child. Maybe if others just saw Rafe around her and thought—

Then he heard Rafe's voice raised again, and he put his eye back to the peephole.

"Don't you see how they're using you?"

"They hope I'll help you. That's all."

"Help me." The bitter sounds of Rafe's laughter spilled from him.

"Sit here by me," said the girl.

Rafe kept up his pacing, coming so near the other side of the peephole that Caedon flinched back. It was hard to see the small hole from the other side, though, concealed in a knot in the wood planking of the walls. And in the state Rafe was in, Caedon was pretty sure he wouldn't spot it.

"Shall I massage your temples, Leofric? It's very soothing. We don't need to do anything. Just sit here by me and let me help you. Your head aches, I warrant."

"It does," Rafe muttered.

"Sit here."

That's right, breathed Caedon. *Go to her. Sit beside her.* His own task was clear but delicate. Keep Rafe strong enough to tup the girl, but weak enough so he was unsteady on his legs, aching and feverish.

She had him on the bed now. She was leaning over him.

"Let me show you something I learned of the king," she said.

"No!" said Rafe.

No, thought Caedon. The wrong note to strike. Even from across the room, he caught the revulsion in Rafe's voice.

But he was wrong. She had the lad helpless now, and he did his duty.

Caedon slumped down on the bench in the outer chamber. *Nine Spheres,* he thought. *Rafe may not have the stamina for this, and I might not, either.*

There was a stirring inside the bedchamber, and Caedon got himself quickly outside it. He leaned against the wall, trying for an unconcerned look.

Rafe burst through the door. "Dark Ones take you, Caedon," he snarled, and then he was away down the corridor.

Caedon found himself laughing helplessly. He wasn't laughing at Rafe. He was laughing at himself. Gaining Rafe's cooperation had turned into hard work. He got a grip on himself and pushed open the door to the outer room.

Bertrys was standing just outside the bedchamber, her eyes snapping, wrapped in a fur robe.

"Mistress Bertrys—" Caedon began.

"He's impossible!" she said. "He insults me, my lord. He calls me vile names."

"You want to give up on him, then?" said Caedon.

She calmed down. A small smile began to play about her lips. "No," she said.

"Good girl," Caedon said. Then, "I brought you a little something."

A turning of the moon later, Caedon was in the small garden beside the suite of rooms where Bertrys and Rafe enacted their nightly struggle.

Some nights Bertrys prevailed. Some nights Rafe did. Caedon prayed to whatever gods there might be that each night would find Bertrys the victor. He wanted her to succeed with Rafe. Of course he did. That was the largest part of it. But there was another reason. When Rafe won out, Caedon knew he would face a long fatiguing session with the lad, bringing him to see his duty and the consequences if he didn't do it.

Suppose I fuck her, he had thought to himself on more than one occasion. *If I'm the one who gets her with child, but everyone thinks it's Rafe, won't the outcome be the same?*

But then he'd have to get himself somehow in the mood to do it—as difficult in its own way as getting Rafe in the mood. *Why should I have to do it?* he thought resentfully. Rafe needed to do his duty.

There was another reason. Caedon's mind shied away from what it was. To bring himself to bed the girl, he'd inevitably think about those other times. The deception he had practiced on Diera. And if he thought of that, he'd inevitably think of— His guard would be down, and he'd think of it. He was sure he would.

Here he stopped himself in a panic. He couldn't allow himself the luxury of thinking about it, that thing hidden deep in his mind. Not without carefully setting up the proper wards. If Gilles were to turn his attention to Caedon, just at that moment, all would be lost. So when his mind turned of its own accord in that dangerous direction, Caedon deliberately moved his attention to some neutral object. He was becoming quite skilled at doing so.

Caedon sat in the little garden now, though, and felt a thrill of anticipation. Rafe and Bertrys were both coming to see him this morning. They had both stayed the entire night in the little bedchamber, and now they had something to tell him. Caedon was pretty sure he knew what it had to be.

The late summer flowers burgeoned over the trellises and stone walls of the garden. Their scent was delightful.

As the two came in and he pointed them to seats across from his own, Caedon suddenly raised his hand. "Listen," he said.

They sat still and all three of them strained to hear.

From far away came the faint call of a bird.

"The last cuckoo of the summer," he said, closing his eyes and smiling.

"They say some hear the cuckoo into early harvest-tide," Bertrys said after a moment.

"That would be something to remember," said Caedon, opening his eyes. "By now, almost all those birds have flown."

"Where do you think they go, my lord?"

"Wherever they go, I suppose," said Caedon. "Who knows?"

Rafe sat silently frowning.

"Well, now," said Caedon, his tone turning brisk. "Here the two of you are. What do you have to say to me."

"I'm with child!" Bertrys said. "And Master Leofric is here to ask you something."

"What's that, Leofric."

Rafe's voice was ironic. "I think you know, my lord."

"Indeed no. Tell me, young master." *I'm going to force you to say it,* Caedon thought. After this, he'd be able to feed again. Really feed. He felt his blood beginning to rouse to it.

"I must ask your lordship's permission to marry this girl," said Rafe dully.

"You see how he treats me, your lordship," Bertrys burst out.

"Now, child," said Caedon, giving Rafe a sharp look of warning. "You mustn't mind him. It's just his manner."

"Well, it's an ill manner," said Bertrys. She looked on the point of tears.

"No matter, mistress. He'll wed you—won't you, Leofric?—and all will be well."

Rafe said nothing.

"You have my permission to marry this lovely young girl, Master Leofric," said Caedon, "And I will give the bride a rich marriage gift. And the child a gift as well, when it is born. Perhaps you'll name the child after me."

Rafe gave him a weary, hostile stare.

You'll pay for that, my lad, thought Caedon with relish.

"Here's a little preliminary gift," he said to Bertrys, passing her a small leathern bag of coin. "For bridal trimmings and cloth to make yourself a new kirtle."

"Now that I'm bought and paid for, my lord, may I return to the castle?" said Rafe.

"Indeed no," said Caedon. "I'll need you here with me a bit longer, Master Leofric. But I'll call the cart so that you may go back to your lady, Mistress Bertrys."

"Thank you, my lord," said Bertrys, ignoring Rafe's tone, all smiles now.

But, Caedon saw with satisfaction, Rafe was looking at his shoes in an attitude of resignation. And, Caedon saw, when Rafe raised his eyes to Caedon's, of dread.

CHAPTER TWENTY-ONE

Justice Under the Spheres

Diera

D iera had gotten the earl's lady's agreement that Master Leofric could take her out on one of the drives she loved so much.

"And now that you have Mistress Bertrys with you, I'm much easier in my mind about your drives with that young man," said her ladyship. At Diera's startled look, she continued, "Now, Your Highness, I was sure you'd never forget yourself and your position, and of course Master Leofric has our good Lord Caedon's confidence—" she paused delicately. "I'm sure you never noticed it, but the way that young man looked at you—well, some days it made me wonder."

"Oh, your ladyship!" Diera exclaimed.

"Now, now, dear child. All is well. Just a foolish notion young men sometimes get. It was clear there was no harm in the lad. And now he is hard taken with that little Bertrys, and now they will marry. What could be better?"

"What indeed?" Diera murmured.

"When I heard the news about the two of them, I was hoping she'd soon be a wife. How diverting, to plan a little wedding for her. But that lad. I confess, Your Highness, I worry on your little maid's behalf, marrying a man so delicate in health. Master Leofric has had another of his episodes, I hear. He seems to have recovered, though, if he's well enough to drive you around the countryside. You and his blooming bride-to-be. Perhaps they'll soon be wed after all." She gave Diera a little hug. "Go out now and enjoy these last fine days. I'd go myself, the weather is so lovely. But no, I have to see to Mildburg's arrangements. Her betrothal will be announced very soon."

"I'm glad to hear it, my lady."

"Well," the earl's lady concluded, "Ill health or no, Master Leofric will be a father soon, from the looks of things, so he and Bertrys will have to be wed soon." She stopped and put her hand on Diera's arm. "My dear. You didn't know?"

Diera shook her head mutely.

"My dear child," said the lady, dropping her voice. "I hope you haven't conceived an affection for this lad."

Diera shook her head again. "I'm just surprised."

"No? All for the best, then. A married couple in your service. Very proper."

"Yes," whispered Diera.

When Diera went out to the stables for Rafe to hand her into the cart, though, Bertrys was nowhere around.

"Where is Bertrys?" she summoned up the self-possession to say, in a placid voice. "She was just with me. We were to meet here at the stables for our excursion."

"She was taken sick, my lady," said Rafe, holding out a hand.

She accepted his help and stepped up into the cart. Then she released his hand as if it had turned unexpectedly into a poisonous serpent.

Her cheeks burned with rage. "They say a woman's stomach is delicate at times like these," she said, trying to control the mordant that had crept into her voice.

"Yes, well," said Rafe. His tone was dry. "Perhaps that's why she's sick, then." A dangerous look had come into his own eye.

Before Diera could exclaim, he was on the wagon seat and had whipped the horses into an unaccustomedly brisk trot toward the castle gates.

As they barreled down the road away from the castle, Diera closed her eyes and clenched her hands hard on the rails of the cart. But tears of anger forced themselves past her eyelids anyhow, however hard she tried to stop them, and rolled down her cheeks. She dashed them away impatiently with her hand.

She wasn't paying attention to their surroundings at all. Not to the fine weather around her, just the tumultuous inner weather, when she realized Rafe had driven down the little-used lane where they stopped when they needed to talk. He pulled up under the trees and turned on the wagon seat to look back at her. His eyes burned into hers. She was shocked at how unwell he looked.

"Why are we stopping here?" she made herself say coldly.

"We need to talk, my lady."

"Do we?"

"You know we do. You know they forced me. Caedon forced me."

"Is that even possible?"

He blushed deeply. "Unfortunately yes, my lady."

"Well, then. Here we are. What do you want to say?"

Without asking, he had clambered over into the cart with her and reached out to take her hands.

She let him, hating herself.

"Diera. I despise this, what I've had to do. We talked about this, you know. This is the very reason I told you I needed to end it. This." He smiled bitterly.

"Oh, Rafe," she said. "I didn't think—"

"No, you didn't, did you?" His voice turned suddenly savage. "But let's leave that. I need to get you out. I've gotten word to Avery, and he's working on something, but I'm not sure he'll be able to act fast enough. Remember what I told you? How carefully you're watched? The roads are watched. If we can slip through the forest, maybe we can do it. Maybe."

Diera raised her eyes to his, somberly. "I beg your pardon, Rafe. I truly do." Her eyes filled with tears. "I can see by looking at you that Caedon has been at you again, doing whatever he does to you. You're in more danger than I am."

"But I'm not the heir to Artur," said Rafe. "So it doesn't matter as much, for me. It matters for you, the danger you're in. You're Artur's heir," he insisted.

"I'm not his heir. I'm a woman," said Diera, surprised.

"We're looking for your brothers, lady. That too. But you have probably thought this yourself. I've no time for niceties, so I'll say it outright. Your brothers are probably dead. You're your father's heir. The heir to the throne."

"That can't be, Rafe. By law it can't."

"The law is wrong, Your Highness," said Rafe. "And we all know it."

"I'm no queen."

"You will be, if there's any justice under the Spheres."

"I don't believe it, Rafe," said Diera. "I don't believe there is."

"There's something bigger at stake than kings or queens. But if we're to fight it, we puny beings underneath the Spheres, we need to have just rulers to help us do it."

Diera wasn't sure what Rafe meant. "What's at stake, Rafe?"

"Do you know what's meant when we pray for the Children's balance?"

Diera thought about it and shook her head. "I suppose I've always believed that justice is meant by that phrase."

"Yes, but justice is making things right, not just in ordinary matters, but in the big things, too. Balance is the force that holds up the Spheres. If balance is disturbed, if harmony fails, the structure falls apart. The world underneath the Spheres will be crushed, and everything we are, and everything we love, will be crushed with it."

"That's a terrifying thought," Diera murmured.

"Balance is at stake here, Diera." He stared at her. "You don't know what I mean, do you?"

She shook her head no, and he smiled at her. "Here we sit in this silly painted cart, having a philosophical discussion. We need to act in the small ways we puny beings are able to act. We're wasting time. I have a route in mind. Let's go. Let's get you out of here."

"Right now?"

"Right now." He swung out of the cart and helped her out. "Follow me," he said over his shoulder, and headed off into the forest.

After an astonished moment, she followed him, picking her way over downed limbs of trees, brambles that caught at her kirtle and cloak, holes—animal dens, maybe—that threatened to turn her ankles.

She was soon winded. "I'm not used to this," she gasped.

"I'll slow the pace, lady, but we don't have much time."

"Rafe," she said. "Look at you. You're in no condition for this, either. You can hardly stand."

"I'll force myself, lady. This may be the only chance we have. If I can't continue, I'll explain the route, and you'll go on without me." He gave her a hard look. "Your uncle's orders."

"I'll do what you say on one condition."

"What's that?" His voice was impatient. He tugged her along.

"On the condition that you stop referring to me as lady. On the condition that you use my name."

A very faint ghost of a smile crossed his features. It was gone so fast she wasn't sure she even saw it. "Yes, my lady," he said. "Yes, Diera."

She grabbed him by the shoulders then. She pulled him down to her and kissed him deep. "I beg you to forgive me, Rafe. What I said to you. What I thought. What I've made you do."

He seemed to pull back from her, but then he caught her into his arms and was kissing her back. They were crying, both of them.

"I can't stand this, Diera. I can't stand it," he whispered. "You must be safe. I'll do anything to keep you safe. Anything." He looked up into the trees and laughed. "Children keep me. Children keep us both. The fate of the Spheres hangs in the balance, and this is what I care about most."

"I don't care about any of that, about what's happening with the Spheres. I care about you, Rafe."

"Listen, Diera. When all this is over, I won't be here. No, stop," he said, putting his hand to her mouth. "I won't. You have to think how you'll go on. You must. Promise me."

Diera found she was shaking her head. "I'll make no such promise."

"Promise me," he insisted. "You'll be a queen. You'll have to think about the big things then."

"Suppose I am? Suppose by some strange circumstance I become queen. I'm just one lone woman. I won't be able to do much by myself, and then, the way all of us go, I'll go too."

"But while you're here, you must work for justice. Work for the balance that keeps the Spheres intact. Then hand it off to the next. In a long chain, one handing it off to the next, and the next, no one giving up. No one stepping aside. Beside us ordinary folk, there stand powerful ones underneath the Spheres, and above them, too, more powerful than you can imagine. Some of them are out for their own power. We puny ones, we may be weak, but we have each other. For balance, Diera." He took her hand. "Promise me."

"I promise," she breathed. She wasn't even sure she knew what she was promising. The words he spoke sounded so strange and unlikely. But she saw he meant them, and she realized how deeply she trusted him.

He gave her a quick kiss. "We have to hurry. They'll be missing us soon. Let's go."

They moved forward again, slashing their way through dense groves of saplings intent on holding them back; underbrush; once for a blessed time a quiet grove of trees where the sun slanted down past the big trunks to a gentle forest floor carpeted with moss.

Rafe pulled up at a sandy spot. In the distance they heard the rushing of waters. "If I'm not mistaken, we're in greatest peril here. These are the limits of Treddian's lands. Here's where we'll find armed men posted." His voice was low. "Look, now. If I fall, and you have the chance, you must keep going."

He bent and with a twig he drew her a quick diagram in the grainy soil. "Here's the river, see. Get over the river. Keep going down it, follow it down, not up. You're going to have to get over it."

"How?"

He looked up and saw her despair. His gray Sea Child eyes crinkled. "Dark Ones take you children of the Child of Earth. You can't swim, can you?"

She shook her head no.

He brought her hand to his mouth, kissed it, and grinned. "You're going to have to get wet, Diera."

"Oh, no," she said, dismayed.

"Oh, yes. Look, just keep following the river." He tapped with his twig at his diagram. "Around here, there's a ford. The water is pretty shallow. Wade across."

She shook her head doubtfully.

"You must do it, Diera."

"I won't be afraid. You'll be with me," she said, setting her chin stubbornly.

"Yes, but in case I'm not."

Impulsively she pulled his bent head over to her and crouched down beside him. "I love you, Rafe."

He swayed in her arms.

Alarmed, she looked at his pallor and felt how he trembled.

He put her gently aside and rose. He tapped again at the diagram. "Memorize this, Diera. Get across the river. Then get down it on the other side. If you have to sleep in the woods, do it. But keep walking. You'll come to a town, after a while. Cwen is there."

"Cwenegund? Lyn's old nurse?"

"Yes. She's one of us. I'm not sure how you'll do it. Maybe pay someone to take a message to her. You won't be able to walk right in. There are guards set, and you have to have proper identification. But if you can get word to Cwen, you will be all right." He felt in his belt pouch and produced a coin. "Here, this should do it."

She laughed a little. "I brought no coin with me, when we left the castle."

"Do you have my diagram committed to memory?"

She nodded, and he rubbed it out with his shoe. "Let's keep going."

"You're ill, Rafe."

"I'm fine now. I've had a rest."

She put a hand to his cheek. "You're burning up."

"Let's get me to the river, then, where I can cool off. If we get there together, I'll swim you across." He turned to resume walking, but when he looked back over his shoulder at her, he stopped. "Your eyes are enormous, do you know that? I could drown in them, and we of the Sea Child don't drown. It will be fine. Let's keep going."

They hadn't gone far, though, before he raised his hand and then put a finger to his lips. He steered her to a rock outcropping and motioned. She crouched down.

"Stay here," he said, his voice just at her ear. "I heard something. I'm going to see." He crept away from her. The forest had become thick again. She marveled how noiselessly he went.

After too long a time, when she found she was seized with terror and uncertainty, she saw him, easing back to her. He nodded off in the direction where he had gone. "A patrol over there," he murmured at her ear. "Three of them." Then he pointed silently in the other direction, and he was off through the thickets again.

When he came back, his face was white. "Five over there. They're patrolling the border between here and the river. This way. As silently as you can."

They began to move cautiously forward. Every furlong or so, he motioned her to crouch down while he reconnoitered forward. Then he came back to her, and they went another furlong.

On the third of these assays, a voice directly to the left of them called out sharply, "Who's there? Stop in the Earl Treddian's name."

Rafe grabbed Diera by the hand. "Run," he said to her hoarsely, and they began blundering forward through the forest as fast as they could.

Behind them, Diera heard the voices of men to left and right, calling to each other, and their heavy bodies rushing just behind them. Her blood hammered in her ears.

"Run!" Rafe said, shoving her on.

She looked over at him.

His breath was coming hard and labored. His eyes rolled up into his head, and he fell forward with a crash, stretched out face down in the clutter of underbrush.

The crashing of their pursuers grew louder, right on them now.

It's no use, thought Diera blankly. She stood over Rafe and waited.

An instant later, the first of their pursuers pushed through the trees. "There they are," he cried.

Armed men moved to surround her.

Diera lifted her chin. "Thank the Lady," she said to them all. "We were lost in this forest, and Master Leofric has fallen ill."

CHAPTER TWENTY-TWO

Away She Must Fly

Diera

"Why am I here, my lord, and not at the earl's castle," Diera demanded.

Caedon was stalking back and forth before her, like some enraged cat. He didn't answer.

"What have you done with Rafe."

"You think anyone will believe that? You two heard some cuckoo in the woods and got lost following it?" he snarled. "You think everyone is an utter babe?"

"It was the only thing that came into my head. We did hear a cuckoo," said Diera, remembering.

"That's a weak cupful of posset, Diera."

"It's all I could come up with at the time."

He strode to her and put his hands on her shoulders, gripping them hard.

"How dare you touch me, sir."

He ignored this. "You are a brazen puss, you know that, Diera?"

"Take your hands off me."

He did, flinging away from her in disgust. "Do you know the time this is going to cost me?"

"How is Rafe?" she asked again.

"Foolish lad. He was much too weak to go marching off through the woods like that. What was he thinking."

She looked at him, exasperated. "What do you think he was thinking."

"He's in the hands of the healers, if you have to know. He has a troublesome fever."

Diera sank down before the hearth stones in relief. "What will you do to him?" she asked after a moment.

"You'd be better off wondering what I'll do to you," he said, the strange amber of his eyes flashing.

"How troublesome?" she asked suddenly.

"The fever? They can't get it down. He needed to be careful, and instead—"

"Let me help. Let me see to him."

"Certainly not."

"What can I give you, to let me?"

He swiveled around to look at her. Then he shook his head. "Tempting, but no." He began muttering to himself as he paced.

"The wedding postponed," she heard him saying, and "Dark Ones take them both, the besotted fools" and "Just end it."

"End what?" she demanded sharply.

He didn't reply. He shouldered out of the room, and she heard the bolt being rammed to.

She sank to the hearth, shivering, and the tears began to come. She let them. She silently wiped them away, but they just kept falling.

She thought about the menace of the woods, her hand in Rafe's, their breath coming hard in their ears. Far off, the call of a bird, a lonely sound piercing the green silence. *When sun's no longer high, away she must fly.* Some snatch of a rhyme she had heard somewhere.

Now there was the sound of the bolt scrawing as someone drew it back. A woman came into the room then, bearing fresh clothing.

The woman curtseyed. "Let me see to you, lady. Then his lordship will take you back to the castle."

Diera let herself be dressed, combed, brushed, put to rights.

"There now, your ladyship. You look grand," said the woman, curtseying again and withdrawing.

In a moment, Caedon thrust into the room. He looked her up and down coldly. "Are you ready?"

She nodded.

She let him lead her unresisting to his cart. They jolted off in the direction of the castle.

"Stick to your fopdoodle story about the cuckoo, Diera," he told her. "You heard it in the woods. You demanded Master Leofric take you to it, so that you might see it, ignoring his obvious illness, hard-hearted woman that you are. The two of you got lost. Master Leofric fell over. You called and screamed until Treddian's men heard you and rescued the two of you. You're not to say how far into the woods you went."

"What about the men who found us? They'll know the story for a lie."

"Let me worry about them. Do you understand what you're to say?"

She nodded.

"Good," he said. As the cart pulled up into the castle's stables, he turned to her. "And you're going to beg that girl's pardon, for endangering her betrothed on your silly whim."

"I will," said Diera. She looked over at him. "And in return?"

"In return, I may, just may, decide not to strangle you the moment Audemar delivers you into my hands."

"Not good enough, Caedon. Tell me what I want to hear. Otherwise, I'll let the whole castle know what really happened."

"Not that they won't realize immediately what did," he bit out.

"That's immaterial, isn't it? They'll need a fiction to cling to, won't they. So. Tell me what I want to hear."

"Very well. I promise not to harm that stupid lad."

"What a liar you are."

"I promise not to harm him right now, and to get him nicely healed up. That's the best you'll get from me, Diera," he said.

"You won't punish him?"

"Eventually I will. You too."

"But not now."

"No," he said, and made her a sweeping bow. "Now let's get to board, and let me see you convince them."

"You're joking. They won't be convinced."

"I don't mean that," he said fretfully. "Let me see you convince them to swallow down your improbable tale and not spit it back out in disgust. Let me see you get them to pretend they think it's the truth. Let me see you behave yourself without causing me further trouble."

"Done," she said.

Diera sat silently among Treddian's family, looking straight ahead. To one side, Bertrys sat glowering at her, barely able to contain herself, as always. Behind Bertrys stood Rafe. It was the first time she'd seen him since the incident. Thank the Children, he didn't seem damaged. Apparently Caedon had kept his word. Rafe stood upright behind his betrothed, and whenever Diera dared flick her eyes in his direction, she thought she could tell his color was better. The slight tremor she had noticed in his left hand seemed to be gone.

She'd discovered a little tactic she could use, whenever anyone appeared to be on the point of asking her about the day of the attempted escape. She had discovered she could pretty convincingly cause herself to faint. She'd had to use this tactic earlier in the evening, but now—or so everyone thought, or pretended to think—she had revived.

While she was supposedly in a dead faint, she heard the earl's lady say, in an undertone, to Treddian, "However will we rid ourselves of her now? If the king expects our help in marrying her off, how will we ever find her a proper husband?" Diera didn't hear any answering reply. Then the lady's voice again, more insistent. "If it turns out she's prone to fits?"

Finally Treddian's bored voice. "That's Audemar's problem, my dear. But I'll take it up with Lord Caedon. I'm sure he'll have some ideas."

"Not our son," said his lady. "I'll not hear of his marrying her, and you can tell that king I said so. As for her." She had looked down at Diera. "I'd like her out of here. She's a bad influence on the girls, and now with Mildburg's betrothal about to be announced—"

"A bad influence?"

"You didn't believe that fopdoodle story of hers, surely."

Diera had moaned and fluttered her eyelids then, and everyone had crowded around to murmur comforting words and help her to a chair.

Now she sat in the chair, looking blankly around her.

"My cloak," she croaked out. She watched as Bertrys peevishly detached herself from Rafe's side to go looking for it.

Diera exchanged the barest of glances with Rafe. *We tried. I tried,* she strove to tell him with her eyes. But she didn't dare do anything obvious.

As the days passed and the air grew cooler, signaling the turn into harvest-tide soon to come, the eyes that cut in her direction then quickly away whenever she entered a room, the whispers that abruptly stopped as she went by, began to lessen. The gossip mill of Treddian's household found other grist to grind, and life swept on in all its boredom and regular tasks. Food to prepare. Yarn to spin. Cloth to weave. Clothes to stitch up and wash and mend.

The ladies of the castle performed none of these duties. They had other occupations. Forever and always, they had their embroidery by them.

Diera forced herself to take up her needle and silk.

"A la," said Mildburg, the oldest daughter, once, as she watched Diera bent over her latest embroidery project. "You're no good at all at it, are you?"

Diera looked up from her stitchery. The daughters were all good-hearted girls. She smiled. "No. My woman used to try and try to get me to do better. She failed. As you see." Diera waved the snarled piece with its crooked stitches at Mildburg.

Mildburg covered her mouth with her hand and let out a snort. Then she fell over in giggles.

Diera laughed too. "You'll make a proper wife for the Lord Beorhtric. Look at your own lovely work."

"I can hardly wait for the betrothal feast," Mildburg said breathlessly.

Diera could. The longer the preparations for Mildburg's festivities dragged out, the longer it would take for the earl's lady to approve the wedding of Rafe to Bertrys. The earl's lady had taken a fancy to arranging the whole thing herself, as if it were a thrilling production at one of the puppet theaters at the fair.

But first things first. First, the much more magnificent wedding of her daughter. A production orders of magnitude more magnificent than any pretty entertainment she'd fashion around the wedding of these underlings.

Diera patted Mildburg's hand. "Your marriage festivities will make a fine occasion, I'm sure of it," she said. "Everyone says Lord Beorhtric is a fine proper man."

"I haven't met him yet," said Mildburg. She suddenly looked uncertain. "He's pretty old, I think."

"I met him once, when I was a child," said Diera. "He was a strapping, upstanding warrior. His looks were most distinguished." As she said this, she thought with pity that he must be quite a bit older now.

She thought harder. Beorhtric. There was something she'd heard about him. Some bit of scandal.

Then she recalled what it was. He was the man Lyn was betrothed to. Odelyn, Lord Piers's oldest daughter, the one John loved. When it became known about Lyn and John, Beorhtric set out to kill them both, to clear his honor. The king had forbidden it. John he sent into exile. Lord Piers had killed his own daughter with his own hands, to satisfy his own honor as the father of damaged goods, so then Beorhtric couldn't do it himself.

Diera had to suppress a shudder.

"He had a wife," said Mildburg. "She died."

"In childbed?" said Diera.

Mildburg nodded, looking frightened.

He'd had two, not counting the doomed Odelyn, Diera remembered, and both had gone the same way. "You're a young healthy girl, Mildburg. You'll give Beorhtric many strong sons, I'm sure of it, and he will love and honor you."

The girl brightened then. "And the wedding will be magnificent," she said. "Father has promised."

"I'll rejoice with you," Diera assured her.

"You're like a sister to me, Your Highness," whispered Mildburg.

Diera embraced her fondly. "I never had any sisters," she said. *What a wonderful thing*, she thought, *to live a normal life and fall perfectly, easily in with all of your family's expectations.*

Rafe walked through the hall where she and Mildburg sat together. Diera couldn't help it. Her eyes followed him. Her heart thumped in her chest.

She bent quickly over her embroidery.

When she looked up again, she saw Mildburg was regarding her silently.

Mildburg put out a sudden hand and squeezed Diera's.

Diera had to blink back tears.

She doggedly stabbed her needle into the silk.

CHAPTER TWENTY-THREE

A Conundrum

Caedon

Y ou've played me false, mistress," Caedon said softly to Eris.

"I have not," she said, looking him straight in the eye.

"How do you explain these rumors I hear, then?" said Caedon. He heard his voice grow testy, and he hated that. He didn't want Eris to see how easily she got under his skin.

"What rumors are those, my lord?"

"You know perfectly well what I'm talking about. The rumors I hear about Ailys and that boy."

"What boy."

"You're trying my patience, Eris. You know perfectly well what boy."

"What do you care, lord? He's not your target."

"He was carrying a lot of gold, I hear. Now Ailys has it. I do not have it."

"Lord, you don't need gold," said Eris.

It was true. He didn't. But it galled him that his own creature would turn around and help Ailys.

"You work for me, not for Ailys," he said.

"This was a private concern, lord," said the girl.

"Oh, aye? A member of The Rising handed over to that woman and not to me? The Rising's gold handed over to her and not to me?"

"You don't need the gold. And now it's not in the hands of The Rising. You should be pleased."

He couldn't help it. A rage rose in him, and he backhanded her.

She stood glowering at him with her hand held to her jaw.

"He's not just a member of The Rising," she said. "I told you. He's my brother. He's my best friend."

Caedon found he was breathing hard. "How touching," he said, trying to keep himself from hitting her again. Suddenly he wanted to beat her and beat her and beat her, until her very features were unrecognizable. He made himself steady his breath. He gripped his hands hard on the carved arms of his chair. "Avery is your brother, too," he pointed out.

"Not in any way I count it," she said.

"Let's see how well you do, then, delivering the other members of The Rising into my hands."

"I'll do it easily."

"Bold words. Easily, you say. You've gotten John to me. That's only one of them. What about the earl?"

"You'll have him too, lord."

"When?"

"Soon," she said.

"And Avery? And that other man, the peasant?"

"Conal's not a peasant, lord, as you know very well," said Eris with a smile.

"Yeoman. Peasant. What's the difference? When will I have them?"

"Soon."

"How?"

"I'm working on it, lord."

"Good. But you know, this Walter fellow—"

"My friend. My brother."

"He's one of the Six, I hear. One of their leadership. Whatever your plan was, it failed. He's back with them now. He has to go, Eris. They all have to go, and he's one of them."

"They call him one of the Six, but they don't treat him like one. They know he's little more than a green lad. They tell him what to do, and he does it. He's not really one of the leadership, just their errand boy. But anyway, whether he is or he isn't part of The Rising's leadership, I'll never betray him, lord."

"Yet you betrayed him to Ailys."

She stood silent.

He regarded her through narrowed eyes. "But you didn't, did you? Not by your lights. Is that what you thought you were doing, with that lad? Getting him away from me?"

"I thought Ailys would keep him safe."

"Safe from me," Caedon persisted.

"Safe from the wars. Ailys could keep him out of it."

"She didn't."

"She's a fool. It was Dru," Eris said bitterly. "Dru got him out again, and back into danger. You'll have him next, lord."

"Who, Dru? The earl? I want the boy."

"You're wrong. You do want the earl."

"I want the boy, Eris."

"You can't have him. That's my price."

"You're trying to dictate terms to me, Eris?" He looked at her with curiosity. "You're a study, Mistress Eris. You've helped me with Diera more than once, and she's as much kin to you as Wat is. More or less. As I understand it, she was your childhood friend as much as Wat was."

Eris looked at him with a smirk. "Diera. She thought she was my friend, maybe. I never made that mistake."

Caedon tapped his fingers on the arms of his chair, staring at her. "You go after any woman you think will go after Wat, don't you?" he said softly. "Diera. She doesn't love Wat, you know."

"I know," said Eris. "She loves Rafe. Did you know he's a spy under your very nose?"

"You think you're very clever, don't you, Eris. Yes, of course I know Rafe is spying for The Rising. Tell me something I don't know, Eris."

Eris looked nonplussed at this.

"Keep out of the Rafe matter, Eris. You'll just mess things up. I have my own plans for him." Caedon was still thinking about

Diera. "Diera doesn't love Wat, and besides, he's her uncle. But she's too close to him. Closer than you."

"No one is closer to him than I am," she said sharply.

"And that girl. The one I heard about, a turning of the moon or so ago. Wat's new partner. Now his dead partner."

Eris stood looking at him with her lower lip pushed truculently out.

Caedon's eyes opened wide. "Nine Spheres," he whispered. "That was you, that night. The night Ailys betrayed Odelyn and John. You're the person who told me where I'd find Ailys's little maid. What was her name? Keelie," he remembered. "I stopped along the road to ask directions to her house, and that was you. You were the one who told me."

"My price," said Eris. "My price is Wat."

"So. Here's something I completely fail to understand. Maybe you can enlighten me," said Caedon. "It's Ailys. You know why she wanted him. She wanted the gold, true. But why wouldn't she have had the lad killed, and simply taken it? It's because she, being Ailys, wanted more than the gold. She wanted him, and you gave him to her." He fixed Eris with a fascinated look. "Why? You knew what she wanted him for," he repeated.

Eris shrugged. "You know the lady well, my lord."

"She's all appetite."

"She's not all appetite."

"She has a large appetite. We can agree on that, I think."

"We can."

"Why feed Wat to her? If he's a friend and brother so dear to you that you'll kill any woman who looks at him twice, it doesn't make sense you'd hand him over to someone like Ailys without a qualm."

Eris shrugged again. "Are we finished here, my lord?"

Caedon couldn't even be angry at her insolence. Not now. She was too fascinating to him. He thought about taking her to Gilles and seeing what Gilles would make of her. Gilles might very probably be able to use someone like Eris. He decided that once The Rising was done for, he'd take her to Gilles for training.

Or he'd kill her. Whichever. It depended on how much she provoked him and when she did it.

He waved a hand at her. "Go, then. I'll hold off on Wat, for the moment. We'll discuss him later. No promises about my long-term plans for the lad. In the meantime, I want the earl."

"He's yours, lord," said Eris, and whisked away.

Caedon sat for a long time gazing into the crumbling turves at his hearth, as they glowed into mere embers.

I'm wrong, he thought. *It's not that Eris will kill any woman who looks at Wat twice. She can serve him up as the daintiest morsel on the plate of the most voracious woman, and she won't turn a hair while that woman gobbles him up.*

It's exactly the opposite of what I've been thinking.

Wat himself was the key, Caedon realized. *Eris will kill any woman whom Wat looks at twice. And she doesn't care if it's friendship or if it's love, or even if it's just casual attraction. As for Ailys. There's no possible way a young man like Wat would be attracted to a woman like Ailys. It's not in him. The lad*, he thought, *is some kind of insane idealist, like all those people in The Rising.* The gods knew why they held to such notions against all the evidence under the Nine Spheres of the way the world really works, but they did.

Once he worked out the conundrum, Caedon could take himself off to bed. He really would have to see about getting Eris across the Narrows to Gilles. He promised himself he would. Eris was her own one-woman weapon, and he was learning every day how to wield her more skillfully than the day before.

But Wat. He did want that boy. He wanted the whole set of those brothers. He'd taken the little one. He'd taken John. Wat was the last piece in the set, and Caedon wanted him.

He thought with regret of the little one, Aedan. The boy had been at exactly the right age. Caedon had intended to send him across as a present to Gilles, but the ham-fisted men he'd assigned to do the fighting had botched it. Caedon had been able to send the shell of the boy only over to Gilles. A nice gift. But not the best gift.

With Wat, Caedon intended to do the same thing he'd done to John. With this difference. Something in John's core had eluded him. He didn't intend to make the same mistake with Wat.

When, later on, he talked the matter over with Gilles, Gilles just laughed at him. "You're obsessed, my boy. Why?"

Caedon had a hard time saying why.

"You know why I wanted John dead. He was never going to cooperate with me, so I wouldn't have been able to own him in that way. But if I had had him dead, I would have enjoyed him very much, and I could have unraveled some of his mysteries. You did well there, my dearest lad," said Gilles, "even though you were thwarted. Your intentions were good. It wasn't your fault that you couldn't send the body to me. And you're right. The little one would have been a nice gift for you to have given me, and you did manage to salvage the remains and get them to me. Don't think I don't appreciate you and how hard you tried to please me." Gilles put out a hand and ran it affectionately down Caedon's cheek. "You always please me." Gilles regarded Caedon with a smile. "This other brother, though. What do I care about this Wat fellow?"

"But I want him," Caedon said stubbornly. *And,* he thought suddenly, *I wanted John, and I didn't get him. Not really.*

True, Ailys had tried to undermine his efforts.

But John himself had been the real block to Caedon's desire. Some strange kind of resistance he was able to put up, even when completely destroyed and depleted. It gnawed at Caedon that he'd never been able to figure out why.

"Ah, humanity," said Gilles. "So foolish. But so very sweet." He caressed Caedon. "Come with me, lad," he said. "We'll play, and then when I've worked up an appetite, I'll feed."

Caedon's mind uneasily skated around the matter of the ward that kept his secret safe, and then skated away. Even with the ward in place, it wouldn't do to think about all that directly. It was too dangerous.

But he was struck with a thought that had been hovering in the back of his mind for some time now. A very different thought. A thought about Rafe.

"Mighty lord," he said shyly.

"What is it, my dearest lad?"

"You know that full body thing you do, through the pores?" Caedon was almost sorry he had asked. The look Gilles turned on him was so nakedly hungry.

"Yes," said Gilles. His pointed red tongue darted from his mouth and just as quickly back. "Yes, I do."

"Teach the manner of it to me, lord?"

"Nothing would give me more pleasure," Gilles purred. "Let me demonstrate."

CHAPTER TWENTY-FOUR

No Respite

Dru

Dru was huddled with Avery and Conal, talking their plans over. He spotted Wat headed across the dooryard outside the cottage with his bow, to practice.

"Wat," Dru called out. "Come over here to us."

Wat stopped and swiveled around. He headed in their direction instead. It caught at Dru's heart, seeing the hangdog look he had about him. It was always there, these days, sometimes more noticeable than others.

Wat blamed himself and blamed himself and blamed himself. He couldn't stop doing it. Dru and Avery and Conal had talked about it. They'd all decided only time would cure Wat of it. They'd decided the wrong tactic would be to coddle Wat. They decided they'd treat him exactly as if he weren't beaten down by lugging that heavy burden along with him every day.

But we do, thought Dru. *We do coddle him. I know I do. I can't seem to help myself.*

"Sit here by me, Wat," said Avery.

Wat folded his long self up to sit by the three of them.

So like John, thought Dru, with a catch in his throat.

"But I'm not John," Wat had burst out at them all, one time. One of them must have said something about it, implied it somehow. "I'm nothing like John."

Conal was the one who had stopped his outburst. He'd seized Wat around the neck and slung his arm about Wat's shoulders. "Of course you're like your brother. Of course we'd see it and love it in you. But mostly, Wat, you're yourself and we love you for yourself."

Now they all looked at Wat.

"We've had word," Avery told him. "The army has come south. We've placed men here and there about the countryside, and on our signal, they'll assemble."

Wat looked from one to the other of them. "Will it be enough?" he said carefully.

They all saw what he was not saying. *Because of me, because I let the gold get away from me, this army of ours is pathetically small. How can we possibly win against Caedon? Because of me, how do we even have a chance.*

Conal was completely matter-of-fact.

If anyone can keep to our promise to one another, thought Dru, *Conal can. Conal really doesn't mean to coddle Wat, and for the most part, he's not doing it.*

"Not if we tried to fight the kind of battle we fought in the north," said Conal.

Wat nodded, looking bleak.

"You know, Wat," said Avery. "We would have lost that battle if not for John."

"And we don't have John," said Conal. "It's not just the numbers, lad."

That, of course, was the wrong thing to say, thought Dru. After all, the burden of not being soon enough to save his brother far outweighed anything having to do with mere gold. There was no right thing to say, apparently.

"We don't have John. We don't have the coin. How can we think of doing it, then," said Wat in a flat voice.

"I'll tell you how," said Conal. They put their heads together and talked it through.

Torrin, Lorel, Eris roamed back and forth across the dooryard going about their ordinary tasks.

The four of them dropped their voices. "Someone is betraying us," Dru said to them all. "We don't know who it is. Probably someone one of us here at the cottage trusts. Inadvertently, we're probably saying or doing things that tip this person off, and then the person gets to Caedon. Someone in Torrin and Lorel's village, maybe. Someone Eris trades with, when she's bringing back information. Dark Ones take it, maybe even someone in my village that I only have the most casual acquaintance with, but who watches my movements and understands what they mean," said Dru.

"Someone maybe Cwen works with," said Avery. "Or someone following Wat from tavern to tavern, fair to fair, when he's on his circuit. Someone like that girl."

They all went quiet. No one wanted to talk about her. *So many things you can't talk about around Wat*, thought Dru. *So many ways to step in it.*

But who was the betrayer? How did it happen? That was the important thing right now, not Wat's tender feelings. *Child help me, I'm starting to resent the lad*, Dru said to himself. *I must not do that.*

Dru thought about the days Wat spent in the hands of Ailys, raving out of his head with fever. What might he have said, and who might have heard him say it. He didn't bring that up, though. One more piece of blame Wat could pile on himself. If it was so, that Wat had revealed something in that state, there would have been absolutely nothing he could have done about it. But try telling that to Wat.

From what the lad had said, he'd been taken completely off-guard. No way to defend himself. Then he found himself in Ailys's hands.

Of course, thought Dru. *More of the betrayer's work. Someone must have tipped Ailys off to Wat's whereabouts and importance.* He doubted very strongly Wat would have let anything slip during his time at Lunds-fort, so Ailys must have found out about Wat some other way. He remembered what Wat had told him. How Ailys had seemed to know him when she saw him at Mabire's hearth, and how unlikely it was that she would have.

Of course Ailys was in league with Caedon. All of them were as sure as they could possibly be, without direct evidence, that Ailys had played a major role in Artur's assassination.

Ailys must have been holding Wat for Caedon. It was just damn good luck Dru had gotten to the lad before Caedon had. They had all been enraged at the idea of Wat in Ailys's hands, Eris most of all.

Poor Eris, thought Dru. *She is as protective of Wat as a mother.* But then he thought, *as a lover.* He brushed the thought away, disgusted at himself for even harboring such a notion.

"So," said Conal. "Here's the way our campaign will go."

Dru pushed aside his worries about Wat, about Eris, and about the betrayer to listen.

"We establish dummy troop movements and emplacements," Conal said, using a twig to sketch out a little diagram at their feet. "Caedon will hear about that through our betrayer, whoever he turns out to be, and we'll decoy Caedon's forces away from the real action." Conal carefully rubbed the diagram out with the toe of his shoe.

"Meanwhile," Dru said to Wat, "the real action will be broken up into many small quick strikes aimed at disorienting the enemy and causing chaos. Caedon won't know where we'll strike next."

"We'll do a lot with a little," said Wat.

"Exactly," said Avery.

"And Wat," said Conal. "We're going to beat them."

"Here's when we see whether our plan will work," said Dru to Wat. He and Wat would be teamed up at one place, leading one small group of attackers. Avery and Conal would place themselves at a different spot pretty far removed from Dru's and Wat's place. And at another place off to the flank of Caedon's army, Torin, Lorel, and Eris would be leading their own group.

For now, Avery and Conal had stationed their small cadre at a high spot in the hills where they could look out over Caedon's entire encampment. Caedon's commander had taken their bait so far. His troops were acting as if they believed Avery's army was about to attack in force. Dru felt a moment of regret that Caedon himself was not leading his army against them. But they'd blacken his eye nonetheless.

Avery angled over to their group through the brush and boulders and moved up and down their line. "You know where you're to go," he said to Dru and Wat. They nodded. They saw him cross the ridge to Torin, Lorel, and Eris. From where they lay along the ridge, they saw Eris suddenly stand up and the others hastily pull her back down.

"Nine Spheres," Dru muttered.

"What?" said Wat.

"Is it possible Torrin and Lorel could have forgotten to brief Eris? She came back from her scouting expedition late last night."

Conal strode past, looking harried.

"Conal," said Dru. Conal circled back to them. Dru nodded over his shoulder in the direction of the place where Lorel, Torrin, and Eris crouched. "Something going on with Eris?"

"A communications mishap only," said Conal, his smile tight. "It's all straightened out now. Torrin and Lorel thought I'd be briefing Eris, and I thought I left it up to those two to do it. Too much on my mind. I must have forgotten to tell them about it. We just worked everything out, though. Now Eris knows where she's supposed to be."

Conal left to finish informing someone down the line about some supply matter.

"That's not like Conal," said Wat.

"A lot on his mind," said Dru.

"Well," said Wat, "as the bards say, all's well that ends well."

They turned their attention back to the field below them.

"That's a lot of men," said Wat. "They outnumber us five to one."

"Ha," said Dru. "Caedon's underestimating us. That's not even Audemar's full army down there. Caedon isn't taking us seriously. He's soon to learn he has made a big mistake." He looked over with concern at Wat. "Are you worried, lad?"

"What? No," said Wat.

Dru turned away, relieved. Then he turned back and really looked at Wat. Wat had spoken truly. He wasn't worried. *And that*, thought Dru, *is the really worrisome thing about it*. It was as if Wat were waiting to throw himself into a suicidal trap, and wanted to do it. Wat had a strange blank look about him.

"Wat." Dru shook him roughly.

Wat turned to Dru. His eyes stared through Dru and past him, to some other place.

"Wat, it's not going to be like that. They're not going to destroy us. We're going to destroy them." He gave Wat another shake. "Wake up, Wat. We're going to decimate those men down there. And you're going to help me do it. I need you here to help me do it. Understand? Don't let me down, Wat." He knew his voice was vibrating with the anger he felt.

Wat colored up. "I won't," he promised.

"Good. Don't," said Dru shortly. "Work out your own private grief somewhere else," he said roughly. "Not here. Am I clear?"

"Yes," said Wat.

Dru hugged Wat to him fiercely. "You're good, Wat. Conal and I taught you ourselves. We know. We're trusting our lives to you. Save the self-doubt for some other time, Dark Ones take you."

Wat gave him a sidelong, shaky grin. "I'll do it, Dru."

Thank the Child, thought Dru. *The lad was going to be all right.* "Take it out on them," he said, pointing down field.

"I plan to," said Wat.

Avery's low whistle floated over the ridge.

"Here we go, lad," whispered Dru. "With me?"

"Yes," Wat whispered back.

"Good, because I'll beat you bloody, afterward, if I find you've held anything back."

"I won't," said Wat.

Dru stood in a half-crouch and said to the men and women around him, "Hold, everyone. Hold until I give the signal. Avery's group is going to decoy those men away. We're going to wait. Understand?"

On the left flank, Dru, Wat, and their cohort watched as Avery's and Conal's soldiers ran yelling and shrieking down the hill at the enemy. Dru saw that over on the right flank, Torrin, Lorel, and Eris were waiting as well.

As the enemy began to flow up the hill to meet the group in the center, Avery and Conal led their men in a slow retreat up-range, their bowmen shooting downhill, killing and wounding enemy troops and horses as they went.

Dru stood up. He motioned to his group. "Move out," he yelled. They went on a fast run down the ridge and then up into the hills. In a long encircling action, they came upon the enemy from the rear. "We know this terrain," Dru pointed out as he and Wat jogged beside their troops. "Caedon's men don't." Their own troops were on foot, not horseback, dodging among boulders and down narrow mountain defiles. "Our work this summer, scouting the place, is paying off for us now. Caedon has just brought his forces up from the east over the past sen'night," Dru said to Wat.

From all the way across the gorge, Torrin's, Lorel's, and Erin's people had begun sending down a rain of arrows upon the enemy from a completely different angle than Avery's and Conal's attack. Caedon's men were moiling about in a confused mass down in the valley. It was becoming clear to them how useless their horses were in such terrain.

"Down there, they don't know what's going on," shouted Dru to Wat. "Just the way we want it, lad."

Dru and Wat had led their fighters almost to the valley floor by now. Caedon's bowmen spotted them and were starting to pin them down under heavy fire.

"Come on," Dru screamed to his group. "We're going forward right through them."

Caedon's men were looking behind them, ahead of them, un-certain where to focus their attacks. Dru saw them starting to panic. Dru and Wat led their fighters forward, ravaging the enemy in front of them. Caedon's men turned and began to flee. Dru and Wat followed.

But as the fighting intensified, Dru realized they'd moved into the midst of Caedon's main force. They were encircled. Dru motioned to his men. They threw up some of Caedon's abandoned baggage wagons to make themselves a temporary fortification and kept firing.

"We're going to run out of arrows," Wat told Dru, his jaw set in a tense line. "We could shoot until we run out, take out as many of the enemy with us before we surrender or we're overrun. Give the other two groups the time they need—"

"No," said Dru. He glanced behind him, where the enemy were drawing up more men. "And we can't retreat."

"Only one other way," said Wat, and he grinned. "Forward."

"Forward!" Dru shouted at his troops. They surged ahead. Dru realized it was the last thing the enemy were expecting. The men of Caedon stumbled around in confusion as Dru and Wat and their group fought through and up the hill to disappear into the rugged broken land on the right flank. "Scatter and meet up at the original spot," he called out hoarsely.

To their enemies, it must have looked like their group dissolved into thin air.

The bewildered enemy were then set upon by Torrin, Lorel, and Eris's group, and Avery's and Conal's soon joined in.

A threatening sky boiled up into thunderheads, and lashing rain poured down onto the battlefield. Dru's group knew the land well. They met up at their spot, streaming with water, thumping each other on the back.

In the valley, the enemy floundered in a sea of mud and rain.

"We're going back down," Dru shouted, gesturing.

Wat was doing a quick head count. "One lost, looks like."

"And we took many of the enemy out. Good work," cried Dru above the crashing of the storm. On a run, they circled around to the enemy's flank again. While the enemy troops were engaged in fending off Avery and Conal in the center, and Torrin, Lorel, and Eris on the right, Dru and Wat took them from the rear, shooting down many before they realized where the lethal barrage of arrows was coming from.

"Pull back," Dru called out. It was going on twilight. Between the dusk, coming earlier now at the beginning of harvest-tide, and the unrelenting rain, it was too hard to see their targets. They withdrew to a stand of trees just behind the enemy.

Dru leaned against a tree with his hood up to keep out the rain, as much of it as he could. He stilled his breathing. He let his mind settle. At home, harvest was coming. He'd get back to Elsebet and the girls after the battle, and they'd bring in the crops. Then, as he and Elsebet had promised each other, they'd take the girls to Cwen.

He thought of Jillie, and Mirin. Jillie, so joyous. Life hadn't taught her its cruelty, not yet. He prayed to his Child it never would. And Mirin. He remembered their parting, before he returned to Avery and to war.

"Father, I had a dream," she said to him. Elsebet was occupied with Jillie in the cabin, and he and Mirin had stepped outside into the sunshine.

He remembered his heart seizing as he looked at her. John had known things. Mirin knew things. What had it brought John but sorrow? What would it bring his girl, his dear girl, so gallant and brave?

"In my dream, a storm was coming, Father," she said to him, shivering in spite of the warmth of the sun. "A big storm, and it swept everything away. All of us. Our cabin. Everything. And then I couldn't find you. I couldn't find you and Mother. And I couldn't find Jillie. She was lost, Father."

"It was just a dream, Mirin. Just a bad dream."

"Everything," she insisted. "And Jillie was lost to everything."

He remembered pulling her to him and kissing the top of her head, holding her hard until her distress lessened. "Sea Child keep you," he whispered to her.

A day later, he left for the wars.

Dru shook the droplets of rain from him, and shook the memory off too. He couldn't think of it now. After the battle was over, he'd think of it and what to do. He settled back more comfortably against the tree. Dimly across from him, he saw Wat was doing the same.

Now they'd wait.

The rain ceased; the air cleared. A brilliant moon rose over the field of battle. As the enemy sagged in exhaustion, Dru looked around. He saw his own fighters were at the point of exhaustion, too. He moved from fighter to fighter. "We're all worn out, but dig deep. Find something extra. We're attacking."

He and Wat led their group out of the woods at a run, in an onslaught that caught their enemy off-guard.

Even with the moon this bright, the light was too treacherous for their bows. They all drew their swords and fell upon the enemy, slashing at them, grinding them down into the mud, trampling and thrusting.

"Keep going," yelled Dru. They fought their way from behind right through the enemy center. "Fast!" he yelled. With the element of surprise, and the speed his exhausted fighters managed to summon up, they outran the surprised enemy and, as before, melted back up the hill and into Avery's and Conal's force.

"All you varlets, get a little rest. As soon as it's dawn, we attack them again. Give them no respite. Keep at them," said Conal, going from group to group.

The moon edged under the tree line. They huddled together, trying to rest. Dru was even able to snatch some sleep.

At first light, they strung their bows and attacked again. The demoralized enemy turned and ran, leaving many dead on the field behind them.

Dru sent Wat and a few others down the field to gather every usable arrow they could find and bring it back to him.

As he watched Wat go, Dru began to smile. The broad set of Wat's shoulders, the snap of his eyes told Dru everything he needed to know.

Then Dru joined Avery and Conal, and all the others. They pounded on each other in congratulation. Covered with mud, their clothing sodden, they sent up whoops of triumph, eyes flashing from grimy faces.

A quick count told them the tale. Only ten of The Rising lost, and below them, hundreds of Caedon's men lay dead on the field in the valley.

Dru stood on the ridge to meet Wat as he toiled up the hill, sheafs of arrows in each fist, more in the quiver at his back. Wat couldn't stop grinning, and neither could Dru.

Later on, at the hearth in the cottage, the mood was joyous.

"We beat them!" Everyone kept saying it, over and over.

Only Conal was a bit subdued.

"This is your moment, Con," said Avery. "You did this. Your strategy."

Conal smiled a little and went over to Avery to embrace him.

"What is it, Con?" Dru asked him privately, later.

"We did it. I'm glad. I'm proud of everyone, especially young Wat." They both looked over at him, where he was laughing and talking with the others. "But Dru—"

Dru started to realize what Conal was going to say. Everyone was ebullient, in the aftermath of victory. Conal was thinking ahead.

"It's not enough, Dru. We did a lot with a little, just as we said we would. It harassed the enemy, but it didn't make a major dent in them. They didn't even field their best troops against us. What happens when they do?"

They sat together looking soberly at each other.

"Caedon wasn't even there," said Conal. "I'd like to meet that man. I'd like to stand toe to toe with him. I'd like to see which of us came out on top. I'd like to think I'd be the one." His expression was bleak. "That fight I dream of. I've dreamt of that fight since—" He drew a ragged breath. "It's for The Rising, of course. But it's personal, Dru."

Dru realized. He knew the time Conal meant. He knew Conal had dreamed of fighting Caedon for years. Since that time

Caedon had arranged a vicious little trap for a boy, and lured him into it. Since that time Caedon tried to damage Avery. And succeeded.

"It's not going to happen, that fight," said Conal, his voice dropping low. "Caedon knows better than to let it happen."

"We do what we can," said Dru at last.

"We do what we can," Conal repeated.

They both looked over at Wat again.

"This has been good for Wat, at least," said Dru.

"Yes," said Conal.

As they both sat scrutinizing him, Dru saw a new confidence in Wat.

But, he thought uneasily, *there's a hardness there.* It wasn't there before. He no longer saw trust in Wat's blue eyes. Eyes that used to be so guileless.

And Dru had found something.

Before they left for the battle, Avery was rummaging through the niches in the cottage, looking for his brooch. He kept it carefully hidden away unless he needed it, on an occasion like this one.

"Look," he said softly to Dru, calling him over. "It's the box with Johnny's rebec. Wat has nearly finished mending it."

"I've been helping him these past few nights," said Dru. "It's important to Wat."

"Oh, here's my brooch," said Avery, drawing a stone crock from the back of the niche and shaking something that dropped with a metallic clinking out of it. Then, "No," he said. "I put the brooch in the next niche over. I remember now." He had slipped this clinking object back in the crock, shoved it back into the niche.

Dru had seen, though. It was the armlet of that girl.

What is it doing in that crock, in that niche? Dru thought.

Then he realized. Wat must have found it. Wat must have put it there.

What have we done to ourselves, all of us, searching for justice? he thought. *What have I turned myself into?*

What had become of Wat's trust?

Dru knew Wat trusted him, and he was glad of it. He knew Wat trusted Conal and Avery and Rafe.

What about his sister, Eris? They had been very close. Dru thought Wat still trusted her.

Dru wasn't sure about Eris, himself. After some things he'd seen at the battle, he wasn't sure he trusted her.

"We're all Wat's brothers," he said to Conal. "We've all taken over from Johnny, as much as we can. Wat did well in this battle, and look at him now. He sees he can hold his own, and hold up his part in The Rising. But how will he continue? Suppose we're not around to help him? I don't think that sister of his will help him much."

When Dru thought of Eris, and thought of the dead girl's armlet, the turmoil inside him threatened to overwhelm him.

Conal put his hand on Dru's arm. "It's unavoidable, Dru. Wat worked through that bad time. Now he has to keep figuring it out for himself. One situation at a time, one hard decision after the other."

"Don't we all." Dru stared down miserably at the packed dirt of the cottage floor and hoped to his Child the good things he was doing outweighed the bad. "If only Johnny were here," he murmured.

"You know," said Conal, his eyes thoughtful. "In some ways, I feel he still is. I feel he's with us, Dru. Do you find that fanciful?"

"No," Dru whispered. "I feel the same."

CHAPTER TWENTY-FIVE

A Bowl of Broth

Diera

The entire castle was agog with preparations for Mildburg's wedding. The event gave Diera many little tasks to
perform, and those took her mind off other things.

Bertrys's swollen belly, for example.

Bertrys still was made to attend her, even though it was clear
neither one of them wanted it. That was uncomfortable. Bertrys
oozed resentment and malice.

And really, who would blame her, Diera said to herself. *I am the
woman who tried to take her betrothed away from her. The one who*

endangered the father of her unborn child. And keeps on doing it, or so it seems to her.

Whenever she thought no one was looking, Diera scrutinized Rafe. Did he seem better, or worse? Was Caedon keeping his promise not to harm Rafe further?

Once Caedon caught her looking. He imperceptibly shook his head. Diera had quickly dropped her eyes.

The day for which Mildburg longed finally did come. A sen'night before the event, her betrothed, the Lord Beorhtric, came up from his lands east of Tambourne to participate in all the festivities.

Because of a mighty storm and some kind of fierce battle involving a horde of lawless bandits, Mildburg had not been able to journey to Tambourne for her betrothal feast. She had been terribly disappointed.

"I forbid you to travel, my child," said Treddian. "We won't go. The roads are far too dangerous, with those brigands rampaging over the countryside."

They were sitting at the hearth after the board had been cleared, as usual.

"But Lord Caedon's army has chased them away," said Mildburg petulantly.

Diera saw a quick look pass between Caedon and Treddian.

"Many of them escaped Lord Caedon's mopping up parties and are lurking in the forests between here and the Riverlands," said her father. "Their minds are bent on kidnap and ransom and thievery and murder."

Diera drew in a breath. *It's a lie,* she thought. She was not sure how she knew it. Looking at Caedon's expression, somehow she did.

As she went about the castle in the next few days, she heard snatches of rumor from servants and others she happened to pass. A battle had been fought. A battle involving The Rising. And The Rising had won it. Caedon was lurking in disgrace at his manor or here at the castle. He dare not show his face at court.

Diera's heart would have risen at the news, except for one thing.

Rafe was nowhere to be seen.

She knew what that meant. He was lying ill at Caedon's manor, and he was ill because of Caedon.

Caedon thinks Rafe knows something, thought Diera. Something about the attack.

He probably does know something, she thought.

Every time she looked in Caedon's direction, at the thundercloud that had permanently settled on his expression, her terror rose, especially when Rafe did not return.

At last she steeled herself to question Bertrys.

"Mistress Bertrys," she said, as she sat in her rooms trying to force herself to go to bed. Every night she fought the same battle. She went to her bed, she tossed restlessly, and then she either suffered through terrible dreams or gave up, seized a robe, and went to sit by her hearth until dawn. By then, she feared going to bed at all. She knew she'd face many candle measures of torment.

"Yes, my lady?" said Bertrys, turning her perpetually sullen eyes on Diera's.

"How is it with you, mistress? Will your child be born soon, do you think?"

"Not for some turnings of the moon yet, Your Highness."

"Surely the earl's lady will arrange for your marriage soon, though," Diera persisted.

"She's taken up with the Lady Mildburg's wedding," said Bertrys.

"That must cause much anxiety for you, and for—for Master Leofric," Diera got out. Then she realized she shouldn't have said anything.

She saw Bertrys couldn't contain herself. The girl stood up, holding her belly with both hands. Her eyes blazed. "How dare you mention him to me. He's ill. There. Does that content you?"

"No, Bertrys, I—"

"You know very well, my lady. He's being punished. Probably for some mischief you got him into. The good Lord Caedon has had to punish him. If my babe is born without a father, it will be because of you, I don't doubt. I hope you are satisfied." Bertrys flounced out of the room.

So Diera was left in even greater terror than before.

Part of her thought she should insist Bertrys be chastised for her insubordinate behavior. But another part of her said, *No, leave it.* That part of her knew, miserably, that Bertrys must be as frightened as she was over Rafe. Diera knew she herself must seem like some powerful, threatening presence to Bertrys. Bertrys probably saw Rafe's true feelings. She probably thought of Diera as some malign rival. How could she not?

When Bertrys came back into her presence later in the day, Diera saw she was fearful of what Diera would do to her now that she had answered back. When Diera did nothing, Bertrys became ever more insolent. Diera let her. What did it matter.

Caedon was damaging Rafe. What did anything matter beside that?

So I must go to Caedon, she thought.

After the board had been cleared the next night, she looked over at Caedon and summoned up all her courage. "My lord Caedon, a private word with you, please."

"Oh?" he said, frowning at her. "Oh, indeed, a private word. What could you have to say that you can't say in front of the earl and his wife, who are standing in the stead of parents to you?"

Diera looked nervously to Treddian, where he yawned by the hearth, patting his expanding stomach, and to his lady, fixing her with beady, curious eyes.

"It's to do with my marriage prospects, Lord Caedon."

"Ah," he said.

There, she thought. *He won't want to talk about that in front of Treddian, because anything he says in public could be used to thwart his private interests.*

"My lord. My lady. If you'll excuse us, I'll take Her Highness for a turn about the pleached garden."

Treddian nodded indifferently. His lady subsided, disappointed, into her chair.

Caedon offered Diera his arm and escorted her to the little enclosed orchard garden just past the stable and mews at the very edge of the castle's outer bailey.

A sliver of moon hung by its golden chain from the Spheres.

The early harvest-tide air was warm that night.

Diera stood listening. "The cuckoo isn't singing now." The thought somehow filled her with sorrow.

"Nine Spheres, the way you talk, Diera. Maybe those who know you well really do believe you headed into the forest in search of some fopdoodle bird."

"Caedon," she said. "You promised."

"You mean about Rafe?" He laughed. "My promise didn't extend to traitorous behavior. Treason against the king."

"Suppose he did know something about that battle. What could he possibly do, pent up here? You've kept a close eye on him, Caedon. You know he couldn't have gotten any word to The Rising or aided them in any way."

"So. You don't want to talk about your marriage prospects. You want to talk about this." He regarded her under hooded eyes, his face shadowed in the dim light of the moon. "You certainly seem to know a lot about it, Diera. That battle. What battle? What do you know about anything? Is there more than one traitor here?"

"I knew nothing about the battle, lord. I didn't know it was going to happen, I didn't know it was happening. I didn't tell anyone anything."

He had seized her by the wrist and was digging his fingers into her flesh.

She stood with her head bent. Then she looked into his eyes. "I knew nothing," she insisted. "I didn't even know there was a battle until I heard the servants gossiping about it. A battle The Rising seems to have won."

"The Rising." He pushed away from her, contempt in his voice. "They're a bunch of outlaws. That's all they are."

"I have no opinion about that, lord. I know nothing about it, beyond the common knowledge that it exists. I'm not here to talk to you about that."

"What, then. About Rafe, I suppose."

"Yes." She tried to keep control of her emotions, but she felt she was failing. "Will you kill him? Are you killing him?" she burst out.

"Not yet. As soon as he marries that girl, then I will. That's all the use he is to me, now."

"So he'll have to be fit for the wedding. Fit to stand before the priest of the Lady in the temple."

Caedon looked over at her and began to laugh. "Indeed, you are right, my dear. I'll have to ease off on him, at least that much."

"May I see him?"

"Why?"

"To make sure he is well."

"Certainly not."

"I swear this to you, Caedon. If you make me desperate, I'll do something you'll really regret."

"What can you possibly do? You're weak, friendless. You're completely in my control."

"Not completely."

"Pretty much."

"Your threats don't scare me any longer, Caedon. If I did away with myself, I'd find the means. I already have the means." *Suppose he realizes I'm bluffing?* she thought, but she pressed on. "Your witch Labinia left me the means. She didn't realize I saw some of the things she was doing, so she was careless with her—her materials, I suppose one might call them. But I did see. And I have them. You say if I do away with myself, you'll kill Rafe. Well, you're killing him anyway, aren't you. So your threats mean nothing to me now. I tell you I have the means, Caedon."

"What means? I'll have you watched, Diera. You'll never be able to do it."

"And if you're wrong? I tell you I'm desperate, Caedon. You're killing the man I love. You raped me and took my child from me, and that child lies long dead. You've done every ill thing one person can do to another. There's nothing more you can do to me. I don't fear you any longer."

Caedon stood shaking his head. He blew out a breath. "I don't need this," he muttered. "Not right now."

"So will you let me see him?"

"Very well. I'll take you to him tomorrow. Now stop being a torment to me."

Me, a torment to you? Diera nearly cried out. But she looked at him hard and had to conceal her surprise. Indeed it seemed she was tormenting him. She saw that now. Why in the Nine would he feel tormented by her? He was the tormenter.

She didn't have time to puzzle out the vile mystery that was Caedon. Instead, she made herself completely cold. "When tomorrow?"

"I'll bring my cart over in the morning. Will you be satisfied?"

"Yes."

"Well, then," he said, and stalked out of the garden.

In the morning, he took her to his manor. He led her to a small room and let her into it. He stood at the door, watching.

The room was warm. Rafe was hunched in a far corner, shivering, a robe drawn about him.

"Rafe!" she cried. She ran to him and gathered him into her arms. Let Caedon watch. She didn't care.

She put Rafe's head on her shoulder and stroked him and murmured to him. Then she held him a little way from her and looked into his eyes.

Rafe stared blankly ahead.

He didn't know her. He didn't know anything. But he was alive.

"You swine," she said over her shoulder to Caedon.

He didn't reply.

"Give me something to feed him. Broth or something."

"Get it yourself," said Caedon. She heard him striding down the corridor.

Diera carefully pulled the robe about Rafe's shoulders, which felt as thin as blades under her hands. She didn't want to leave him.

She stepped into the corridor and looked down it. The kitchen, she recalled. She went out into a courtyard and over to the kitchen shed. A bondswoman looked up, startled.

"I need a bowl of broth for Master Leofric," she told the woman.

Silently, the woman dipped up a wooden bowl of something in the kettle over the fire and handed it to Diera.

"And a spoon," said Diera, making her voice even. She felt she was at the limits of her patience.

The woman found a spoon and wiped it off on her apron. She handed that to Diera, too.

Diera got herself back to the small room and crouched down beside Rafe. She spooned up some of the broth and guided it to his mouth. He turned his head away, shook it.

"No, my darling. You must eat this," she whispered in his ear.

After a moment, he let her feed it to him, and he swallowed.

"That's right," she murmured. "Just like that. Now a bit more."

Spoonful by spoonful, she fed him and as she did, she stroked him, his head, his arms. When the bowl was empty, she pulled him to her and nestled him against her and crooned to him.

After a long time, she heard him sigh, and he put his head over onto her shoulder.

She didn't dare to move.

Then she realized Caedon was back in the doorway. How long had he been watching there?

"Touching," he said. "Now it's time for you to go, Your Highness." His voice had the usual mocking edge.

She looked up at Caedon. "How long before he recovers?" she said, keeping her tone as neutral as she could.

Caedon shrugged. "A sen'night more, perhaps."

"What do you do to him?" she snapped.

"Nothing you'd understand."

"How do you know he'll recover?" Now he had frightened her.

"That's how long it takes."

"And you're sure about that?"

"Completely. If I'd wanted a different outcome, I would have arranged for one."

"You're a monster."

"Let's go," he said sharply. "Time's up."

"You've done this to him time after time. I know it. I know it well, Caedon. How can anyone survive this?"

"We can. We can and we do."

"We?" Diera looked at him, startled.

"Never mind. Perhaps, after you and I are wed and you've given me a child, I'll teach you how. Time's up, Diera. Get to your feet before I drag you. You're going back now, Diera. You've seen. You've played heroic nursemaid. Now you're going."

She turned back to Rafe. His gaze seemed just as blank as before. *It's going to kill me to leave him here*, she thought. But she knew she must.

She arranged Rafe's robe more securely around him. She ran her hand tenderly through his long, disheveled hair, pushing it off his forehead, hot and fevered, and she tucked his amulet on its thong into the neck of his loose tunic. She stood then and let Caedon lead her from the room.

As he handed her back into the cart, he stared at her with a malevolence that chilled her. But she saw something else underneath. Jealousy, perhaps.

CHAPTER TWENTY-SIX

The Woods Shall to You Answer

Diera

D iera felt sorry for poor Mildburg. The closer her wedding came, the more frightened the girl looked. Since she hadn't been able to travel to Tambourne for the betrothal, she'd only met her future lord, Beorhtric, a sen'night before she was to wed him.

And he was indeed old. For an old man, though, he was hale and upright. Diera thought she remembered him from her grandfather the king's board, years ago. He was of middle years then. Now past them.

Beorhtric claimed to remember her, too. "Ah, Your Highness, I remember you when you were only a small girl at Tam Fort. It delights me to see you now," he said, as everyone gathered for the marriage.

"You are kind, my lord," said Diera, dropping him a curtsey.

Her parents urged Mildburg forward then. "And here is your bride, my lord," Treddian said.

"A lovely flower," said Beorhtric.

Mildburg looked like she might faint.

"Courage," Diera whispered to her.

She turned aside and seized Diera's hand. Her own was icy cold. "Now at last I know how you feel," she whispered to Diera.

Diera looked at her inquiringly.

"When your fits come on you," said Mildburg.

"Oh," said Diera. "That. To be sure."

They all made ready to go to the temple of the Lady Goddess down the hill from the castle. The wind had whipped up. There was a hint of chill in the air that hadn't been there even a sen'night earlier.

As they rode down the forested path to the temple, Diera listened. No bird called. The forest, which had echoed with birdsong only a turning of the moon ago, was silent.

As they came down to the flat bottomland below the castle, though, flocks of blackbirds rose from the fields where the crops had all been harvested, leaving the chaff for the birds to pick over. The birds called in their rasping voices, rose, settled, called, rose again, settled.

Everyone was stiff in embroidered finery. Beorhtric took the trembling Mildburg by the hand and they knelt before the Lady Goddess's priest. He joined their hands and said the proper words over them. The rest, Diera included, murmured the proper responses.

And it was done. Mildburg was a wife. The earl's lady glowed with pleasure at her side. Diera could see she was already eyeing her second daughter speculatively. Poor little stunted Ceolwen, with her innocent blue eyes and her stammering speech, would be next.

Now for the feasting.

The lady of the earl had gone all out. Her chief steward, the pompous Master Charlo, brought over from the Baronies with his sophisticated ways, directed a fleet of blue- and brown-clad servants in the presentation of dish after dish.

Jellies of swans with gilded beaks and feet. Quarters of stag and boar. Meat pies. Jugged hare. Plums, delectable plump islands in a sea of rose water filling a vast silver bowl.

Diera could hardly bring herself to taste anything. At a table far to one side sat some of the better class of servants, including Bertrys and, beside her, Rafe.

Even from where she was sitting, Diera saw he hardly looked recovered. He was gaunt and pale. He moved haltingly. His bride-to-be was blooming with health, swollen high with their child.

With a thudding in the pit of her stomach, Diera realized. Now that Mildburg was off the earl's lady's hands, she'd turn her attention to her pet project, creating some kind of play-acted wedding for Bertrys. A kind of rustic spectacle for the gentles to chuckle at and enjoy. And then almost immediately afterward, so it seemed, Bertrys would give birth to her child. After that. . .

Diera felt her face grow hot, then suddenly chill. She wondered if she were about to faint in earnest.

After that, Rafe would no longer be useful to Caedon, and Caedon would kill him.

Swinging onto the bench beside her, Caedon himself nodded to all the guests. Under the table, he possessed Diera's hand and squeezed it.

"I saw where you were looking, Diera," he murmured in her ear. "I know what you're thinking."

"Remember our bargain," said Diera, getting the words out past numb lips.

"I do. Oh, dear girl, indeed I do."

After many candle measures of feasting, Beorhtric seized Mildburg by the hand and stood, dragging her up after him.

"I thank you all, my lords. My ladies. My bride and I are tired. We'll take our leave."

This pronouncement caused good-natured cheering and joking.

Diera saw Mildburg had turned white.

Treddian stood up and toasted the couple, and his lady joined in. She clapped her hands.

Master Charlo came to stand beside her ladyship. He bowed.

"Master Charlo will lead you to a comfortable chamber, my lord," she said to Beorhtric.

More cheering and joking.

Beorhtric helped his bride off the bench, and to the sound of a pipe played prettily by one of Treddian's court musicians, they moved off behind Master Charlo to the bridal bedchamber.

"Poor girl," said Caedon.

Diera looked over at him. "I'm surprised to hear you say so."

"I'm not completely heartless, as you seem to think. Anyone can see it. The girl is frightened nearly to death."

"She is."

"At least she's not a royal bride. I hear your grandmother's wedding to the king was quite raucous and crude. But then, you folk over here have that reputation."

"While you of the Baronies are, I hear," hissed Diera, "so very civilized."

Caedon laughed. "So we are, my darling bride-to-be."

"You don't know that Audemar will agree to our marriage. He may not. Especially not now, after the disgrace of that battle. Two failures in a row, and at the hands of The Rising, that disorganized band of thugs." Diera had drunk down her mead. She was feeling reckless. She didn't care whether she angered him or not.

He tightened his hand on her thigh. "Careful, Diera," he said, and smiled pleasantly at her. "But anyway, you're wrong. I'll persuade Audemar to give me what I want. I have the means, and he's as witless a monarch as anyone with brains ever served."

"You, I suppose, being the one with the brains."

"I like this, Diera," said Caedon. "I enjoy jousting with you in words like this. Enjoy it very much. You're not the green girl you were. I'll win, you know, and then I'll claim my forfeit."

Talk buzzed about the table. Mostly bawdy talk about what the vigorous old Beorhtric was doing to his child-bride Mildburg.

"She'll stay here with her parents, though, and Beorhtric will go back to his own lands tomorrow," Caedon said.

"Really? That's a good thing. The poor girl will be a piece of wreckage by tomorrow," said Diera. "But why?"

"Beorhtric and Treddian decided between them. The roads are still too dangerous. And Mildburg is so young that she'll stay with her mother a while longer."

"Dangerous roads." Diera looked over at Caedon with a cynical smile. "Those pesky bandits again."

"You're enjoying this, testing me," said Caedon. "I'm enjoying it too. I'm already planning what I'll do to you, once I get you to myself."

Her fate was intertwined with his. She saw it. She prayed to her Child that it not be true, but it was true, and in ways she had an inkling she didn't even understand. But he didn't frighten her any more. "I'm tired, my lord," she told him coldly. "Pray you excuse me."

She rose from the bench. He shrugged and turned to the person beside him. Behind her, she heard the conversation veer away from bawdy comments on what the newly wedded couple were doing and over to the serious matter of politics.

Diera headed out into the cool air of evening. She was almost never alone now. Thank the Child Bertrys was occupied at the feast. Caedon had set Bertrys to watch her closer than ever.

Bertrys, Diera realized. That was another reason Rafe was doomed. Caedon had a willing instrument set to watch her now. He didn't need Rafe for that task any longer.

She stood in the gallery leading along the outer bailey of the castle and breathed in the night air.

Then she stood rigid. A touch at her elbow.

"Rafe," she sobbed, turning to him and burying her head against his chest.

He stood there silently, stroking her hair.

"Is it true, that you came to me in my illness?" he said at last. "Or did I dream you? Caedon just laughs, when I ask him."

"It's true. I made you eat some broth. You didn't know me, Rafe. I was so afraid."

"Deep down, I did know you," he whispered. "I knew it. I knew you were there. Let's move away from this place. We'll be seen."

"It's so dangerous for you to be anywhere near me."

He took her by the elbow and guided her down to the bailey and into the pleached garden. It was dark now. It was the dark of the moon, and the moon had withdrawn her face.

"Caedon is going to kill you," she whispered.

"I know."

"As soon as your baby is born."

"I know."

"What must we do, Rafe?"

"There's a plan."

She sucked in her breath. "How do you know?"

"I had a visit from my brother."

"Your brother?"

He laughed quietly. "From Wat. He has been masquerading as my brother for a year or so now. A few of the guards know him. Or think they do."

"Wat's going to get you out?"

"We're going to get you out, Diera."

"What about you, Rafe?"

"I'll be helping to do it."

"So we'll escape together," she breathed.

"If the gods are kind, maybe we will," he said.

"The gods are kind. The Children are kind, Rafe."

She could feel more than see it, but she knew he was smiling.

"My Child is kind to me. I know it," he said. "John knew it. Before Caedon took him, he told Wat, and then Wat told me. We talked of it the day we lay John to rest. So I know it." Then he said, low, "Marry me, Diera."

"With all my heart," she whispered back. "But who would allow such a thing?"

"Suppose the two of us are the only ones necessary to allow it."

"Yes," she breathed. "Shall we do it? Let's do it right here."

He took her by the hand and led her to the center of the garden. He knelt to her. "I, child of the Child of Sea, pledge you my hand, and all my worldly goods, which in fact I am wearing at the moment, and my heart, Diera."

She knelt facing him. "I, child of the Child of Earth, pledge you my hand, my goods, which in fact have all been taken away from me, and my heart, Rafe."

"You must use my real name."

"Rafe isn't your real name?"

"No, it's the name Audemar insisted on calling me, when I came over here as a boy, and it stuck. He couldn't deal with all those Baronies sounds and syllables. The same name, in the Baronies, is Raoul. My name is Raoul."

"I pledge myself to you. Raoul," she whispered, rolling the unfamiliar syllables on her tongue.

Diera felt how strange it was to say that. But everything was strange. They both looked strange in the dim light, strange to themselves and to each other.

"Now we must kiss," said Rafe. "We have no ring, so we must swear our love on this." He pulled the thong he always wore over his head and piled it into his palm. She put her palm over his. Between their hands, she felt the little amulet he always wore, nestled there.

"What is this? You said it's from your family."

"It's a small bird, but not the blackbird of The Rising. It's something I've worn most of my life, a little bird called a martlet."

"Swearing on this, I feel as though I'm swearing on your life," she whispered. And then they both swore, using the little bird for sign and symbol.

"Now we are wed," Diera concluded.

"No one will part us now. They may try. They may succeed, on this side of that river. But not forever."

"Not forever," she whispered, taking the amulet on its thong and pulling it back over his head, arranging it so the little bird dangled next to his heart.

They embraced. She felt how thin he was in her arms. She wanted to weep, but she couldn't stop smiling. They belonged to each other, and the Children had given them Their blessing.

He began to rise to his feet. "We'd better get back before someone misses us."

"Wait," she said, pulling him back down beside her. "Stop. Listen. Did you hear that?"

They knelt side-by-side for a moment, their faces lifted to the dark sky. From far away there was a faint, two-note call.

"A cuckoo, this late? Not possible," he said. "Must be some other bird."

"Maybe."

They stood then, and remained still. They listened for a long time. But they didn't hear the call again.

CHAPTER TWENTY-SEVEN

Like Cattle

Caedon

E ris, his best source of information, had finally located
Earl Drustan and his family for Caedon. "And high time,
too," said Caedon, pursing his lips with displeasure.

"Sorry, your lordship," she had muttered. She didn't sound
sorry. Not sorry enough. Insolent, as always.

"Meanwhile," he said, trying to contain his rage, "you kept a
valuable piece of information from me. About that battle. You,
everyone, all my other people I had out there, watching. All of you
said the forces of The Rising were a small, ill-equipped group of

ill-assorted, ill-trained fighters who would hardly pose a threat. You were all wrong."

"That's what all of us thought. We were deceived."

"By whom?"

"It was Conal," she said sullenly.

Caedon felt his rage fading. "Conal," he said grudgingly. "A worthy opponent."

"Worthy or not, you would have had him, lord. But—" It was clear Eris was having trouble keeping her own rage in check. "He's on to me, lord."

"He's told the others about you?" In that case, Caedon wondered, what good was she to him? He could do away with her. He'd enjoy it.

"No, he didn't tell the others. He can't do that."

"Why wouldn't he."

"Avery has a blind spot. He loves his kin. I suppose that's why Audemar is so offensive to him. A man who would betray and kill his own kin. And I'm Avery's kin. Conal knows Avery won't hear anything against me. Unless Conal has direct evidence against me, he doesn't stand a chance. He doesn't have that evidence."

"Yes, I see," said Caedon. *Oh, well,* he thought. He'd just have to postpone the pleasure of giving Eris her comeuppance. He looked at her moodily. "Avery must think Audemar is some kind of freak, an aberration. Foolish boy. Plenty of people underneath the Spheres will turn on their own."

"Don't call him a boy."

"You're right. He's not a boy," said Caedon. "I see that now. And with Conal beside him, he's doubly dangerous. So then. Conal is on to you. How do you know?"

"They had the strategy of that battle carefully worked out, lord. They knew exactly what they were about. But beforehand, Conal sent me away on some mission. I accomplished it. Some trivial matter, getting information about grain storage in Withiel. While I was gone, they shared their strategy with everyone. Not the direct confrontation I was led to believe they'd planned. Instead, quick strikes from unexpected directions. Wearing your forces down. Sowing chaos. Moving faster than your troops did. Conal's task was to brief me as soon as I returned. He somehow forgot."

"I see," said Caedon. "So you were actually at this battle? You actually fought against me?"

"Yes, lord. Your men were easy pickings. You should work on that."

"Don't push me too far, mistress," Caedon muttered. His ire began to rise again.

She was paying him no mind.

"As to this troublesome earl." Caedon shoved his emotions aside in order to concentrate. "Tell me of him. You've discovered his whereabouts?"

"The Rising kept Earl Drustan's location a closely guarded secret. I think only Avery knew it. But they had to slip up sometime, and now they have. When your lordship did away with John, Avery was so upset he said some rash things, in his anger and grief. He probably didn't even realize what he was giving away, but I've been working on possible locations for many seasons now, and when they sent someone off to warn him, the last piece clicked into place. I understood at once."

"Well, then," said Caedon, grudgingly. "I suppose you've earned a reward."

"And of course my best source of all is Wat."

"He doesn't realize, I hope."

"Oh, no," said Eris, smiling her cynical smile. "He has no idea." Then she had shrugged. "If you expect good work, you have to realize. These things do take time."

Caedon wanted to smack the insolence out of her.

She rose to go. "You miscalculated, lord, with John," she said.

"That's none of your concern," he told her.

She shrugged.

"Besides, I thought you told me John was the heart of The Rising. Now he's dead."

"He was the heart of The Rising. Even in death, lord, he still is."

"Nonsense," he told her. "People don't follow a ghost. Get out of my house, and don't return until you have something to offer me. Something more useful than nonsense."

Without a word, she bowed and left him. He watched her go. As soon as Eris's usefulness waned, he thought, he'd take pleasure in destroying her.

He'd given up the idea of sending her to Gilles. She was too annoying.

At the moment, though, he was pleased, in spite of her impertinent manner.

Oh, yes, he thought, smiling to himself now. With the help of this source embedded under the very noses of his enemies, he'd tracked down the earl and his family. Now, it was only a matter of time.

With relish, Caedon set out to perform the important task of crushing Earl Drustan. He wouldn't have dreamed of leaving such an important task to others, or to deprive himself of the pleasure of seeing to it himself.

He rode out with the soldiers and watched as they set fire to the tiny cabin where the earl and his family had been living, a small place on a squalid little farm in a squalid little village. He watched as the poor former earl, the dirtiest of peasants now, staggered out of the burning timbers with his wife and child. Watched as the man tried to shield his wife, and watched as his men cut the Earl Drustan down. Then she too, his wife. She was one of them, he discovered later. One of The Rising too. She was a woman only, so she didn't matter.

But then as he sat enjoying the spectacle of the carnage, he stood up in his stirrups. Alarmed, he raised his hand, and his men came rushing back to him.

"I thought I told you. Don't harm the child." He turned furiously on the captain of the patrol. Clumsy oafs of soldiers had already killed one child he wanted. John's youngest brother. Now they were thwarting him again with their lack of sense.

"Pardon, lord!" cried the captain, kneeling before Caedon on his horse. "The little girl ran between her parents. We tried to avoid striking her, but—"

"Incompetent half-wits," Caedon snarled down at him. "Bring the body here." Gilles could do something with bodies, too. The child might not be a complete waste. That young boy's body hadn't been.

A soldier brought the girl's limp little form to Caedon. Caedon saw with amusement how the fellow cradled her. Sentimental fools, every one of them.

"Here she is, lord," the man said. "But I think she's still alive."

With an exclamation, Caedon leaped from his horse. Below him in the meadow, the soldiers were moving down to the edge of it to investigate something. Maybe they'd found the older girl. Caedon paid them no mind. "If you find the other girl, kill her," he said over his shoulder. Then he turned his attention to the little one.

The soldier carrying the child laid her down in the dirt of the dooryard and Caedon bent over her. She was exquisite. Just exactly right. Just exactly the right age. He put out a hand and touched her. He felt her all over. Her eyes fluttered open.

Caedon smiled down at her. "Don't fear, little girl," he whispered to her. "You're with me now."

Thank whatever gods there might be, or none of them if there weren't. The girl was fine. A healer had to nurse her back to health, but that was fairly easily done. Once she was a healthy child again, he had her taken to his manor and put into one of the rooms he kept for such a purpose.

"Is she ready for company? Will she understand me when I speak to her?" he asked the healer woman in whose hands he'd placed her.

"Yes, lord. She's sitting up and taking nourishment. She has started to ask where her parents are."

"Good work. I'll go in to her now."

The woman stood outside while Caedon moved quietly through the door into the room where he was keeping the little girl.

"Hello, child," he said softly as her head whipped to the door. She cowered back.

He came to the bed and sat on the side of it. He took her hand.

"You've been very ill. What is your name?"

"Jillie," she said. "I'm Jillie. Where is my mother? Where is my da?"

"Dear child. How hard this is to hear. You are so young and don't understand how cruel the world can be. Your mother and father decided they didn't want you any more, especially when they saw how damaged you were. They gave you to me."

"Bad men hurt them!" she cried.

"Maybe you dreamed that, while you were sick," said Caedon. "No. They gave you away."

Jillie began to cry.

Caedon gathered her tenderly to him and stroked her, feeling her all over, how lovely she was. "There now," he said. "There, now."

As the days went by, Caedon felt an almost dizzy sense of joy. What pleasure he'd have, getting to know this little girl who had fallen into his hands. What pleasure he'd know, slowly cultivating her, savoring her. In fact—and strange that this was happening with a girl child, because he might more easily expect it of a boy—there was something especially taking about her. Something deeply unusual.

He and Rafe had been Gilles's chosen, his most-beloved children. Gilles had spared them, unlike the other children he took, because they were such delicious food, worth the effort of further careful harvesting.

Caedon was amazed at his good fortune. Silently he praised Gilles. This girl-child might be Caedon's own carefully cultivated feast.

In spite of the unpleasantness of the battles he'd lost, the violence he'd endured, Caedon was beginning to reap the rich rewards of his ever closer connection with Gilles. Gilles's gifts had saved him in the first battle, shielding him from John's song and then from capture in the river. Later, Gilles had shielded him during the attack by John's would-be rescuers. The shield couldn't keep Caedon from all his injuries, but it kept him from the fatal blow that Wat was about to inflict on him.

Wat would pay, thought Caedon. And Rafe, of course.

Now the debacle of this last battle had set him back. But it was a gnat-bite only, and soon Audemar would be over his pique.

Meanwhile, the powers Gilles granted Caedon were showering him with more, and still more.

This child.

Drustan dead in the dirt. By now, Caedon thought, the earl was no longer even that, his flesh perishing away into the earth it came from, he and that woman rotting away unburied where his men had dragged the two of them, lying underneath the sun and rain like downed cattle until the procession of the ages saw to it their very bones turned to dust. So much for the music of the body.

One thing troubled Caedon, and one thing angered him. The trouble came of course from Rafe.

Who else? he said to himself, disgruntled.

Before Rafe could marry that girl, that little Bertrys, she had given birth to a misshapen thing already dead. Now Caedon had to start all over again with the lad, but of course everything had to wait while Bertrys recovered her strength. Caedon knew he would have to ease off Rafe and resume the tiresome hectoring it took to get Rafe to do his duty.

Meanwhile—Caedon shook his head, remembering. On the day it had happened, the poor young woman lay whimpering in the hands of her healer, and Rafe stood slumped outside Bertrys's door.

Caedon was savage with disappointment. He supposed he shouldn't have goaded Rafe, not at a time when they were both feeling dangerous. "So, Master Rafe. Ready yourself to try again. In the meantime, you might want to praise whatever weakling gods you worship that you'll get a few more seasons of life as a result of that girl's misfortune."

As he said this and turned with a cynical smile in Rafe's direction, the world suddenly upended. Without a word, Rafe had turned on him. His fingers, surprisingly strong, were fastened about Caedon's windpipe, and Caedon felt a pounding pressure behind his eyeballs.

"You dark poisoned thing," Rafe whispered in his ear as he bore him down to the stones of the floor.

Caedon felt himself fighting, lashing out with arms and legs, but it was as if someone else were doing it. He felt strangely removed, as if he were watching it all from somewhere above, up by the ceiling.

His breath was completely stopped.

But some dim place in him saw Rafe didn't have the strength to follow through to the end. Caedon fought harder. Desperation gave him the strength.

Rafe's grip relaxed, just enough for Caedon to draw in breath.

"Diera," he rasped out. "She'll die. I've given orders."

The safe word, he thought to himself. *My best control.*

Rafe's arms dropped to his sides. He rocked back on his heels from where he had been leaning down on Caedon with all his strength.

By that point, Caedon's manservant, attracted by the noise of their scuffling, had yelled for the guards, and they rushed to pinion Rafe and help Caedon to his feet.

Caedon stood grasping at his bruised throat and staring at Rafe. There was a courage in the lad still. Fight left in him. Just when Caedon was sure it was all pressed out of the lad, there it rose again. Caedon supposed that was the thing that kept Rafe dear to Gilles. Some reckless gallantry in him.

"Put him to the sword, lord?" said one of the guardsmen.

"No, take him to a cell," Caedon got out in a hoarse whisper.

As they started to lead Rafe away, Caedon put out a hand to stop them. "You understand?" he whispered to Rafe. "You understand I'll come to you later, as soon as these bruises have healed."

Rafe looked blankly into Caedon's eyes. Caedon was about to summon the energy to strike him for it, but then he realized Rafe was far away. Rafe was somewhere else.

"Take him to a cell," Caedon got out to the guards.

There would be a little interval, he realized. Some time before Bertrys was well enough for Rafe to tup her again. If only he could end the lad now, thought Caedon. But no. With the defeat of his forces and Audemar's displeasure, Caedon knew he would have to postpone his demand that Audemar give Diera to him to wife. Caedon would have to keep on using Rafe, and so using Bertrys. And so he would have to force Rafe to try again to get a child into her belly.

Caedon determined to make the most of the time he'd have with Rafe. At least there would be that pleasure.

After a while, Rafe was walking the castle grounds again, and Caedon and Bertrys were collaborating again on their difficult task. But, as always, Rafe was so much trouble that any advantage to Caedon just barely outweighed the trouble it took to gain that advantage.

The thought galled him.

Something else disturbed him, and he didn't know what to make of it. In spite of his continued attacks on Rafe, depleting him more and more deeply; in spite of Diera's hopeless position, the two of them seemed—not content, certainly not content. Serene, somehow. He tried and failed to thrust his unease about the two of them away from him.

He set out to uncover what it was, and to thwart and destroy it. But before he could, an event happened to anger him. Anger him deeply.

To placate Audemar in the aftermath of the latest defeat of his soldiers against The Rising, he'd had to give up his prize, the little girl. Had to let her be transferred to Treddian's custody. Someday, he was sure of it, he'd get her back. Meanwhile, he knew exactly where Treddian was holding her, and he kept watch. Once, bribing her minder, he was able to slip into her cell there and enjoy her for a few delicious candle measures.

Soon, he'd have her all to himself again. Caedon was a patient man. He could wait. The pleasure would be all the greater, once she was in his hands again.

But his troubles with the little girl distracted him from the odd undercurrent of feeling nagging at him about Rafe and Diera.

He resolved that he would unravel this mystery soon. He'd punish them both.

On the whole, in spite of the trouble and the anger, Caedon felt a surge of optimism. He was winning. Gilles would reward him richly.

CHAPTER TWENTY-EIGHT

Warded

Caedon

As Caedon recovered his place in Audemar's regard, he saw it was time for him to pay his true master an overdue visit. Besides, Gilles was dangling the promise of more gifts he'd be willing to give to Caedon. Caedon, though, would have to do his part and give Gilles the feast he loved the most.

So on a beautiful harvest-tide day, Caedon set out to cross the Narrows. As he stepped off the cog onto the small boat that would take him to shore, he engaged a healer to look after him during the fortnight and more of recovery, an ordeal he shuddered to think on. Gilles hadn't fed from his favorite food in such a long time. He was hungry.

As soon as Caedon healed, he'd take passage back across the Narrows. Audemar had seen things his way at last. Caedon would return to Treddian's castle, and there he would wed Diera. He'd end the Rafe problem permanently, and then he'd strategize about the best way to use Diera. Kill her? Create a figurehead ruler out of her and use that camouflage for his own designs on the realm? There were maybe other uses to which he could put her. He'd have to talk it over with Gilles.

But first things first. Before that journey, Caedon had another to make. Caedon looked around for a driver he'd depended on for years. There was the man. Caedon stopped for a moment and concentrated hard, looking deep inward. He stepped into a protected inner space and drew it securely in after him, warded and secret. Then, once he felt himself ready, his outer self, the one the world saw, waved the man over.

The man drew up his cart and hopped down off the wagon seat. He pulled his forelock and bowed to Caedon. He summoned a dockworker, and together they loaded Caedon's gear into the wagon.

Caedon breathed in the air of the Baronies with delight. To hear his own language all around him, to see these familiar scenes. It was a tonic to him.

Now he climbed into the wagon.

"Your usual road, my lord?" said the driver.

"Not this time," said Caedon. "The peninsula."

They jolted away. They stopped at an inn for the night, where Caedon heard the very different language of his childhood spoken alongside the Baronies speech.

Hearing this old peninsula language called up such memories, as it always did, some fond, but most of them as terrible as nightmare.

Caedon brushed these memories aside. They had nothing to do with his life now.

In the morning, he resumed his travels. Around mid-morning, he and his driver came to a small village.

Caedon got out of the cart. He handed the driver a bag of coin. "Here, my good man. Go back to that inn where we stayed, and keep my things safe. In the morning, return to me here, and I'll resume my journey."

The driver pulled his forelock, turned his team, and left Caedon standing in the road.

Once the man had driven out of sight, Caedon proceeded on foot into a little village not too much further up the coast. As he walked along, he checked to make sure he had tucked himself securely away in that inward place he'd discovered seven years earlier. He allowed himself to go to it only on rare occasions, and so far, Gilles hadn't caught him out.

Every time he did go into that hiding place, he took an immense risk.

If Gilles is paying attention to me the moment I move out of his scrutiny.

If Gilles notices me disappearing from awareness.

Then Gilles would have questions. If that ever happened, Caedon knew he would be done for. The wards he set around his hidden inner space stayed secure only because Gilles didn't know they were there. The instant Gilles suspected they were, he could smash through them easily.

If Gilles withdrew his protections from Caedon, Caedon knew his enemies could destroy him, even if Gilles didn't do it personally.

He thought of the battle that Avery had won with John's help. They were on the point of catching him and killing him, but Gilles had protected him from them. Suppose, just when he thought he was safe from John's shriek, Gilles had whipped his ward from Caedon. Caedon, like the others, would have been destroyed.

Caedon realized how much Gilles would have enjoyed that instant of realization.

You defied me, and you thought you'd get away with it. No. Here. I have delivered you to your enemy. That's what Gilles would tell him in that moment.

Caedon shivered. He had a premonition he'd face such a moment. Not right away. Someday.

He stopped in the road. He could turn back. He could force himself never to come here again.

Instead, he moved forward.

As he moved down the road toward the tiny hamlet, his pulse pounding, he thought of the moment, seven years ago, when he'd first hidden from Gilles. He remembered preparing himself, taking himself to an inward room where he'd never dared go before.

For a few seasons and more, he'd allowed himself to come up to the threshold of this inner place, to make sure he knew his way. But he'd never allowed himself to step over that threshold, and in. He'd never allowed himself to close the door behind him.

Now. Caedon remembered himself thinking it. *Now!*

This inner hidden chamber. This place no one could follow him. Now that he was in it, he dared think it. This place where even Gilles could not follow him. He'd discovered it by chance, practicing the skills and gifts Gilles had granted him. Surely Gilles didn't realize he'd made such a place available to his underling. It was a slip-up. Gilles was not all-powerful, all-knowing. He seemed to be, but he was not. *He's a powerful mage, most powerful of all, maybe,* Caedon thought. *But he's not a god.*

When Gilles shared his gifts with Caedon, an opportunity opened to Caedon that Gilles had not foreseen.

Just thinking that thought made Caedon feel a wave of nausea and fear.

Seven years ago, his burden in his arms, he realized he had to take the risk, right then, or not at all. Seven years ago, he had stepped over the inner threshold with his burden. Once he had known himself safe and hidden, he had come to this same small village to leave his burden here.

At first he decided he'd never be able to return to examine the treasure he had secreted. He'd have to be content just knowing Gilles had no idea of its existence.

A year later, though, he felt a powerful compulsion to come back. There was great danger, Caedon knew. Even if Gilles had been paying attention, even if he felt the moment when Caedon disappeared from his view, even if Gilles questioned him closely once Caedon stood before him, Caedon could maybe tuck his actions away into the hidden place inside where Gilles would not even know they existed. Perhaps even then he'd be safe from Gilles, and then the treasure he had hidden away in the village would be safe.

But that was pure speculation. Caedon was taking a huge risk in going back to that place. It was madness to go back there.

This is a good time, he remembered insisting to himself, that next year. Gilles had traveled to some other plane. His eye was probably not on Caedon. It could be on him, even from that other far plane, Caedon realized, a trickle of sweat beginning to form on his upper lip, his forehead, the pits of his arms. It might be.

But he felt compelled to take the risk.

How strange, he remembered thinking. *I who always have my own advantage at the forefront of my mind.* The compulsion to take this risky step outweighed even that. *Where did it come from?* he wondered. *I must be*, he thought, *a man like any other.* He knew from his training with Gilles that he should banish this idea entirely. And he knew, from his childhood, that he was not in fact a man like any other. Gilles was teaching him how to face it. *But there are ways that I am*, he thought, with wonder, and he realized he didn't even feel ashamed.

That first time, if Gilles had bothered to notice, he would have seen Caedon go to the village, even into the house, before blinking completely out of Gilles's awareness. Caedon counted himself lucky Gilles's attention must have been elsewhere.

The second time, Caedon was much more careful. He'd made sure to cross the threshold into hiding as soon as he set foot on land, so even the journey to the village would be closed off and warded from view.

When he had known himself to be hidden and safe, only then had he risked walking up to the door of the same small cottage he'd visited the year previous.

The goodwife of the house had opened the door. "Your lordship!" she had exclaimed in the language of the Sceptered Isle, making a deep curtsey to him. She was a worthy woman of the countryside outside Londs-fort, where everyone spoke both that language and Baronies speech. "We didn't look for you here."

Caedon closed his eyes, remembering.

"You know why I'm here, surely, goodwife," he remembered himself telling the woman of the house.

"Indeed, your lordship. I'll get him, shall I? Would you like some refreshment?"

"No, I don't need anything," he'd said, his heart oddly thumping in his chest.

The woman had disappeared down a corridor of the house.

He thought about that time now, six years ago. He remembered the tread of the goodwife coming back up the corridor, and how his heart had hammered in his chest. She'd entered the room leading a small child of about three years.

"Here now, baby," she had said to this child, switching to Baronies speech. "Here's someone who wants to meet you." She'd looked over at Caedon. "Good Lady, how many pet names we have for the sweetling. Seeing as he has no name. But my lord, I must tell you, he is the most loving child."

Caedon had sat gazing at the child. "Bring him here." He remembered how hard it was to get the words out.

"I'm following your instructions, lord. I'm using Baronies speech with him. That shall be his first tongue, as your lordship has ordered." The goodwife had led the little boy to Caedon and put the little hand in Caedon's hand, outstretched.

Caedon remembered bending to look into the tiny boy's face. He remembered the moment the child had looked up into Caedon's eyes. Caedon remembered how dizzy he felt, gazing down into the boy's face, just as if he were looking into a mirror. The strange amber eyes of the boy, fringed with the thickest lashes. Caedon had scrutinized the boy. Did he see anything of Diera there? Perhaps. But mostly what Caedon saw was himself. Himself as once he had been.

"Do you have a name for the boy?" The goodwife's voice had come at him as if from a distance.

Caedon remembered putting out a finger to stroke the tender cheek of his son. "I'm your father." *Je suis ton père*, he had whispered to the boy. *And no one will have you. You will stay perfect, just as you are.* He'd gotten the boy away from the wet nurse where Labinia had taken him. He'd told Gilles the boy had died of plague and paid Labinia off to corroborate his lie. He'd told Diera the same. Then he'd taken the child here, and brought the goodwife over from Lunds-fort to care for him.

Luckily, Labinia was dead. Not even the most persuasive of inducements could lead her to betray him now. And the goodwife had no idea she was doing anything more than caring for the motherless babe of some gentle who paid her well to do it.

"Sir?" The goodwife's voice again. "What shall you call him?" She had switched back to the tongue of the Sceptered Isle.

"I'll call him Yann," Caedon had said.

"John?" the goodwife had asked. That was the Lunds-fort version of the name, and the goodwife, a stolid woman of the countryside surrounding the city, hadn't understood.

Caedon had shaken his head. "Yann."

He remembered how the goodwife had gone away muttering in her strange borderland patois, "John. Yann. It's the same, isn't it?"

Caedon hadn't paid attention. His gaze was rapt on his son. "No one will have you. Only you yourself. You'll grow straight and strong. I will love you and take care of you always," he had whispered. He had bent down and kissed the boy, and the boy had put up his little arms around Caedon's neck. The boy would know fineness and honor. He'd know the skills of a warrior. He'd learn the sword. Caedon would teach him everything.

Caedon remembered the shudder that had wracked him. *Everything. But not that.*

He'd teach Yann his letters. He'd show him all the treasures of the Old Ones.

Three years later, when Yann was six, Caedon had come back. He remembered the wave of terror that had surged over him. Looking at his perfect son, standing before him at the perfect age, Caedon had shivered with terror that Gilles might somehow know, in spite of all precautions. Might somehow reach out his arm and seize Caedon's son away from him. This was the dangerous age.

But now, today, they were past that, three years past, and nothing had happened. Gilles did not know.

Caedon knocked.

A boy came to the door, straight-limbed, slender, Caedon's own amber eyes in Diera's beautiful oval of a face.

"Yann."

"Father," said the boy, embracing him.

"How I have missed you," said Caedon. "How I have longed to be here with you."

A deep-hidden memory from his own boyhood swam up to him from far inside. A memory of the early days with Gilles.

A memory of a tutor who placed Caedon's hands on the strings of an instrument. Not a rebec. A harp, the type people played around here.

Perhaps he'd engage someone to teach Yann the pathway to the Spheres. He would. He'd do it. He'd have someone teach Yann music.

He knew he himself would never be able to listen.

But Yann's pure voice, the strings of his harp, his song would mount to the Spheres where the stars revolve, the place from which they gaze down in their compassion upon the poor small stunted creatures crawling broken across the earth.

Caedon wondered whether, in that high place, there might be pity even for him.

Epilogue

In a little meadow, a girl screams out in horror, and the blackbirds scream too. Her parents have been killed in brutal ways. The killers have taken her young sister. She flees with nothing to her name, only the rebec Johnny taught her to play. She wanders the world underneath the Nine Spheres, searching for her sister, searching for the one true inward thing Johnny has charged her to find.

Across the boundary in the Land of the Dead, John watches over her, and so do her father and mother. But they can do nothing to help her, only love her from across that stream.

She must do it herself, and the thing she must do, under the Nine Spheres, is the hardest undertaking the Children ever set. There will be perils along the way.

She must find a sister and a queen. Those tasks will be hard enough.

Harder still, far harder, she must find the path that leads to herself.

READER, Before you go!

The sweep of the ten novels in the interlocking Storm-clouds/Harbingers series starts with the sighting of the comet of 976 CE, recorded in the British Isles. Except for that one reference, we know almost nothing about this hyperbolic comet, known as x976, but it did show up, and you can read about it in the historical record.

The events of these novels progress from the appearance of x976 to the famous sighting of Halley's Comet in 1066 CE. Halley's, one of the most-studied comets in human history, seemed to the people of the British Isles in 1066 to presage the regime change ushered in by the Norman Conquest, and it was observed in the Americas, too. These two comets frame my series of novels—with this difference, that the sightings of the two comets in my novels occur in the fantasy-verse, not in real-life history!

All ten novels are available at amazon.com in paperback editions and for Kindle. For more information about the novels in the series, and for a playlist that includes many of the songs the characters play and sing, go to my author web site, www.janemwiseman.com. To see the way people, places, and things may have looked in the Stormclouds/Harbingers world, go to my Pinterest boards: *Medieval Life—Gyrfalcon*, *Medieval Life—Shrike*, *Medieval Life—Stormbird* (for the **Stormclouds** series); *Medieval Life—10th Century* (about *Blackbird Rising*), *Medieval Life—Halcyon*, *Medieval Life—Firebird*, *Medieval Life—Ghost Bird* (for the **Harbingers** series);. *Medieval Life—Martlet* and *Medieval Life—Nightingale* (for the **Betwixt & Between** companion series). Also *Medieval Life—Dark Ones*.

The "flavor" of the three series varies a bit. The novels of the Stormclouds and Betwixt & Between series are a bit darker and more adult, while the novels of the Harbingers series are a bit more YA/NA in flavor. Even though, chronologically, the Stormclouds novels come first, you may begin either with the Stormclouds novels or the Harbingers novels, and may want to read the Betwixt & Between novels last. *Dark Ones Take It*, the standalone origin story of the series villain, is a pretty dark read.

The Novels:

A Gyrfalcon for a King (Stormclouds, book 1) : King Ranulf may be cursed, a curse of his own making, through his own misdeeds. Which of his sons will redeem him and which will be his undoing? Artur, the crown prince, scholarly and retiring? Audemar, the second son, conspiring to unseat him? Avery, the third son, alert to the dangers that surround the throne? Or John, Ranulf's bastard son—John the minstrel, John the mage.

The Call of the Shrike (Stormclouds, book 2) : Ranulf's true-born son Prince Avery and his bastard son John band together with three friends in the guerilla action they name The Rising. The young warriors of The Rising set out to right a great wrong that threatens the realm. They face a mighty enemy—not the enemy they thought they were fighting, but one more dangerous than they could ever have imagined.

Stormbird (Stormclouds, book 3) : The ragtag band of The Rising faces near-impossible odds in its quest for justice. How can the

Six hope to prevail when they fight without resources; when they are picked off one by one? When they face an evil man backed by an unimaginably evil force? John's young brother Wat must take up his brother's fight, struggling against not only the powerful enemies of The Rising but his own self-doubts. Meanwhile, in the grasp of their enemy, Caedon, the Princess Diera must do the same.

Blackbird Rising (Harbingers, book 1):   An orphaned young girl, a band of spies and assassins, a sister lost, a queen found—in the midst of chaos and treachery, Mirin must somehow learn to trust. Only then can she fulfill the mission John the minstrel left her. Only then can she live up to the promise and the magic of her music.

Halcyon (Harbingers, book 2) : On the run, Mirin and Wat try to carve out a new life together. But when everything is taken from Mirin, she must find the strength to go on alone. Her music sustains her, and so does the mysterious power of the fisher-bird, the harbinger of her god.

Firebird (Harbingers, book 3) : Keera has one goal—avenging her parents—and boundless confidence. After all, she has her magic powers, and they are second to none. When she finds she must fight her battle with only her wits and her grit, how can she possibly prevail? But the girl has friends: an old mage who helps her, a young man with a twinkle in his eye who can't get her out of his mind—and a ghost.

Ghost Bird (Harbingers, book 4) : Keera and Gwyl voyage in Gwyl's dragon ship to the heart of a new continent. But their enemies from the world left behind are not done with them yet. The two of them have to fight for the life they want, pursued by a powerful evil, relentless and closing in. Lucky for them Keera is an ornithomancer like her mother, Mirin, and like her uncle, John—the kind of mage who calls upon the mysterious powers of birds.

The Martlet is a Wanderer (Betwixt & Between, book 1)   : Who is Silence? He can't speak to tell anyone the role he played in the conspiracy called The Rising, and he can't remember it anyway. He knows only that he needs to find two people: a friend, and a woman who means more to him than life itself. How can he possibly carry out this mission? Especially since he might be dead. (The events of this novel take place in parallel with *Halcyon*.)

The Nightingale Holds Up the Sky   (*Betwixt & Between* , book 2) : Say you've been kidnapped and dragged to the underworld. Say the man who loves you wanders the realm looking for you. Say he finds a way in. But suppose you don't want to be found. As for the fate of the realm in the grip of evil, the fate of the world underneath the Spheres; as for justice—suppose you forge your own. (The events of this novel take place in parallel with *Halcyon* and *Firebird*.)

Stand-alone novel in the world of the Stormclouds/Harbingers series:
Dark Ones Take It , *being the origin story of Caedon and his brother, Maeldoi.*

Caedon and Maeldoi are gwrgi—creatures who look like the rest of us, except for their amber eyes. When they get into a rage, they transform. Like werewolves? Not exactly. To an out-of-control bestial form of themselves. As they reach manhood, the dangerous age, the brothers are separated. Caedon is adopted by Gilles de Rais, a powerful mage with powerful se-crets, a sorcerer who values Caedon's rage and schemes how to use it. Maeldoi is taken off by his fellow gwrgi to be taught how to control the rage inside him. **Brother against brother** . When Caedon and Maeldoi meet again, the fate of the Spheres Them-selves hangs in the balance.

About the Author

I hope you have enjoyed *Stormbird*, Book III of the Stormclouds series, the prequel series to the Harbingers fantasy novels. Please leave a review of my novel on amazon.com, goodreads, and other web sites and groups for readers and book lovers. I care about what my readers think! Please visit my author page on www.amazon.com and my author web site, www.janemwiseman.com. Follow my blog about speculative fiction, www.fantastes.com.

Jane Wiseman splits her time between urban Minneapolis and the Sandia Mountains of New Mexico. She loves fantasy in all its forms, enjoys her family, reads all the time, and writes in many different modes. As for fantasy, she writes books that she would like to read. She also paints.

A NOTE OF ACKNOWLEDGMENT

Thanks to my wonderful daughter, Margaret Govoni, for your editing eye, especially in the early stages. You steered me away from many mishaps and missteps, Margaret. All the remaining ones are mine alone.

Thanks to Bob, marvelous beta reader!

Thanks for all the helpful suggestions I've gathered from a number of online Litreactor workshops, www.Litreactor.com and from other writing workshops, especially Tinker Mountain Writers:

www.hollins.edu/academics/workshops-online-writing-courses/tinker-mountain-writers-workshop-residential/

and the (sadly now defunct) Taos Summer Writers' Conference. The instructors' comments and suggestions were of course incredibly helpful, but I have valued beyond measure the comments and suggestions of my fellow workshop attendees. Thanks to all of you! You may not have been able to save me from all my writing sins, but you saved me from many. Thanks also to the Anam Cara Writer's and Artist's Retreat, www.anamcararetreat.com, on the Beara Peninsula of Ireland. What a peaceful and lovely place to write! Thanks, Sue!

And finally, thanks to all you Norrathians out there. You are my true battle buddies. You know who you are. You are my fantasy friends in the purest sense of all.

Thanks to the following purchased stock photo art and royalty-free art used for the composite cover illustration of this novel:

NOTES ON Stormbird
from the author

THIS NOVEL IS A WORK OF FANTASY, NOT HISTORICAL FICTION, although it is indebted to history.

THE TIME-PERIOD of the novel is roughly early medieval. The novel begins in a geopolitical environment resembling several of the Frankish, Anglo-Saxon, and Scandinavian kingdoms vying for power in the 10th and 11th centuries.

TWELVE REALMS:

THE SCEPTERED ISLE stands in for the united Heptarchy (seven main kingdoms) of mainland Anglo-Saxon England, but also includes the northern part of the realm (Scotland), the Western Isle (Ireland) and the northern isles (islands off the coast of Scotland— Inner and Outer Hebrides, Orkney, and Shetland Islands). It does not include the area around Lunds-fort (London), however.

THE EASTERN BARONIES stands in for a loose confederation of powerful feudal lords spreading across medieval France and parts of Germany. In my tale, the Eastern Baronies also own territory on the mainland of the Sceptered Isle—the land around Lunds-fort (London) and along the eastern edge of the mainland—in addition to their strongholds across the Narrows (the English Channel).

THE SOUTHERN PRIMACY stands in for medieval territories in Italy (as well as Portugal and Spain), the homeland to which the Old Ones (ancient Romans) pulled back as their empire dwindled.

THE LYRE-LANDS stands in for the vestiges of ancient Greece and the lands rimming the Aegean in the medieval era, including that vast metropolis the Vikings knew as "the Great City," Constantinople (Istanbul).

THE REALM OF THE ASP stands in for the ancient Near and Middle East.

THE BURNT LANDS is a vague concept to people of the Sceptered Isle and similar northern realms. It stands in for North Africa and below, through Sub-Saharan Africa, but people in the northern realms know little of these lands.

THE ICE-REALM stands in for medieval Norway and, in a loose sense, the other parts of Scandinavia. Its king wants to add the Cold Lands (Greenland) to his realm.

THE FIRE ISLE stands in for medieval Iceland.

THE MOUNTAIN FASTNESSES stands in for the Alpine regions of Europe.

THE TRADE ROAD FORTIFICATIONS stands in for the old Silk Road of the late ancient world through the Renaissance, stretching along the Eurasian steppes.

THE SILK LANDS stands in for China and southeast Asia.

THE FORGOTTEN KINGDOM stands in for the Indian subcontinent. No one in the Stormclouds/Harbingers world knows much about this place.

ALSO:

UNKNOWN LANDS (the Americas) across the Great Sea stretching to the west. Travelers have come back with tales of these lands, but no one knows much about them.

THE CONCEPT OF TWO COMPETING RELIGIOUS GROUPS , worshippers of the Lady Goddess vs. worshippers of an elemental universe controlled by earth, sea, fire, and sky, is fantasy but based on some actual bits of information about belief systems in the post-Roman British Isles and medieval beliefs in general, especially medieval ideas about the body and healing. These derived from very ancient sources such as the Greek philosopher Empedocles. (Present-day astrologers have their own settled ideas about these matters. I know nothing about their ideas and don't pretend to.) There is a sense that older gods once ruled the lands, but no one remembers much about them.

THE OVERALL CONCEPT OF MY NOVEL'S UNIVERSE is Pythagorean: nine revolving crystalline spheres carry the heavenly bodies (sun, moon, stars, planets) around the earth at their center. This idea from the ancient classical Near East was widespread in the medieval period, obviously long before anyone knew anything about the way the physical universe really works.

THE CUCKOO RHYME that begins this novel is an adaptation of a piece of weather folklore from the British Isles.

SOME OF CONAL'S IDEAS ABOUT WAR are indebted to Tim Harford's book about decision-making, *Messy: The Power of Disorder to Change Lives*, especially the

chapter about the great German general Erwin Rommel's tactics in World Wars I and II. The battle Avery's and Conal's army fights is also indebted to this chapter, especially the description of the World War I battle in 1915 near Binarville in northeastern France, and a 1917 battle near Venice, both of which the drastically outnumbered Rommel won through quick and relentless action leaving the enemy confused and in a state of chaos. Another really important source for me was this blog post by Michael Gross on the ethics of insurgency (and Prof. Gross, a political scientist, has written a book on the subject for anyone interested in learning more):
https://moralvictories.gla.ac.uk/the-ethics-of-insurgency-and-a-close-look-at-just-guerrilla-warfare/

VAMPIRISM is a complicated topic, and it's not just about fanged, blood-sucking, black-clad people who can transform into bats and are chased by buff young California girls or doctors with fake Dutch accents. So-called "psychic vampirism" is described in this article:
https://www.researchgate.net/publication/283273380_The_Psychic_Vampire_and_Vampyre_Subculture

My fantasy version of Gilles is probably more akin to the medieval notion of the incubus or other types of parasitic demons than about vampires as usually depicted in popular culture, and he is also a necromancer.

BASTARDS in the actual historical time-period of this fantasy novel would not have suffered the stigma that John and Wat do, although some of the stigma they endure is due to the particular emotions of their father and not the general practices of the (fantasy) time. In the actual medieval era (which is huge, stretching from the fall of the Roman empire to the Renaissance in the 14th-17th centuries—a period of easily a thousand years), the stigma about bastardy came much later. Here's an article by Sara McDougall that explains the matter quickly and well:
https://aeon.co/ideas/the-strange-story-of-inventing-the-bastard-in-medieval-europe

THE REBEC is a real medieval musical stringed instrument from around the 10th century. The rebec preceded later stringed instruments such as the lute, the gittern, and the citole. Unlike the lute, which is built of strips of wood, the rebec's bowl was carved from a single piece of wood. It may be the precursor to the violin, but musicologists have had a lively debate about this, and I'm not qualified to weigh in. I only hope I don't have any technical details drastically wrong. See *A Harbingers/Stormclouds Playlist* posted on my web site, janemwiseman.com, for what a rebec looks and sounds like.

MEDIEVAL WAGONS didn't have suspension mechanisms, so the ride was very rough and jolting.

CAEDON'S IDEAS ABOUT WAR are indebted to Julius Caesar ("the general of the Old Ones"), *Commentarii de Bello Gallico*.

THE CUCKOO, the song Rhiane sings for Wat, is a version of an old English folk song, Roud 413, with some modifications of my own. A good version of it can be found here:
https://www.youtube.com/watch?v=614L6q88pAM

This song crossed to the Americas, where it became a staple of Southern Appalachian folk music in a slightly different version, which you can hear recorded by many artists (including the very young Bob Dylan, performing it at the Gaslight in 1962). *She Moved Through the Fair* is another well-known traditional folk song, Roud 861. Rhiane wants to sing it, but Wat won't let her because it reminds him too painfully of John. It figures prominently in Stormclouds Book II, *The Call of the Shrike*, and you can listen to it on *A Harbingers/Stormclouds Playlist* posted on my web site, janemwiseman.com.)

THE BOW was one of the most important weapons of the time. From around the age of eight, a medieval boy in the (historical) British Isles would begin practicing to draw a bow (later called the longbow), usually made of the just about perfect wood of the yew, with its inner layer of heartwood and its outer layer of sapwood. There were even laws mandating hours of daily practice with the bow, so that in time of war the monarch would have a trained force of bowmen to call on. Medieval English bows and the tactics of fighting with such bows are complex technical matters. Apologies for anything this novel gets wrong about such a fascinating subject. A good source is Robert Hardy's *Longbow: A Social and Military History*.

Many battles in the British Isles and beyond involved strategies using bowmen. The most famous is probably the 15th century Battle of Agincourt, during the Hundred Years' War (see Juliet Barker's matchless *Agincourt: The Battle That Made England*—and of course the Sir Lawrence Olivier film version of

Shakespeare's *Henry V*, based on research about Agincourt, from which just about every other movie battle scene involving flights of arrows derives), but many battles before and after were decided or materially aided by volleys of arrows from English longbows.

STONE CROCKS, historically, were probably made later than the time period of this fantasy novel.

MEDIEVAL DANCE: Information about dance in medieval times is sparse, communicated to modern researchers through musical texts, paintings, and accounts in written tales. You can find out quite a bit about Renaissance dance. Not medieval. The dance Wat learns is a composite I've imagined using several of these vague medieval sources, especially a brief translation derived from http://www.hs-augsburg.de/~harsch/Chronologia/Lspost11/Ruod-lieb/ruo_frag.html

My Latin is not up to this, so I'm not sure exactly where the excerpt I read comes from in this text. If your Latin is good, and you want to know more, here's where to look!

PEOPLE IN THE 10TH CENTURY BRITISH ISLES WERE FAIRLY TALL, around as tall as people are today, according to archaeological evidence. Nobody is quite sure why, but the most likely reasons are related to nutrition and favorable growing weather for crops. Average height then dropped from about 1200 AD throughout the rest of the medieval period. This web site explains: http://www.ox.ac.uk/news/2017-04-18-highs-and-lows-english-man%E2%80%99s-average-height-over-2000-years-0

MEDIEVAL MARRIAGE AND WEDDINGS: Quite a lot is known about medieval feasts such as those celebrating weddings. Marriage itself, as a legal and socioeconomic institution, is an entire study in itself. I'm indebted to *Marriage: A History*, by Stephanie Coontz.

APOLOGIES FOR MY PETTY AND NOT-SO-PETTY THEFTS! (As always, lawyers, I am playfully using the word "theft" for the literary figure of speech known as "allusion." The technical term for what I am doing with these allusions is the "mashup.") In this book, I stole (and frequently distorted my thievings) from the traditional folklore of the British Isles; from Geoffrey Chaucer; from Thomas More; from Hugh Latimer; from Shakespeare; from eighteenth century poet

Alexander Pope's *The Rape of the Lock*; from the German fairy tale *Snow White*, collected by the Brothers Grimm; from Edmund Spenser's late-16th century marriage poem *Epithalamion*; from the life of Gilles de Rais, a real fifteenth-century French baron who supported Joan of Arc but later became fascinated with the occult, going down in history as one of the most prolific and chilling serial killers (especially of children) the world has known. Gilles de Rais plays an important role in several other novels in the **Stormclouds** and **Harbingers** series.

And a final thank-you to Warren Robinett, the inventor of the easter egg.

an excerpt from: BLACKBIRD RISING

Book I of the Harbingers fantasy series

The story follows the end of *Stormbird*, Book III of the Stormclouds fantasy series.

CHAPTER ONE

Blackbird's Eye

o you remember the day Johnny the Traveler said black-birds are my friends? You may have been too young to remember it, and too much has happened since then. But I want you to try.

I had given Johnny a skeptical look when he said it, the thing about the blackbirds. "The Child of Earth is not my Child," I reminded him.

"I told the blackbirds about you," Johnny replied. "Now they're friends of yours."

Or are they foe?

I hope you do remember the day Johnny came to visit us, Jillie. That was a good day. Then there's the day I hope you don't remember. The terrible day when everything we knew fell burning into ruins. I hope the Children, in Their mercy, have blocked it from your memory. I wish They had blocked it from mine.

The blackbirds flap over the little rise in the meadow to settle and flutter and fuss.

Foe, I scream inside myself when I see them.

Not friend.

Foe.

I hear their shrieking. I stand stunned at the edge of the meadow. Past the flurry of wings and beaks I see our gutted cabin, a thin trail of smoke rising from its roof. I see the soldiers of the king poking around it, the dark form of a man on horseback directing them. Strewn down the furlong of meadow between me and the ruins of our house, I see crumpled piles, maybe cloth, distorted and lumpy. I tell myself I don't know what they are, but in a different part of myself, I do. They are bodies.

Blackbirds perch on them. Five or six. They step delicately on and over the lumpy forms of our father and mother, cut down as they tried to run for the safety of the brushy forest verge.

And there's a smaller bundle, too. *Jillie*, I whisper, and my heart wrenches loose from me. I see, tossed out beside you, a splash of bright yellow. My mother had made you a poppet out of leftover cloth from her new yellow holiday kirtle.

You loved that doll.

From somewhere, I hear a drum pounding. I can feel the pulse beating in my ears, and I realize the sound is my own heart.

The drumbeat is so loud I think the soldiers must be able to hear it, even though they're at the other end of the meadow. Though I know in some sensible part of me that the sound is enclosed inside my body, I still find myself backing into the underbrush and crouching down.

These men patrolling the ruins of our home, they're soldiers of the king. They wear his scarlet livery. They are slashes of scarlet in and about the gray of the smoldering, stove-in cabin, almost gone back to the earth our father hacked it out of. Slashes of scarlet roaming the vivid meadow.

Down the meadow, the hovering birds bob and toss and jerk their heads. *Are they feeding?* I have a powerful urge to rush these birds, scream at them, chase them off the bodies. Something holds me back. That something keeps me alive.

The scene that is spread out before me makes no sense. The pounding drum. The ringing in my ears. Aren't we all loyal subjects of the king, all in our family? We have never done any wrong, not to the king, not to our neighbors. I want to scream at the soldiers and tell them so.

Instead, all words are driven out of me as if some massive dangerous animal has slammed me to the dirt.

From over the meadow I can see the shingles our father had split himself, still glowing on what is left of our roof. In flashes, I have a chilling notion of how the whole thing happened. I feel as if I'm rising, hovering like one of the birds, and I think I see it—the soldiers throwing burning brands on the low roof to force all of you out through the only door.

A blackness comes across me, there in the meadow, and then a flash, and in that flash I see it.

The burning shingles don't collapse at once. Our parents grab at you. You're crying in panic, Jillie. They burst to the door, help you crawl out, and try to run. They don't get far.

The soldiers ride all of you down.

Evil stalks beside these soldiers of the king. Their leader is not dressed in scarlet. He's dressed in black. The way he holds himself is wolf-like. Sinister. Like one of the Dark Ones.

I shake my head to clear it. Now my body is back crouching low to the earth, where it belongs, in its hiding place at the verge of the meadow. I'm in my leather tunic, the one our mother made for me of rabbit skins from my own trapping expeditions, and I'm wearing my brown woolen trousers. Boys' clothes, forbidden but practical for hunting. The tunic, buff and brown and mottled, blends in with the dapples and overlapping shadows at the meadow's edge. And the trousers are the same color as the forest behind me.

If I had been wearing my regular clothes, my kirtle, my white headcloth and apron, I would have stood out against the forest backdrop. I would have been dead by the third step I took into the meadow.

Though I don't understand what I'm sensing or even exactly what I'm seeing, I find myself edging backward into the brush. From there, hidden, I stare and stare at this thing I can barely fathom, something so out of the realm of possibility that I don't and can't believe it.

From where I hide, I see the soldiers moving down into the meadow toward the bodies. As they near, the blackbirds explode upward in a raucous storm of feathers and beaks and claws. I shrink down even lower, flattening myself on the ground as the blackbirds fly over, back into the woods beyond me. One stares at me, as it strafes me, one eye dark, foreboding, the other filmy white with blindness.

From wanting to rush at the blackbirds and flail at them with my hands, I become one of them. I'm rising again, soaring far overhead. I scream and scream.

The soldiers stop, look over their shoulders in my direction. They come down the meadow toward me, and as they do, one final blackbird rises shrieking from the meadow's verge, going at them with talon and beak. They duck back and hasten toward the cabin, where their leader sits his horse.

They mount up, too, and they all ride off.

I watch myself soaring on wide black wings. My eye scans the landscape for the dark leader. My beak opens wide to accuse him, and my talons spread, ready to fasten deep into his flesh.

But the bodies distract me. In a dive that bolts from the zenith of the sky, I arrow down to those bodies, desperate to reach them.

Instead, I slam back into my own body where it's standing stunned now at the ragged edge of the meadow. I'm a girl again. I turn and run. As I zigzag terror-stricken through the trees, something bangs and thwacks against me. It is my rebec, hanging from its shoulder strap.

Everything I've known and loved has just been destroyed. My rebec is the one good thing still with me in a world gone gray and horror-filled.

www.ingramcontent.com/pod-product-compliance
Lightning Source LLC
Chambersburg PA
CBHW021214260626

47172CB00002B/428